And then it all happened at once; the sirens leapt into swooping ear-assaulting life, seeming almost above her head they were so close, and echoing dreadfully in the long empty corridor as the sound of the planes got thicker and even louder. She was running now, which she'd been taught nurses must never do – except in the case of fire or haemorrhage – and ahead of her the doors into Casualty swung wide as someone came out, pushing an empty trolley. She got a glimpse of the well-lit waiting room beyond and tried to run even faster, feeling illogically that would be a safe place to shelter, and then as the trolley-pusher began to move from a patch of darkness to light the noise became unbearable and her ears seemed to burst, and her body to be punched by a huge fist, and she was lying flat on her back and trying to breathe through a thick cloud of dust that seemed to fill her nose and mouth.

She started to cough and splutter then, and at last the worst of the clogging stuff burst out of her nose and she could breathe, and she tried to reach up to wipe her face and mouth; but her arms were caught in her cape and she had to struggle.

'Easy, easy does it.'
'Who's that? What happened?'

Also by Claire Rayner in Sphere Books:

MADDIE
REPRISE
CLINICAL JUDGEMENTS
JUBILEE: POPPY CHRONICLES I
FLANDERS: POPPY CHRONICLES II
FLAPPER: POPPY CHRONICLES III

CLAIRE RAYNER

BLITZ
THE POPPY CHRONICLES IV

SPHERE BOOKS LIMITED

A *Sphere* Book

First published in Great Britain in 1990 by
George Weidenfeld & Nicolson Limited
This edition published by Sphere Books Ltd 1991

ISBN 0 7474 0735 5

Printed and bound in Great Britain by
BPCC Hazell Books
Aylesbury, Bucks, England
Member of BPCC Ltd.

Sphere Books Ltd
A Division of
Macdonald & Co (Publishers) Ltd
165 Great Dover Street
London SE1 4YA

A member of Maxwell Macmillan Publishing Corporation

For Nina and Peter Angel
with love

· 1 ·

The explosion, when it came, was not so much loud as long, Robin told herself, attempting to use logical thought to control her fear, while at the same time trying to keep her head down and the child in her arms safe as he struggled and screamed at the top of his voice. And then as her ears sang shrilly, she decided it had been loud after all; very loud, a great cracking thunderous roar; and also suffocating. Clouds of plaster dust were filling her nose and mouth and small Billy wriggled against her apron front and began to make choking noises; and automatically she upended him and thumped his back, crouching there behind the big dressings cupboard, until he spluttered and at last, to her intense relief, gasped and then began to bawl again.

'Are you all right, Nurse Bradman?' The voice was high and sounded distinctly annoyed. 'Nurse Chester, where are you? Staff Nurse Puncheon – where are the baby nurses? We'd better start the count at once – '

'I'm here, Sister,' Robin managed, though her voice was husky because of the dust, and coughing, she straightened herself gingerly and peered over the top of the dressings cupboard to see what was happening down the ward, as Billy settled to a steady wail. 'And I've got Billy Cooper – '

'And I've got both the Davidoff twins,' came from somewhere behind Robin and she turned her head gratefully at the sound of Chick's familiar drawl, to see her standing there with a kicking toddler under each arm – both of them laughing and clearly believing the whole episode had been entertainment provided just for them – and a face as white as a ghost out of which her eyes peered like the holes in the skull of the skeleton in the nurses' lecture room.

'Oh, Chick!' Robin said and managed to laugh: 'You look absolutely ridiculous – '

'You should see your face, honey bun!' Chick retorted and came towards her, hoicking the Davidoff twins up on to her broad shoulders as she did so. And then giggled softly as she caught sight of Sister Marshall, who was picking her way over the piles of rubble in the middle of the usually perfectly shining floor. 'Oh, look at the Old Bat, will you? Now that really has to be the funniest thing ever. Worth being in a raid for, that is.'

And indeed, Sister Marshall did look absurd, her angular body in its usually crisply starched blue dress and huge sleeves looking as though it had been dusted with a giant sugar powderer, and her face, as white as her cap and strings, peering out ferociously between them at her ruined ward. And Robin giggled too.

'I can't see what there is to laugh at, Nurse Bradman!' Sister Marshall said tartly. 'Now, get that child out of here and into the first undamaged ward you can find and then come back here at once and we'll start to clean the place. I can't have this sort of thing going on in Annie Zunz Ward, and I won't stand for it!' And she peered upwards as though the mere power of her voice would penetrate the cracked ceiling and send the German planes scuttling back across the Channel.

And why shouldn't it? Robin thought, making her way through the rubble towards the big double doors at the end, following the other nurses now emerging from their hiding places, each with a child or two in their arms; she scares the hell out of everyone else, from the consultants down to me.

2

'She's taking this personally,' Chick murmured in her ear as they managed to get to the doors. 'Honestly, she's the best secret weapon this country has. Churchill ought to pack her in a bomb and send her over to Berlin and drrop her there. Then it'd all be over and I could go home and – '

'You dare,' Robin said and reached out and punched her friend's arm affectionately. 'If we have to have a war to keep you here, then I suppose we'll have to have a war – '

'Stop that chattering, nurses, and hurry up!' Sister Marshall called down the ward behind them and with a soft groan Chick escaped through the double doors on Robin's heels.

Outside in the wide corridor it was even worse. There was rubble everywhere and a reek of old plaster and dust and somewhere beneath it the ominous smell of gas, all mixed up with the usual hospital smells of carbolic and Lysol, because the operating theatre at the end of the corridor was working full tilt, even though the raid was still on. The nurses there were frantically scrubbing instruments and bowls out in the corridor, using great buckets of disinfectant, because their sluice had been battered to uselessness an hour or two earlier. It had been one of the worst evenings ever, and Robin, stumbling a little as they reached the stairs, thought muzzily – it must be after eight thirty. Time I was off duty, surely? And then laughed aloud at the silliness of the notion of ever getting off duty in all this hubbub.

And hubbub there was. Somewhere outside the shattered windows where glass fragments hung precariously on the criss-crossed paper strips, people were shouting and there were bells ringing furiously as yet more fire-fighting equipment arrived, while inside there were the wails of the frightened children, although the Davidoff twins were still chortling as Chick bounced them on her shoulders and went hurrying down the stairs, picking her way as surely as a goat on a mountain-side.

3

Robin followed her gratefully, as usual. Ever since she had started as a very frightened junior probationer at the London Hospital in the days of the phoney war last September, when nothing much was happening and people were telling themselves optimistically it would all be over by Christmas, Chick had been her mentor, her friend and her supporter. And Robin felt a sharp pang of guilt as she thought how much she needed her; if she hadn't happened to have been caught here that September when she'd been touring Europe, she'd have been safely at home in Toronto now, and Robin would have had no one to call her friend – but it was selfish of her to be glad Chick was so far away from her home and family. And, ashamed, she pushed the thought away.

The ward below was full of extra cots and the nurses there were bustling about, trying to settle the now thoroughly aroused new arrivals in some sort of order. Here there was dust, as there was everywhere in the hospital, Robin imagined, but the place hadn't been damaged and she marvelled at how well the old structure was holding up. Their floor, she knew, had been badly knocked about, but even so, wasn't totally unusable, and she relinquished Billy to the care of a second-year nurse of Marriot Ward staff, and turned to go, as Chick, the Davidoff twins now ensconced side by side in the same cot and looking as though they were about to add their bawls to everyone else's, came and grabbed her arm.

'Better get back,' she said. 'That old fool'll kill herself before she'll go off and leave that mess behind. I hate the very sound of her name, but we'll have to help her.'

'Oh, she's not that bad,' Robin said as they made for the door. 'Considering how old she is – I mean, she stood up to last week's bashing well enough and got us all straight again, and now this – you can't help but be sorry for her.'

'I rather think I meant something along those lines,' Chick said with some sarcasm. 'Anyway, we'd better get back. It's not over yet – I haven't heard the all clear,

4

have you? – and Staff Nurse here says she's heard there's another gas main fractured over the road and that could go too. It was that which caused the damage to this wing, it seems, not a direct hit or anything – '

They were half-way up the stairs again by now, the other nurses following with their aprons crumpled and their caps askew, looking like a flock of ruffled geese, and Robin said anxiously, 'A gas main? Then why did we get so damaged and Marriot Ward didn't? I mean – '

'Ass!' Chick said indulgently. 'We're on the main road side, right? Marriot faces out back. So we got the impact. It'll be the same on the second and first floors too – Spruce and Willow'll be pretty shook up – '

'Not so bad for them. They're adult wards – ' Robin said.

'And full of pretty sick people.' Chick sounded grim. 'They admitted dozens after Sunday's lot. Come on, kid. We'd better get going. There's a lot to do, and the Old Bat'll be sure to try to get all the children back up here before the night's out.' And she pushed open the big double doors to Annie Zunz Ward and went in.

The lights were on again now behind the makeshift blackouts that had been put up, and down at the far end of the ward Robin could see the burly back of Todd, the ward orderly, fixing the last of them. And not for the first time marvelled at the speed and strength of the man. He said little – though when he did it sounded agreeable for he had a soft Scottish accent that Robin liked – but worked doggedly, no matter what was asked of him.

There had been times when Robin had wanted to protest at the sort of jobs Todd was given; the dirtiest and most effortful were always saved for him, and not just because he was a man and a big one at that. There were other men working in the hospital as porters and orderlies, but they were never treated as harshly as Todd was; but they weren't conscientious objectors. Robin stifled her impulse to go down to help Todd and went instead to find Sister Marshall for instructions. It was none of her business why the man wasn't willing to serve in the forces, like every other man with any shred of patriotism and hatred of the Nazis, and anyway he always looked so dour when you spoke to him that it put you off, she told herself.

But he was a great worker, and as the long hours went on in a frenzy of Sister Marshall-inspired cleaning and sweeping and checking of supplies, as the cupboards and cabinets which had been upended and shaken into total disorder were set right, she had many occasions to be grateful to him. Just as she and Chick were struggling to get a particularly heavy cabinet back into position, he appeared beside them and with apparent ease got the thing exactly where it should be; as Robin reached to get at a high shelf that needed cleaning but couldn't quite manage it, he arrived beside her, all six foot three inches of him, and dealt with it for her. And though he did no more than nod his awareness of her thanks and said not a word, she felt better because he was there.

At three o'clock they stopped and Todd was sent to fetch tea for them all from the canteen in the basement, where the big shelters were, which he brought in a great enamel jug, a thick brew of particularly strong tea well laced with sweetened evaporated milk and extra sugar. And although at first Robin found it revolting, she discovered it gave her a powerful lift and took a second mugful, curling her now filthy hands round its comforting warmth contentedly. Sister Marshall, with some huffing and puffing, unearthed a tin of chocolate biscuits for them all and they sat there, half a dozen nurses and the bad-tempered Staff Nurse Puncheon and now much less annoyed Sister Marshall, recovering from it all.

Outside the flames still flickered in spite of the efforts of the firemen, as they could see when they turned out the lights and lifted a blackout from one glassless window and looked out across the road. The once familiar row of shops and buildings there was pitted with gaps where bombs had fallen, so that it looked like an old man's teeth, and heaps of smoking, flaming rubble replaced the tobacconist's and the pub on the corner where the housemen sneaked off to get some rest and recreation and the more racy of the nurses sometimes joined them. Chick looked mournfully at the tobacconist's and sighed.

'Bang goes my best black-marketeer,' she said gloomily. 'He always had a packet of Weights under the counter for me. Now what'll I do?'

'Give up smoking?' Robin suggested and Chick threw her a look of mock horror.

'Do you want me to give up living?' she said. 'Listen, what'd life be worth without sneaking off for a crafty drag behind the Old Bat's back?'

'She's not so bad,' Robin said and looked back over her shoulder to see where Sister Marshall was in the dimness. 'Those chocolate biscuits had to be hers, you know. They were never supplied by the Bursar's office.'

'Oh, she's not such an old toad,' Chick said carelessly. 'Listen, hon, when do you think she'll let us off duty?'

'Fourpence gets you a quid she'll make us wait till four and then fetch the children back to have their treatment here before their breakfasts.'

'But there aren't any windows. They'll freeze!'

'Hardly,' Robin said drily. 'It's been as hot a September as anyone can remember – and that's not just the bombs. No, you'll see. She can't bear not to have her patients under her own eyes.'

And so it was. By the time they were allowed to go off duty, the children, in the cots and beds that Sister Marshall had somehow repaired or scrounged, with Todd to help her do it, were back in Annie Zunz and bouncing around shouting for attention with as much verve as if they'd not lost half the night to the German bombers, and Robin had scurried about among them with clean nappies and bottles of milk and rusks as though she had five feet all running at the same time, with each one of

7

them aching miserably. She felt as though she had been working for uncountable hours.

And indeed she had; yesterday should have been her last day on duty, which meant she should have gone off last night at eight thirty, to come on in the morning and work till noon, and then off to bed ready to come back with the Daughters of Dracula, as everyone called the night staff, at eight o'clock. As it was, she had, like everyone else, worked a straight twenty hours and she was beginning to feel very odd in consequence. Her head was spinning and her eyes felt heavy and gritty, but she didn't feel sleepy any more. There had been moments during the night when she hadn't been able to hide her jaw-cracking yawns, finding it impossible to avoid Sister Marshall seeing her gaping wide, but Sister Marshall who, for all her famous tetchiness and demands for perfection on her ward, was a good enough soul as everyone agreed, had pretended not to notice and sent Todd to get some more tea for them all.

But now, as the pearly light of the late summer morning crept through the cracks in the blackout and Todd could at last take the hideous things down as the hospital carpenter arrived with boards to close off some of the windows, and some precious glass to reglaze enough of them to give the ward some daylight, Robin was on the point of exhaustion. Together with Chick and Staff Nurse Puncheon and the three first-years, Moriarty and McCulloch and Brown, she stood drooping in front of Sister's desk, waiting to be sent off duty at last, and yearning for rest. And Staff Nurse Puncheon snapped at her, 'Stand up straight, Bradman, for heaven's sake. We don't want Sister seeing you looking like that, do we? And do tidy your cap! Busy or not, you don't have to look like a guttersnipe.'

Robin reddened and pinched Chick's arm hard, knowing her friend was about to make some sort of retort, and that would never do; unlike Sister Marshall, the Staff Nurse, a singularly sour young woman with heavy overhanging front teeth that gave her a perpetually angry look, and a rather spotty complexion, was never known to be anything but thoroughly vindictive. To get on her wrong side could be disaster for any young nurse, especially one who had straight teeth and a smooth complexion. That was well known to raise Puncheon's ire to fever pitch. So, they both subsided and Robin did all she could to straighten her cap and stand up straight, as Sister Marshall, by some miracle looking as neat as she always did, came hurrying along the ward towards them.

'Well now, nurses,' she said briskly. 'You've all done very well. I'm most impressed by your efforts, and reports of your good work will go to Matron. Thank you very much. We've been lucky – none of the children were hurt and they will soon be doing very well again, though they'll need some extra naps today, no doubt. For yourselves, it's high time you went. Nurse Puncheon, you may take the rest of the day off, and I won't expect to see you till seven tomorrow morning. I can get a relief to hold the fort – '

'Oh, I'll work, Sister,' Puncheon said, with the sort of radiant and self-sacrificing smile on her face that always made Chick mime violent vomiting. 'It's no trouble to – '

'No, Staff Nurse,' Sister Marshall said firmly. 'I have made the arrangement I want. Nurses Chester and Bradman, you are due on night duty, are you not? Take tonight off, and report on Wednesday night. I will deal with Matron's office on that. You are both to go to Casualty. Take care of yourselves down there. It won't be as easy as it was here, you know.'

'No, Sister,' said Chick and glowed, tired as she was, and Robin was amused. Old Chick loved to be where the biggest hubbub was, adoring the busyness of Casualty, though Robin herself shrank from it; anything could come in through the great doors to the vast tiled waiting hall, any sort of injury and any sort of danger; but if Chick was to be there too, she told herself, she could cope well enough – perhaps.

' – if you don't mind, Nurse Bradman.' She heard Sister Marshall's voice and realized she had been talking to her and reddened.

'I'm sorry, Sister, I was – I didn't hear.'

'That was very apparent. Go to bed, nurse, at once. I've told the rest of you when to return on duty. Now go and have a good breakfast and take care of yourselves. You'll need all the energy you've got to see you through the rest of these difficult days. But it's all excellent training for you. Make the most of it.'

And Robin again managed not to laugh aloud at the familiarity of Sister Marshall's harangue and went gratefully trailing over to the Nurses' Home for the bath and bed she so ached for. It had been another hellish night, but they'd survived it. They could again.

· 2 ·

Considering how exhausted she had been when she had fallen into bed at seven, Robin slept poorly. The noise from the streets outside made by the lorries and fire appliances still trying to deal with the effects of last night's raids, and the heat of the September afternoon that built up steadily in her small room on the ground floor of the Nurses' Home, combined to make her toss restlessly and dream fitfully. And at two in the afternoon she gave up the struggle, and rolled over on to her back to lie with hands clasped behind her head, staring at the golden glowing blind over her window, and letting confused thoughts drift in and out of her head.

She'd never get any studying done for the Anatomy and Physiology exam, she told herself, and considered for a while getting up and spending the rest of the day studying till it was time to go on duty; and then banished the idea as fast as it had come. The work would have to be done eventually, air raids or no air raids, with the October exams looming, but she couldn't be expected to do any work today, not after last night's efforts, shaky though her knowledge was of the heart, its arteries and nerve supply and the structure and function of the eye. Maybe they'd have a quiet night on Casualty and she'd be able to do some then, she thought optimistically; and then grinned at herself in the dim afternoon light. Quiet, on Casualty, in these incredible days? A ridiculous notion.

11

Her mind drifted away; she should have phoned Ma before falling into bed, weary as she had been; Ma always fretted so when there were raids – and when weren't there, these nights? – and she'd be getting herself into a proper lather. I'll call her soon, Robin promised herself drowsily, and let a picture of her mother and the Norland Square house unfold in front of her eyes. The small room on the second floor that was hers with all her childhood dolls and books still scattered about; the nursery at the top of the house, with its rocking horse and doll's house, and the contrast of the drawing room on the first floor, with its exotic, if now rather shabby, decor of Bakst fabrics and eastern cushions. Her own father had designed that room, Ma had told her, and both she and David wanted to keep it that way as long as they could, though it had been done so long ago – before the First War even, the Great War, as they called it. Ha! thought Robin, remembering last night; it couldn't have been greater than this one, and went on with her memory's tour of the house that was home. She ended in the comfortable cluttered kitchen down in the basement with its scrubbed wooden table and the old rag rug, washed almost white now, in front of the shiny blackleaded range, and old Goosey pottering about and making a fuss of everyone who came within reach. Robin's lips curved; dear old Goosey must be over eighty now, and still thinking she ran the house for her beloved Mrs Poppy and Mr David and the children, when in reality she was as much a burden to Poppy as a help. Not that anyone would ever dream of letting the old darling know that. Her place in the Deveen family was too important for that.

Deveen, thought Robin and yawned. Would I like to be called Robin Deveen now? They'd asked her, just after they'd married, what she wanted to do. She could have changed her name to match her stepfather's and mother's if she chose; but even at the age of only eight she'd known what she wanted.

'It wouldn't be fair, would it, David?' she'd said, and the grown-up Robin, in her crumpled hot bed in the Nurses' home in Whitechapel Road could almost hear her own childish treble in her memory's ears. 'I mean, I know I never saw my father and he never saw me, but he was my father. Mummy explained about that. It wouldn't be right, would it? Not after him being in the Great War and everything.'

'You're absolutely right about that, Robin,' David had said gravely. 'I couldn't agree more. You are *absolutely* right. But I'll tell you what – you can borrow my name if you ever need it. Okay? There may be times when it could come in handy to have another label to use. You never know.'

Robin had laughed at the time, quite convinced that was just another of David's sillinesses, but he'd been right. There had indeed been lots of times, when Chloe was being particularly ghastly, when Robin had yearned to stop being a Bradman, the way Chloe was, and had wished to be a Deveen like David and Ma. Like the time Chloe had got divorced; and at that memory Robin turned over in bed with a convulsive movement and tried to banish Chloe from her mind.

But she wouldn't go and Robin lay curled on her side, still staring at the oblong of golden blind and thought about Chloe. So beautiful, so selfish, so unkind, so thoughtless, the nastiest sister – well, half-sister – anyone could possibly have. The divorce had been awful because Chloe, out of sheer horridness, according to fourteen-year-old Robin, had reverted to her single name, and plastered it all over the newspapers. Going to school all through that summer had been frightful, simply frightful. The other girls had stared at her and whispered as one nastiness after another came out in court and was published with lip-smacking relish in papers like the *Daily Mirror* (oh, the shame of it!) and the *Daily Sketch* (oh, the even greater shame!). Which had been a strange experience for Robin, because she had always been popular with everyone as a lively person and a good hardworking one, too. Chloe had made it all so horrible that Robin had begged her mother to take her away from school and Poppy had been inclined to refuse ('It's such a good school, darling, and you're doing so well. This'll soon be forgotten, honestly it will!') but it had been David who had made it possible to go on, and get over it, and prove his Poppy was right.

'You have to give people the chance to be themselves,' he had said in that soft American voice of his which never changed, however long he lived in England and which Robin had come to love as much as she had once hated it. 'Chloe is what she is, a sad and sorry lady, and we just have to live with that. Pretending she isn't your sister won't help. You'll know she is, you see, and that means other people will too. Stick with it and you'll like yourself a whole lot more than you would if you tried to duck out. Give it a shot, anyway.'

And she had, and they had been right, Ma and David; it had ended with Chloe divorced and given lots of money from it – because her husband had been immensely rich, as rich as he was nasty, it seemed – and everyone at school had got all excited about Fay Wray in *King Kong* and swooned over Greta Garbo in *Queen Christina* and forgotten the Chloe fuss and that had been that. Chloe had gone on her usual way, though she hadn't married again (thank heaven, thought Robin), and everything had been fine.

Until the war had started and it all got so horrid, if in a different way. And Robin turned on to her back again and scowled at the blind. The first days had been so disagreeable, what with Ma and David having to do so much with their work, and at the same time persuade Lee and Joshy to be evacuated. Lee had been sensible enough but Joshy had not, and had screamed and sulked and made no end of a fuss.

'For all the world,' Lee had said with all the scorn of a sophisticated eleven-year-old, 'as though he were four instead of eight. Do shut up, Joshy. You're making it worse for everyone. I'll be there to look after you.'

Poor old Joshy, thought Robin as she saw the image of her small half-brother scowling in her mind's eye, the shock of black hair that always fell into his eyes in its usual tangle and his dark eyes staring pugnaciously through it. Poor Joshy. Twice he'd run away already; and twice they'd made him go back. He must drive Goosey's nephew potty, she thought, trying to keep an eye on him on that rambling farm in Norfolk. She remembered it well, from the times Goosey had taken her there to visit when she'd been small and Ma and David had first married. She'd hated it at first, had been angry with David for taking up so much of Ma's time when Robin had always had her to herself, but it had got easier and easier as time had gone on and now the thought of life without David was insupportable. And she smiled at the blind, thinking of her stepfather, who always managed somehow to make her laugh.

Jessie, she thought then. She makes me laugh too. And suddenly sat up in bed. There was no hope of sleeping any more, she told herself as she swung her legs out. And I'm absolutely starving. She hadn't realized it, but she was empty because she'd been far too weary to eat when she'd come off duty this morning. The answer was either scrabbling for whatever she could get in the canteen – pilchard sandwiches or something equally revolting – or taking a cab up to Cable Street, to see what Auntie Jessie had to offer.

And she hummed a little as she scrambled into her new trousers – bought especially for being in the shelters, if she ever got caught in a raid when she was off duty – and the cream silk blouse Ma had made for her out of one of her own old ones. She felt and looked cool and she leaned towards her mirror to brush her curly hair into some sort of order and made for the corridor.

And as she closed her door softly the adjoining one opened and Chick put her head out and grinned at her.

'Two minds with but a single,' she whispered, for they were on the night nurses' floor, and making any sound at all was considered a crime fit for hanging by Home Sister. 'I'm absolutely starving – are you going on a recce?'

'I can do better than that,' Robin whispered back. 'I'm going down to my Auntie Jessie's. Do you want to come?'

'Do cats eat kippers?' Chick retorted delightedly and came out of her room. She was wearing trousers too, a very racy pair in checks with a matching cotton shirt which she'd bought in New York in the last summer before the War broke out and which she had brought on the long tour of Europe she had planned. Robin had only a hazy knowledge of her life in her own country but had a distinct impression that Chick came from a rich family. She certainly seemed to have plenty of cash and had none of the problems some of the other nurses had, lacking adequate support from their families. But she never showed off or made reference to such things, so neither did Robin. It was one of the most comfortable things about their friendship, she thought. You talked of what you wanted to, and didn't have to talk of things you didn't want to. She herself had told Chick lots about her family and had indeed taken her home to Norland Square to meet them but she had never told her of the awful Chloe. That would be too shaming –

The street outside sobered them both. The smell of explosives still hung in the air, and everywhere they looked dust motes floated in the long rays of the September sun to create a golden haze over the battered buildings. Across the road the last of the flames had at last been extinguished, leaving behind the heavy reek of wet rotten wood and newly distributed mildew as well as the hint of coal gas that still hung around; and Chick shivered a little even in the sunshine and tucked her hand into Robin's elbow.

'Come on, kid. We'll leg it down to Cable Street. I can't imagine there'll be many buses this afternoon, one way or another, and it'll add to an already terrific appetite – it shouldn't take long – '

It didn't, as they stepped out with long strides, and even in the smoke-filled reeking air, laden with the smell of demolition, and even walking past the wrecked buildings that seemed to be everywhere, Robin felt the vigour that exercise always created in her, and the sheer delight in being alive that was so much a part of her, and knew a moment of guilt. She shouldn't feel so when all around her was destruction and death; but then she felt better, because people they passed smiled and waved, and some of the air raid wardens, who knew all the nurses from the hospital by sight, spotted them as they went past a particularly high pile of rubble and waved and shouted cheerfully. Even the shops had cheeky signs on them; 'Special Sale, Courtesy the Nasties' read one in a shoe shop and on a china shop, 'Business as bloody usual. To hell with Adolf.' With that sort of attitude in everyone around her, it was all right, she decided, to feel tolerably good. And her step lengthened and they went belting arm in arm along the tired battered road until Chick gasped and laughed and complained of breathlessness.

'Are you sure your aunt won't mind me coming too?' she said as soon as she could talk easily. 'I mean, what with shortages and all – she can't stretch her rations that far, surely? A woman on her own – '

'I wouldn't worry about that,' Robin said blithely. 'She'll not worry, you can be sure of that – she's only happy when she's feeding people. That's why she runs a restaurant. She'll be all right – '

'Black-market?' Chick said and grinned at her. 'No, don't look like that! From all I hear everyone who can does and everyone who doesn't wishes they could. People always try to do the best they can for themselves when times are hard.'

'Not my Auntie Jessie. She's the straightest person you ever saw. Says what she thinks when she thinks it. And she certainly wouldn't black-market. She says you don't

17

have to – she gets lots of fish and so forth and she manages fine. I hope you like fish – '

'I like food,' Chick said simply. 'All I can get. God, I'm hungry! I'd kill for a hot dog.'

'She might even manage that,' Robin said and grinned at the look of sheer greed that crossed Chick's face. 'She runs a delicatessen, remember, and they have all sorts of odd foreign things in them, don't they?'

'Foreign! Don't you dare call me foreign! Daughter of the Empire, that's me, fighting for the Mother Country, or some such. Foreign, forsooth – I'll have your guts for garters, you talk to me that way – '

'Of course you're foreign,' Robin said cheerfully. 'That accent of yours, you could cut it with a knife, and the clothes you wear – you never saw anything like *that* in Swan and Edgar's, now, did you?'

'You're damned right – I never saw anything I'd be caught dead in in Swan and Edgar's – listen, is it the next road on the left or – '

'Good for you, remembering! Yes, it is. And here's hoping Jessie's got something ready to eat and doesn't have to start making things. I don't think I can wait another moment – '

They ran the last few yards, bursting with an energy neither knew they had, and stopped outside the neat shop half-way down Cable street. Over its fascia a sign read, 'Jessie's Best Foods' and below that an elegantly painted hand pointed to the right and a smaller sign that read, 'Trade Counter. Ring Twice'.

'Oh!' Chick moaned ecstatically and lifted her nose to the air. 'I smell pickles and pastrami, I swear it – '

'And salt beef and cheese and a lot of other goodies besides. Come on.' And with a proprietorial air, Robin ushered her friend into the shop.

It hadn't changed in all the years Robin could remember. She had first been brought here as a very small child and she could still remember the bewildering effect of the shelves full of exotic-looking packages and tins and the long glass-covered fitting below the counter where dishes of the most remarkable concoctions waited to be weighed out into small measures: cream cheeses and chopped herring mixtures, rows of different kinds of pickled fish and sides of rich rosy smoked salmon and umpteen different kinds of sausages. There weren't any sausages there now, for they had come from France and Italy and Germany in the old days before the War, and supplies had vanished with the first air raid, but there were instead dishes of delectable-looking salads and piles of crisp rolls, some garnished with scraps of fried onions and some round and glistening with a rich golden brown crust and holes in their centres, and Chick looked at those and crooned, 'Oh, as I live and breathe, bagels! Am I in London or New York? Who is the angel who did this? Let me at 'em!'

The woman behind the counter, who had been serving an elderly customer with a pot of cream cheese, came and peered at her, and Chick looked up at the wizened little face under its mop of highly regrettable yellow curls, which looked so ferociously out of place that they made the shop look almost toylike, and grinned widely. 'Hi,' she said. 'I'm the bagel maven!'

'Maven?' Robin said, mystified, and smiled at the little woman who now saw her and was coming out from behind the counter in an eager bustle. 'Hello, Lily. Are you well?'

'All the better for seein' you, lovey! There, but you look tired! The way they work you down there, it's a sin and a crime, that's what it is. So, what's this already? I ain't never seen this one before, have I?'

'I think you've always been at the restaurant, or in the kitchens,' Robin said. 'This is my friend Chick Chester. She's been here with me before. What's a whatever you said, Chick?'

Chick's face split in a wide grin. 'Maven. A connoisseur, ducky. One who knows all there is to know on a subject. Here's me, a good Toronto Catholic, and

I know more Yiddish than you do, and you're part Jewish!'

'Not difficult to know more than I do,' Robin said and felt a sudden pang as she always did when the subject came up. 'I know damn all about it. No one ever taught me – '

'So what?' Lily said comfortably and led them towards the back of the shop. 'You got enough on your mind, ain't you? Listen, your auntie's in the kitchen. See yourself through, eh? And you want to eat? I can get a plate or two ready here for you both or you can talk to your auntie and she'll have maybe hot – '

'Both!' Chick said greedily and followed Robin through the little room at the back of the shop and out of the big doors which led to the preparation kitchens that spread to the other side of the establishment.

Here was bustle of a high order and the two girls stood hovering in the doorway for a moment, watching. There were long metal preparation tables and huge ovens and cooking hobs and sinks and, everywhere where they could be put, long shelves crammed with pots and pans of all sorts and sizes. Standing at each of the preparation tables were women, all of them clearly well over fifty, wrapped in voluminous overalls and with their hair tied back in cotton scarves, chopping vegetables, mixing salads and cakes and beating eggs. In the middle of them stood a woman who was not wearing an overall, even though her dress, of rich crimson silk, was clearly an expensive one, who was rolling pastry with lusty thumping strokes, and pulling at it with big capable hands.

'There, you see? *That's* how I like to see my strudel dough – so thin you could read the newspaper through it. None of your heavy great slabs for Jessie's, and don't you forget it, dolly, don't you ever forget it – ' And the woman beside her muttered, but reached for the rolling pin and took over the pulling and thumping of the pastry under the other's very watchful eye.

Looking at her, Robin experienced the wash of feeling that Jessie always created in her; she looked so comfortable, so sure, so reliable in a hard world, with her great size, and her magnificent bust pushing so imperiously against the silk of her dress. She looked older now, of course she did, for her hair, once so vigorous and thick and exuberant, was whiter and much less pleased with itself, and the vast bulk that had always distinguished her seemed to have collapsed in on itself a little. But there was still a great energy in her and she displayed it to the full as she lifted her head and caught sight of the two girls in the doorway.

'Boobala!' she shrieked. 'It's my boobala! Come here, you dolly, you – come and give me a hug. Have you eaten? Of course you haven't eaten – listen, what'll you have? Fish? I got a bissel the best fried plaice you ever tasted – or there's some chicken, gedampt just the way you like it, and I got some oil, I could make you some chips. Oh dolly, it's good to see you!' And she folded Robin in a huge rosewater and frying- oil and fish-scented grasp, burying Robin's head in that ample bosom and squeezing her till her ribs seemed to crack.

And Robin, who had once found those hugs a bit overwhelming, gave her back as good as she got, and hugged her with all the fervour she had in her. Never mind air raids and the hateful Staff Nurse Puncheon and aching feet and sleeplessness; this was what living was all about.

· 3 ·

'Sugar,' said Mrs Crighton in loud patrician tones. 'I must have sugar. You can't run a canteen without sugar, now can you? Be reasonable, Mrs Deveen!'

'I'm trying to be,' Poppy said, controlling her anger as best she could. This woman made more fuss than all the rest of the volunteers put together; the sooner she could be shifted somewhere else the better for all of them. If she had to find another canteen somewhere for her, she'd do it, damned if she wouldn't. 'I'm afraid it's you who is being a little less than reasonable. I simply *can't* get any more. They're having enough trouble with supplies for people to get their ration as it is. I've managed to get some saccharin, however, and – '

'Saccharin?' Mrs Crighton actually snorted. 'What good is that? It won't give these poor creatures any nutrients, will it?' And she rolled the word round her tongue with relish. 'Nutrients are what it's all about, surely?'

'No it isn't,' Poppy snapped, her patience at last exhausted. 'It's about providing a few minutes to sit down and rest with a cup of tea and a sandwich or two before they have to go back and work again. They understand that even if you don't. And I really must say' – and here her control totally slipped and she let her anger show, well aware of her self-indulgence – 'I really can't understand how so much gets used when I'm not here. You'd almost think some people were taking it home with them.'

Mrs Crighton looked at her with a face of stone and then, very magisterially, took off her frilled apron.

'That does it. I shall leave now and I shall not return. If you can do no better when your errors of management are pointed out to you by an experienced person than hurl insults and accusations, then it is better that I take my valuable services where they will be appreciated. You will have to find someone else to handle tonight's shift; I shall not be here. Good afternoon, Mrs Deveen!' And she went stumping out of the canteen as a few weary firefighters and air raid wardens, crouched over their tea and tired buns, watched her with dispirited eyes.

'Good riddance to that one.' Maria, the tall and rather thin helper from the other end of the Whitechapel Road sounded deeply satisfied. 'Rotten old bat – and I reckon you was right, Mrs D. She's been 'elping herself to more sugar than anyone's got any right to. A little bit's fair enough, but not 'ole packets, like!' And she mopped the counter with a vicious sweep of her dishcloth that wiped the haughty Mrs Crighton out of existence, and looked smug.

Poppy sighed. She knew they all took some of the supplies as their perks; and she couldn't blame them. The rations were getting less and less and so much had disappeared from the shops that feeding the weary families that still remained in the East End was a major problem for a housewife, especially if she was working as well and so had no time to queue at the shops. Perhaps she shouldn't have been so tough on Mrs Crighton; a pair of hands was a pair of hands, after all, and for a moment she considered going after her and asking her to come back.

'If you only knew what she's been like, when you're not 'ere!' Maria went on. 'You'd think she was a duchess, honest you would. I mean, you muck in with the rest of us, you do, but not Madam 'Igh and Mighty Crighton. Oh, no, not 'er! Sits there and says she's supervisin' and makes a bleedin' pest of 'erself. Listen, Mrs D, I can stay on if you like, for a bit, till five maybe, but I got to get 'ome then. My old man, with 'is back an' all, 'e can't get me old Mum down to the shelter, and there's the kids to think of an' all – can you manage on your own tonight? There ain't no one else to 'old the fort, that's the thing. Mrs Barnes got 'erself bombed out yesterday and she's been sent off to 'Igh Wycombe or some such place and Mrs Knott, she's 'ad to go and take care of 'er sister's kids on account their mum's gone into the 'ospital for her sixth and 'aving a bad time of it.'

Poppy stood there in the canteen she had worked so hard to set up and run in the cellar of the abandoned dress factory in Plumber's Row, and wondered how much longer she could go on. It was almost an academic exercise, as though she weren't thinking about herself at all, but about some other person who was Poppy Deveen and who was trying so hard to keep her life together in the middle of the hell the world had become. The children away – and she ached with the misery of missing them; her serious, sensible Lee and little Josh, who always seemed to be so cocky and self contained, but who was (as who could know better than Poppy?) so often frightened inside – and David, in whom all her security and peace rested, away again on impossible trains and so tired that she could have wept for him, and no phone call from Robin this morning and God knows what had happened to her, and now Mrs Crighton –

But she didn't weep and stopped the academic thinking, because it was a waste of time and she had work to do, and said as briskly as she could, 'That's very good of you, Maria, I do appreciate it. I'll be back by five, I promise. And if you can find any of your friends and neighbours who'd be interested in helping out, do tell them. I really don't think I can recruit people from the West End any more.'

'I'll say not,' Maria said sturdily. 'Toffee-nosed bitches like that. 'Oo needs 'em?'

So much, thought Poppy wearily, for the Dunkirk spirit and all of us pulling together to win the war and all the rest of it. It was just the same as it had been last time, with middle- and upper-class people working in canteens and behaving as though they were doing a huge favour to the exhausted ordinary soldiers who were going through hell to protect them, and the resentment that had caused in the rank and file, and she closed her eyes and looked back almost twenty-five years to the eager girl she had been in her FANY's uniform and her determination to help win the War to End All Wars, driving her ambulance around France – and opened them again to look at today's reality.

It had all seemed rather unimportant at first, a very flat anticlimax to all the worry. Once Chamberlain had made his announcement of war and that first siren warning of a raid had turned out to be a false alarm, nothing much had happened. All those months of the Phoney War when the children had come back to London from being evacuated and David had spent his time as usual in his Fleet Street office and Robin at the London Hospital had seemed so happy and useful, though it was a pity she had to work so hard; Poppy had thought with deliberate optimism that it would be all right this time, a sensible war, over by Christmas. But she had known in her heart that it wasn't to be that way, and when the bad times came and the Germans went pushing through Holland and Belgium, and Poland had fallen and then eventually Dunkirk had happened to waken everyone up to what it was to be like, and the fear of invasion had gripped even the most optimistic, she had rallied fast and got herself as organized as she could. The children had to be sent off to Norfolk again, with the usual fussing and flailing from Joshy but Lee's calm acceptance to sweeten the wretched business, and they had checked the strength of the shelter in the back garden at Norland Square and started to persuade Goosey to go with the children to Norfolk. Not that anyone had for a moment expected she would; for Goosey, dearly as she loved the children, the place she had to be was Norland Square. Hadn't she lived there for more than forty years? It would take more than a nasty little jumped-up Hun like that creature with the silly moustache to get her out of it, she had said firmly – and that had been that.

Her mother had been no better; Poppy had gone to Mildred's house in Leinster Terrace and begged her to go to the country, in case of bombing, but she had refused to hear of it.

'I am seventy-four, Poppy, and therefore living on extra time. If it is meant for me to die in an air raid, then so be it. I can't leave here – Queenie would never go and how could I leave her? I have my own responsibilities as you have yours. I'll take care of myself, be assured. You have enough to do.' And she had rung for Queenie to make more tea, and flatly refused to discuss the matter further.

Poppy had worried about Jessie too, for she wasn't nearly as young as she pretended to be. Seventy-five, Poppy had told her very directly, isn't exactly a youngster. And Jessie had laughed and pooh-poohed her and pointed out that the business had to be kept going and that it was work of great wartime importance, at that.

'Where'll the poor things go when they're home from the trenches on leave?' she asked. 'They've got to have somewhere to enjoy themselves. So Poppy's and Jessie's have got to keep going. I'll supply a canteen too, if you set one up. There – will that make you feel better? Then you'll know I can't just go off to the country like some babe in arms – any more than your Mama will. I'm as stubborn as she is, and a lot more useful – '

And Poppy had thrown up her hands and stopped arguing. This war was not going to be at all like the last one, with its trenches and regular troopships over the channel; she knew that, but why try to explain to Jessie? What good would it do?

So she had set up the canteen and settled to dogged work at the two restaurants, struggling to get food supplies for them, somehow managing to keep going and to look after Goosey and David when he was home,

26

which was less and less often these busy days, for his paper sent him all over the place to report what was happening. He even had to go to France to join the BEF in the early days, but glory be, had been sent home again before the retreat had turned into the danger of Dunkirk's beaches – and she shuddered now at the memory of those dreadful days in June.

And then the raids had begun; and Poppy looked around at the few people using her canteen at this time of day, and could have wept for them. Arthur Brook, the warden from the post on the corner of Stepney Way, was sitting half asleep in the corner over a cooling cup of Bovril, his face greyish white with fatigue and the inevitable layers of dust from the piles of rubble, and beside him the lanky shape of his son Freddy, a sickly youth who'd been turned down for the army because of his health and now worked seventeen hours a day helping the rescue teams. He'd have been better off in the army, Poppy thought with compunction, looking at the boy's sleeping face with its lax lower jaw that revealed his apologies for teeth. He'd have had an easier time with them. The other people in the canteen were in no better shape; exhaustion hung around all of them like a veil that blurred their shapes and their features and Poppy thought – I've got to keep going. This is just about the only place they get any time to call their own, between raids.

And she nodded quietly at Maria and said, 'I'm going over to Cable Street, to my aunt's. You've got the phone number? Great – I'll try to see if she can spare some sugar from her supplies, but I know she's badly off too. Take care of what there is for me, Maria, I can't manage any more wastage – '

Maria nodded and let her eyes slide away from Poppy's direct gaze, but that didn't matter, Poppy told herself. She'd got the message and she'd act on it.

The walk to Jessie's was, as always, a dispiriting experience. The smell alone was enough to plunge a person into despondency. Old buildings don't break up

27

kindly, she thought, as she picked her way carefully along Coke Street, making for Backchurch Lane on the other side of Commercial Road. They die as noisily as they can, and leave a dreadful smell behind. And then there was the gas and the cracked sewers and sometimes she even thought she caught a whiff of the sickly sweetish smell of dead bodies, so familiar to her from the last war, but she refused to even consider that. The rescue teams were incredible; they got out every last dead body as well as the living survivors. She had to believe that, they all did. And then she remembered the awful day when the branch of Woolworth's in Commercial Road had suffered a direct hit when the shop had been full of people and they hadn't attempted to clear the site. They'd just sealed it off and left it to Nature to deal with the results –

She shook herself mentally and stepped out faster, reaching the end of Backchurch Lane at last and looking across Cable Street to her aunt's small shop and kitchens, the place where the whole business had begun, and she stopped for a moment and let herself remember. All those long hard years of looking after Robin and then David and the babies as the business had grown and blossomed even through the long depression years, until she had thought that at last there was no more need ever to worry again. They'd always be able to make a good living. Better than that even, maybe a lot of money, opening a fourth and then a fifth restaurant – and again she gave herself that mental shake and crossed the road. This was September 1940, not Happy-Ever-After-Time. When the war was over it would be different perhaps, but right now there was work to do. A lot of it.

She nodded cheerfully at Lily Harvey as she went through the shop, and Lily, who was serving a customer, waved to her to wait so that she could tell her something, but Poppy just smiled at her and went on; Lily always had something special to say. Whatever it was, it could wait, and she couldn't. There was a lot to do between now and getting back to the canteen before five o'clock to send

Maria heading home to Shadwell and to prepare for the German planes to start their usual evening visitation.

It wasn't until she got into the kitchen and saw the three of them that she realized just how anxious she'd been. Robin was sitting perched on a high stool at one of the preparation tables, a plate of casseroled chicken in front of her, into which she was digging with great relish. Beside her, her friend Chick was equally occupied, while Jessie sat facing them both, her chin propped on her plump hands as she beamed with satisfaction, watching her food being appreciated.

'Robin!' Poppy cried. 'You didn't call me this morning! What happened?'

Robin looked up guiltily and managed a smile, though her mouth was full. 'Oh, darling, I'm so sorry! I was so dead to the world, I simply couldn't bear to wait for a phone and there was only one working. Some of the lines are down. I'm sorry, darling, truly I am – but I'm fine – '

'I've been frantic,' Poppy said, more sharply than she meant to. 'It really is a bit selfish of you, you know. It wouldn't have hurt to hold on for a little longer to let me know you were all right – '

A slightly mulish expression moved across Robin's face and Poppy thought: oh damn, damn, damn, I've done it again. Why can't I keep my stupid mouth shut? And she thought confusedly about how it had been with her own mother all those years ago and how long it had taken them to become, if not close, at least friendly towards each other, and somewhere deep inside she hurt. Was it to be like that with her beloved Robin and she? It couldn't be. I can't be like Mildred, I can't. It won't be the same for us –

'I told you. I was absolutely flattened. We had a ghastly night – '

'Oh, I'm sorry to fuss, darling,' Poppy said and came and stood behind her and put an arm around her daughter and set her cheek against her hair. 'It's just that I've had a perfectly foul time with one of the women at the canteen,

29

over sugar, and I have to take her shift tonight and they've sent David off somewhere ridiculous, Hull or somewhere. I do try not to be a bore, though, over you, I really do.'

Robin put down her fork and returned her mother's hug. 'It's all right, fusspot. I'll forgive you. Thousands wouldn't,' she said lightly, but there was a shadow between them all the same, and Poppy thought – oh, Lee, I do miss you. And then felt guilty that she should be thinking of her second child in such a way at such a juncture. Surely she didn't have favourites? It would be a dreadful thing if she had. Mothers shouldn't.

'So, listen, Robin, your mother's right. It ain't nice you don't call her. You know how she worries,' Jessie said.

'Then she shouldn't,' Robin said sharply and went on eating. 'I'm a big girl now, Auntie Jessie. Twenty-one, for pity's sake – an adult. Don't you start! Ye gods, Chick, you're lucky, you know that? You can't be got at because of not phoning often enough!'

'I wish I could be,' Chick said quietly and Robin flushed a little and went on eating, with a decidedly mulish look on her face now.

'So, what's news, Jess?' Poppy said, feeling the need to discharge the tension that had sprung up in the little group of women. 'Did the fish turn up?'

'Miracles happen, dolly, miracles really happen! I got all the plaice I wanted, and some halibut too, believe it or not! Come and see – ' The big woman slid off her stool and went waddling over to the cold rooms on the far side, with Poppy walking behind her, their heads close together.

'Listen kid,' Chick said as soon as they were out of earshot. 'Where do you get off being such a sourpuss? So your Mom wants you to call her? What's so terrible?'

'Oh, they're all the same!' Robin said and threw down her fork. Suddenly she wasn't hungry any more. 'If it isn't Ma, it's Jessie, and if it isn't her, it's Goosey and David's the worst of the lot. It's like – it's like being in a hothouse.'

30

'People get anxious in wartime,' Chick said, putting on the voice of a BBC lecturer, very heavy and portentous, and then returning to her own light tones. 'Haven't you noticed that? They kinda look round for something or someone to be anxious about and they pick on people. I dare say that's it.'

'You idiot,' Robin said and laughed in spite of herself. 'Okay, okay – not another word. I'll call my mother every hour on the hour, all right? Don't you start nagging or I really will go into a decline.'

Chick finished her chicken, doing everything but lick the plate. 'I'll see to it you do. Listen, do you think your aunt could spare me some of that strudel? It looks good enough to eat.'

'Help yourself,' Robin said proprietorially again. 'She's a lovely old darling, actually, and only fusses when Ma does, and she won't fuss over strudel. No, not for me, I've had enough. Mmm? What is it?' And she turned her head because Lily from the shop was prodding her.

'Where's your ma?' she demanded and her little head bounced so that her absurd hair seemed to bounce too with a separate life of its own. 'There's someone here wants to see your Auntie Jessie and your Ma won't be best pleased and I saw her come through.'

'She's in the cold rooms with Auntie Jessie. Who is it, Lily?'

'Least said soonest mended,' Lily said darkly and stood hovering, staring over her shoulder, clearly undecided, but then she caught her breath and went hurrying back to the door, because it had opened again and someone was standing there in the shadowy corridor outside.

'Come back into the shop, you idiot,' Lily said urgently. 'We don't want no arguments around here today, whatever else happens. On your way – I'll tell Jessie when – '

'What is it, Lily?' Jessie and Poppy had come out of the cold rooms and were standing looking at Lily's expressive back and she turned and looked at them and held her arms out in a pathetic attempt to hide the person she'd been talking to. But she needn't have bothered because he sidestepped her and said easily, 'Hi Mom. And Poppy! Well, well, well. Long time no see.'

'Heavens above!' Chick whispered into Robin's ear. 'Who is that gorgeous man? He looks like some film star, I swear. Did you ever *see* anyone so good-looking?'

· 4 ·

Jessie's reaction would have been funny if it hadn't been so obvious that she was distressed. She looked at the man in the expensive suit and the wide-lapelled camel-hair coat flung oh-so-casually over his shoulders, and her face lit up as though someone had switched on a lamp inside her, and she made to move towards him; and then stopped and looked over her shoulder at Poppy, and her face fell ludicrously.

Poppy stared at him with a face like stone, and Robin looked from one to the other in great interest as Chick leaned over and breathed into her ear, 'Who is it?'

Robin grimaced her lack of knowledge and Chick murmured, 'Nice! Hope he's available – ' as the man pulled his coat off with an elegant sweep of one arm and dropped it on the nearest preparation table before walking lazily over to Jessie.

'Well, well,' he said and bent and kissed her on each cheek. 'Who'd have thought it. Imagine finding you with visitors!' And he turned and looked at Poppy and lifted his brows. 'Hi there, Poppy! So how are things with you?'

He had a marked American accent and that made Chick sit up even straighter and Robin nudged her with a sharp elbow. Chick's refusal to behave in a circumspect way over men she liked the look of always made Robin blush for her. It was so very un-English, she would tell her scoldingly, and Chick would laugh and promise to

33

mend her ways, but here she was, doing it again: and the tall man caught her eye then and smiled, a lazy curling of the lips that showed a dimple at one corner of his all-too-perfect mouth and made Chick almost burst with delight.

'And who have we here? Two pretty ladies – I guess the Good Lord's watching over me today. Introduce me, someone!'

'Girls, it's time you were on your way, isn't it?' Poppy said and Robin stared at her mother in amazement. She'd never heard a voice as hard and indeed downright rude emerging from her, and she got to her feet and said deliberately to the tall man, 'It seems we have to introduce ourselves. I'm Robin Bradman, and this is Chick Chester, my friend. Who are you?'

'Well, well! So you're little Robin, hmm? I've heard a lot about you.' And he looked over his shoulder at Poppy who was now looking very pinched about the mouth. 'It's good to meet you,' and held out his hand to Robin to be shaken. 'And you too – Chick, was it?'

'Yes, indeedy,' Chick said fervently and stuck out one hand and shook his vigorously. 'Where are you from? My part of the world, I think.'

He put his head on one side and looked at her quizzically. 'I doubt it. I'm a Londoner, you know? Brought up in these mean streets – '

Jessie, who had regained some of her self-control, made an odd little sound at that and the man looked at her and laughed. 'No offence meant!'

'You sound American,' Chick said. 'Me, I'm Canadian.'

'Ah, one from the wilderness, hmm? Great little place, they tell me. Never been there myself, mind you. Me, I like the sophisticated life, you know? New York, that's my natural home.'

'Who are you?' Robin demanded again, somewhat chilled by the man's insolent manner and he grinned again and looked at Poppy.

'Okay if I say, Poppy?' he said teasingly. 'I mean, I wouldn't want you at me like a wildcat. You were bad enough over little Chloe – God knows how you'd be over this one!'

Poppy moved forward and to Robin's amazement her fists were actually clenched, and, alarmed, Robin slid off her stool and took Chick's arm in one firm hand and urged her past the man towards the door.

'I'm not sure I'm interested,' she said in a high voice, trying to ignore the memories that were pushing at her now, the half-explained things she had overheard as a child, the hints that had been dropped by Lily, that most inveterate of chatterboxes, and she didn't want to know more. Whatever it was it had upset her mother badly and however cross Poppy sometimes made her, Robin loved her mother dearly and would not willingly hurt her. And she hurried across the room and kissed Poppy and said quietly, 'We must go, darling. We'll be on duty soon and I've got to sort out my uniform and do some studying. I promise to call you as soon as I get off duty tomorrow – bye.' And she went then and hugged Jessie and kissed her, realizing as she did so that for once her aunt was unaware of her. Her attention was completely fixed on the man who was now leaning against one of the preparation tables, picking at a tray of strudel and watching, with clear amusement, all that was going on. And looking at Jessie's face Robin thought – she's getting awfully old, for her face was drawn and pinched and sagged miserably.

'Take care of yourself, Auntie Jessie,' she said gently and then with a jerk of her head at Chick made for the door and Chick, unusually subdued, followed her.

There was a little silence when they'd gone and then Poppy said tightly, 'How long have you been back?'

Jessie looked almost despairing at that, and made a move towards her and then pulled back and turned to the man and then almost tottered as she moved away from both of them and went and sat on the tall stool

Robin had just vacated, and then leaned her head on her hand. Neither of the others seemed to notice; they were staring at each other.

'Well, now, let me see,' he said lazily and picked up another piece of strudel. 'It was June, as I recall – '

'Then how the hell did you get here?' she flared. 'They stopped ordinary passenger crossings from America well before then!'

He lifted his eyebrows and then with great delicacy cleaned his sticky fingers on a silk handkerchief.

'Did I say it was this year?' he murmured. 'It was June '38. Wasn't it, Ma?'

'I told you not to come here unless I made an arrangement!' Jessie said and her voice was thick. 'All I want is peace and quiet, the chance to live the way I want with the people I want and no trouble! All you had to do is keep out of the way. Why make a *tummel*?'

'A *tummel*?' he said, looking at her with his brows raised.

'You know what I mean – don't try and make a fool of me, Bernie! I didn't want any rows or arguments. All I asked of you was you should keep out of Poppy's way. And here you are – you know we usually get together this time of the day!'

'I got tired of it,' Bernie said offhandedly. 'Why should I hide from my own cousin, hmm? A man can visit his mother with a bit of a business proposition without having to hide away as though it were some sort of crime!' He snickered then. 'Not that it's entirely kosher, I can't deny, but you know how it is. Hard times mean hard deals.'

Poppy had moved away to stand leaning against the table near Jessie. Her face was still pinched and white and her eyes glittered a little as she looked at Jessie.

'He's been here two years?'

'Yes,' Jessie said after a moment. 'Yes, I did my best, Poppy! But what could I do? He turned up on my doorstep looking like such a nebbish – terrible clothes,

36

thin as a rake, what would you expect me to do? Send him away?'

'After what he did to you, I rather think I would have expected it,' Poppy said.

'What I did to her? You mean to your precious Chloe, don't you? Not that I remember her as being all that hard to deal with. She wanted what she got as much as I did, if you see what I mean. She wasn't exactly a shrinking blossom when I met her, you know. Hanging around nightclubs at her age – '

'I'm not interested in anything you have to say!' Poppy flared. 'Not now or ever! You treated Chloe abominably and you gave your mother hell! She broke her heart while you were in that prison, do you know that? I was glad to see you there – it was where you belonged. I only wish they'd kept you longer. But she's your mother and she suffered hell because of you – '

'So how could I have sent him away, Poppy?' Jessie looked up at her, and her eyes were reddened with unshed tears. 'Hmm? Like you said, I'm his mother! How could I send him away? And how could I cause you pain? So I did the best I could. I told him to be careful, not to let you find out that he was here, everything'd be fine. And now look at how we are!' And she bent her head over her hands and this time let her tears go, and after a moment Poppy bent over and held her close, letting the old woman cry her heart out on her shoulder. And Bernie stood and watched with a faint grin on his face.

Eventually Jessie's tears slowed and changed to occasional hiccups and she sat up and mopped her ravaged face, as Poppy went over to one of the hobs where a coffee pot stood bubbling gently, and fetched it, together with a mug.

There was a silence as Jessie sipped the coffee and then, looking better, set down the mug.

'Well, Bernie, what have you got to say for yourself?'

'Me? What should I have to say?'

37

'Listen, you didn't come here at this time just to make mischief?' Jessie looked sharply at him then. 'Or did you?'

'Would I do that?' He opened his eyes wide and then laughed. 'Well, all right, maybe I would. Only I didn't. No, I had to talk to you fast. It's important. Believe it or not, I tried to keep out of Poppy's way. I don't like rows no more than you do. But she hung around so long I had to come through from the shop. There's a limit to how much of Lily's chatter one man can take.'

'So, what's so urgent?'And Jessie glanced uneasily at Poppy, who was still standing staring stonily at him.

Bernie shot a sharp glance at her too, and then looked back at his mother. 'It's nothing all that much, no big deal. It's just that I need some warehouse space and I want to rent yours. It's hard to find anywhere these days that's really safe, you know? And you've got all these cellars here – '

'We're using them as shelters,' Poppy said shortly.

'All of them? Hardly. As I recall, those cellars go not only right under these buildings but half-way under Cable Street as well. It's an enormous space.'

'So? It's enormous. We're using it ourselves for storage.'

'All of it?'

'That's none of your business.'

'I'll pay a decent rent,' he said with a studiedly casual air. 'A more than decent rent. You can have twenty pounds a week.'

Poppy blinked. 'Twenty – are you mad? That's a crazy amount for a cold cellar!'

'But it's a dry cellar as well as cold, isn't it?' he said quickly.

'Yes,' she said. 'That's why we use it to store our dry goods – '

'Right. Then it'll suit my needs too.'

'What do you want them for?'

'I told you. Twenty quid a week.'

'How will you use them, damn you? Don't be clever with me!'

'Twenty quid a week, and no questions asked,' he said and turned away. 'Take it or leave it.'

'I'll leave it,' Poppy said at once. 'You can't think I'd let you have our premises to use any way you like, do you? With your record? I'd have to be mad to do that.'

He looked at her for a long moment and then sighed. 'Always the perfect little angel, eh, Poppy? Well, suppose you mind your own business? This is my mother's place, not yours and – '

'Like hell it is,' Poppy snapped. 'I'm an equal partner in this enterprise, as you ought to know by now if you've been in London all this time. Jessie must have told you – '

'I did,' Jessie said weakly. 'Honestly, I did, Poppola. I told him you'd never agree – '

Poppy whirled on her. 'You mean you knew about this – this whatever it is he wants our cellars for?'

Jessie looked miserable. 'He's talked about it before,' she mumbled.

'Why didn't you tell me?' Poppy said. 'After all, if it's such a good business deal, shouldn't I be allowed to consider it? Twenty pounds a week for accommodation we don't otherwise use has to be good business.'

'I didn't think you'd like it,' Jessie mumbled and Poppy said angrily, 'What did you say?'

And this time Jessie shouted it. 'I didn't think you'd like it!' and there was a ringing silence.

Poppy sighed then, a deep sucking in of breath that seemed to weaken her, for she stood there with her eyes closed, leaning against the table and trying to regain her composure. Then she said as steadily as she could, 'Then it's all starting again.'

'How do you mean, starting again?' Jessie began to bluster. 'Who's starting anything again? I told you, I wouldn't do nothing you don't like. You're equal partners with me, and I wouldn't never do nothing to

39

upset you. But when my own son comes asking, and it seems harmless enough, what am I – '

'Harmless?' Poppy opened her eyes and glared at her. 'Since when were any of this – this – since when did he ever suggest anything that was harmless? Good for him maybe, but hell for everyone else around him. Every time – '

'Not this time,' Bernie said smoothly and came and stood beside his mother. 'Suppose instead of spouting off like some busted water main you listen for a few minutes, hey, Poppy? Just listen and hear what I'm offering and what for.'

'I told you, I'm not interested in any offer you have to make, now or ever,' she flared. 'After the sort of things you did in the past? Ye gods, when you were only sixteen you tried to embezzle money from your mother, and everything you've done since confirms what you are. A slippery liar at best, a downright crook at worst. You can double your offer of rent, it won't make any difference – '

He smiled, totally ignoring her taunts. 'I won't double it, but I could go up fifty per cent.' He spoke with a fine judicious air. 'Which, seeing it's a perfectly reasonable bit of business and not particularly slippery, is as fair an offer as you'll get anywhere. These are bad times, Poppy. Make the sunshine when you can!'

'Poppy, at least listen!' Jessie said pleadingly. 'Do me a favour, dolly! Let him say what he has to say and if you still say no, then no it is. I can't say fairer than that, can I? You understand, Bernie?' And she turned and looked at her son, her face pouched with anxiety. 'If Poppy don't like it, then I don't like it. But for God's sake, the two of you, get this sorted out. I can't go on like this, squeezed like some piece of stringy old salt beef in a sandwich – ' and she tried to laugh at her own weak joke and only managed to twist her face into a grimace and produce a half sob, half hiccup.

40

There was another little silence and then Poppy said, 'All right. So what's this deal you're offering, Bernie?'

'That's better!' he said and folded his arms, leaning against the table, and Poppy couldn't help but notice how good he looked. He must be – she worked it out quickly – almost forty, and yet he looked as handsome as he ever had, with the lustrous dark eyes and the thick glossy hair, now gently sprinkled with a little white at the temples in a way that greatly added to his charms rather than detracting from them. The dimpled mouth looked as delectable as it ever had, and she felt again the stab of regret she so often had in the old days, that someone so beautiful could be so all round dreadful a person, evil, even; and she thought fleetingly of her stepdaughter Chloe and what he had done to her, and at once stopped seeing his beauty and was aware only of the need to be ever vigilant when considering anything he had to say.

'It's like this, Poppy.' He smiled winningly. 'Since I came back I've been making a living as best I can, a little deal here, a little arrangement there, just the sort of things I could pick up. It wasn't easy after all those years in the state pen in Maryland! I may not have a prison record here, but word gets around, you know? So I had to do the best for myself I could – '

'Get to the point, I haven't all day.' And she looked at her watch pointedly and was startled to see how late it was: almost five. She'd have to go soon, have to get over to the canteen. 'Hurry up,' she added harshly. 'I have to leave.'

'It's all very simple. I've got a consignment of dried fruit coming in from America. I managed to get space on a merchantman on its way to Oslo – never mind how, but I can tell you it's flying a Swedish flag and it cost me plenty to get my stuff on it – and I have to store it somewhere safe. Another of these bloody raids and my money could go up in smoke, my whole investment. And it's a big one. All I want is to store it here in Mum's – in your cellars so I can sell it later on – '

'Why not sell it now? There's a market I imagine. You could get it out to shops fast and then you wouldn't need storage.'

'There's too much for that. Anyway, I can't get enough petrol just now to deal with distribution. And to be honest I'd like to hold on a bit. The price could get better.'

Her lips curled at that. 'Hoarding food, Bernie? Where *do* you get your nice little ideas from, I wonder.'

He grinned unrepentantly. 'So I want to get the best return on my investment I can! Is that such a crime? Listen, Poppy, it's no big deal! Let me rent the cellars for a few weeks – it's all I want. I can let you have some of the stuff for your own use – '

'I don't want anything from you!' she said with blistering scorn.

'But your canteen? Yes, I know about it. Mum told me. A few pounds of raisins'd come handy surely? I can even get you some eggs and a bit of sugar and butter. Then you can make all the poor little wardens and firefighters nice puddings – '

She opened her mouth to refuse and then stopped, too disgusted to say all she would have wanted to.

'Forget it,' she said. 'I want nothing black-market. I haven't needed it to break the law yet, and I'm damned if I'm going to now, just for you.'

'There's nothing illegal about dried fruit, Poppy!' Jessie said. 'Is there? This I thought you could take and be glad of it. He said he won't charge you – I mean, it's hard to get these days! Sugar and butter I grant you, they're rationed and I wouldn't touch 'em either – but a bissel dried fruit and some eggs? Where'd the crime be there? It's good business, dolly! – I want some for the kitchens, I can tell you. Make a deal already, Poppy – let's make an arrangement and then we'll all be happy – '

It started slowly and far away as it usually did and all of them lifted their heads and then as it got louder and the sickeningly familiar swooning wail came closer Poppy said, 'Oh, to hell with it. Do as you like, Jessie, I have to go – I promised to be back at the canteen by five and it's nearly that now.'

And she turned and made for the door, grabbing her coat from the back of it and slinging it on as she went.

'Poppy!' Jessie shrieked and got awkwardly to her feet. 'A raid's started – don't go out there – are you crazy? Come down to the cellar with me, Poppy!'

But she'd gone, leaving the door swinging behind her, and Jessie sat down again, her face a mask of fear and misery. And Bernie looked after her and smiled.

'Well, that's that then!' he said with great satisfaction. 'I'll start shifting the stuff in first thing in the morning.'

'If it doesn't get bombed tonight,' Jessie said. 'Like my Poppy!' and began to cry again.

'Oh, it won't,' he said and stretched widely. 'On account it's not coming off a ship but from Birmingham. Got to tell Poppy the best sort of story, eh? Not to worry, Mum – just leave it all to me. And right now, let's get down to the cellars – now we've got all this sorted out we don't want to get ourselves killed, do we?'

· 5 ·

The sirens were still wailing as Poppy emerged into the street, and went hurtling across it and into Backchurch Lane. She was calculating feverishly as she ran; there were usually a few minutes grace after the sirens went this far west. Most of the raids were centred on the docks, much further east, and though the planes came this far, often it took a few minutes for them to get here. If she managed to run fast enough, she'd be in the canteen basement in time to avoid being hurt.

And as she ran she prayed incoherently somewhere deep inside to the God she wasn't even sure existed: Please let me get there safely, please let me not be killed and make sure my Robin's safe and back at the hospital by now – and again she started working out how far the two girls had had to go, and whether they'd have reached their destination in time. And felt a little better, for they were long-legged healthy girls and anyway would have the sense to take shelter well in time to be safe, even if they hadn't got as far along the Whitechapel Road as they needed to be.

She was still running, but her attention had slipped, and in trying to dodge a hole that had been made in the pavement a few days earlier she swerved, caught the heel of her shoe on a piece of rubble and went sprawling, to lie there winded for a second or two, not quite sure what had happened.

Someone hauled her to her feet and dusted her down, scolding all the time in a croaky rumble.

'Look at you, lady, just look at you, running around the streets and the sireen blowin' off fit to bust itself! Come on now, into the shelter 'ere and no muckin' about. We'll get you safe, come on now, lady.'

She got to her feet awkwardly, very aware now that her knee hurt abominably. She looked at the torn silk stocking there and could have wept; she had only one more pair left and after that, heaven knew where she'd get a further supply.

'I'm all right,' she muttered and pulled away from the man's restraining hand. 'I've got to get to Plumber's Row – don't stop me – I've got to get there – '

' 'Ere, if it isn't Mrs Deveen!' the voice said and for the first time she peered at the dusty face under the warden's tin hat and said gratefully, 'Arthur! What are you doing here?'

'My job, Mrs Deveen,' he said promptly and shook her arm. 'Which is to get the likes of you to safety. Now come on. We ain't got more than a few seconds till they start chucking it all down.'

'I've got to get to the canteen, Arthur – help me!' she said and turned and began to run and after a moment he came thumping after her.

'You won't be no good if you gets there dead!' he bawled. 'And you will, yer go runnin' around like that with no 'at on. 'Ere, take mine if you gotta go– ' and he caught up with her and took his tin hat off and thumped it on to her head. It smelled of hair oil and tobacco and she grabbed the brim as it slid around on her and held on, and gasped gratefully, 'Bless you, Arthur! Will you be all right without it?'

'I will,' he said and stopped running to shout after her, 'I got another at the Post. Run for it, you 'ear me? Run like the bleedin' clappers!'

And she did.

Robin and Chick had nearly reached the hospital when the sirens began and Chick lifted her head and said in surprise, 'But it's not dark yet!'

45

'Maybe not, but they're still coming,' Robin said grimly. 'Here we go again! Do we shelter or run for it?'

Chick was craning at the sky. 'Run for it,' she said after a moment. 'There's nothing to see yet and I've heard no explosions. It's only a few hundred yards or so now. Step it out, kid – '

They hared along the Whitechapel Road, wheeling in and out of the other running people, and Chick, with her much longer legs, was well ahead by the time they reached the hospital gates, and after one reassuring look behind her to make sure Robin was there, she disappeared through them, aiming for the entrance to the big shelter across the main courtyard.

Robin was pounding behind her, her breath coming rather short now, and she looked down at the ground at her feet as she ran, afraid of tripping up, and then almost fell as she went charging into someone to one side of her and just regained her balance as a hand grabbed her elbow.

'Hey, watch where you're going,' someone shouted and she caught her breath, startled, and looked to see what had happened, and saw a large battered perambulator laden with bundles and boxes and, pushing helplessly on the big curved handle, a very dirty and bedraggled old man.

He was almost weeping, and his nose was running dispiritedly into his straggling whiskers as he pushed impotently on the pram. The person who had grabbed her elbow said then from behind her, 'The wheel's broken – leave it, you stupid old geezer' – and Robin peered over her shoulder to see one of the hospital porters standing there.

'You go on in, Nurse!' he shouted at her and gave her a push and then began to run himself, and still the old man pushed on his pram and whimpered helplessly as it listed alarmingly and refused to budge.

'Oh, do come on!' Robin cried, for now the noise had begun. Somewhere ahead of them, away to the east, the all too familiar sounds of explosions came crumping through the summer air, and she knew it was only a matter of moments before they'd be overhead, those crawling ugly planes with their loads of bombs that came spiralling so lazily and deceptively out of the sky, and she pulled on the old man's arm in an attempt to dislodge him and carry him to safety.

But still he stood there, stubbornly pushing at his unresponsive pram and wouldn't let go, and Robin almost wept with fear for her own safety and the frustration of dealing with such mulishness. And she shouted furiously, 'Will you come to the shelters, you stupid old man!'

And then suddenly there was someone else there, and she almost gawped as a large arm reached over her shoulder and hauled the pram upright and the old man managed to push it, and together the three of them began to run awkwardly towards the hospital gates. And when they got there the tall man behind picked up the pram bodily and hauled it across the yard as he panted at Robin, 'Get him inside, will you – I can manage this for him.'

And then they were all tumbling into the big shelter as the warden, shouting furiously, waved them in and then banged the door behind them, and they stood there in the dim light of the rows of oil lamps, gasping as they tried to catch their wind.

'Oh, Robin!' Chick was beside her then, all compunction and anxiety. 'I thought you were right behind me! What happened?'

'I – ' Robin began and then shook her head, still trying to get her breath.

'Nurse Chester!' A voice came out of the crowd, which had been making a fair amount of noise as it chattered, and it was unmistakeably that of Sister Marshall. 'Come here and give me some help with the twins, will you? You're the only one who can stop their shrieking – ' And indeed the noise of crying children was a strong obbligato to the overall sound, and Chick made a face and said hurriedly, 'Are you okay, kid?'

Robin nodded gratefully. 'I'm fine,' she managed and her voice was husky with the effort of speaking. She hadn't realized just how hard to run it had been and how much she had almost had to carry the old man, who for all his frailty had been a considerable weight. 'Go on – I'm fine – ' And Chick with one last squeeze of Robin's hand was gone, back into the depths of the shelter where Sister Marshall had all her Annie Zunz patients collected under her careful eye.

The old man was taken away then, down towards the far end where there was a small oil stove where hot drinks could be made, and she watched the warden take him, grateful to be rid of him, for he had started to smell rather heavy in the thick air of the stuffy shelter.

'Ye gods, but it fair reeks in here,' the tall man said and Robin turned to him eagerly.

'I'm so grateful to you!' she said. 'I didn't know what to do. I couldn't have left him but it was all getting so noisy – ' And almost on cue there was a loud crump and the walls seemed to shake as the lamps went rolling wildly on their hooks, sending great shadows up the walls and illuminating frightened faces, all staring upwards. The chattering had stopped for a moment and then it started again, louder now and more defiant as the shelterers caught their breath and managed to relax a little, and someone at the far end of the shelter started to sing 'Daisy' and one after another people joined in, a little raggedly at first but then with more and more assurance.

'It was no bother to me,' the tall man said and Robin peered at him in the dimness, startled, for now she recognized his voice.

'Oh' she said. 'It's you!'

'As far as I know,' the tall man said courteously and then smiled and she thought – why, he's quite young! All the times she had seen him on Annie Zunz Ward he had seemed to be a man well into his thirties, with his dour glare and his tightly-held lips, but now the smile revealed rather endearingly misshapen teeth and stripped years off him.

'I'm sorry, Todd,' she said. 'I hadn't realized.'

'No reason why ye should, Nurse,' he said and the years climbed back into his face, as he shut his mouth tightly.

'Oh, please, don't call me Nurse like that! It's as though I were on duty, and I'm not. Not until eight at any rate. Call me Robin,' and she stuck out her hand. 'I can't tell you how grateful I am. You saved that old man, but you did me a good deed too. I'd be out there yet, arguing with him, if you hadn't come and grabbed his pram.' She turned her head and peered into the pram, where it was set against the only available patch of wall. 'What do you suppose is in it that he hung on so hard?'

'Everything he owns, I imagine,' he said and shook her hand awkwardly and then let it go and stood erect against the wall, his arms dangling at his side, staring at her. She could see him more closely now as her eyes became accustomed to the change in the light levels and she was puzzled. He was a little paler than she remembered seeing him on the ward, and was sweating. His forehead and upper lips were beaded, and she rubbed her own face, a little surprised. It was warm in here, but not that hot –

There was another crump and again the lamps swung wildly but the noise was less and there was a drop in the level of chatter to a low murmur as they all strained their ears to hear, and then another crump came noticeably further away and shoulders relaxed and people started to talk again and to laugh and sing; and Robin too took a deep breath of relief and slid down the wall to crouch on her haunches, since there were no spaces on any of the benches.

'Weren't you on duty this afternoon, Todd?' she asked, trying again to make conversation even though it was obviously going to be as difficult, she told herself a little wryly, as walking over a ploughed field in silk dancing pumps. 'I thought you'd have been up on the ward – '

'I'm transferred to night duty tonight,' he said a little gruffly, as though the words were being dragged out of him. 'Casualty.'

49

'Oh!' she said brightly. 'Me too! Will you like it, do you think? I'm not sure, but Chick – you know, Nurse Chester? – she's going to Cas too, and she says it should be interesting.'

'Oh, aye, it'll be that for sure,' Todd said. 'If you regard it as interesting to see people with their limbs blasted off and their eyes fairly sucked out of their skulls.'

She shrank a little at the savagery of his tone, and stared at him. He too was now leaning against the wall in a crouch, in the usual way that people used when they couldn't find anywhere to sit, and she could see his eyes gleaming in the shadows.

'I didn't mean that,' she said in a low voice. 'Of course I didn't. It's awful, all of it. But we do our best to help them and – '

'Oh, aye, I'm sure you do. I'm sorry. I shouldna' ha' said that. It's just that I get so angry – ' He caught his breath and then stopped. 'You'll not want to listen to me blethering on about it,' he said then in a flat tone.

'Of course I do!' she said. 'I'm always interested in what people have to say.'

'Even a stinkin' conchie like me?'

She flushed and was glad he couldn't see it in the dimness. She had felt scorn for him when she'd first heard why he was an orderly, and she couldn't deny that, but he had been so helpful and brave enough out there in the Mile End Road. Many another man would have left the two of them in order to take himself to safety, rather than carry a great dead weight like that pram in order to persuade a frightened man to take shelter.

'Of course,' she said, 'I'm interested in people of all sorts.' She tried to smile then, hoping he could tell from her voice that she meant kindly. 'That's why I'm a nurse. Because I like being with people. It's not because I like to see people in pain or anything. I just like being with them.'

'Aye? Well, I'm glad to hear it,' he said and lapsed into silence.

They stayed there for a while listening to the crumps of bombs becoming ever fainter, and longing for the all clear, and then she said, 'Tell me, Todd, why are you a conchie?'

'Ye gods, do you have to call me Todd like that?' he burst out and there was real venom in his tones. 'I'm no' your servant!'

She stared at him in amazement. 'I'm sorry – I don't understand what you – '

'If it's too much trouble to call me *Mr* Todd then – '

'Mr Todd?' she said. 'But isn't that your first name?'

He was the one who stopped short.

'What did you say?'

'I said I thought Todd was your first name. I'm sorry if I've offended you, but it was the only name I ever heard anyone call you and – '

'Ah, to damnation wi' it!' he said and shook his head. 'I've made a fat fool of mysel', have I not? I'm sorry, Miss Bradman, I meant no – '

'My name is Robin,' she said steadily. 'I told you that.'

'And mine is Hamish.'

She caught her breath, a sudden desire to laugh bubbling up in her. It wasn't the odd name, well, not really; but it wasn't a common one and what with the events of the afternoon and the oddness of this whole conversation, it was all she could do to regain her composure. But somehow she managed it and said gravely, 'I'm pleased to know it, Hamish. And I'm sorry I didn't before.'

'No need to fash yerself,' he said and smiled again and his uneven teeth glimmered in the dimness and then she could laugh.

'Such a funny word! I know it's Scots, but I never know exactly what it means – '

'It's no' Scots so much as French,' he said. 'Did ye not do the language at school? *Ne fâchez vous* – don't disturb yourself, don't be angered – we've a good deal of the French in Scotland. Dour, d'you see, comes from the French for hard – *dûr* – and there are others – '

'You're a very interesting person!' she said and again reddened. 'Oh, I'm sorry! That sounds – I didn't mean to be so rude. It's just that on the ward, only seeing you do the buckets and scrub the pans and so forth – '

'Aye,' he said grimly. 'Always the dirtiest jobs they can find for me. Because I'm that dirty thing, a man with conscience.'

There was a little silence and then she said, 'Tell me about it.'

'What's to tell you? I canna' fight and kill. Indeed, I will na'. It's as simple as that. So I came here to work instead.'

'But you can't want the Nazis to take over the world?' she said wonderingly. 'They will if they can.'

'Aye, so we're told,' he said. 'And have every reason to believe. The way they're behaving now is – it's sickening. But all the same I believe all life is sacred. I canna' take it, nor can I inflict pain. It's not a thing I can do. So, I do this work instead.'

'It's a pity you're not a woman. Then you could be a nurse,' she said, and he laughed.

'Oh, I could join the army and say I wanted to be a stretcher-bearer or a medical orderly, but there's no guarantee that they'd let me. And I might find myself with a gun put in my hands and then what? Do I turn and refuse and make it worse for the other men? Better to stay here. As for training as a nurse – I could for the mental hospitals, I dare say. They use male nurses. But I don't want that. After this horrible war is over, as God willing it will be, I'll be back to university.'

'Back to – '

'I want to take my master's degree. I've got my bachelor's. I'm a biologist,' he said simply and she stared at him again, seeing him in a whole new light.

'But what a waste to be emptying bedpans and scrubbing crappy mackintoshes!' she said. 'Why aren't you doing that sort of work now? It must be more useful than this – '

He shook his head. 'The only sort of work that is useful in biology right now is warfare,' he said bitterly. 'They're even thinking of germ bombs. It makes me sick – faugh!' And he made the expressive sound deep in his throat and she felt a little chill of cold move in her.

'I see,' was all she could say, and that weakly, and he laughed then.

'It's difficult for you to understand. That I can hate the Nazis for the dreadful things they're doing and yet not feel able to take up a gun against them?'

There was a silence and then she said. 'Well, yes. I'm sorry, but I do. It's just that – I thought we all had to be in this together.'

'I am in it,' he said. 'Aren't I? Here at the hospital. Even scrubbing babies' crappy mackintoshes is a contribution, isn't it? It releases people like you to do more important work.'

She managed a smile. 'I suppose so. I wish I really understood though. I have so many friends, you see – ' And then she stopped.

He nodded. 'I know. In the services.'

'Yes,' she said. 'One's in the Navy.'

He made a face. 'Oh, God, that's awful. I'm sorry.'

'Yes,' she said. 'Me too,' and then stopped suddenly. 'Are you religious? Is that it?'

He laughed. 'Because I call on the name of God from time to time? Bad habit that. Just slang for me, I'm afraid. Me, I'm a real freethinker. Agnostic, you know? Not an atheist, mark you. That's as arrogant as being a theist – I mean, swearing there's no god is the same really as maintaining there is. Neither side have any evidence either way. Me, I don't know, and don't care too much. I think people matter most.'

She leaned forwards then and touched his arm, suddenly overwhelmed with gratitude. 'Oh, I am glad you said that. I think I'm the same really. I've never talked about it, but it matters to me. I mean, I think about such things sometimes. Especially when – '

53

She was never to know why she did it, but the words came tumbling out of her.

'I'm a quarter Jewish, you see. I had a Jewish grandfather. I have this Jewish aunt – well, great-aunt really. She's lovely. But my father, and now my stepfather – they're just the usual English thing, you know, Church. Not that they go much, but they belong and I sometimes feel a bit bewildered by it all.'

'I can well see you would,' he said. And then lifted his head. Somewhere outside the long-awaited wail had started in the distance and they listened hard and then it started up close by and the shelterers took a deep sigh of relief and got to their feet, reaching for their knitting and their books, and talking and laughing loudly in deep relief that this was another air raid over and done with and they were not hurt.

'I'd love to talk some more about this,' Robin said, a little shyly, and she straightened her somewhat creaking knees and brushed the dust of the shelter wall from her trousers and shirt. She didn't look at him.

'Aye, well, mebbe we can at that,' he said. 'If there's time in Casualty. Not that it'll be likely.' He squinted outside as the warden came and opened the door. There was the all too familiar dust in the air again and the sickening reek of cordite, and he sighed. 'If it's like this now, God help us all when it gets dark – ' And then his eyes glinted with humour as he looked at her. 'If you'll forgive my use of the deity's name!'

She laughed too and then watched as he went walking away across the courtyard, his long legs covering the ground quickly, as she waited for Chick to emerge with her armful of Davidoff twins. What a very odd day this was turning out to be, she thought, as she looked up at the sky, now a rich blue with the last rays of the September afternoon. Even among odd days which were the normal thing now, this one had given her a great deal to think about.

·6·

By seven o'clock, Poppy's battered knee had swollen
so badly she had to limp, and she felt dreadful. There
wasn't time to think about it as the first all-clear of the
night offered only a half hour's respite before the warning
wailed its swooping notes again, but it sat at the back of
her consciousness like a thick black cloud that threatened
to overwhelm her at any moment.

Maria had gone when she had reached the canteen,
leaving a note that said cryptically, 'I been and gone I
had to see you tomorrow as per arrangements as usual
yrs truly Maria Randall (Mrs),' and there had been a knot
of wardens on their way on duty waiting and clamouring
for their evening meal before they went. She had barely
had time to put on her apron before she was dishing out
the mince and potatoes that Maria had mercifully left
bubbling ready on the stove.

The first wave of evening regulars went and she had
a moment or two then for herself, and she used them
to take off her stockings, pulling the tattered threads
from her bloodied knee very gingerly, though it stung
dreadfully, and then putting on iodine and a makeshift
bandage. She was almost in tears of pain by this time and
had to be very firm indeed with herself as she swallowed
a couple of aspirin and then limped around the canteen
collecting dirty dishes and washing up, and leaving the
serving counter clean and ready for the next onslaught.
To be so upset and tearful just because of a fall? It was

ridiculous. And then she sighed and began to slice bread with some ferocity.

It wasn't the fall; of course it wasn't. It was that wretched Bernie who had upset her, and she brooded over him as she spread the margarine and then fish paste to make the piles of sandwiches that would vanish in no time once the night raids started in good earnest, as they very soon would. You could almost tell the time by those wretched planes. But it wasn't the raids that had upset her, nor was it the fall. It was definitely Bernie; and the more she thought about him the more ferociously hard and fast she worked.

He was hateful, totally hateful, she told herself. To have come slinking around Jessie as he had, and to have been here in London for two years without her knowing it – and then a different sort of anger filled her. How could Jessie have been so devious with her? To have hidden the fact so well had been an act of downright betrayal, she thought hotly, a dreadful thing to have done to her –

But she couldn't sustain her anger for long, not against Jessie. As she had said herself so piteously, what was a mother to do? The fact that Bernie had behaved disgracefully didn't alter the fact that he was her son, and a much beloved one at that. It was inevitable that Jessie would try to protect him.

As long as he didn't go near Chloe again, Poppy thought and then stopped spreading fish paste to stare sightlessly ahead. Chloe was hardly her problem any more. Since her marriage and that dreadful, indeed positively disgraceful and all too public divorce, she had lived in her own flat, a very handsome if rather small place, in Bryanston Square. She was her own woman now, for good or ill. How could it be otherwise? She was thirty-two, well beyond her stepmother's control. But for all that, Poppy felt a responsibility for her. When she had married Chloe's father, in those dark and painful days during the last war, she had taken on Chloe too, like it or not. She had been a dreadfully spoiled child and remained

56

so, whatever Poppy had tried to do for her, and though her affair with Bernie and the miserable outcome of it had brought her a little closer to her stepmother, still she had gone her own headstrong way; and Poppy sighed and bent her head again to her sandwiches.

Maybe it wouldn't all start up again, she told herself then, trying to be optimistic. Chloe's no longer the silly girl she had been a dozen or so years ago. What with her job at the War Office (what was it? wondered Poppy – something vaguely secretarial was all she knew, and that it seemed to give her an amazing amount of free time) and her special friends there, she had become a decidedly snobbish young woman. She went out and about only with senior officers, and rarely deigned to go below the rank of major, though she would sometimes be seen with a captain. Lieutenants were certainly of no interest unless they happened also to be rich in their own right, or titled (and there had been one or two of those, Poppy remembered) so perhaps she would scorn a civilian like Bernie, even if he did try to make contact. Poppy cheered up then even more as another thought bubbled up; because he hadn't attempted to do so yet and he'd been back from America for two years, maybe that boded well?

The sirens began their closer clamour then, and she lifted her head and waited fearfully, and then almost at once the other noise began; the roar of guns from the ack-ack batteries that had been set up well to the north, in Hackney's Victoria Park, and which were loud even at this distance. She sometimes doubted that they did any good; she had never heard of a plane being brought down by one of them around here, but it was like the searchlight that sprang up as the planes came over. They made people on the ground feel that at least someone somewhere was trying to fight back. The worst thing about the raids was the feeling of being so utterly helpless, crouching in shelters like terrified rabbits in burrows, while the Germans overhead sat there like scornful winged demons, raining down death and horror.

Heavens, she thought, I must be low to be thinking such morbid thoughts, and pulled back her shoulders and took a few deep breaths to restore her to her usual state of common sense. The aspirin had started to have an effect so that her knee just throbbed heavily now, but her mood had lifted a little; and it was just as well it had. There were more crumps as bombs fell somewhere fairly near and then she heard the shriek of the bells as the fire engines came thudding through the streets overhead.

They'll start coming in soon, she thought, the walking casualties and the people caught outside the shelters and the workers and drivers – and she sighed, and checked that both the urns were full and bubbling and that she had the milk ready in the cups. Preparation, she always told her staff, was the key to fast service, and she had to be sure not to forget it herself, now she was working on her own. And for one brief moment she even regretted the absence of the egregious Mrs Crighton.

But only for a moment, because the door was pushed open as the first people arrived – a fireman leading one of his mates who had a blackened face and whose eyes were half closed above swollen cheeks.

'Got a blast from a gas flare,' explained the fireman after he'd settled the injured man at a table. 'Can you take care of 'im for us till the ambulance can take 'im? There's bin a direct hit over at Fieldgate Street, by Vine Court. They're digging 'em out now. The Warden's post 'as gone an' all – '

She lifted her head quickly. 'The Post? What about old Arthur?'

The fireman shook his head and began to make his way back to the door. 'Sorry, ducks, but he was one of the dead ones. Three there was. Was he a friend of yours?'

'Yes,' Poppy said dully. 'A friend of mine – ' And she looked over her shoulder at the tin hat Arthur had given her and which was hanging on the hook behind the side door and thought – please, don't let him be dead because he didn't have his tin hat –

'Rotten luck it was,' the fireman said. 'Crushed right across his chest, he was. Never stood a chance, lying there looking just as he usually did, only with this bleedin' great rafter across him.'

'Not – not his head then?'

The fireman looked at her sharply. 'No, love. Does it matter?'

'He gave me his tin hat to get me back here safely – I was caught outside in the alert at five o'clock – '

The fireman shook his head and opened the door. 'Never give it a thought, ducks. He was wearing one.' And went. And Poppy took a deep shaking breath and carried a cup of very hot sweet tea over to the man sitting so quietly slumped at the table.

He was shocked, but as far as she could see the damage to his face wasn't too bad and as she went and collected cold wet cloths to put across his forehead and to pat on his flaming cheeks, she was grateful again for the nursing experience she had been given during the last war as part of her FANY's training. First Aid Nursing Yeomanry, she thought as she worked on the injured man, and got a sudden vision of herself in the uniform, and then banished it. She was just a canteen supervisor in this war, one with a bit of first-aid training, admittedly, but only a caterer and cleaner-upper. She had enough on her plate without getting notions about getting back into uniform again. And she patted the grateful fireman on the shoulder and left him to sip his tea as again the doors opened and another group of people came in.

From then on it was bedlam. She poured tea and refilled urns and made more and more sandwiches and was grateful when some of the men collected the used cups and saucers and plates for her and brought them back to be washed up. Being single-handed on a night like this was hell; but it did at least have the virtue of keeping her mind off other, more personal things.

Or did until around eleven, when one of the ambulance drivers, his face streaked with dirt and his uniform blood spattered, came and asked for 'some tea and a bit of grub, ducky. I never got no dinner today on account I overslept after last night being such a bugger, beggin' your pardon for the language, and I ain't et nothing since ten o'clock this morning.'

'Oh, dear,' Poppy said and her face crumpled. 'There was some mince and potatoes but that all went ages ago. I've only these few sandwiches left – '

The man picked up one of the thin sandwiches mournfully and lifted a bread slice to inspect the filling.

'Fish paste,' he said lugubriously. 'Nothin' to eat since ten o'clock and all I get now is fish paste. Don't it break yer 'eart? What I'd like to 'ave, if I coud 'ave what I liked, would be a nice fried egg samwidge. My old Mum, she used to give 'em when I was tired and couldn't eat a proper big dinner. "Eggs, Sid," she used to say to me. "Eggs is nature's treasury of food, eggs is. As full of meat as anythin' could be an' as good as steak." An' she'd fry' me an egg in a nice bit o' butter and put on a bit o' pepper, you know, for a relish, and slap it between two big slices of new bread and I tell you, that was a meal that was.' And he sighed. 'Never mind, ducks. No eggs around these days for the askin' is there? Not down 'ere in the East End anyway. All gone up West, I dare say, to the clubs and the fancy caffs where they can get big money for 'em. I'll 'ave this and be glad to get it. Never say no if there ain't somethin' else to say yes to, my Mum used to say – '

'Your Mum talked too much, if you ask me,' the next man in the queue growled. 'I'll 'ave one of your sandwiches missus, and be glad to get it. An' a cuppa char – ta, ever so – '

Eggs, she thought as she set to work to make another pile of fish paste sandwiches, spreading the thin pink mess as carefully as she could at high speed. Egg sandwiches – what a delight it would be to give them to these exhausted hungry people when they came in. She could get a big griddle from home and have it ready on the stove; it wouldn't take that long to fry eggs and put them into prepared bread and butter – well, margarine – and so give people the extra nourishment and pleasure they needed, doing the sort of dreadful jobs they had to do. And the figure of Bernie standing there in Jessie's preparation kitchens and murmuring about eggs and butter and sugar rose in her mind and with it a sense of desolation. Was there to be no end to the bad effects that man could have on her, no end to his intrusiveness? Now he was tempting her to start to shop on the black market, and that was dreadful.

'What's so dreadful?' A corner of her mind became a whisper so intense it was as though she could actually feel a hot breath on her cheek. 'What's so dreadful? You wouldn't be taking it for yourself, would you? That *would* be dreadful, like the hateful Mrs Crighton pretending to be so virtuous while steadily stealing sugar from the stores. This would be for the people here and no one else. To make them a sustaining sandwich – that wouldn't be such a crime, would it? Better the stuff comes here to you and the people who deserve it than goes off to the West End and the fancy clubs and caffs to fill rich men's stomachs, rich men who were well out of reach of the bombing – '

Her mind was still whirling with it all when the midnight shift turned up as they always did, in a tight cluster, having dodged their way through the raids to get there. They were close neighbours who lived at the other end of Mulberry Street, only a couple of hundred yards from the canteen, but it still took courage to venture out of their home shelter to get here, protected though this cellar was, and especially brave of Agnes Clewitt who was so typical a little spinster that Poppy sometimes thought she'd been invented rather than born like other people. But here they were and Joyce Jasper, the largest and noisiest of

61

them, waved to her vigorously as they came in pulling off their coats and hats, for they always dressed as though they were to brave a blizzard even on the hottest of summer evenings.

'I 'eard about that Madam Crighton leavin' you in the lurch,' she bawled cheerfully as she pulled on a large flowered apron. 'Maria, she popped in an' told me on 'er way 'ome. Old cow! I 'ope she gets a direct 'it, that I do. Not that she's likely to get that, tucked up in bloody Bayswater like she is.'

Poppy, who also was safe from bombs tucked away in her old home in Holland Park which had suffered not a single raid, was uneasy at that.

'That's a bit much, Joyce,' she said, trying not to sound too reproving. After all they were volunteers, and she needed them badly. She couldn't be schoolmarmish with them. Too risky. 'She's not a nice woman, I know, but all the same – '

'That one, a direct 'it?' Rose, a plump little woman who bustled about the place like a demented bee, gave a little snort. 'Some fine 'opes! She'd frighten any bleedin' bomb into goin' straight back up where it come from.'

At which they all laughed and got to work, clearing tables and washing up, stacking up the clean plates, and peeling potatoes ready to make another pot of mince. It was dull fare, but they made it as savoury as they could, with some of the herbs and spices Poppy had brought from her jealously hoarded home stores, and the men and women who used the canteen seemed to enjoy it.

'I'll try to get some more meat tomorrow,' Poppy promised as Rose tipped the last few pounds of pallid minced beef into the pot with some onions and carrots and sent savoury smells drifting through the air. 'My aunt maybe has some – '

'See what else she's got while you're at it,' Joyce called jovially from the washing-up sink. 'Bit o' butter and some sugar instead of this lousy saccharin stuff.

62

Curls your teeth, that does – ' And Poppy managed a mechanical smile and escaped then into the roaring, burning, shrieking night outside.

This was the worst part of the journey home, always was. She had to get herself to Aldgate East Station to pick up the night bus that was going west. There were no more trains, of course; they stopped around ten-thirty by which time the tube stations were jammed with sleeping shelterers. The authorities had tried to keep them out but had had to give up the unequal struggle, because several hundred determined Londoners clutching rugs and bottles of water and packets of sandwiches and storming each and every station were not easy to stop; and Poppy applauded them. There had been far too little shelter accommodation provided when all this started, and when shelters were destroyed what were people supposed to do? The Tube was a perfect answer to the people, if not to the authorities.

No, there would be no train but with luck the bus would be there, and she would use the ten minutes or so it took her to hurry through the streets to the station, while bombs were dropping not far away and she could hear the uneven drone of the enemy planes overhead, to pray wordlessly for the bus to be there.

Tonight in fact wasn't too bad at all. There was a lull in the bombing and the bus was indeed there, ready and waiting to set off on its last journey of the night only ten minutes after she got there. Some nights it was a half hour wait or longer before it would go, so she felt fortunate tonight. Until again the words that Joyce had thrown at her so cheerfully rang in her ears.

Would it be so reprehensible to get supplies from Jessie that had originated with Bernie? He'd offered to give them to her, in addition to rent. Well, if she took it as food for the canteen, instead of paying for it for herself, wouldn't that wipe out the sin? And there was no doubt her people here needed it more than his horrible customers possibly could, whoever they might be.

She sat in a corner seat and leaned her head against the window of the bus, feeling the curled edges of the sticky paper which criss-crossed the panes and which were there to prevent shattered glass from flying about dangerously, and didn't care whether it caught her hair or not. She was too tired to do anything but rest and maybe fall asleep. She always woke up when the bus got to Piccadilly Circus, where she could pick up another bus, or even sometimes a taxi, to Holland Park. With luck she'd grab half an hour now, and then another – she worked it out; bed at one thirty, up at seven thirty meant another five hours or so – so it wouldn't be too bad –

But she couldn't sleep even though she usually did, and after a while sat up and stared unseeingly through the bus window and the impenetrable darkness outside, remembering the days when cheerful street lights and shop fronts had winked back at travellers, and buses themselves had been moving beacons in a dark world. Now with their pallid blue lamps inside and head-lights reduced to a faint yellow cross outside, it wasn't even possible to read and so divert yourself that way. All you could do was think your own gloomy thoughts and try to see some sense in a world gone crazy.

A world gone crazy, she thought then, and tried to remember how it had been before all this started. Lee, lovely solemn sensible little Lee, at her good girls' school and working hard, and outrageous bouncing Joshy, not working at all and causing all sorts of fusses at his infants' school. Her lips curved as she remembered the way on his first day there he discovered that it made the whole school laugh if he stood in the playground and filled his new cap with water from the drinking fountain and then put it on, so that the water cascaded all down his face, and had gone on and on doing it to mounting juvenile applause until the teacher had realized what was going on and rescued the sodden child and sent him home to his mother in someone else's cast-offs, at least two sizes too big for him, and looking as though butter wouldn't

64

melt in his wicked little mouth. Such happy days, she thought. There they'd all been, she and the children and dear, dear David who was so safe and reliable and so perfect a husband, even if he wasn't as exciting as her first husband Bobby had been, and even if he didn't arouse in her the same sort of passion she had felt so long ago – don't think about that, Poppy, she adjured herself then. Think of the good old days, the happy days, the days last year, last century, indeed, when all this wasn't happening.

She must have fallen asleep eventually, because the conductor was shaking her shoulder and urging her to get off, and she staggered blearily out onto the street and again had a moment of good fortune, for there was a taxi with his flag up and she seized on him gratefully, ignoring the expense, and sent him on his way to Norland Square. And managed to sleep again, as the cab went rattling along the Bayswater Road.

But then she was there, in the dear familiar square, and she padded wearily up the front steps and reached into her bag for her keys, scrabbling deep among all the detritus there; and then froze.

There had been movement in the area below around by the dustbins and the potted ivies that grew up the wall to reach the railings, and she peered down, her heart thumping sickeningly loudly in her ears. There had been so many tales of the looters and robbers who, driven out of the East End by the bombing, were coming west to steal from luckier householders. David had told her that it was a very real risk, even though such incidents were never reported in the Press.

'Bad for morale,' he had explained. 'The last thing the government needs is a class war, but it's happening all the same. People are angry in the East End at the way the well-off seem to be better off even as regards the raids – so watch out, darling. Be careful – '

Now she stood there icily still, staring down at the area; and then her courage returned, and moving stealthily, she set her key in the lock. She could get in fast and if there was someone in there, could call the police.

But she stopped then, angry with herself, with the man, if that was who it was in the area below, and most of all with the world gone mad around her, and pushing all caution aside, she leaned over the railings without stopping to think and called, 'Who is it? Who's down there?'

There was another rustle and then a clang as a dustbin lid went flying, and she caught her breath, furious now.

'Whoever you are, come out. I have a truncheon here and I shall use it!' And her hand curled round her small handbag and somewhere in the back of her mind she registered amusement at her own silliness. 'Do you hear me? Out here with you!'

There was yet another clatter and then a movement, and she strained her eyes to see; and then she did see. A round white face with a pair of dark eyes staring up at her with a mixture of expressions in them; trepidation and hope and cheekiness and sheer cold terror.

And she caught her breath and stared back, and her aching knee and her thumping headache and her general fatigue all melded together to make her hugely, furiously angry. And without stopping to think she shouted, 'Joshy? Oh, Joshy, you *naughty* child! What are you doing here again? You know you're supposed to be in Norfolk! Joshy, honestly, I could kill you!'

· 7 ·

He was very subdued as she took him upstairs, dropping
her coat and bag in the hall first, and into the bathroom.
He was filthy, and despite the warm evening, shivering with
cold, and a hot bath was an obvious must; and she ran
the bath and helped him undress and then, after adding a
handful of her own special and almost unobtainable bath
salts as a sort of gesture of partial forgiveness, lifted him
into the scented silkiness. He lay there wreathed in steam,
the dirt floating off him and his expression smoothing
out a little as he relaxed, but still quiet and watchful,
answering her questions at first with just monosyllables
and delivering those in a low voice, very unlike his usual
clear treble.

'Did you leave a note to tell them you were coming
home? Does Mr Gosling know?'

'No,' he said and didn't look at her, bending his head
to watch his hands as he rubbed soap into them.

'Then they'll be worried.'

'P'raps.'

'Oh, Joshy, you are – what time did you leave?'

'Tea-time, I think.'

'Did you have any tea?'

'No.'

'Are you hungry?'

'No.'

'You're fibbing – you're starving! You always are!'

His eyes flicked up then and she caught a glimpse of

their darkness and almost melted, he looked so very anxious, and impulsively she leaned forwards and kissed him.

'Oh, Joshy, you truly are a wretch!' she said fondly. 'What am I to do with you? Give you some hot anchovy toast, I suppose, and a big cup of Horlicks – '

His eyes glinted again, this time with cautious pleasure. 'Yes, please, Mummy,' he said and then looked away, still seeming fearful, and she was filled with even more compunction.

He was only nine after all, a small boy, albeit a resourceful and brave one. It wasn't easy to find the right train and get yourself on it – and off it – without a ticket, and then to cross London from Liverpool Street station, in the middle of the raids, to go to Holland Park: and she had a sudden vision of him being caught in a raid and at once her resolve was hardened. To see this small and so precious pink and slippery little body crushed under the rubble of bombed buildings, to see these soft downy cheeks scarred with burns – it was a dreadful prospect. And she got to her feet and said crisply, 'Well, we'd better get on with it. Out you come, and then I'll make you some supper – '

He lifted his chin and said in a small voice, 'Please, Mummy, can I have a bubble?'

She stopped then and looked down at him, and after a moment he held out the soap to her and she sighed and sat on the edge of the bath. It had been such a ritual part of bath time all through the toddler and small boy years; how could she refuse him now?

She took the soap and made a rich lather on both hands and then, holding her forefingers and thumbs close together opened them slowly and gently until a triangular film of bubble, glistening, irridescent, trembling with promise, hung there between them, and she held out her hands and Joshy blew gently on it. The film bulged and swelled and then rounded to become a bubble that drifted away from her hands and went floating through the steam that rose from the bath to hang above them for a moment, bouncing gently in the movement of the air, and they both watched it, holding their breath.

And then it floated away and touched the tiled wall of the bathroom and disappeared, and Joshy sighed and Poppy got to her feet and said prosaically, 'There you are, then. Now, out you get and dry yourself very carefully. There are pyjamas on the heater and you can put on Lee's old dressing gown from the airing cupboard. I'll make your supper – '

As she sliced bread and toasted it, and then spread it with his favourite mixture of Gentleman's Relish and butter – using some of their precious and dwindling stores – and then watched the milk for the Horlicks bubble up the sides of the enamelled pan on the cooker, she brooded over what to do.

He had to go back, of course. There was no question of that. London was a lethal place now. He had to be safe. She couldn't go on if anything happened to her precious children and she hardened her jaw as she saw again that glimpse of dark eyes staring up at her from the area and the fragment of a moment when she had wanted to celebrate his return and reach out and hold him and vow never to let him out of her sight again. But she couldn't do that. It would be too wickedly selfish. He had to go back; there was no other way.

He appeared at the head of the stairs down to the kitchen, wrapped in the pink fluffy dressing gown that had been Lee's, and which was still too big for him. His dark hair was tousled and his face glowed pinkly from his bath, and once again her bones seemed to dissolve within her as she looked at him. All she wanted to do was take him up in her arms and hug and hold him and never let him go.

But she had to be a good mother, a sensible mother, a protective mother and she nodded at him and said crisply, 'Here you are, Joshy. Supper. Come and sit down now and eat it all up. And then bed. We'll talk tomorrow about getting you back to the farm.'

He came down the stairs a little clumsily and she saw that he had put on a pair of his sister's slippers, too; rather large fluffy ones with pink pompoms on the toes and he was finding them very awkward, and she watched his slow progress down the stairs and saw in his shadow the rumbustious toddler he had been, rushing around the house like a small and very excitable engine, and sliding on his belly down stairs because walking was too slow for him, and behind that image the baby who had lain in his pram in the sunshine of the garden making scribble noises at the birds which chattered in the trees above him. And she took hold of the edge of the table with both hands and held on. I mustn't make it too nice for him to be at home, she told herself, I mustn't. I must make him understand how important it is he goes back, I must be firm, I must be firm, I must –

He reached the table and pushed the scrubbed wooden chair a little nearer and sat down, and pushed up the sleeves of the gown which had fallen over his hands again, and reached for his supper. Poppy, who had made some tea for herself, sat and watched him as he ate, clearly very hungrily indeed, and said nothing as she thought about the next stage.

He couldn't be sent back alone. The fact that he had managed somehow to get himself on the train and off it at Liverpool Street without any money didn't mean she would be justified in sending him back alone, albeit with a ticket; and then she couldn't help it, and had to ask him.

'How was it the ticket inspectors didn't catch you, Joshy?'

He didn't look up and waited to swallow his mouthful before answering, clearly mindful of the manners he had been taught. 'I hid in the lavatory,' he said.

'But the inspectors always open the lavatory doors, or knock on them if the engaged sign's up, and wait – '

Now Joshy did look at her and a hint of wickedness shone in his eyes. 'I hid behind the door and made myself ever so thin,' he said. 'And when they pushed the door open they didn't see me.'

She looked at his small body, wiry and healthy but undoubtedly thin, and sighed. It really was too easy for him altogether. 'And at Liverpool Street?'

'I looked all anxious and said my Mummy was just ahead, and he let me through.'

'I'll bet he did,' Poppy said. 'Joshy, you know it's naughty to tell lies!'

'Not always. Daddy said it's sometimes necessary. If you're caught by an enemy soldier and he says, "Are you an English boy?" it's better to say, "Nein, mein Herr. Ich bin ein Deutscher Jünge." That's safer, Daddy said. In an emergency, Daddy said – '

She sighed. 'I know what Daddy said. He wasn't telling you to tell lies, though, Joshy – that was just a – a game of pretend. You know that – '

'Not really, it wasn't,' Joshy said and swallowed the last of the thick Horlicks. 'It could be real if they invade, couldn't it? And if they do I want to be here with you, not in horrible old Norfolk.'

'They aren't going to invade – ' Poppy said uneasily, aching somewhere deep inside at the way small children had to grow up in this fear that shrouded them all. 'Not now. It was before – everyone was afraid they would – in the summer, when the weather was easier for them – '

'It's still quite summer,' Joshy said with devastating logic. 'Isn't it? Ever so warm and summery. And if Hitler wanted to invade us a few weeks ago, then he still does, doesn't he? And he'll get to London before he gets to Norfolk and I want to be here with you where all the fun is and – '

'Fun!' Poppy said and almost laughed. 'Fun, Joshy? This is a war we're talking about – '

'I know.' His eyes glowed and he pushed his plate and mug away. 'Oh, I know all about it, Mummy. After school me and Danny and Edward from the other farm and Jerry Hopkins and the others, we play at invasions and I'm always the aeroplanes over London and I drop a bomb

71

on Hitler, right on him, kerpow, and stop him from going any further and then – '

'Joshy, war is not fun. War is dangerous and – it hurts people.'

'It kills them too,' Joshy said happily, and glowed even more brightly. 'It squashes them flat and makes them all bleed and scream like the pigs on the farm when they're killed. Edward saw them do it and he told me how they – '

'Joshy, I don't want another word,' Poppy said, holding up both hands to ward off his words. 'Killing is – it's dreadful. And being hurt is dreadful. It isn't a bit like the games you play with the boys after school. You mustn't think it is, ever. We sent you to Norfolk with Lee because we love you both so much and mean to keep you safe. No one will so much as graze your knees if we can stop them, and – '

'I keep on grazing my knees,' Joshy said swiftly. 'Look – ' And he pushed back his chair and began to roll up his pyjama legs. 'See? Big grazes. So wouldn't I be better here than getting all grazed then on a horrid farm, where there's just smelly old cows who do lavatories in the yard and geese who keep chasing you till you fall over in the smells and – '

'Joshy, stop it,' Poppy said. 'I didn't mean that getting a graze was so dreadful. I was just trying to explain why we sent you to Norfolk – and why you have to stay there till the war's over and it's safe to come home to London.'

He sat there with his head down and let his pyjama legs slither down till they almost covered the pompoms on the slippers.

'Do I really have to?' he said then, and there was a piteous note in his voice. 'Have I absolutely ever so much all the time got to?'

They had taught him that phrase, she remembered, as she stared at him, feeling helpless. Taught him it was what you said when you went through your bedtime ritual; 'Do you love me?' 'Of course I love you.' 'How much do you love me?' 'Absolutely, ever so much, all the time – '

'Yes, darling,' she said gently. 'Yes, you do. Because I love you absolutely ever so much, all the time, and that means I have to keep you safe. We miss you as much as you miss us, and we wish even more than you do that this horrible war was over and we could all be together again. But what can we do? There *is* a war and we have to do the best we can and not fuss too much.'

She stood up and came and bent down beside him and picked him up and he wrapped his legs round her waist and she thought with a pang – he's growing. He's taller than he was in the spring – and she held him tight as he buried his face in the junction of her neck and shoulder the way he had done as a fretful toddler, and held on equally tightly. They stood there for a while in the quiet kitchen where the light reflected off the gleaming black planes of the old range in the fireplace and on the dishes arranged so neatly on Goosey's old dresser, and said nothing. And then she carried him up to his room and put him to bed and kissed him, and he fell asleep even before she'd left the room, with all the abandonment of a weary child. She was weeping a little as she went downstairs to the hall and the telephone.

It took her over an hour to get through to him. The office was supposed to be always manned, or rather womanned these days, for David had had to take on a rather sour middle-aged woman to act as his second-in-command instead of the eager young would-be male journalists who had once flocked to work with him, but who were now all in the armed services; but tonight the phone rang and rang in her ear and she stood there in the hall of her shabby old house, staring down at the now rather dingy black and white tiles of the floor – for Goosey couldn't get the right polish for them anywhere – and imagined the phone on his desk, ringing through the empty rooms. And her tired mind ran away with her and she saw the rooms as stripped and bare and David gone for ever, gone somewhere out of reach the way Bobby had gone, and felt the desolation of being totally and helplessly alone in a hostile world; and had to hold on very hard to her common sense to avoid going headfirst into a state of panic.

But she managed it at last. She made herself some tea – oh, she thought, these interminable cups of tea! – and went back to sit in the hall on the battered old carved chair they had found in the Caledonian Market and brought home in such triumph that time when she had been so heavily pregnant with the little boy now sleeping so deeply upstairs, and dialled again.

And this time he answered and she could have wept with relief.

'Darling! I've been ringing and ringing, it must have been an hour. It's almost three in the morning – can't you get home tonight?'

'Is it likely?' he said wearily. 'I've been trying, believe me. But I've got some good pictures from the raids and some stories about Americans caught here and I've been trying to get the stuff cabled over. I've been at the Embassy all the time. I can't think why Mrs Humphries isn't here – she should be – '

'Well, no one's been there – I've been trying for ages. Listen, David – '

'Bloody woman,' he said fretfully. 'I'll have to find someone else, though don't ask me where or how. But God knows what might have been coming in! They're still working in the office in Baltimore and they could have been sending cables and heaven knows what I've missed – '

'That's the least of your problems right now,' she said crisply. 'Joshy's here.'

There was a little silence and then he spoke with a much brighter tone in his voice. 'Joshy? He's run away again?'

'Again,' she said wearily. 'What are we to do with him?'

'The little wretch,' David said softly and there was a note of pride and delight in his voice that made Poppy sit up very straight indeed.

'David, now, stop that! I've been trying so hard to show him in every way I can that this isn't on. He's got to go back – you can't mean to allow him to stay here! You've seen what the raids are like!'

'They're all to the east – '

'David, you can't – for God's sake, they could reach here as easily as they reach the East End and probably will! How can you even consider it?'

There was a little silence and then he said dully, 'I know. You're right, of course. It's mad to even – but it's just that I hate to think of him so unhappy that he'll do this so often. This is the third time, for pity's sake!'

'Don't I know it?' she said grimly.

'How is he?'

'A little subdued. He knows I'm not pleased – '

'You're not being – '

'Being what?' she said and her voice was a little high. She was desperately tired and all she needed now to set her fuse off was any sort of remonstrance.

'Oh, you know, darling! A bit firm – '

'He needs it.'

'Of course he does. But he needs loving even more.'

'I'm well aware of that. I've given him lots of attention since I found him here – '

'But lots of disapproval too.'

'Of course. He's got to understand he can't just do what he wants. He can't, David. You must understand that – '

David sighed gustily in her ear. 'Oh, I dare say you're right. You usually are. But I'll never get used to you Brits, you know. You're so – oh, you're so goddamned tough with your kids! They never seem to get away with anything, poor little tykes – '

'And from where I stand American children get away with a deal too much,' she said tartly. 'Listen, are we going to stand here at three in the morning arguing the toss about transatlantic child-rearing methods?'

He sighed again. 'No, darling. I'm sorry. It's just that – Jesus, I miss that kid!'

'Do you think I don't? I *hurt*, I want them here so much – '

'But they can't stay in London. You're right, of course. You always are, sweetheart.'

'So you keep saying, but you don't always mean it,' she said. 'The question is, how do we get him back there? I can't go, you can't go – '

'I'll think of something,' he said. 'Maybe Goosey – '

'Out of the question. She's too old and far too decrepit. Those trains can be hours late and you're lucky if you get a seat and – '

'No, I know. Damn it all! I'll have to work something out. Look, Poppy, doll, go to bed. You must be really bushed.'

'I'm dead on my feet,' she said then and yawned, hugely, and was aware as she hadn't been at all aware so far of just how much she ached for sleep. Her eyelids felt as though they had been lined with lead shot. 'I'm supposed to be at the canteen at seven – '

'To hell with that!' he said vigorously. 'Someone else'll have to do your shift – '

'I could ask Joyce to hold on a bit till Maria gets there,' she said dubiously.

'Then do that. Call her now. And then go to bed. I'll be there as soon as I can. Be nice to him, sweetheart.'

'I'm being as nice as I dare,' she said. 'I want to hold him and kiss him to pieces – but he's got to know he's in the wrong. He's got to go back and be safe.'

'I know,' he said. 'Goddamn it, I know! See you soon, doll – ' And the phone clicked in her ear and she yawned again and picked it up to call Joyce.

And when she'd made the necessary arrangements and Joyce had promised cheerfully to recruit her sister Madge from over Hackney way to muck in, she sat there in her little wooden chair in the hall too tired to make the effort to climb the stairs again and go to bed.

And that was where David found her at seven o'clock when he came home.

· 8 ·

Robin's first night on Casualty, she decided, had been complete and utter hell.

She had come on duty at eight thirty sharp, after eating dispirited porridge and toast and marmalade in the nurses' dining room – for it had been decreed that night nurses breakfasted in the evening and took their dinners in the morning – to find the department alive with activity. There had been a slanting hit on a small tenement house just off Sidney Street, and seven people had been buried in it. All of them were out now, and all of them were in the Casualty department, three of them children who were shrieking in fear and rage and loneliness for their mothers, both of whom were in separate cubicles and suffering from various injuries, while the other survivors, two battered old women, sat in a corner glowering at everyone and demanding to be taken home.

No one, it turned out, had been able to convince them they had no home to go back to, so it was small wonder that Sister Priestland, the small and very round Irish Sister in charge, was in a state of high tension. She was flashing around her department from cubicle to cubicle and through the crowded benches in the waiting room – for in addition to the Sidney Street hit there had been plenty of other incidents causing injuries among civilians as well as wardens and firefighters – like a small tornado in a rage and Chick, standing at Robin's elbow, looked around at it all and breathed an awed, 'Oh, my Gawd!' in her ear.

Sister caught sight of them and came rushing across the tessellated hall towards them with her heels slapping on the ground like gunshots.

'Are you the two new nurses on my list? Right, let's get you to work. What're your names?'

They murmured their responses, trying not to catch the eyes of the curious waiting patients who were now all staring at them with great interest, for want of anything better to watch. At which Sister Priestland snapped, 'Do speak up! This is a noisy department whether I like it or not, and I don't, preferring calm and quiet, but there it is – so you have to make yourself heard and understood! Now, you, Chester, go and help Staff Nurse Meek deal with those wretched children – I see from your report from Sister Marshall that you're very good with them – and you, Nurse Bradman, had better come with me and we'll see what we can do with you. Sister Marshall said you were good with your hands and kept your head well. Now let me see you do it.'

And she fled across the hall again towards the far cubicle, with Robin breathlessly at her heels, and plunged through the curtains of where there seemed to be a great deal going on.

That was the point at which Robin felt she'd descended into hell. She'd seen blood and broken flesh before in her first year at the London, especially since the raids had begun, but she had never seen anything like this, and she felt herself whiten as the curtain swished to behind her.

The woman on the high examination and treatment couch was young – possibly not much older than Robin herself, but she looked dreadful. Her face was a yellowish white and she was breathing rapidly and shallowly as her eyes, wide and glazed with terror, flicked from one to the other of the men on each side of her.

They were doctors, and they were working with their heads well down over her right leg, and neither of them paid any attention as she yelped in pain at one of their actions; and Robin looked at the leg and tried to keep her head clear.

It had, it seemed at that first glance, been severed half across at the thick part of the calf. In spite of the mass of bright red muscle and the pumping of blood that was covering the whole area, Robin could see the pale rich gleam of naked bone, and her own flesh crept in sympathy at the sight of that huge gash with its outwardly pouting lips, and she pulled her eyes away and made herself look questioningly at Sister Priestland.

'Right, nurse,' she said, and her voice seemed a little approving now. 'Come and look after this cubicle for the night. Take care of this poor girl while her wound is repaired. They'll be putting on plaster afterwards, I suspect, but they'll tell you. I've got an even worse one in the next cubicle – Oh, and nurse – the baby's all right.'

With which cryptic remark she was gone, leaving Robin standing paralysed for a moment. But only for a moment. Moving as carefully as she could across the slippery floor, which was awash with blood, she went gingerly round the doctor in front of her, and managed to reach the head of the couch, and stretched her arm to put her hand on the woman's shoulder.

At once she turned her head and opened her eyes, for she had been lying with them grimly closed, and looked up at her and somehow Robin managed to smile. If she paid no attention to the horror of the wound that was now so easily seen from her new position, she'd be all right. She wouldn't be sick, she wouldn't. She'd be able to do her job and do it properly – and she leaned over the woman and whispered, 'Hello, dear. What's your name?'

The woman gasped and moaned as one of the doctors did something that hurt and he looked up for a brief moment and muttered, 'Sorry, love, but we had to get that artery, that was – well, anyway, you'll be a bit better now. We've stopped most of the bleeding. Give you a transfusion soon and you'll feel all tickety-boo – '

79

He looked at Robin and lifted one eyebrow comically, and Robin managed to make a small smile in response. She knew who he was from the eyes she could see above his blood-spattered mask and rubber apron: Mr Landow, the surgical registrar who had once come to Annie Zunz to do an emergency tracheotomy on a choking baby, and had told her approvingly that she was deft because she had been able to help him when he reached out his hand for an instrument and Sister had been unable to reach it for him. It helped to know at least one face in this alarming charnel house, and she looked back down at her patient, feeling at last a little less queasy.

'Did you hear that, dear? The surgeon says you'll soon be much better. It's – you've hurt your leg, you see, and it's bleeding a bit. But they've stopped it now and they'll give you some blood to replace your loss and then you'll be feeling quite different – '

'Amy – ' the woman whispered and Robin bent to hear her better. 'What is it? Is that your name? Amy? It's such a pretty name – what's the rest of it, can you tell me?'

The woman rolled her head restlessly on the pillow. 'I'm Betty – ' she said and now her voice was strengthened by a spurt of anger. 'Betty Roydell, seventeen Sidney Street, London E.1. – Betty Roydell – ' Her voice ran away then, and she closed her eyes tightly and yelped again and Robin risked a look downwards at her leg.

It was looking a little more like a human limb now, and less like a piece of butcher's meat on a slab. The two doctors had stopped the bleeding and one of them was now mopping away the last of it, while Mr Landow was preparing a curved needle with catgut, and Robin looked at him and at the great gash that she could now see ran right round the calf from the inner side of the knee almost down to the ankle on the other side, and instinctively tightened her grasp on Betty Roydell's hand, which she had slipped into hers without even realizing she'd done it.

Betty opened her eyes again and said loudly, 'Amy? Where's Amy – ' and suddenly Robin understood.

'Is that your baby, Betty?' she said and the woman stared at her with hot eyes and said urgently, 'My baby? – Amy?'

'Sister says she's fine,' Robin said, but still the woman looked agitated and had opened her mouth to speak again, when the babies across the big hall, who had quietened down, possibly because of the sort of magic Chick always worked with children, started again. A long wail of misery filled the air and beneath her fingers Robin felt the woman's hand relax.

'That's all right, then,' she said and closed her eyes again and this time seemed to go to sleep, and Robin smiled at Mr Landow almost in triumph as though she had achieved something, when of course she hadn't. But they all seemed to feel better.

It took the two doctors half an hour to stitch the deeper layers of the wound and then to repair the surface, using syringe after syringe of local anaesthetic as they went.

'Can't use a general,' Landow muttered when she ventured to ask why. 'Not only because the bloody theatres are jammed with even worse cases than this, God help us, but because in her state she'd never survive it. She's lost over two pints I reckon – check whether it's down from the lab, will you? The blood we ordered for her – it should be here by now.'

She checked and found it was, and then helped them set up the transfusion and saw the now restless Betty sent to the wards, while her baby, who it seemed was suffering little more than a bad fright, was admitted to the children's ward to wait for her. Sister Marshall was a good soul, and never objected to taking in such children if she had space.

'And even if she hadn't,' Chick murmured at Robin as she hurried past her on her way to the ward with Amy and another baby who had to be admitted for the same reason. 'She'd put 'em up in the bath. See you at the midnight trough – '

But they didn't get to their midnight meal. Robin, swathed in a vast red rubber apron, had to clean her cubicle first where the thick clotted blood, which lay everywhere and which also spattered up to the ceiling, took a lot of removing, and she'd no sooner finished than another wave of casualties arrived, this time people who had been gassed when a main was fractured and there was a great panic to get respirators on them all and to repair the injuries they had collected at the same time.

At one point in the ensuing hubbub Robin became aware of Hamish Todd working like a man twice even his considerable size, bodily carrying full-grown people from trolley to cubicle through the busy waiting room, because it was quicker than trying to manoeuvre the big agony wagons, as everyone at the hospital called them, fast enough. He caught her eye as he settled one of them in her cubicle and said, 'Good evening Nurse Bradman,' in as calm and courteous a voice as if they had encountered each other at a vicarage tea party, and she would have burst into laughter if it hadn't been for the man on her couch, who was beginning to emerge from his semi-coma and was rolling around restlessly and also starting to retch. She reached for a kidney dish but too late, and as a mass of half digested food and quantities of heavy beer hit her newly cleaned floor and walls she could have screamed. By which time Hamish was away collecting more people to take them to cubicles.

By the time that man had recovered enough to be carried up to the ward that had been set aside for gassed cases, up on the top floor of the far wing, and she had cleaned the malodorous mess in her cubicle, it was past midnight, and somehow she had no appetite.

Casualty was still bursting at the seams with patients and staff, and she saw no reason to bother Sister Priestland for instructions. She just stayed in the cubicle she'd been put in and dealt with whatever cases the ambulance men came and dumped there. She would clean up superficial wounds as best she could and make the patient as comfortable as possible and then go and try to find a doctor she could drag to her cubicle to see what more needed to be done. There were notes pinned to each patient's garments, obviously collected on their way in, and not knowing what had to be done with them, she simply wrote on each the time, and what treatment had been given and sent them on their way, some to be admitted, but more and more, as the pressure came off and the raids dribbled to an end, to homes if they still had them, or to the emergency centres if they hadn't.

Quite a lot of them went no further than the benches in the middle of the waiting room and stretched out there, and Robin was anxious about that. Surely it wasn't permitted in this busy department? But Sister Priestland, still hurtling around like a thing possessed and doing the work of three, saw them and said nothing, so neither did Robin. And her respect for her new Sister went up a notch.

At half past five Chick came across the at last quiet waiting hall, where the only activity seemed to be a few faint sounds from people twisting and turning to make themselves as comfortable as they could on the hard benches, and shook her head at her. Her apron was smeared with blood, her curly hair was in an uproar and her cap looked as though it just had been squeezed, then stamped on and finally pinned back on her head.

'Children,' she said briefly as she caught Robin looking at it, and then groaned. 'Do you remember something called food? I'm sure I had some once. Right now though it's like a mirage. My poor belly – hollow as a – '

'Nurses!' Sister Priestland appeared at their side with all the suddenness of the fairy queen in a pantomime. 'There are sandwiches in my office. And coffee. Come and get it at once. No, I shall remain out here to keep an eye open. Go and get your food. At once!'

Gratefully they went and found the small cluttered office filled with comfortable fug and a number of

83

people. The two doctors, Landow and Mike Smith, a sandy-haired round-faced man of great charm and sweet temper, Staff Nurse Meek and the senior probationers Jenner and Dollis, and the laboratory technician who had spent a hectic night cross-matching the umpteen pints of blood that had been needed for transfusions, as well as making sure there were enough bottles of normal saline and dextrose to keep the shocked patients alive. They were all smoking and hazy blue wreaths hung over their heads and added to the heat; but no one seemed to mind.

'Ah!' said Dollis, a large girl in thick glasses and with her cap pinned severely at the front of her head. 'The new bugs. Come over here, you two, and find a corner. It's all right to smoke – '

'Thank God for that,' Chick said gratefully and curled down in the corner. 'But I need food more – '

'Sister's a gem,' Dollis said. 'Lots of watercress for sandwiches from somewhere – help yourself.'

They did, and sat there munching in a comfortable silence while the men talked in a desultory fashion of the cases they'd dealt with and the nurses just stared into space. They were all too tired to talk, but it was good to be there with them, Robin decided, and reached for another sandwich from the depleted plate.

And then stopped and looked around again.

'Where's Todd?' she said. 'Isn't he taking a break too?'

'Todd?' Staff Nurse Meek raised her eyebrows at her. 'Who's Todd?'

'The orderly,' Robin said. 'The one who carried all those patients through the waiting room because they couldn't get the trolleys through. He's worked so hard – I've seen him. He must be starving.'

'Oh, he'll get his somewhere else,' Nurse Meek said and reached into her dress pocket for another cigarette. It was still quiet outside in the waiting hall and there seemed to be no rush at the moment.

'Where?' Robin said and Chick poked her in the ribs, but she paid no attention. 'There isn't anywhere else, is there? If you don't go for your meal at midnight or at half past, where else can you go?'

'Really, Nurse whatever your name is,' Meek snapped at her. 'I don't see what the orderly's work has to do with you.'

'Nothing,' Robin said steadily. 'But it just doesn't seem right that – '

'That what?' Meek said dangerously. Never, thought Robin in the recesses of her mind, was a person more ineptly named. She had a sharp little face that was pretty sometimes but now looked foxy with anger. She had lifted her head so that the special bows of the fully-trained nurse showed clearly under her chin and Robin felt herself quail. But she couldn't stop now.

'That what?' Meek repeated and Robin took a deep breath.

'That he is not allowed to come and share the break with us,' she said. 'He's worked just as hard as we have. Harder, I think – '

'Really? That's your opinion is it?' Meek said acidly. 'Tell me, did Sister Marshall welcome the opinions of junior probationers on her ward? Or did she just step back and let you run it?'

'Who is Todd?' Dr Landow said lazily, and looked at Robin with a ghost of a wink. 'Someone special?'

'Not in the least special,' Meek said sharply. 'Just an orderly – some conchie they've stuck us with.'

'You're not stuck with him!' Robin flared at her. 'He's a very good man who works hard and – '

'Dear me, do I hear the wings of love or whatever breaking on the turgid air and all that rot?' Mike Smith said and laughed. 'Stooping to conquer a bit, aren't you, dear? You can do better than a conchie orderly, I'd have thought.'

'It's nothing of the sort,' Robin cried, her face crimson with embarrassment now. 'It's just that it doesn't seem

85

right when we've all worked the same that we don't all get the same sort of break and something to eat and I just wanted to know – '

'Well, it's none of your business,' Staff Nurse Meek said furiously. 'Much more of this and I'll have to talk to Sister about you! And you won't like that one bit!'

'End of fuss,' Dr Landow said lazily and got to his feet. He was a tall man with a shadow of dark stubble across his chin and cheeks, and a rapidly receding hairline, and he had an air of authority about him that stopped Staff Nurse Meek, who had opened her mouth to speak again. 'I'll take the absent Todd the remains of this great feast and our young nurse's conscience will be satisfied and our staff nurse's sense of propriety won't be outraged. Everyone had enough of Sister's delectable watercress sandwiches? Splendid. The remains shall serve as a banquet to our despised – and prized – orderly.' And he went lounging out of the small room bearing the plate and the coffee that Chick, acting with speed if not prudence, had poured into one of the tin mugs.

There was a silence and then Staff Nurse Meek, her cheeks suddenly much redder than they had been and her eyes very bright, said sharply, 'All of you nurses, it's time to get this place tidied. At once, now. I'll deal with you later, Nurse Bradman. Or rather, Sister will. Now get this place cleaned up at once.'

And clean up they did. By the time the day staff came through the big double doors with their clean aprons glittering in the morning sunshine, and their caps neatly set on well-brushed hair, the casualty nurses looked like the skivvies they had been for the past two or three hours.

Their work had been to some effect, however. Nurse Meek had chivvied the sleepers out of the waiting room while Sister Priestland was out of sight dealing with a member of the nursing staff from the operating theatres who had splashed her legs with pure carbolic acid, and had harried the four junior nurses mercilessly. Dollis and Jenner had been furious with Robin for having so provoked the staff nurse and muttered unpleasantly at her as they passed her, and altogether Robin had felt wretched.

But she knew she had been right, and that had helped her a little, and if anyone argued more with her about it, she'd stick to her guns, she told herself firmly, even with Sister if she had to. It had been abominable to ignore Todd when they'd had their break, quite abominable, and she scrubbed and polished even harder every time she thought of it. It was worth all this nagging and dislike to have stood up for a principle, really it was.

Or so she tried to convince herself, but by the time she came off duty, bedraggled and exhausted, she wasn't quite so sure. All around her the hospital buzzed and hummed as the day got under way and the rubble began to be picked up in the battered streets and houses that surrounded it. She stood there blinking in the sunshine and wondering bleakly why she bothered. It was too wearing altogether to work here, and maybe she should do as Poppy wanted her to do and leave London and find somewhere peaceful and safe, out of the line of fire.

But then she pulled her cape more closely around her and set off to trudge to the Nurses' Home and a bath and bed. It was silly to stand about thinking when she felt like this. She'd never think clearly that way, and she dragged her weary feet on and was hardly able to turn her head when Chick came after her and fell into step alongside.

'Heavens, I've been looking everywhere for you. Why weren't you in the dining room?'

'If you think I can face shepherd's pie at this hour of the morning, you've another think coming,' Robin said. 'If only we could have two breakfasts it wouldn't be so bad, but the sight of all that awful stuff – and the cabbage – at eight in the morning – I just can't handle it.'

'Night Sister'll have your guts for garters,' Chick said cheerfully. 'I answered roll call for you this morning, but she looked up a bit sharpish when I did it. I won't get away with it again. No more shirking! Come and sit with us at least, even if you don't want to eat. Then you can find out about your own off-duty.'

'Mmm? What off-duty?'

'See what I mean? They've changed the schedule, ducky. You've got three nights off starting tonight! So you needn't face old Priestland and that repellent very unMeek madam, and by the time you get back maybe they'll have forgotten all about your waving the banner for Todd. Whatever got into you?' Chick looked at her curiously as they reached the foot of the stairs to their rooms. 'I didn't think you cared that much about him.'

Robin made a face. 'I don't. I mean I've nothing for or against him. I just thought it was rotten to treat him as though he hadn't worked as hard as we had, just because he's an orderly.'

'Oh, you're such snobs, you British! That's why I like you, kid. You ain't! I'll back you up if the fuss starts again. Good on you, anyway. Goodnight, or good morning, or whatever. Remember to phone your Ma, for heaven's sake.'

'I'll do better than that,' Robin said, suddenly energized. 'Of course I will. Now I've got nights off, I'll go home! There! See you in a few days, Chick!' And she went hurrying up the stairs feeling much better than she would have thought possible, after such a night of utter hell.

· 9 ·

The house was blissfully quiet when Robin got there and she stood in the hall breathing in the familiar smells of floor polish and brass cleaner and flowers – for there were vases of rich red and bronze chrysanthemums from the garden set on the polished hall tables – and listened. There was a faint clatter of dishes from below and she smiled; dear old Goosey twiddling about at something or other; and then a new scent reached her, of baking this time, and her smile widened. The absence of shepherd's pie and cabbage inside her was making itself felt, a little noisily. Goosey would like nothing better than to have someone to feed, and she threw her coat on to the hall stand and dropped her weekend case on the floor and went clattering down to the kitchen to be hugged by a delighted Goosey and fussed over as though she were still three years old. Very agreeable, Robin thought, balm to a wounded soul, and luxuriated in it.

Not until she had wolfed a great plateful of French toast – for Goosey unearthed a precious egg from her secret hoard – and followed it with vast cups of tea, did she stop to check on the rest of the family. And was amazed to be told that both Poppy and David were at home and fast asleep.

' 'Ad a terrible night they did, bless 'em both,' Goosey said, and sat down at the table herself and poured a cup of tea from the chipped old brown teapot into her favourite cup, which she'd bought long ago on a seaside holiday in Yarmouth and which held fully half a pint. 'There's Mr David comes 'ome at seven this mornin' just as I'm about to get things goin' and there she is, Mrs Poppy, poor soul, fast asleep on that there chair in the 'all! I ask you! Sleeping on that chair! I said to her, I did, when she goes up to have a bath and I take her a bit o' breakfast, I told her, that's no way to take care of yourself to win the war, is it? No matter what's happened to young Joshy and no matter what they say – '

'Joshy?' Robin's head came up sharply and the sleepiness which had been creeping back disappeared. 'What about him?'

Goosey shook her head lugubriously. 'Done it again, ain't 'e? Just like last time. Mind you – ' and her attempt to be censorious faltered and vanished, to be replaced by a wide proud grin that showed all too clearly the teeth she no longer had. 'You got to 'and it to him. A right young limb 'e is, and clever! They don't come any cleverer than our Joshy.'

'Run away again?' Robin asked sympathetically.

'Course 'e has! Yer Ma had a bad time of it down that canteen of hers last night, and then comes home dead tired and there he is down in the area and waitin' for 'er. Told me, she did, this morning when I got her into bed. Couldn't hardly move she couldn't, she was that stiff. But she said he'd got to go back o' course. Shame really.' Goosey got to her feet with an audible creaking of her old stays. 'When he just don't want to. It's not that my brother's boy's not good to him and to our Lee, of course he is, but it stands to reason the poor little things want to be with their Ma and Pa, don't it? It's flyin' in the face of nature, that's what it is, to keep these children so far away from their own. We've had no bombs here, have we? They're all down in that nasty East End of yours.' And she looked at Robin sternly as though to blame her for the pasting that was being suffered by the slums in which she worked. 'If it was up to me, I tell you straight, I'd keep the children here and make sure we all got down in that nasty shelter whenever there was any hint of trouble and we'd all be fine and young Joshy wouldn't have to keep on upsetting everyone by legging it the way he does. And my nephew,' she went on with an air of great virtue, 'my nephew could take on some other of these 'ere evacuees what'd be glad of the chance to go and live on a farm like his. Ducks and geese and there's chickens and all – but there it is, no one don't want my opinion, do they? I'm just an old woman and no good to no one, not when it comes to opinions, though I can cook and clean and so forth o' course – '

Robin cut in hastily to stem the tide of chatter which was threatening to turn into an all too familiar diatribe. No one knew better than Robin just how much of the housework and cooking Poppy had to do now that Goosey was so old and frail, and equally no one knew just how much the old woman tried to convince herself and everyone around her that she was still the prop and stay of the household that she always had been.

'Listen, Goosey, where is he? Joshy, I mean. Has he gone out to play or something? Because – '

'Him, gone out? Not a bit of it. Fast asleep still, isn't he? Up there in his bed looking like every angel you ever saw, as pink as a picture that he is. He was always the best-looking of all you babies. Goosey should know, because didn't I have the care of all three of you? But no one never asks me for an opinion – why should they? I'm only old Goosey, been here for ever – '

She went on muttering to herself as she began laboriously to wash the last of the dishes Robin had swiftly taken from the table to the sink, and only stopped when Robin kissed the back of her old neck, which smelled as it always did of baby powder and lavender water, and made for the stairs.

'I'll go up and see him,' she said. 'I've missed the little wretch dreadfully. And it's high time he was up, surely – '

'Didn't get to bed till well after one, or maybe it was two, this morning,' Goosey said. 'And he'd been on the run all day. He might well be sleeping yet.'

'It's ten o'clock now – so he's had eight hours at least. Do start some breakfast for him, Goosey. Have you another egg to manage some French toast for him? He loves it – I'll be down with him soon – '

And she ran up the stairs eagerly. She had always adored her small brother, from the moment she had first seen him, a crumpled creature with a furious expression on his face, the day Poppy had brought him home from the hospital. Lee had always been a little remote, a self-contained child with a strong will of her own and a tendency to be silent and watchful, but Joshy had always been delightful, confiding, friendly and just wicked enough to be amusing. To see him before she curled up for a day's sleep herself would be lovely.

He was already awake when she put her head round his door, sitting on the edge of his bed and struggling to tie his shoelaces tight enough. Even at his age he still found that a problem and his big sister was one of the few people he allowed to know it, and he grinned cheerfully at her over his shoulder as she said, 'Joshy!' in a delighted voice, and stuck out one leg.

'I knew someone'd come if I tried on my own first,' he said. 'And I'm glad it's you. You won't give me a row, will you?'

Robin crouched in front of him and expertly lacing and tying his scuffed brown shoes, laughed.

'Ma been giving you a tongue-lashing?'

He made a face. 'Sort of.'

'I'll bet. You are a wretch, Joshy. You know how she worries – tell me, how'd you do it this time?'

He launched into a graphic account of his escapade, and she stayed there sitting on her haunches in front of him and watching his eloquent face as he chattered on, and marvelled a little. She was used to children from her work at the hospital, and of course from Lee, who at two years his senior had been the first small child she'd ever had much to do with; but none of them had ever seemed to her to have his ready wit and sharp intelligence. One day, she found herself thinking now as he mimed for her the way the ticket inspector had slammed open the lavatory door behind which he had been hiding, one day he'll be famous. He'll do something very special with his life. He's that sort of person.

Joshy finished then with a sudden descent into gloom. '– So Mummy found me and said I'd got to go back. I had a lovely supper and everything but she says I've got to go back. It's not fair.'

Robin got to her feet a little stiffly. 'I'm sorry, Joshy, but it is, you know. It's dangerous in London. I was in a raid the other night and last night – well, the injured people in Casualty – it was dreadful.'

'Lots of blood?' Joshy said and his eyes glowed.

'Lots,' Robin said. 'And no, I will not tell you the details, so stop gloating. You're a revolting child, young man, that's what you are. If someone came and spilled all their guts at your feet you wouldn't turn a hair, I suspect – '

'Course I wouldn't!' he said disgustedly. 'It's what wars are about, isn't it? That's why I want to stay home. To be where it's all happening and see all the fun.'

'Not to be with us? With Ma and Pa?' Robin was genuinely curious, for he had always been a most affectionate child as well as being as normally bloodthirsty as any boy of his age, and he looked at her and then away and made a face.

'Course I do,' he said gruffly. 'That's mostly why I want to stay here, but I can't tell them that, can I? They'll get all worried and that's no good to anyone. I thought if I showed them how brave I am and everything they'd let me stay because they'd know then that nothing that happened would upset me. They'd think I'd be all right and – '

'You're missing the point, Josh,' Robin said as gently as she could. 'It's not the possibility that you'd see something nasty and be upset that worries them. It's the possibility that *you'd* be the something nasty and bloody that they'd see. You could be hurt, love, killed even.'

Joshy stared at her, invincible in his belief in his own immortality. 'You haven't been hurt or killed,' he said. 'Have you? And you're down in the East End where it's much worse, and you're working in a hospital where there are all sorts of disgusting germs to give you dreadful diseases, and you haven't caught any of them.'

'Haven't I just,' Robin said with considerable feeling. 'Didn't I have the most appalling flu last year, caught from the hospital?'

'Well, so did we all, didn't we? So it wasn't just the hospital, it was everywhere. Anyway, they couldn't hurt me, those bombs. I can run ever so fast. And anyway, there are the shelters, aren't there?'

'They're not always all that safe,' Robin said, remembering the night last week when a shelter had had a direct hit across the road from the hospital, and all the fifteen people in it had died. 'You'll have to go back, Joshy. You know you will.'

He looked triumphantly at her and shook his head. 'Well, maybe, but not yet. I don't know when. I heard Ma and Pa talking last night. They came in to see me and I sort of stayed asleep, you know what I mean. And they were saying there's no one to take me back. Pa's got his work and Ma's got the canteen and Goosey's too old. So there it is. I'll have to stay a while, at least.'

She looked at him consideringly. 'I'm afraid it isn't, my love.' And she reached out and hugged him. 'Don't hate me for it. But I've got three nights off. I could take you. And I will, because it just isn't safe enough for you in London. No, don't look at me that way. Believe it or not, I'm on your side. But I also know what your tricks are, so go back you will. And I'll take you. But not right now. I need some sleep in the worst way, and Goosey's making some breakfast for you in the kitchen. So, on your way sweetheart. Big sister needs some time to herself.' And she slapped his bottom gently as he stood up reluctantly and went over to the door, his head down and his feet dragging.

'I should have guessed no one'd understand,' he said mournfully. 'It's always the same. Not fair – ' And he went out of the room and down the stairs, slapping his feet noisily on each step as a form of protest – it always annoyed Goosey dreadfully when he did it – leaving Robin wanting to weep for him. It is really a rotten time to be a child, she thought. At least she could be part of it all, and feel she was useful. Or could most of the time, for she remembered suddenly the expression on Staff Nurse Meek's face when she had argued with her about Todd, and she sighed. Going to Norfolk with Joshy could be fun really. She might even decide to stay there with him, and to hell with the hospital and nursing. It was a thought –

But one not to be thought, or at least not now, and she went across the hallway to her own familiar room and went to bed. There was no way she could cope another moment without some rest. And she was asleep almost before she pulled the blankets above her naked body, for she had been too weary to go down to fetch her things from the hall.

'I'll tell you what,' David said. 'We'll have a holiday. Tomorrow everyone has to get back to work – me to the bureau and your Ma to the canteen and you to the farm. That's your war work, really, Joshy, isn't it?' Joshy opened his mouth to speak but his father rushed on, preventing him. 'So what say we all go out to dinner tonight, hmm?'

Joshy was immediately enthralled. 'To a restaurant? I mean, a real one, not Mummy's or Auntie Jessie's?'

David laughed as Poppy made a little face, but it was clear she wasn't upset. 'I think so. We could do better than at an hotel, I think. I wonder – ' and he looked thoughtfully at Joshy. 'Is it time you tried Chinese food, do you think?'

Joshy's eyes widened and Robin laughed. She remembered how exciting it had been the first time David and Poppy had taken her to a Chinese restaurant. It had been back in those days when she hadn't been absolutely sure how she felt about David, whether she liked him for being fun or hated him for being so important to Poppy. That night learning from him how to eat with chopsticks had helped to resolve the problem.

'He'll show you how to eat with chopsticks, Joshy,' she said. 'It's fun. You're allowed to pick the bowl up and hold it under your chin – '

Joshy snorted with laughter. 'Will Goosey be coming? She'd have a fit if she saw me do that.'

'No,' Poppy said. 'Not Goosey. She doesn't really like foreign food and anyway she likes to get to bed early. Will that help, Joshy?'

His face lost some of its sparkle as he glanced at her and then he sighed and nodded. 'I suppose so. I mean I've got to go back anyway, so there it is. I might as well have some fun out of it all while I'm here. There isn't any in rotten old Norfolk.'

'Fiddle de dee,' Poppy said crisply. 'It's there if you look for it. Fun comes from inside you most of the time anyway. When you go anywhere at all you always find yourself waiting on the step when you arrive.'

Joshy stared at her. 'That's soppy,' he said. 'I mean, I don't want to be cheeky or anything, but it *is* soppy.'

'It's very wise, my son,' David said and leaned over and tugged him to his feet. 'As you'll realize one day. Come on. We'll kick a ball about in the garden for a bit and then get changed. Poppy, you can get someone to stand in for you tonight? Under the circumstances?'

'What else can I do?' Poppy said. 'Sometimes it's just – well, not to worry. Jessie said she'd go and keep an eye on things, which is good of her. I've asked Flo and

Edna not to let her do too much, but you know how she is. And I just hope there aren't any bad incidents tonight. At least she'll be safe there. I worry myself sick about her at Cable Street. She never uses her shelter, you know?'

'I thought she went to her cellar?' Robin said.

'If she feels like it. But too often she doesn't. At the canteen she'll be fine, though. It shakes a bit but even close hits leave it secure.'

'I worry about Auntie Jessie,' Robin said after a while and went over to the drawing-room window to look down into the garden where David and Joshy had arrived and were now kicking a battered football with a great deal more energy than accuracy. 'She's so stubborn – Ma. tell me about the man at Auntie Jessie's.'

'Man? What man?'

'Oh, come on. You know who I mean! He turned up at Auntie Jessie's the day I was there with Chick and you looked like thunder. He knew who I was and said something about Chloe. Who is he and why do you loathe him so?'

There was a little silence and then Poppy said shortly, 'Private, my love. Private.'

'Oh, Ma, come off it. This is me, remember?'

'Could I forget? Well, I suppose – it's just that he's – oh, he's such a chancer! Not as scrupulously honest as he might be, and nasty with it.'

'That doesn't tell me who he is. Just what he is.' Robin looked over her shoulder at Poppy. 'Come on, Ma. Spill it!'

'Oh – ' Poppy made a face and went and curled up on one of the big multi-coloured cushions by the empty fireplace. 'I suppose you'll find out sooner or later. He's Bernie – '

Robin frowned. 'Bernie? I've heard of him before – '

'Possibly,' Poppy said drily. 'He's Jessie's son.'

'That's it! I knew I'd heard hints from – well, never mind. I just knew there was something about him! So

97

he's Jessie's, is he? He must have had a simply gorgeous-looking father!'

Poppy lifted her brows. 'As a matter of fact, he gets his looks from his mother's side of the family,' she said a little frostily. 'Your grandfather – my father and Jessie's brother – was a very good-looking person and Jessie, when she was younger – and anyway, look at you. You're no slouch!'

Robin went pink. 'Thanking you kindly, ma'am,' she said as lightly as she could. 'So, he's Jessie's son and he's a bit of a chancer, not too honest. Is that why you loathe him so? And where does Chloe come in?'

'Enough,' Poppy said. 'This is turning into gossip.'

'Mm.' Robin's eyes glinted with amusement. 'And isn't it fun?'

Poppy laughed in spite of herself. 'Honestly, Robin, you're as bad as Joshy sometimes.'

'I wish I had half his intelligence and a quarter of his charm,' Robin said. 'He really is something rather special.'

'He is, isn't he?' Poppy smiled at her daughter then. 'You all are. And it's lovely to see you so attached to him. Half-brother and all – '

'To quote an expert,' Robin said lightly. 'Fiddle de dee! He's my little brother completely, and there's an end to it. Now tell me about Chloe. Don't keep changing the subject.'

'I can't,' Poppy said uncomfortably. 'She's your sister too, and – '

Robin made a face. 'Now she really *feels* like a half-sister. In fact a quarter, or less. She can be so – oh, you know what I mean.'

'I do and I don't want to talk about it.' Poppy was more uneasy than ever. 'She's a – I mean she's a private person now. Lives her own life. We don't see much of her and it's horrid to gossip about her – '

'I see,' Robin said shrewdly. 'So she and Bernie were some sort of – '

'That's enough, Robin!' Poppy was on her feet. 'I'm going to bath and change. It's high time I dressed properly. I've been slopping around like this for far too long.' And she tugged at her dressing gown. 'You could do with something different too. Have you anything with you from the hospital you can wear? Or would you like to borrow something of mine?'

Robin pulled at her skimpy green siren suit. 'I can't go in this?'

'You know perfectly well that – ' And then Poppy stopped. 'You really can get me so agitated, Robin! Time you grew out of that at your great age.'

Robin laughed. 'I know. Isn't it awful? But at least it means I'm old enough to wear that little green number of yours. The suit – the one with the silly hat to match.'

Poppy made a face. 'I was going to wear that – oh, all right. I'll make do with the black.'

'And very nice, too,' Robin said as they made for the door. 'You look like a femme fatale in it. I'll need some stockings too. Any possibility of those?'

And arguing amiably over clothes they went upstairs. Talking about Chloe clearly wasn't on the agenda today, Robin thought privately as she chattered on about the use of a string of pearls that Poppy had and which would look splendid with the green suit. Sooner or later she'd find out about the link between her and the amazingly good-looking and highly dubious cousin. Be nice, and persuade Ma, that was the secret, but not now. Now they were going out as almost a family to eat exotic food and have some fun, war or no war.

· 10 ·

Joshy was for once in his life silenced with awe by the restaurant to which David took them. The place was full of bead curtains and low lights and carved wooden partitions between the tables, all painted in bright green and red and gold lacquer, and the smell was extraordinary; Robin identified ginger and cinnamon and garlic and then had to give up as the scent, exotic, delicious and highly promising, overwhelmed her, and then laughed aloud as she caught sight of Joshy with his head up, snuffling the air like a small hedgehog.

The place was full, with blue and khaki uniforms predominating among the diners, and there was a great deal of noise as people laughed and chattered, but the owner, a round man with a smile almost as wide as his teeth were white and with the most oriental of eyes and brows, welcomed David as though he had every table available to him and his party alone, and led them to a large round one almost in the middle of the restaurant.

Joshy was even more enthralled to discover that the centre of the table, far from being rigid, was a roudabout, and he reached forwards and pushed on it and it turned indolently on its axis.

'It's called a Lazy Susan in America,' David explained just as he had once explained to Robin long ago. 'I don't know what it is in Chinese. Anyway, the thing is, Chinese food comes in lots of different dishes and everyone helps themselves into their own bowls. The Lazy Susan makes it easier for everyone to get what they want without stretching all the time.'

Joshy turned it again and then dug into his pocket and pulled out a rather battered wooden model of a Spitfire. 'Old George – he's the cowherd on the farm – he says the trouble the Air Force has is that it can't find enough places where it can build ever such long runways to take off on and land on,' he said, and reached forward with his Spitfire. 'Look, Pa, if I turn the table this way, and then make the aeroplane land from the opposite way, see? The aeroplane sort of stays in the same place but manages to run enough to land safely, and still it doesn't take up as much space as a long runway, would it? It'd be a sort of round runway, wouldn't it?'

David said nothing, staring at him, and Poppy and Robin were silent too, gazing at Joshy's absorbed face as he pushed the Lazy Susan from the left and brought his toy plane in to land from the right. 'Mind you,' he said then. 'You'd have to have some sort of cooling system, wouldn't you, because of the friction on the wheels making them too hot? And you'd have to have special equipment on the wheels for landing, to make sure the plane sort of went round in a curve instead of straight because it'd go off the edge if you didn't have something to guide it – '

He sighed then and pushed his plane back in his pocket. 'I'll have to think about that. Maybe George'll help me make a Lazy Runway.'

'George will make you one?' David said a little weakly, still staring with some awe at his son. 'Did he make that Spitfire?'

'Mmm? Oh, a bit of it. He sort of showed me how and then I did it. I say, where's the lavatory? I really must go to the lavatory.'

Poppy smiled. All his life Joshy had been passionately interested in lavatories and had never failed to visit a new one when he could. 'You won't find any bead curtains or lacquer there, you know,' she said. 'There's a sign on the wall over there – see?' And Joshy nodded and scrambled down from his place and hurried away, his small legs, sun browned beneath his short trousers, looking plump and healthy as he moved.

'I say, he really is something, isn't he?' Robin said after a moment. 'He scares me sometimes, he's so bright.'

'Me too,' David said. 'Or is it just that I don't remember how I used to think? Maybe all boys think like that – '

'And girls,' Robin said. 'I mean, I'm admiring Joshy because he's clever, but I don't think he's clever just because he's a boy. There's more to brains than sex, you know!'

'Well, yes, of course,' David said. 'I wasn't being – I just thought that Joshy seems to have the promise of a fine mind and I wasn't sure if I was right or whether it was just the way boys think. I wasn't criticizing you.'

'Hmm!' Robin said and Poppy laughed.

'He's better than most men, you know, darling,' she said. 'I get so many people throwing their hands up in amazement because I can run a business and don't look like something out of Madame Tussaud's Chamber of Horrors. David's not like that – at least I don't think so – '

'Hey, after all these years, you can say that?' David said indignantly. 'Of course I'm not! Ye gods, where'd we all be without women in this war? They're filling all the gaps the men in the services have left behind and – '

'Yes – and what will they do when the war's over, hmm? Go back home to be good and quiet again?' Robin said. 'I was listening to some of them at the hospital – the women who're taking over the porters' jobs. We've only got old men there now, and these women, and one of them was saying it'd be just like last time. When the war was on, she said, no one could be nicer to women than the men were, but as soon as it was over, it was a matter of get back where you belong – stop taking our jobs away.'

David shook his head. 'Not this time,' he said confidently. 'It has to be different this time.'

'I wish I could be so sure,' Poppy said unexpectedly. 'In some ways it's getting worse. I mean, I know more women have jobs now and so forth and are in the Army and all the rest of it, but there were men in the restaurant the other day complaining that women's real war work was looking wonderful, to cheer the chaps up when they come home on leave – '

'You see?' Robin was triumphant. 'It isn't easy for us, after all – and you thinking boys better than girls is just another – '

'Hey, pax, pax!' David held up both hands. 'Believe me, I mean no such thing. And isn't it time we started to order? I yearn for noodles in my bowl rather than talking about the contents of male and female noodles, if you'll forgive me a lousy joke.'

'Darling, calling that a joke is to over-qualify it,' Poppy murmured and began to read her menu. 'Ye gods, David, how do they manage this in times like these? Shrimps and lobster? Who's catching them at this time of the year? Who's got the time – '

The proprietor materialized at her left shoulder. 'I'm afraid there is no shrimp and no lobster available today, Madame Deveen,' he said in a richly emollient voice. 'There has not been for some time. But I leave these items on the menu just to encourage the hopes of better times to come. I can give you many agreeable dishes however. Some sweet and sour pork balls and a soft noodle and chicken dish – not a lot of chicken you understand, but some, and there are many ways with vegetables of course. I have some good won ton and a few spring rolls, filled with the best of bean sprouts which I grow myself from the small store of Mung beans I fetched from the docks only three days before the commencement of hostilities – '

Joshy came back and joined in the ordering ritual with much delight and was given his first lesson with chopsticks by the round-faced proprietor and proved himself very deft. And Robin caught David's eye and

103

he lifted his brows comically and spread his hands wide as if to say, 'You see? He just is a superior person.' And she grinned back at him. Boy or girl, brain differences apart, it couldn't be denied that there was a certain special something about Joshy.

They had been eating for five or perhaps ten minutes or so, prodding excitedly into one dish after another as they came up and were put on the Lazy Susan, when the big bead curtains over the main door rattled again and moved and a noisy party came bursting in. There was a blur of khaki and bright blue and a good deal of laughter that sounded to Robin decidedly alcoholic. She had spent enough nights on Casualty in her first year at the hospital, before the raids had begun, to have heard that on Saturday nights, and she recognized it again. And then there was a peal of high feminine laughter and her back stiffened suddenly. She knew that sound, and she lifted her head and looked, and Poppy, who was sitting opposite her caught her eye and said softly, 'Is it?'

'I think so – ' Robin said and ducked her head, as though she didn't want to be seen and then, a little ashamed, raised it again. She was being ridiculous; and as the noisy party came barging past their table on a wave of brandy-scented air well laced with a heavy musky woman's perfume, she smiled carefully and said, 'Hello Chloe.'

Chloe hadn't seen them, but now she stopped and stared and then tugged on the sleeve of one of the men in her party and made him stop too.

'Darling,' she said and her voice was high and she used an exaggerated drawl. 'Do see who's here! The family, no less!'

'What's that?' The man was a captain, and his uniform was very well pressed, even dapper. He wore his hair sleeked well back and rich with brilliantine and he had the square face, Robin decided, of the sort of man you saw in toothpaste advertisements. Quite good-looking at the first glance and desperately dull at the second. 'Your people? Well, well. Good show, what?'

Robin felt her lips quirk. She'd lived in the East End long enough now to find herself filled with disdain at the sort of people her patients would label with loud scorn as 'toffs'; and here undoubtedly was a toff. And a stupid one at that, she decided, because he was looking at them all with a sudden glassy stare. But then she realized he wasn't stupid, but in fact rather sharp, because the glassiness came from brandy, rather than from any inner lacks.

'How de do, sir,' the man said and held out one hand to David. 'A pleasure to meet you, Mr er – '

'Deveen,' Chloe said loudly. 'My stepfather, sort of.' She giggled then. 'Actually, dearest, I'm a poor 'ickle orphan, don't you know, but Poppy here's my stepmother and after my poor old dad died she hurried off and married David here, so he's a sort of second time around stepfather, I suppose.'

'With no control over her at all,' David said easily, and smiled at Poppy, and Robin could see the reassurance he was trying to put into that look. 'Maybe you'll do better, Captain er – '

'Stanniforth. Colin Stanniforth. You're an American then?'

'Indeed, yes.'

'I see. Over here to see when your lot are going to come on in and join in the fun? Bit of a problem, some of your people, aren't they? Want to sit there all cosy on the edge of the Atlantic and to hell with what's going on this side? Never mind though. We can manage well enough, eh?' And he laughed rather loudly, his glassy eyes now fixed on David's civilian suit.

'I'm a journalist,' David said levelly. 'Writing the most honest account I can of what's going on here on the British side of the Atlantic. I could perhaps persuade a few of the isolationists back home to think again. It's certainly what I'm trying to do – '

'Oh, darlings, no boring shop talk, for God's sake. Too bloody boring to be true!' Chloe said loudly and looked challengingly at Poppy, who had reddened a little at her language and glanced uncertainly at Joshy. He, however, was ignoring all of them, intent instead on chasing a pea round his bowl with his chopsticks. 'So what are you all doing here? I thought the young one was off being a vaccie somewhere? Ought to be in bed anyway.'

Joshy, aware now that he had entered the conversation and having successfully speared his pea, even if he couldn't get it in the right way between the tips of both his chopsticks, glowered at her.

'I ran away, if you must know,' he said sourly. 'Honestly, Chloe, you do look soppy. All that stuff on your face. You don't look like that when you come to tea at our house.'

Chloe looked thunderous and David laughed. 'Oh, dear, isn't it sad when brothers and sisters fight, Captain Stanniforth? Still it must be a comfort to you to know that Chloe's family is so honest with her!'

'Eh, what? Oh, yes, absolutely, yes.' Stanniforth said and gave a bark of puzzled laughter. 'I say, Chloe, better be joining the others, I'm afraid. They're getting a touch restless, the natives – ' And indeed the rest of their party had started banging on the table with spoons to attract their attention and everyone else in the restaurant was looking round. Robin was mortified but Chloe seemed to regain her composure at once and positively preened.

'Such a fuss. Can't leave them for a moment but they're yelping,' she said. 'Just like you, Joshy. As I said, time you were in bed, isn't it? You're looking positively hagged. But then, so do you, Robin. You need some makeup, dear – let me know what you want to spend and I'll put you in touch with my chap. A dear little man – gets all sorts of goodies over from America mostly.' She flashed a sharp little glance at David. 'I dare say you're much too busy to think of such things for her, eh, David? Not even for Poppy – ' And she threw a slightly contemptuous glance at Poppy's subtle makeup. 'Well, dearest, must fly. See you soon, hmm?' And she swept off, taking Stanniforth with her, and soon the noise from the other table where they and their friends were ensconced doubled, and everyone else returned to their own food and stopped staring.

'Why does she do that?' Poppy said in a low voice. 'She's not exactly marvellous when she comes to see us at home, but whenever we run into her when we're out she behaves as though we're something to be ashamed of – it's too bad of her – and Joshy, you didn't help. I've told you never to make personal remarks.'

'Well, she did it first,' Joshy said passionately.

'I didn't hear anything to make you so – ' Poppy began, but Joshy looked even more thunderous.

'She made a personal *look*,' he said. 'She looked at me the way Mrs George looked at me the time I fell in all the cow muck and came into the kitchen and dropped it on the floor and the – '

'Joshy, darling!' Poppy said and closed her eyes, for his voice had been loud enough for the people at adjoining tables on both sides to hear and look amused, and David laughed.

'Forget it all,' he said amiably. 'This is our holiday, remember? Tomorrow it's trains north and all the other miseries, but right now here are quantities of noodles and vegetables and even, I suspect, some more sweet and sour pork left. Joshy, will you have some fried rice first? Look, it's got real undried egg bits in it – '

They settled down to finish their meal and no more was said about Chloe. But Robin was very aware of her and sat and brooded a little. Did she really look so awful? It was all right for Chloe in her comfortable safe office job with all the time in the world to spare, or so it seemed, to look so wonderful – and Robin couldn't deny she did, to a very marked degree – but no second-year student nurse at the London could possibly compete with her. Which saddened Robin a good deal. She wasn't vain, but she took a healthy interest in her appearance, and she could still feel that cool stare of Chloe's raking her face, innocent of any makeup as it was. She'd really have to take herself in hand, she thought then. I can't have someone of her age looking so much better than I do –

And then felt another stab of anger; because wasn't she now doing exactly what she had complained to David about – which was thinking like the silliest sort of girl? Modern women were supposed to be different, to be serious and hardworking, not flibberty and makeup-mad like Chloe; yet here she was, as modern as anything and wanting to look like her man-mad stepsister –

It was a very confused Robin who filled her bowl with the last of the noodles and set about competing with Joshy to see who could eat them in the tidiest way. Very confused indeed.

· 11 ·

By lunch-time, Poppy had seen Robin and a rather white-faced and stonily dry-eyed Joshy off at Liverpool Street station, and wept her way back to Jessie's Cable Street premises in a taxi. Parting with him again had been hell and his own attempts to hide his distress had only added to her own sense of misery. But, she told herself, as she pushed her half crown into the taxi driver's hand, go back to safety he'd had to. However painful, it was better for everyone involved, it had to be, and she felt a great surge of gratitude for Robin's good-heartedness in spending one of her all too precious off-duty days looking after her little brother's needs. And that feeling helped her in her resolve to think no more about Joshy. To do so would be like pulling the scab off a festering wound. She wouldn't, couldn't do that. Instead she would concentrate on other matters; and now she sat at Jessie's side going through the orders with her so that they could share their resources between their restaurants as scrupulously as they could. The time she had lost at the office because of Joshy's escapade hadn't after all resulted in the muddle and confusion she'd feared; Minnie, the bookkeeper at her own restaurant over in Knightsbridge, had kept things going there beautifully, and hadn't had a single quarrel with old Horace, the head waiter – a remarkable circumstance on its own – and at Jessie's restaurant in Duke Street, Ollie, the chef Jessie had found in an Indian restaurant in the Old Kent Road and who had turned out to be the best cook of classic Jewish food in the whole of London, had been equally capable. So now the two of them sat hunched over their books at Cable Street, while that much smaller restaurant, too, almost ran itself, with Lily to keep an eye on it.

'I tell you,' Jessie said lugubriously. 'If it wasn't for this war and we could get all the supplies we need, we could be coining it, really raking it in, you know that? I'm turning customers away here and at Duke Street, just like you are in Knightsbridge, and I'm here to tell you it's making me plutz – '

She stopped then as Poppy lifted an eyebrow at her. 'All right, it's making me choke with aggravation! The money we could be making – '

'If there wasn't a war on, Jessie darling, there'd be more restaurants around and not so many customers. It's only because of rationing that more people try to eat out these days. So stop thinking you're losing a fortune. You're not. What we have to work on is this problem of supplies. And not just for the business. There's the canteen to think about too – '

Jessie looked at her sideways. 'I sometimes get the feeling you worry more about the canteen than you do about the business.'

Poppy was silent for a moment and then said levelly, 'Perhaps I do. It's my war effort, Jessie. I have to take it very seriously.'

'The restaurants are war work too,' Jessie pointed out. 'We give soldiers and all like 'em on leave places to go to, fun places they can take a girl and be romantic. It's an important thing, that. Morale and so forth. They go on about it on the wireless, and I listen and I feel good. I think, Jessie, my girl, I think, you're building morale, that's what you're doing. Even here in the East End which ain't so glamorous and I'm the first to admit it, even here I do a sort of war work. Old Marky – you know the one – who's partners with the Harris fella whose wife Sarah had the fits – Marky was telling me he's working eleven, twelve, even thirteen hours a day, he's got so many orders for naval uniforms in. And after that he's got to make for the Army – if it wasn't for this little place here, my little restaurant, he says he'd starve, on account he hardly ever gets to go home. So you don't have to get so agitated over your canteen – you're doing war work here.'

'Yes I do, Jessie.' Poppy pushed the books away from her and leaned back in her chair to stare very directly at her aunt. 'Do you mind?'

'Mind? Of course I don't mind – I'm just saying you don't have to run yourself skinny to do extra war work when you're doing it anyway with the business.'

'The business makes money. It's our living – or part of it. David's doing well enough, but with two young children to plan for – and there's Robin too, entitled to some sort of future cash – well, I need the money. And work which earns it, I can't see as a real war effort. So the canteen – '

'I know. You work all day here and then half the night there to make sure they may all get a cuppa, you don't have to tell me – '

'I want to give them more than cups of tea,' Poppy said. 'Sandwiches and so forth aren't really enough either. Though I did manage to get half a dozen tins of corned beef promised to me this morning. I called the Ministry of Food and they've got me on their priority list, they said, while the raids are so bad. But I still can't get enough. Last night, Maria and Flo and Edna got through everything. I'm down to less then two pounds of tea – that won't last half tonight's push – and a couple of pounds of margarine. Thank God for the corned beef – I haven't even any fish paste left! And then there's sugar and milk – oh, it's getting worse and worse.'

There was a little silence and then Jessie said, 'Uh – I got a few bits and bobs in my special store you could have. For the canteen.'

Poppy looked at her and then down at the books again. She knew perfectly well what Jessie was offering. Her

111

special store had always been the one she kept for the kitchens where she prepared the dishes the business sold to delicatessens all over London for resale to their customers (at considerable profit, somewhat to Jessie's chagrin). It had always been a vital part of the business – indeed, it had been the first extension after the little shop in Cable Street – and though now in these difficult times its output had dwindled, still it was functioning, and functioning well. So it came as no surprise to Poppy that Jessie still had a little hoard of something tucked away in one of her capacious cellars.

But there was more to it than that. Though neither of them spoke about it at this point, both knew of the other's awareness of the fact that these stores had been amplified by Bernie. Neither of them had spoken of him since that morning when he had appeared in the kitchens. But Poppy was sure that Jessie had been thinking about him and what he had asked her to do even more than Poppy herself had. And it was wrong, wrong, wrong to help him in any way. Poppy felt that with a deep passion. And yet, for the canteen –

'I could manage maybe a few pounds of margarine – as much as ten even. That'd go a long way in sandwiches, hmm? And there's a bit of tea, too, and sugar – '

'They use saccharin – '

'Oh, do me a favour, Poppy! There ain't one of these people you look after down there likes that nasty stuff! They'd all rather have sugar – and it's good for 'em, too. Gives energy, don't it? And if they don't need energy to get people outa the rubble and to put out fires, I don't know what they do need. Don't be so proud, dolly! Let me do my bit of war work too, and give you something for the canteen.'

'Is it yours to give, Jessie?' Poppy said levelly. 'That's what's worrying me – '

Jessie began to bluster and at last their inner thoughts were out in the open. 'So, maybe Bernie did bring me an order – is that such a terrible thing? Why shouldn't he do his bit, too? He may be a chancer, my Bernie, but sometimes the way you go on about him, you'd think he was the devil in shoes – '

'He's behaved very badly in the past, Jessie. Treated you like – I'm entitled to be suspicious. I don't want to carry on like those people who never forget a man's past, once he's tried to reform himself, but the trouble is that as far as I can see, Bernie's no more interested in reforming himself than in – in joining the Army.'

Jessie reddened. 'You know he can't. They told him at his medical – he's not suitable – '

'I'm sure they did,' Poppy said a little sardonically. 'Just as I'm sure *he* made sure that he wouldn't be. What was the method he used, Jessie? Told 'em he was a bedwetter, did he? Or that he preferred men to women? They're the two surefire ways of getting yourself an exemption grade, or so they tell me.'

'Listen,' Jessie flared at her. 'Your father served in the Army and much good it did him. Your mother's brothers, too – didn't some of them get killed last time? And what about your Bobby? If a man can get himself out of that sort of danger then I can't see it's no crime. In fact, he'd be crazy not to.'

There was a little silence and then Poppy said wearily, 'Oh, I suppose so. I can't pretend I'm one of those people who think everyone ought to turn himself into cannon fodder. But it does make me furious to see someone actually profiting out of the war and giving nothing back – '

'So help him!' Jessie said triumphantly. 'Take the stuff I've got down there, free of charge, and there's some eggs too, on account he's fetching me twelve dozen a week from some farmer he's got down in Essex somewhere, all legal on account they're not standardized sizes or something, and that way we make sure Bernie's doing his bit too.' And she stared hopefully at Poppy.

Poppy couldn't help it. She began to laugh and after a moment Jessie's anxious expression lifted and she laughed too.

'Honestly, Jessie, you're such a mug where Bernie's concerned! He's a villain, you know he is, because he's treated you just as badly as everyone else. Worse really, and yet you keep on trying to cover for him and make excuses for him and – '

'What else can I do?' Jessie said. 'I'm his mother.'

The laughter stopped and there was a silence and then Poppy sighed. 'Oh, all right. I feel sick about it, but I feel worse about having nothing to give them when they come in during a raid and look so battered and – all right, I'll take it. But it's against my better judgement and – '

'Sure, sure,' Jessie said soothingly. 'Sure. So come down and we'll see what we can fetch up. Bring those boxes there, dolly. It'll take some shlapping up, this stuff, and the boxes'll make it easier.'

The cellars were cold and damp, with little rivulets of moisture running down the walls in the long corridor that ran from one side of them to the other, but behind the snugly-fitting wooden doors that led to each enclosure, all was dry though still very cool. They had built these well, Poppy thought as she followed Jessie down to the last door on the right, which was her special store.

The big woman fumbled with her keys for a moment, and then pushed the door open and reached inside for the switch, and light sprang up from a single dusty low-powered bulb overhead.

The cellar was shelved all round, and stacked on them were piles of assorted goods; and Poppy stared round, fascinated. In all the years she had worked with Jessie, this storeroom had been sacrosanct, used only by Jessie herself, and Poppy had never felt any need to intrude in that little corner of secrecy. Why shouldn't her aunt have it, after all? They might be partners now, but originally the whole business had been Jessie's and she had shared it with her niece out of sheer generosity. The least Poppy had had to do was respect this small area of her privacy.

Jessie was looking round and her voice seemed to have softened as she spoke, as much to herself as to Poppy.

'It makes me feel safe, all this, you know. When we were kids, me and Rae and your father Lizah, rest their dear souls in peace, we used to go without, often and often. Those were hard times. It ain't good being hungry – and then I began to collect a bissel here, a bissel there and when I had things safely locked up it helped me feel better. Not so lonely – and now it's hard times again and I got my store and to see the shelves all full, it takes the frightened feeling away – '

Poppy said nothing but reached out one hand and touched Jessie's shoulder and Jessie turned and looked at her, an oddly appealing little look.

'Try not to get mad with my Bernie, Poppela,' she said. 'He helps me feel better, filling up my stores this way. I know it's crazy, that it doesn't make no difference now, what with all the money in the bank and all, but there it is. Old habits die hard.'

'I understand,' Poppy said. 'Mildred used to be the same, I think – '

'Your ma?' Jessie snorted with laughter at that. 'Listen, your ma, she never felt nothing like the rest of us. I tried so hard with her, to find out when she was worried, but she never said, not her. Not even when she was a bit of a girl, living with me in my old house and waiting for you to be born, even then she never showed no – '

'Well, I've found out since,' Poppy said. 'When she was living in Holborn with me – when I was little – I get flashes of remembering that house sometimes, and the smell of it, the cakes she baked, all coconut and chocolate and lemon and – well, anyway, she told me the best times were when she had the table covered in fresh cakes and rolls waiting to be delivered to her customers. She could pretend they were her own stores, she told me, and that made her feel better.'

She smiled a little crookedly then. 'To tell you the truth, Jessie, I think we're all the same. I get a sort of satisfied feeling when the larder's well stocked, and I know Goosey does. I used to think it was a family thing but – '

'Never,' Jessie said firmly. 'It's women, ain't it? Listen, what will you take – here's margarine. I've got another box at the back, here, see? – '

For the next half hour they wrangled over what Poppy would take as Jessie pressed goods on her, and Poppy demurred; but at last the boxes were filled, with sugar and jam as well as the margarine, and with a great pack of American processed cheese.

'Give 'em Welsh rarebits,' Jessie counselled. 'Put a slice of onion on, for a relish, and they'll be that happy, you won't know them. And after that a few biscuits –' And she dived to the back of the furthest shelf, and pulled out a large tin of rich teas. 'These aren't easy to come by no more, they aren't, McVitie's hand-packed novelties. These'll be as fresh as the day they left the factory, believe me. They got nothing to do with Bernie so you can take them with an easy conscience, all right? Now the eggs and then we'll drag this stuff upstairs – '

Poppy had given up arguing by now and let Jessie add twelve dozen eggs, small bantam ones, but eggs for all that, to her collection and together they dragged the now weighty boxes along the damp outer corridor, after Jessie had carefully locked up.

On each side the other cellar doors stood closed and each of them, Poppy noticed now, had brand new padlocks on them, and she said to Jessie, 'Why such big locks?'

Jessie didn't look at her, keeping her head down over the box she was dragging. 'I don't know. They're the rooms I rent to Bernie.'

Poppy said nothing, but she thought hard. Jessie's private cellar was capacious and high, and well-shelved; the piles of things she had taken for the canteen had made hardly a dent in the stock; if these other cellars – and she had counted them long ago and knew there were seven – were as well stocked, then the amount of stuff Bernie had down here was enormous. And she bit her lip, hard, needing to keep silent for Jessie's sake.

'He's paying twenty a week rent. I agreed it, okay?' Jessie said then a little pugnaciously.

Poppy shook her head. 'Nothing to do with me, Jessie. For my part you can count that as personal income and – '

'No,' Jessie said furiously. 'No! It goes through the books all right and proper, income for the business. I won't hear another word about that. Listen, can you manage this box up the stairs if I take the eggs?'

'I can manage,' said Poppy and at last admitted defeat. How could she not? Wasn't she now as much a conspirator as Jessie in Bernie's dealings? She felt sick about it, even when the other workers at the canteen clustered round with oohs and aahs of delight when she delivered her hoard; even when that night the firemen and rescue teams showed how delighted they were with the new expanded menu. At least the food was going to the sort of people who ought to be having it, and not to West End types who slept safely in their beds at night and hardly knew what it was like to go without. But still she felt grubby.

It was almost eleven o'clock and the raids were filling the streets with noise and the canteen with clamouring workers in need of refreshment, when the phone rang and Poppy, who was nearest at the moment, picked it up. She could hardly hear anything above the general hubbub and stood there with one finger jammed in her ear while she tried to hear the thin voice clacking on the phone.

'Ma – oh, Ma, thank God I'm through! I've been trying for ages, for absolutely ages – it just rang and rang – '

'Robin? Robin, what's the matter?' Poppy's voice sharpened with apprehension.

'It's all right, darling. Joshy's fine. He and Lee greeted each other like long lost explorers and Mr and Mrs Gosling were super to him. Told him firmly it wasn't to happen again but didn't make him feel miserable. He's safe in bed – it's me who's the problem – '

'What problem?' The line crackled and swooped in Poppy's ear and she stamped her foot in sheer frustration as she called her daughter's name over and over again; and then, blessedly, she was there once more, and talking fast.

'Did you hear that, Ma? I can't get back till ten tomorrow at the earliest, there's some sort of trouble on the line down towards – do you understand, Ma? Tennish they say now – could be later – told me to – ' And then the line died for good, and no amount of jiggling on the instrument's rest brought it back.

Poppy gave up trying to reach the operator and hung up, feeling a warm glow. Robin had gone to enormous trouble, clearly, to phone her, and she felt a stab of guilt as she remembered how she had complained at her for not calling one morning when she had come off duty exhausted. Clearly her complaint had hit home, for the child had obviously had a most difficult job getting her call through from Norwich. And she stood staring out into the hubbub of the canteen, thinking of Robin and aching to see her soon.

Well, she'll be back tomorrow, after an appalling journey, she told herself, and she would do all she could to fuss over her and make her comfortable. After all the trouble she had gone to for her family, it was the least her mother could do. And she went back to making fried egg sandwiches for black-faced firemen and exhausted rescue workers with a new energy. Bad as this war was, there were good things about it; and the closeness it gave to family ties was one of them.

· 12 ·

Robin woke with a start as the train again pulled to a shuddering halt, and tried to look at her watch. Her arm had gone to sleep, agonizingly, and she could have cried out with the painful tingling of it as she tried to pull herself away from the heavy sailor who was sitting beside her and who had fallen asleep against her almost as soon as he'd got on the train at Ipswich. She managed to peer at her watch at last, trying to make out the time in the thin light thrown from the single blue bulb overhead, and couldn't. And then stopped trying, because the other people jammed into the compartment were stirring, reaching over each other's heads for kit bags and coats, while outside in the corridor she could just make out a slow movement of people past the compartment. Had they arrived? She tried to see out of the window, through the lattice work of strips of sticky brown paper that had been fixed over it to stop broken glass fragments from flying around should the train encounter a raid, and at last managed to make out the scene beyond.

There it was, the broad and shabby platform, the metallic advertisements for Bovril and Mazawattee Tea and 'The Pick-wick, the Owl and the Waverly Pen, they come as a boon and a blessing to men' beneath the criss-crossed ironwork that spelled Liverpool Street, although of course there were no signs up with that name on them, not during these invasion-fearing days. It would

119

never do for a German spy, dropped by parachute, the Ministry of Information told them all solemnly on the wireless, to discover where he was. So never give a stranger instructions how to get anywhere. Just call the police if anyone asks–

At last the sailor woke up and stretched and grinned at her blearily. 'Where are we, love? In London? That's all right, then. My leave can really begin now. Come on Tosher –' And he leaned across the compartment behind the ample rump of a large man who was trying to push his way to the door, to poke an equally somnolent sailor on the opposite side.

She tumbled out on the platform at last, feeling as though she'd been through a battle. And indeed in many ways she had. It had taken fully eleven hours for the train, already five hours late when it left, to limp its way down from Norwich, stopping for long inexplicable waits at signals set between dull empty fields, and sometimes sitting in wayside halts for even longer. She had long ago finished the package of sandwiches Goosey's nephew's wife had made up for her – and she hadn't really enjoyed them since they were of rather fatty bacon which even though she was dreadfully hungry, she couldn't manage – and she was appallingly thirsty. Getting to the train's lavatory through the crowded corridors, where soldiers slept on the floor with their heads on their kit bags, and weary civilians propped themselves against the windows to get what rest they could, had been a major operation, and there hadn't been more than a trickle of rusty water in the taps when she got there anyway. She'd been grateful for the chance to empty her bladder and had crept her way back to her precious seat, well aware of her good fortune in having it, to make the best of a bad job. Now she stood on Liverpool Street station looking like a ragamuffin and – at this point she looked up at the clock above her head which was, blessedly, going, and felt a stab of apprehension – three hours late back on duty after her nights off. There would be all hell let loose when she got there, she knew, in spite of Poppy's phone call. And she thanked her guardian angel that she had at least been able to get through on the phone after she'd totally failed to make a connection with the hospital itself, to ask her to warn the Matron's office as well as Sister Priestland what had happened to delay her.

She managed to pick up a crowded bus outside the station and swung on to it gratefully to strap-hang all the way down the dark Whitechapel Road, until they were all turned out about seven stops from the hospital, because the siren went. She took a chance, though, and went on, half walking, half running, to get there. If she did all she could to get on duty with the least waste of time, she told herself breathlessly, they'd be sure to understand the problems that had delayed her and there'd be no fuss after all.

Fortunately the raid that had been warned was happening well over towards the docks, so she got to the familiar bulk of the hospital, looming against the night sky, without any difficulty and belted for the nurses' home to scramble out of her dirty clothes with much gratitude, splash water around wherever she could and climb into her uniform. What she would have loved was a bath, but she couldn't indulge herself; it was now almost midnight. If she could get on duty in time to relieve the others for the midnight meal, surely all would be forgiven–

Casualty was as hectic as ever when she got there, and she had mixed feelings about that. It might have been easier for Sister to forgive her if they'd had a quiet night, but busy like this – maybe Sister hadn't even noticed she wasn't there? With which highly optimistic thought Robin plunged into the hubbub and set to work. She took it on herself to head for the same corner cubicle to which she'd been assigned on her first night on Casualty to find it occupied by a small and very grimy child with a severly grazed knee, in which pieces of gravel were embedded, and waiting tearfully for someone to come and deal with him.

So she did. She smiled at the little boy and talked to him as cheerfully as she could as she washed the knee with copious amounts of Eusol, and then began, very delicately, to forceps out the biggest bits of gravel she could find, as the child watched apprehensively and she murmured to him as soothingly as she could, telling him some sort of story to distract his attention.

It wasn't until she stood up, straightening her already weary back to turn to her trolley and get more Eusol that she realized she was being watched. Staff Nurse Meek was standing just outside the cubicle, staring in at her above folded arms. Her eyes glittered as she stared and there was an almost triumphant look on her face.

'Well, well,' she said. 'So you've deigned to come on duty, have you? Good of you! What excuse have you got? It can hardly be oversleeping, not after three nights off.'

'It was my train,' Robin said and smiled at the little boy who had started to tug at her apron. 'Maybe no one told you? Oh dear – sorry, Staff Nurse, but may I just finish this? Poor little chap's a bit agitated. Not surprising. He's got half a pound of assorted road in his knee –' And she picked up the Eusol, and turned back to the demanding child.

'You'll do nothing of the sort!' Nurse Meek snapped, and pushed in through the curtain and took the Eusol jug from her hands. 'I'll finish this. Sister'll want a word with you, young woman. We'll have none of your high-handedness here in this department, I can tell you! On your way, now – '

The child began to wail and Robin said quickly, 'Oh, please let me finish doing him, Staff Nurse! He's just getting used to me. I'm rather comfortable with boys of this age – my little brother – '

'I'm not remotely interested in your family affairs, Nurse,' Meek said icily. 'I told you to go to Sister. Go at once. And you, young man, stop that caterwauling immediately. I never heard such a fuss! Be a man, for heaven's sake – '

And Robin had to go, burning with rage though she was. The child had settled so well with her, and to see Nurse Meek, efficiently and delicately though she performed the necessary treatment, making the child howl like that upset her a good deal. She was almost in tears herself, what with Meek's behaviour and the fatigue from her journey, as she went marching across the crowded waiting hall towards Sister's office.

Sister was standing outside it, talking to one of the doctors as she came up, and she cast one glowering glance at her and said with great chilliness, 'Nurse Bradman? I see! Wait here. I shall deal with you shortly,' and returned her attention to Dr Landow, who looked at Robin with a friendly grin. But Robin couldn't return it. All her apprehension had come back at the sight of Sister's face, so set and angry under the confection of lacy frills that was her cap. Oh please, she prayed wordlessly, please let Ma's message have been detailed enough, please let Sister understand it wasn't my fault –

Landow went away then, nodding affably at Robin, and Sister Priestland, her eyes snapping, drew herself up to her very unimpressive height, tilted her head and stared up at Robin.

'Well, Nurse! And what have you to say for yourself?'

'I'm frightfully sorry, Sister. As you heard, the train I was on coming back from Norwich was dreadfully delayed. There should have been one overnight I could have got, but there was an incident on the line somewhere down near Colchester and – '

'As I heard? Sister Priestland's eyes were almost popping out of her head with fury. 'What do you think I do with my time, Nurse? I work here all the hours God sends, night after night – no off-duty for me, in case you didn't know – and during the day I need to sleep. I have no time to listen to wireless bulletins about trains or incidents – '

Robin, amazed, did the unforgiveable and interrupted her. 'Oh, no, Sister, I didn't mean on the wireless! I mean when my mother contacted you!'

Staff Nurse Meek had appeared on the other side of Sister, holding the notes from the little boy, who was still to be heard bawling lustily all through the department, and lifted her brows at Robin.

'If I may say so, Sister, I heard of no call from anyone about Nurse Bradman's absence. And the office hadn't either, when I reported the fact to them –'

'I'm well aware of that, Staff Nurse,' Sister snapped, not taking her eyes from Robin's mortified face. 'Go and stop that child's noise, for heaven's sake. He needs a little affection, since he was found wandering alone. Go and deal with him and get him up to Sister Marshall as soon as you can.'

Meek reddened and casting a malevolent look at Robin, went, and Sister Priestland stared hard at Robin for another long moment.

'You say a message was sent to explain your absence?'

'Yes, Sister, only it wasn't meant to be an absence. I mean, it was a delay. I had to take my little brother back to his foster home in Norwich, you see, because he ran away again. He hates being an evacuee and no one else in the family could take him. And then the trains –'

'You asked your mother to call?'

'Yes, Sister.'

'Why didn't you call us directly? We aren't unreasonable, you know, but we can't cope with people who tell lies and just don't show a sense of responsibility –'

Robin tightened with anger. 'I do not tell lies! And I was worried sick when I realized I was going to be late. I tried and tried to phone the hospital but I couldn't get through, and the operator told me there were lines down because of the raids, so I tried to get my mother at her canteen as it's not too far from here, and at last I managed it. It took hours to get to her, and the line was dreadful! I'm sure she'd have sent my message. She

124

wouldn't have let me down – she knows how important it is to be where you're wanted when you're wanted.' Robin was well launched now, and her voice rose with her passion. 'She was an ambulance driver and nurse in the last war! She's taught me what's right and what – she got the message here, I'm sure she did – '

She became aware that behind her the buzz of talk and clatter that was so much a part of the Casualty department had dropped to a low murmur as more and more people became aware of the fact that Sister, the Great God of the department, was having a stand-up argument with a junior probationer. The combination of shock and scandalized disbelief and sheer delight in the sideshow had patients and nurses alike agog.

'So I didn't tell you a lie,' she ended lamely in a lower tone. 'It's just some awful sort of mix-up. I wouldn't be late on purpose.'

Sister Priestland was looking at her sharply but there seemed less frost in her now. 'Then why is it, pray, that I have received no such message? Staff Nurse Meek tells me she has not. Must we ask the other nurses?'

'Please do,' Robin said and looked round. She could see Dollis and Jenner on the other side together with the laboratory technician, Peter, and for a moment wondered where Chick was and then remembered that she had nights off, and bit her lip. Which of them would get a rocket now for not passing on an important message? She felt herself between the most towering of cliffs and the deepest of oceans. If someone did confess to forgetting to pass on any message, Sister Priestland's rage would be monumental. And that would ensure that Robin became very unpopular with her fellows; and if no one did then Robin was branded a selfish and indeed rather stupid dodger who played liberties with the truth. It was a mortifying situation to be in.

Sister beckoned imperiously and Nurse Jenner scuttled over, her thick glasses glinting importantly, and with a certain avidity at being included in the little drama outside Sister's office, whatever it was.

'Did you take a message of any kind from Nurse Bradman's mother, Nurse?' Sister demanded. 'I know there have been problems with outside calls on our telephones, or so Nurse Bradman assures me, but I imagine she might have sent a message by hand.'

A little regretfully Jenner denied any knowledge of any message; clearly she wanted to know more about what was going on; and Nurse Dollis took her place for catechism. She was a good deal more wily and denied accepting any message so promptly and with such a sanctimonious air that Robin at once became suspicious. But Sister said nothing, just dismissing her, and looked over the girl's shoulder at the rest of the department. Peter, the lab assistant, had disappeared, and there was only Hamish Todd, standing beside a bucket and mop in the cubicle next to the one in which Robin had been working and staring across with a frown on his face. After a moment he set his mop carefully against the bucket so that it couldn't tumble, and came across the waiting hall.

'Can I help in any way, Sister?' he asked.

'I doubt it,' Sister said grimly. 'I would hardly expect you to take messages of any importance. You're our orderly and as such your duties are entirely domestic and portering. It is the more senior people I need to talk to. You can go and find Peter Rye and ask him to come here, if you please – '

'A message about Nurse Bradman?' Hamish said.

'My mother sent it – I asked her to let Sister and the office know I was held up because of the train from Norwich.'

'Ah,' Hamish said after a moment. 'That message.'

There was a long silence as Sister Priestland stared at him, her eyes so dilated with anger they looked as though they were all pupils.

'You took a message from Mrs Bradman?'

126

'Mrs Deveen,' Robin murmured. She really didn't know why it mattered, but it was something she was so used to doing when people assumed she had the same surname as her mother. Sister Priestland clearly didn't hear her and remained staring at Hamish, who stood there, stolid and quiet, and showing no hint of any discomfiture.

'I – er, I saw a woman standing at the door looking around and she saw me, and not knowing I was just here for the portering and domestic work, you understand, she asked me to take a message from a Mrs Deveen – '

'I see! And you took this message? Have you no sense of any – any proper sense of the way things are dealt with in this department? All messages should be given to me at once, or to my deputy Staff Nurse Meek or to whoever is the most senior of the available nursing staff – '

'I asked the woman to tell you herself,' Hamish said, quite unperturbed by the snapping anger that was being directed at him from the diminutive Sister Priestland. 'But she wouldn't wait. Said she'd been up all the night in the raids and had to be away home.'

'That must have been one of the women from the canteen,' Robin cut in eagerly. 'If Ma couldn't get through on the phone that's what she'd have done, I'm sure of it.'

'Aye,' said Hamish peaceably. 'Aye, that's who it was, all right. A lady from the canteen.'

'Well, Todd,' Sister Priestland said. 'What can I say? Why couldn't you tell me or Nurse Meek?'

'I thought she'd made a mistake, to tell you the truth of it, Sister,' Hamish said, and caught Robin's eye and then let his gaze slide away, almost embarrassed. 'I knew of no Nurse Deveen, do you see, and she said to say that Mrs Deveen's daughter would be late because of the trains and since there's no such person here that I kent, I didna' bother to tell you. Thought she was just another disturbed soul, confused after the raids, you know?'

'Well,' Sister said and seemed almost speechless for a moment. 'Well, I never heard of such impudence! I thought you were a decent sort of man, Todd, in spite of your cowardice and refusal to serve in your country's armed services when you're needed. I certainly didn't think you'd be as stupid as this!'

'Well, there it is, Sister,' Hamish said and suddenly smiled, and it lit his face up so that he looked like a wicked child, for all his bulk. 'It seems you were wrong.'

'Get on with the floor,' she said furiously. 'Go on! And take no more messages and make no more decisions about which you will and which you won't deliver, you understand me? Nurse Bradman, I'm sorry I misjudged you. We'll say no more about it. Away with you to your meal, now, and when you get back take the two cubicles over on the corner, until the others get back and can relieve you on one of them. On your way now.'

'Thank you, Sister,' Robin said breathlessly and escaped, heading for the door, but when she got there, she stopped and looked back. Sister and Nurse Meek had disappeared, and Hamish was swabbing the floor of the cubicle not too far away; and she risked it, and went hurrying across to him.

'How could you do that to me, Hamish?' she said. 'I mean, how could you not tell Sister? Even if you didn't recognize the name, if you'd passed the message on someone would have sorted it out in the office. You really dropped me in it, didn't you?'

'Did I?' he said and leaned on his mop for a moment, looking at her thoughtfully. 'Well, that was in no way my intention. Not after you stood up for me the way you did the other night.'

'Stood up for you?' Robin said and then remembered. 'Oh, the business of the meal break. Well, for heaven's sake, I was just – it seemed all wrong, that was the thing. There was no more to it than that.'

'Well, mebbe not. But I was grateful all the same.'

'Not grateful enough to deliver a message that could have saved me from a rucking,' she snapped and then made a face. 'Oh, drat, I suppose that's not fair. If you didn't know it was about me. Anyway, thanks for owning up in the end. They'll be horrid to you over it, I dare say.'

'It won't be much worse than it's been all along,' he said equably, and started mopping again. 'I can deal with whatever it is.'

'Well, I just – well, all right,' Robin said. 'And I'm sorry it was you that got the – well, you know what I mean.' And she turned to go.

Across the other side of the waiting hall, Staff Nurse Meek was watching with her eyes sharp and glinting a little in the brightness of the overhead lamps, and for some reason that Robin was never to understand she blushed hotly before hurrying off to get her midnight meal. Even though, somehow, she had quite lost her appetite.

· 13 ·

'Dear me,' Mildred said. 'This is a rare surprise these days,' and she looked up at her daughter over her glasses and then returned with some care to her knitting. Her fingers were more gnarled than they had been, and it clearly caused her pain to move the stiff joints, Poppy thought as she bent and kissed her mother's papery old cheek. She put herself through a lot to make those damned socks – and we don't even know if anyone wears them. They looked dreadfully uncomfortable.

'I know, Mama. Don't be annoyed with me – you know perfectly well that I come when I can. But what with the business and the canteen it's not always possible.'

'You could telephone,' Mildred said and Poppy laughed.

'You sound like me having a go at Robin. I suppose it's always the same with mothers.'

'If you find yourself distressed because Robin doesn't phone you, then you should understand how I feel when you fail to do so for me,' Mildred said and then frowned slightly. 'Robin hasn't called me either, for some days now. It isn't like her. I suppose all is well? I imagine I would have heard if it were not.'

'Robin's fine,' Poppy said and sat down gratefully, sinking onto the comfortable sofa that was always there by the fire, but which Mildred scorned, feeling more comfortable in a high-backed straight chair on which she sat looking like a *Punch* cartoon, she was so erect.

'And the reason she hasn't phoned is the same reason I haven't, and why I'm here now.'

Mildred looked up at her briefly. 'Oh?' and again Poppy laughed.

'Really, Mama, I wish you wouldn't put on this performance of being so acid. You aren't at all really.'

'Performance?' Mildred said and managed a hint of a smile. 'What else can I do at my great age but be the age I am?'

'Heavens, you're not that old,' Poppy said bracingly. 'Ten years from now, when you're eighty-four, you can call yourself old. Not yet. Because when you are, I will be too, and I'm not ready.'

'You were saying that the reason for Robin's silence and yours – ' Mildred said, refusing to respond to any comment on her age. Clearly she did take a certain delight in being a typical old lady, and nothing Poppy had to say on the matter would have any effect.

'Telephone damage,' Poppy said. 'They've been down for a longer than usual time. The main exchange building for the East End has been knocked out and they're having all sorts of problems getting it right. That's why I can't call you from the office, and why Robin hasn't, I imagine. Not that I've seen her since she got back from Norwich – '

'You could call me from home,' Mildred said. 'My telephone here is working, so I imagine yours in Norland Square is?'

'No, I can't, even though the phone there is fine, of course. I'm hardly ever home what with the business and the canteen and when I am there you're being an old lady and I'm not allowed to disturb you. You told me never to call you before ten in the morning or after six at night, so there you are! I can only phone you from the office and that one's out of commission.'

'Hmm,' said Mildred, and turned her sock one needle on. The four needles shone a little in the morning light and the bony knuckles looked red and painful. 'What was Robin doing in Norwich?'

Not for the first time Poppy was taken aback by her mother's tenacity. No matter how little attention she might seem to pay to a minor comment, she never forgot it, and always needed full explanations of everything. Poppy, knowing it would be a waste of time to try to gloss over any of the story, launched herself into the tale of Joshy's latest adventure and Mildred, her eyes firmly fixed on her khaki sock, listened and said nothing.

But when Poppy had finished she set her knitting down in her lap and took off her glasses. 'You'll have to start thinking hard about that boy, you know.'

'I never stop thinking about him,' Poppy said. 'Or about Lee. I miss them dreadfully.'

'Of course you do. So do I. But they're where they ought to be, safe and sound. No, I didn't mean that. I meant his future.'

Poppy stared. 'His future? Isn't that why we've sent them both away? To ensure they *have* a future?'

'Of course they will,' Mildred said bracingly. 'I saw the last war, my dear, and I know, just as you should know, that this one will end too and life will start again.'

'I sometimes wonder. This is much worse – the trenches last time, the injuries – the gas – they were dreadful,' and her voice drifted away for a moment as she remembered, because it had been gas that had destroyed Bobby. But then she picked up again. 'But this time, with these awful raids in the East End, it seems much worse to me. You can't imagine what it's like, Mama. I just pray they never come this far. I can't bear to think of you here – you ought to be evacuated like the children.'

'I told you and I tell you again, I'm too old to be uprooted. Here is where I belong and here is where I stay. Besides, I couldn't do it to Queenie. The poor old soul would pine away if she didn't have this house to care for.'

Poppy smiled. Queenie was barely three years her employer's senior, and Mildred persisted in regarding her as totally decrepit, and in some ways she was, for

Mildred was far the better preserved of the two. But Queenie had worked in this house all her adult life, coming to it as a tweeny when she had been fifteen; to take her away now would indeed be an act of cruelty.

'Anyway,' Mildred went on, 'we weren't speaking of my situation. I want to speak of Joshy.'

'I wish you wouldn't. It reminds me too much of how miserable it is not to have him and Lee here.'

'Nonsense. Evacuate yourself if you feel so deprived. Though you'd be a poor creature if you did. A little hardship never hurt anyone. But neglect of talent – that's a different matter.'

'Talent?' Poppy was bewildered. 'Joshy?'

'He's very gifted,' Mildred said and picked up her knitting.

'I know he's bright –' And Poppy launched herself into an account of his invention of a round runway to save space for aerodromes.

Mildred listened and nodded. 'I know perfectly well the child's highly intelligent. It's more than that though. He's musically gifted.'

Poppy shook her head. 'Joshy? Hardly, Mama. When Lee had her piano lessons we tried very hard to start Joshy as well, and he flatly refused to pay any attention at all. I think this time that you've not got it quite – '

'Oh, piano lessons!' Mildred waved a dismissive hand. 'He isn't interested in piano! But he can blow a trumpet.'

Poppy stared at her in amazement. 'He can do what?'

'He said it was a secret and I kept it willingly enough, but he was small then. Now I think perhaps I will serve him better if I speak of it. Just before the war sent them both away, when he was here after his eighth birthday party, you remember? He went up into the attics and he found a horn there that used to belong to your Uncle Wilfred. He'd been given it at some time when he said he was willing to learn, but he never did. So Joshy came down here and I was able to show him the most rudimentary use of the instrument. He showed a most remarkable aptitude – remarkable. We arranged he should come here to play whenever he wished, and so he did, and did quite well, with no lessons at all. Clearly a natural musician – '

'Mama!' Poppy said weakly. 'You amaze me! We tried so hard to find out what he wanted to learn – '

Mildred shook her head. 'It was simply the matter of the material. He dislikes the sort of music teachers make you play, he told me. He is interested in jazz. As indeed I am,' Mildred finished amazingly, and again bent her head to her knitting.

There was a slightly stunned silence and then Poppy said, 'Jazz, Mama? Where do you hear it?'

'Oh, on my wireless from time to time. And I have my gramophone.' And she nodded her head towards the instrument in the corner of the big drawing room. It all looked here much as it had for the whole of Poppy's life; she had come here as a very small child to meet her step-grandmother and her uncles in 1900, forty years ago, and had thought the heavy sofas and chairs and cluttered tables oppressive; and still did. But they suited her mother well enough and so she had never suggested she should refurnish in a more modern manner, though she was well able to afford to do so. Now, looking at the gramophone, sitting somewhat incongruously on a corner table, Poppy wondered if she'd been right to keep so quiet. There were aspects to her mother she had never imagined.

'I believe that Joshy could become an accomplished jazz trumpeter given the chance.' Mildred said then. 'So I think you should be considering how to arrange his future education. He'll soon be old enough for public school. I imagine you'll be sending him to one?'

'When the war's over, I hope so,' Poppy said. 'It all depends on that.'

'It needn't,' Mildred said. 'You should choose a good school for him now, one with a strong musical feeling and one that does not sneer at the modern music, just because

134

it's different. It's highly interesting and Joshy has the right to pursue it. I'd suggest you get the list of schools, when you can tear yourself away from the canteen and the business, and go and see them and choose one. I shall of course pay the fees. No, don't look at me so. I have already decided it. I did little enough for my older granddaughter, and I regret that. She's a highly capable girl. However, she is taking excellent steps for herself. But Lee and Joshy shall have better. I want you to choose schools for both of them, and I think Lee would benefit from one with an art emphasis. She draws very well and has a nice eye for quality – I dare say you and David could pay easily enough for them both, but I have the right, as an old woman, to spend my money while I am able, in the way I choose. I want to do so without undue interference from daughters who should know better than to object.' And still she kept her hands busy over her knitting and kept her head down to watch them.

There was another silence and then Poppy said, 'I'll have to talk to David, of course.'

'Of course. But he's a sensible man. He won't object.'

Poppy smiled then. 'I don't suppose he will, not if you say so. He's ridiculously fond of you.'

'Ridiculously?' Now Mildred did look at her, and Poppy bit her lip.

'I didn't mean that as it sounded,' she said. 'It's just that – ' And Mildred smiled.

'I know,' she said. 'It's easier for him, though, you see. He isn't my daughter is he?' And Poppy smiled and nodded. The tensions between these two had eased a little over the years, but they were still there; their closeness made that inevitable, for Mildred had only had one child and adored her deeply and had been bitterly hurt when Poppy had chosen later in adult life to be closer to her Aunt Jessie than to her mother. But David had in many ways made up for that, and Poppy thought of the generous offer her mother had made and knew that it would be accepted. David could never oppose her, especially when his children would benefit from her actions. And why not? she asked herself then. Why should I feel a chill because my mother wants to be a generous grandmother? Because I'm jealous, a small voice deep inside her said, and she had to admit she was. Her children were hers and she wanted to share them with no other woman.

Mildred had started to talk again and Poppy dragged her attention back.

'That's that then. Now, I want to tell you of something rather surprising. I've had two letters – '

'Oh? Is that so very surprising?'

'These correspondents are. One is the son of my brother, Wilfred – the original owner of Joshy's trumpet – who went to live in South Africa. He was a rogue, my brother Wilfred, lots of charm but rather – well, it was all a long time ago. His son is called Daniel and he tells me in his letter that he is a member of our Royal Air Force now and will be stationed here in England shortly. He could not, of course, tell me when.'

Poppy was intrigued. 'I have a vague memory of Wilfred, I think – '

'I dare say you have. He looked very dashing in his uniform, during the Boer war that was, when your father was so injured – '

'Did Wilfred suffer any wounds like that?' Poppy ventured. 'Or did he return with all his limbs intact?' The thought of men who lost arms in battles always worried Poppy, ever since she had discovered that was what had happened to her father: 'A one-armed boxer,' he'd said to her so often. 'What's the use of a one-armed boxer?' But she mustn't think of Lizah, dead so long now. It wasn't fair to herself and anyway, Mildred was still talking.

'Wilfred,' she said drily, 'was a great deal too careful of himself ever to suffer any undue injury. He went to South Africa sound in mind and limb and never again bothered

136

to write home. However, his son is coming and so we'll have some news, I imagine.'

'It sounds rather exciting,' Poppy said. 'An unknown cousin – '

'Two unknown cousins.' Mildred began to turn the heel of her sock and Poppy watched those slow fingers, fascinated by their skill.

'Two?' she said. 'He has a brother, then?'

'No, this is yet another branch of the family. My other half-brother, Harold, also went to the Colonies, but he chose Australia. I received a letter from his son Harry, as he says he's called, and he is a member of the Australian Army. He too says he'll be in England soon. It's a strange coincidence – '

'Not really,' Poppy said. 'Exciting, I grant you, but not that strange. Soldiers are pouring into the country from everywhere as far as I can tell – New Zealanders and Poles – we get a lot of them in the restaurant in Cable Street. They adore the food. It makes them homesick, they say. And Dutch and Norwegian and French and oh, all sorts.'

'I know. But these are our relations. It's all rather strange to me,' Mildred said. 'Well, once they arrive I shall let you know. And then perhaps you'll be able to come and visit me. Such days are rare now, after all.'

'Mama, stop bullying me.' Poppy got to her feet and bent over to kiss her. 'You know my situation. And now I have to go. I left Jessie to cope alone and I have to go back for a while before I go to do my shift at the canteen. I just hope the trains are still running into the East End. Last night was another appalling one. I just can't see how much longer this can go on.'

'As long as it has to,' Mildred said and lifted her cheek to be kissed. 'And it will end and we'll all start to get back to normal life once more. I do assure you, Poppy, nothing is for ever.'

'I wish I could believe you,' Poppy said, standing at the door and looking back at her. 'I truly wish I could. But from where I am in the East End, it's horrendous. And I have to go back to it.'

'You're a brave woman, Poppy,' Mildred said and looked across the big drawing room at her. 'I am exceedingly proud of you.'

'Are you?'

'I know I may not show it, but I am. And I worry for your welfare, too.'

'I – That's good of you.'

'I may not be as emotional and heart-on-sleeve as your Aunt Jessie, but that doesn't mean that I don't have such feelings. They simply run more deeply, that's all.'

Here we go again, thought Poppy. Jealousy once more. Me jealous of Mama and the children's love for her, and Mama jealous of Jessie and my love for her. Why can't we all just be comfortable with each other?

'I must go, Mama. Take care of yourself and Queenie,' Poppy said.

'I will. And you too, my dear. I need you a great deal, you know.'

'Yes, Mama,' Poppy said and managed to smile as she went, feeling like a child again. It wasn't till she was in the street at last, the familiar old Leinster Terrace with its yellow houses and area railings and the tired plane trees, that she could shake off the feeling, either. And she sighed a little as she made her way down to the Bayswater Road to look in hope for a taxi, which were as rare as hens' teeth these days. Perhaps being a child other people had to look after would be rather agreeable at that; because suddenly she felt very aware of all her responsibilities. This was turning out in many ways to be a much harder war than the last one, because this time there were more people to worry about. And she sighed again as she started the walk down to Marble Arch in the hope of a train, since there were patently not going to be any taxis, and thought about Joshy as a trumpeter with a talent he had never told her about. That hurt a little. And then she corrected herself. It hurt a lot.

138

· 14 ·

Robin came off duty exhausted. The rest of the night, after the fuss over her late return, had been particularly busy, and the combination of that and the tiredness left over from her appalling train journey left her almost paralysed with fatigue. So much so that when she realized that she couldn't call home because the telephones in the hospital were still out of order, she headed straight for bed, even though she knew she ought to go down to Cable Street to reassure her mother she was all right.

'She'll understand,' she told herself optimistically, 'once she realizes about the phones.' And crept out of her bath and into bed feeling at least a hundred years old, as she told Chick when she bumped into her on the night nurses' corridor.

'You look awful,' Chick said with all the candour of old friendship. 'For pity's sake go and get some sleep – '

'Are you going to bed yet? You're on again tonight, aren't you?'

'Mmm, worse luck. No, I'll try and catnap this afternoon maybe – '

'Be an angel then – go down to Jessie's and tell her to let Ma know I'm okay. The phones are down, you see, and – '

'With pleasure!' Chick said at once. 'I could do with some good nosh. Are there any other messages?'

'No,' Robin said and yawned hugely. 'Oh, just a minute though – ask her who it was she sent down here to deliver my message, would you? The one about being back late last night – '

'Oh, God, you weren't, were you?' Chick looked horrified. Of all a nurse's sins, being late on duty was very high on the list of wickedness.

'Not my fault. Had to take Joshy back to Norfolk and it was a matter of trains. I couldn't phone here, so I phoned Ma instead and asked her to get a message down and bless her, she did – but that ass Todd didn't deliver it on. Anyway, tell Ma I got here and I'd love to know who she sent so I can thank her some time.' Again she yawned. 'Oh, God, I could sleep on a nail – '

'Try bed,' Chick said, and shoved her in through her bedroom door. 'It'll be easier. See you at breakfast – '

She woke feeling a great deal better and stretched luxuriously as the clock on her bedside table shrilled, just one minute before the stentorian knocking on her door by the Home Sister, and then dressed quickly. She was ravenous and thought hopefully about breakfast. Perhaps something real tonight, instead of the eternal porridge and toast? Scrambled eggs, she told herself a little wistfully, would be magic, and almost drooled at the thought and that made her laugh. If Auntie Jessie knew how hungry she was, what wouldn't she come up with? Tomorrow morning, after she got off duty, she'd go and see her and perhaps bring back one or two goodies. They'd come in handy for the break in Sister's office if they had another busy night and couldn't get up to their midnight meal. And a supply of Jessie's glorious strudel must surely make people a little more friendly towards her. She hadn't started well on Casualty, she knew perfectly well; making up the lost ground would be no bad thing, and Jessie, dear old Auntie Jessie, could help her do it. Robin was whistling happily as she went hurrying across the yard towards the dinning room and the night's work.

Breakfast – not scrambled eggs but particularly odorous and therefore odious bloaters – was half over before Chick, looking decidedly ruffled, came bursting in. Night Sister looked at her with the sort of horrified disgust normally reserved for child murderers and Chick muttered about the unreliability of her alarm clock and slid into the last available place at the table adjoining Robin's.

She tried to get Robin's attention, only to incur Night Sister's further wrath and when the night staff finally filed out of the dining room on their way to their wards and departments, looking for all the world like a flock of white seagulls, Chick hurried to catch up, but she didn't manage to get through the chattering clusters of nurses until they had reached the big double doors that led to Casualty.

'Robin!' Chick said urgently. 'Must tell you – '

Staff Nurse Meek appeared behind them like the evil fairy in the pantomime, and said loudly, 'What are you two hanging around out here for? You're here to work, believe it or not. Come along at once!' and pushed open the doors and perforce they followed her into a department as hectic as they had ever seen it.

Sister Priestland was already there and bustling about in her usual frenetic fashion and Chick and Robin looked at each other and grimaced and got down to it. There was nothing else they could do. But Chick did manage to hiss at Robin, 'See you at break – the oddest thing to tell you – ' before they were both swallowed into their assigned cubicles.

It was, surprisingly, not the effects of raids that had Casualty busy tonight. It was the usual sort of work that the department was accustomed to do in peacetime; accidental injuries in women trying to cook and clean in cramped, ill-lit and worse-heated rooms; deliberate injuries inflicted on men who got themselves into fights in and around pubs; even a couple of attempted suicides who had filled their stomachs with aspirin. Robin had both of those to deal with and the effort it took to wash out the stomachs of two recalcitrant and very agitated people left her drenched with saline – and worse – and very much the worse for wear. Sister Priestland, spotting her as she cleaned her cubicle yet again, told her crisply to go to the Nurses' Home at once and get herself changed, and Robin escaped gratefully.

By the time she came back it was just gone midnight and there had been a lull in Casualty. The raids tonight, it seemed, were clustered further away than usual, in the docks, and the resulting casualties were being taken to Mile End Hospital. 'Even then, we'll probably get the overflow,' Sister Priestland told her grimly. 'So go to your supper the minute the others get back, Nurse. I don't want anyone hanging about. Just in case – '

Chick had already gone to first supper and as soon as she returned and appeared in the doorway with Nurse Dollis and Nurse Jenner in tow, Robin obediently reached for her cape, ready to go and eat and passed Chick in the doorway.

'Listen, go to the loo as soon as you get back,' Chick hissed. 'I'll see you there. I don't suppose it's that important, but I think you should know – '

'Nurse Chester!' Sister Priestland cried. 'Don't waste time gossiping! If you've nothing better to do you can come and clean this trolley for me. Hurry along now!' And Chick hurried.

Robin ate quickly, grateful for the simplicity of a vegetable pie, and chose not to wait to finish her legitimate half-hour break; she had no idea what Chick wanted to tell her, but she was curious now. It would be worth getting back early so that they could at least have a minute or two to talk, and she wrapped her cape around herself, waved a comprehensive goodbye to the other nurses at second supper, and made her way back down the silent stairs towards the ground floor and the bright lights of the Casualty department.

Around her the hospital was quiet and dim beneath well-shrouded lamps. The windows, blank and shuttered to contain any trace of light that might attract a bomber, seemed to swallow up the sound of her footsteps as she went past them and, ahead of her, the corridor, a particularly long one, looked, she told herself, like one of those illustrations in children's comics, where country roads are shown dwindling away into the distance. A silly conceit, she told herself firmly and hurried on, suddenly alarmed, without knowing quite why.

She became aware then of the sound, a long low uneven buzzing and somewhere at the back of her mind the thought came up as clearly as words on a blackboard. 'Bombers – theirs – close. No sirens – ' and she began to hurry, not quite sure why she was doing so, but clearly aware of danger.

And then it all happened at once; the sirens leapt into swooping ear-assaulting life, seeming almost above her head they were so close, and echoing dreadfully in the long empty corridor as the sound of the planes got thicker and even louder. She was running now, which she'd been taught nurses must never do – except in the case of fire or haemorrhage – and ahead of her the doors into Casualty swung wide as someone came out, pushing an empty trolley. She got a glimpse of the well-lit waiting room beyond and tried to run even faster, feeling illogically that would be a safe place to shelter, and then as the trolley-pusher began to move from a patch of darkness to light the noise became unbearable and her ears seemed to burst, and her body to be punched by a huge fist, and she was lying flat on her back and trying to breathe through a thick cloud of dust that seemed to fill her nose and mouth.

She started to cough and splutter then, and at last the worst of the clogging stuff burst out of her nose and she could breathe, and she tried to reach up to wipe her face and mouth; but her arms were caught in her cape and she had to struggle.

'Easy, easy does it.' The voice seemed to be coming from a long way away and she bent her head forwards, feeling that there were spaces there to let her see, though it was as black as pitch, and thought muzzily – I imagined that! Or it was me? – and again began to struggle to free her arms from the constrictions of her cape.

The voice came louder. 'Easy! You'll have the whole lot down on us!' and at once she stopped moving and tried to peer into the blackness.

'Who's that? What happened?'

'What happened? A direct hit, you daft creature, that's what happened. Are you all right?'

'I don't know!' She was suddenly very angry. 'Who are you calling daft? Who is it? And I can't tell what's happened – '

'Move your legs. Wriggle about a little, only gently, or you'll cause a fall of more rubble. Does it hurt?'

She had obeyed automatically, and this time, her arms managed to get free at least to one elbow and she was able to tug the rest of the fabric clear. And moved her hands forwards gingerly to see what was around her.

'Who is it?' she said again, even though really she knew perfectly well who it was; but her head felt muzzy and her eyes were beginning to smart as sandy tears ran down her cheeks. She felt the wetness of them and put out her tongue to catch them and it was a blessed taste, that saltiness. It seemed to ease away some of the dust that still coated her tongue and filled her nostrils.

'Hamish,' he said. 'Did you no' see me? I was coming down the corridor towards you when it happened – '

'I couldn't see it was you,' she said and then blinked. 'Hold on. I can see a bit now – '

There was a gleam ahead of her in the darkness and she reached towards it, and her hand touched an arm and she pulled back as though she'd been stung.

'It's all right.' He sounded a little sardonic. 'I'm in no state to bite you, you know.'

She was embarrassed suddenly, an absurd way to feel under the circumstances. 'Are you all right? I'm sorry I didn't ask – '

'All right? Well, it's a relative term, you'll agree. I've no broken bones, I can say that much.'

'Nor me. Well, then, we'd better get ourselves out – I can still see that light.'

He seemed to move beside her in the blackness and she thought – I feel like a cat. I can't see and yet I can. She was aware of his shape and bulk now, and it was a good thing to feel beside her. He was warm, too. She could feel his body heat enwrapping her.

'It's a searcher,' he said then and seemed to take a deeper breath. 'It's a torch, see? It's gone – now it's back. Hold on – I'll shout – '

And shout he did, in a way that made Robin need to reach for her ears. And she held them there as he bawled lustily and tried to use her new ability to see in the dark to work out where they were.

As far as she could tell, they were huddled close together beneath something, and she reached up one hand, risking the roar of Hamish's strong voice in her ear, and touched it, and felt metal and then fabric and knew what it was. The trolley Hamish had been pushing. Somehow they were beneath it, and she reached out again, this time sweeping her hand from side to side in a rather gingerly fashion, and felt something else, battered and bent, but undoubtedly a wheel.

She sighed gratefully. These casualty trolleys were made of the heaviest steel; often the porters complained of their weight, and so had she and other nurses. Well, she never would again; the metal surface of the thing was clearly holding up the rubble overhead and was therefore a literal lifesaver, and she felt a great wash of gratitude to it, as though it were a sentient creature; and absurdly, patted the wheel with real affection.

Hamish had stopped bawling and was listening hard and then she felt him relax, just as she did herself, for there was a sound which got louder.

'Okay, mate – we've got you! Sit tight, and we'll be there in two ticks. Just hold on tight there – '

She couldn't help it. She giggled; and then laughed harder and more tears rolled down her face and she could actually feel them making a channel in the dust there.

'As if we were going anywhere!' she spluttered. 'Sit tight! What the hell else does he think we're going to do?'

'I'd like it a deal better if we could do something else,' he said and began to reach out towards the rubble beyond the wheels. There was an ominous sound of movement and another cloud of dust filled Robin's nose and she managed to shout, 'Leave it alone, you ass! You'll have the whole lot in on us!' And she reached down and managed to grab his arm and slid her fingers down it till she reached his hand, and held on tightly.

He kept his fingers very still and then convulsively held on and she said, 'It's all right, Hamish! No need to be scared – '

'I'm no' scared,' he said and suddenly his Scottish accent sounded thicker than it ever had. 'I'm no' in the least scared – '

'Well, I am,' she said, though in fact the first wave of alarm had quite subsided now. She was more irritated than frightened, irritated at the tight crush under the trolley and the difficulty of getting comfortable with her legs curled under her as they were; there was no way she could stretch them out, not without risking a further fall of rubble that could eventually do some more damage, and that wasn't worth considering. Nothing was broken and she didn't think she had any cuts – though she was aware of feeling bruised in places – so there was no longer any need for alarm, especially as now she could hear the cries of the men above and beyond them trying to get down to them, as flickering lights appeared and vanished along the line of rubble ahead.

'Aye, well mebbe –' he said and she felt him pull away from her and pull his arms around him, and a little chilled, she pulled her hand back and tucked it under her other arm. It was the easiest way to sit.

146

'Call again!' a voice shouted ahead and above, and together they shouted. And then, when they were out of breath, stopped and listened, and the voice came down to them, muffled but fully comprehensible.

'Okay, then. We can see where you are. No problem then. Just a bit of rubble to clear. Hold on there and we'll be in in no time. How many of you?'

'Two!' shouted Robin and the voice above called encouragingly back and then there was just the sound of pickaxes and the rattle of shovels on broken bricks.

She sat there in the blackness, trying out her cat's eyes, but she could see no more than she had from the start. Just that flickering torchlight from time to time. But she could still feel him beside her and she said as cheerfully as she could, 'Well, here we are then! How long d'you think they'll take to get us out?'

There was a little silence and then he said shortly, 'I've no way of knowing.'

He sounded irritable and she thought crossly – selfish devil. He's not the only one cooped up here. Why be so sour about it?

And she said sharply, 'Well, try a guess! Half an hour? Or an hour or more? Or the end of the night? At least we won't be going back on duty after this – '

'Oh, will ye be quiet, woman!' he snapped and she caught her breath in amazement.

'Well, you miserable old –' she began and then stopped. Her newly found extra sense had realized something and she sat there, her head up in the darkness, staring with her eyes turned towards where she knew he was, and then slowly, put out one hand and reached for him. His arm beneath her fingers was as tight and knotted as though he were lifting weights, and after a moment she let her hand slide upwards, this time to reach for his face.

It was wet, not just moist with sweat, but pouring with it and she held her hand there for a moment and then without stopping to think let her nursing training take over; and slid her hand away from his cheek, down to

147

his chin and then under his neck until she could reach the pulse in his throat.

He tried to pull his head away from her and she said firmly, 'Keep still!' and amazingly he obeyed.

His pulse, when she found it, was bounding, full and rapid, so rapid that she could hardly count it and she tried to work out how fast it was; and then remembering her own normal pulse was around sixty, put her other hand up to her own throat and checked its rate. It was its usual steady self and she held her fingers against his pulse and compared the count with the speed of her own, and then got it. It was at least twice as fast, maybe faster and she thought – a hundred and twenty a minute. That's very fast for a strong man who does manual work. She could almost hear the voice of the cardiologist who'd taught them when they did their medical lectures.

'Active people have a slower pulse than sedentary ones. An athlete can have a pulse as slow as thirty, at rest, and be a healthy man. Healthier indeed than those of so-called normal pulse of seventy who do not take adequate exercise.'

After a while she let go of her own pulse, but she kept her hand on his and said gently, 'What is it, Hamish? Are you hurt and not wanting to tell me? Please do – I could help – if you're bleeding somewhere at least try and show me, and I'll put some pressure on. They'll be here soon, I'm sure they will. Hear them? They're getting much closer –' And indeed the sounds of diggers getting closer were increasing steadily.

'No,' he said and his voice was husky. 'I'm no' bleeding – ' and then she felt him start to shake, and she let go of his pulse and slid her hand down to get it around his shoulders, and he eased forwards a little to let her and she thought anxiously – he *is* hurt – but he isn't – and couldn't understand her own reaction.

'So long as you're sure you're not bleeding,' she said. 'It doesn't feel like a thready pulse, the sort you'd get with haemorrhage, but it is fast – '

He managed a little gasp that was almost a sigh. 'I'm sure it is! It generally is when – '

'This has happened before?' Her anxiety sharpened again. Had he some sort of heart condition? She wished she'd learned all the stuff she was supposed to about heart disease, but what with the raids and the rest of the work pressure she'd put if off over and over again. If he were to have some sort of heart attack –

'It's not my heart,' he said. 'And don't get anxious about me, for God's sake. Bad enough it is as it is – '

'Well, of course I'm anxious! If you have a high pulse and you're sweating the way you are, you must be ill – '

He seemed to groan and she felt him bend his head forwards on his chest. 'Please,' he said and it came out breathlessly. 'Please, leave me alone.'

'I'd be glad to,' she said tartly. 'Only I can't exactly get up and walk away, can I?'

And again he managed that almost-laugh. 'Oh, for God's sake – '

'You'll be better off telling me,' she said and again held him tightly round his shoulders. To feel the shaking in him was pitiful; he was like a terrified child and she felt a great warmth for him at the thought. 'Come on,' she said, almost wheedling. 'Do tell me –' And this time he really did manage to laugh.

'Oh, God,' he said and he sounded a little hoarse. But his voice was stronger. 'Do I seem as childish as that? How really awful – '

'Oh, damn,' she said and again held his shoulders more tightly in a sort of hug. 'I didn't mean to sound as though I were talking to a child. I just want to help, that's all. And I can't if you don't tell me – '

He drew a deep shuddering breath. 'Oh, for pity's sake, will ye stop your naggin', woman? I'm claustrophobic, if you must know. I'm always like this in enclosed spaces. And I can't do a damned thing about it – '

· 15 ·

They were helped out of their trolley nest just an hour and a half after the bomb fell, to find Sister Priestland waiting for them with a bottle of brandy in one hand and two of the cups from her own coffee tray dangling from the other.

'Ah, there you are,' she said, as they came stumbling out into the bright lights of the rescue workers, as casually as if they'd dropped in for tea. 'You'll be needing this. Now take it and then away to the department to make sure you've no treatable injuries.' And she poured out the brandy skilfully and generously and pushed it at them as the rescue workers began to clear up their gear and make way for the hospital staff who were trying to remove the worst of the mess so the way through Casualty from the main hospital was possible again.

Robin sipped hers gratefully but with a moue of distaste, as Hamish shook his head. 'I don't take spirits, Sister,' he said. 'Thank you all the same. And I'm no' hurt. I'll be back to work then – '

'You'll do no such thing,' said Sister Priestland. 'Not until you've been seen by one of the doctors and passed as fit.' And she looked at the cup of brandy in her hand, then at Hamish, and with a sort of half shrug and half grimace drank it herself. 'It's easier than putting it back in the bottle,' she said and smiled at Robin, a wide sweet smile that made her look suddenly rather vulnerable, and Robin became sharply aware of how

150

heavy a responsibility rested on those plump round shoulders, and was grateful to her.

'I'm fit too, Sister. A bit shaken up but nothing broken or cut.' She moved then experimentally and made a face. 'A few bruises, though.'

'Well, we'll see what the medical men say,' Sister Priestland said. 'Now, come on, and take care as you go –'

They followed her along the wrecked corridor, aware then of what had happened. The roof had come in, clearly, for an awning of blackout material had been rigged overhead to prevent light getting out to bring the bombers back, and everywhere rubble was heaped. One of the rescue men led the little group carefully past the worst of it and then they emerged into the rest of the corridor which was remarkably undamaged.

'A small bomb,' the rescue man said. 'Just one. It's when they come in sticks they really cause a muck-up. This was one left over or something – it was down the docks they laid most of their ruddy Hitler eggs tonight –'

'Small or not,' Sister Priestland said sharply, 'it's done enough damage and caught two of my staff, and I won't have it!' And she turned her head and looked at Robin. 'You shouldn't have been there at the time, for heaven's sake, girl! You were supposed to be at your meal.'

'I came back early,' Robin said and added a little mendaciously, 'in case we got busy.'

'Such stuff,' Sister Priestland snorted. 'You must think me very stupid! You came back early to gossip with your friend, Chester.'

'Oh,' Robin said and could manage no more.

'Well, there it is. Girls!' said Sister Priestland, as though that one syllable said everything necessary. 'She's been leaping about like a scalded cat ever since the incident. She's waiting for you now –'

They arrived in Casualty at last and stood there blinking a little in the bright lights and then there was Chick, bursting across the waiting hall like a hurricane, quite oblivious to everyone else, and seizing Robin by the elbows.

'You wretch!' she cried. 'Getting in the way of a bomb! You ought to know better. You know how I worry. Are you hurt? Are you all right? Have you got any – '

'Nurse Chester, we're all well aware that Nurse Bradman is your very best friend but your anxiety is excessive. Now if you please, a little space and time for the pair of them to be dealt with. Todd, you come to the corner cubicle – here he is, Dr Smith. We need to be sure he has no injuries – '

Hamish was led away, muttering that he was fine, he couldn't think what all the fuss was about, and Robin looked anxiously after him. He caught her eye and lifted his chin a little, looking interrogative and she nodded back at him as reassuringly as she could. He needed to know she wouldn't say a word to anyone about the conversation they had had under that pile of rubble and the casualty department trolley, and she hoped that he had understood the unspoken message she had sent him. But then she saw that a little of his colour had come back and was comforted because he had been rather pallid.

'And you, Nurse Bradman,' Sister Priestland was saying. 'Come here. Dr Landow will check you. Nurse Chester, take her to the cubicle and help her get into a gown and don't exhaust her with your chatter. Now, stop looking so hard done by, Nurse Bradman. You must see we can't let you back on duty till we know you're fit for it. No one can be properly looked after by nurses who are not themselves in peak condition! So it's as much for the patients' sake as yours that it is necessary for you to be medically checked. If necessary, there'll be X-rays. Happily we're not too busy at present, so you'll cause no problems by being a patient yourself for a little while. Nurse Jenner, get on with cleaning those trolleys, and Nurse Dollis, there are drums to be packed. We're short of swabs, and gauze packs and stores. And after that I'll need the kaolin poultices made up for the infected wounds – there's plenty to be done – will you get on with it now?' And she went off in her usual mad bustle and Robin followed Chick gratefully to the corner cubicle, aware of the fact that both the other probationers were watching her with undoubted envy. Clearly they thought it would have been well worth being buried for a couple of hours or so to have had so much attention.

Robin sat on the end of the couch and let her shoulders loosen, aware suddenly of how very tired she was, and how much Sister Priestland's brandy had penetrated to her muscles. She started to shake a little and Chick, looking sharply at her, began to help her undress, untying her shoes and unbuckling her belt, chattering like a train all the time, half scolding, half commiserating.

Robin stopped listening after a while, letting the words roll over her like a tide. She really felt very sleepy now, indeed downright feeble, and she let Chick do as she liked with her, until at last she was stretched out on the consulting couch, wrapped in a gown and wearing beneath it just her panties.

'– it really was, I said, a total mystery, because why did he say he got it if he didn't?'

'Mmm?' Robin said a little dreamily, trying to focus her eyes on Chick's round face. She seemed to be bouncing gently like a barrage balloon on its cables.

'I told you, love – if she didn't realize what it was you wanted and didn't send anyone, how could he have got any message at all? A total mystery – I thought I'd tell you about it, and that was what I tried to do every time I saw you. But of course I couldn't, and then when you go to the trouble of coming back early from your meal so that I could, and then get yourself flattened by a bloody Hun bomb, well, you can imagine how I felt – '

'What are you talking about?' Robin tried to concentrate. It wasn't easy. She had a clamorous need to sleep.

'So I thought, well I'll ask him,' Chick went on, apparently oblivious as she pulled the sheet tidily over

Robin, and checked the examination trolley was ready. 'But damn me if he wasn't flattened by the same wretched bomb! So how could I?'

'Chick!' Robin managed to say it loudly and Chick looked round at her and grinned.

'What is it, ducks?'

'What – are – you – talking – about?'

'I told you! About that message your Ma didn't send.'

Robin blinked. 'Didn't send? I don't understand.'

'It's not difficult. When you phoned from Norwich, you remember? The line was awful at this end, apparently, and she only got one word in three. So she didn't realize you wanted her to call the hospital and tell them you'd be late. So of course she never did.'

'She didn't?' Robin said and closed her eyes, trying to concentrate. And then opened them again to stare at Chick. 'Then what was the message Hamish – I mean Todd – got?'

Chick shook her head. 'See what I mean? That's the total mystery. I'll ask him, shall I? Smith's checked him, I think, by now and I could nip across and have a word – '

'No!' Robin must have shouted it louder than she realized because Chick, who was already half out of the cubicle, turned back and stared.

'What?'

'Leave him be. I'll sort it out,' she said and after a moment Chick let go of the curtain and stood there looking at her with a comically quizzical expression on her face.

'Well, well,' she said. 'So they were right! I told 'em they were screwballs but they were right! You could have said something to me, you know. Damn it, what's a friend for?'

'Now what are you going on about?' Some of the sleepiness had gone, to be replaced by a dullish headache that was beginning to make Robin's temples throb. 'I wish you wouldn't talk mysteries at me.'

'Jenner and Dollis – a right pair of clots they are – said that Staff Nurse Meek, may her cleavage, such as it is, shrivel, was putting it about that you had a tendresse for the orderly, and what a low-class creature you were and so forth, on account of nurses should know better than to consort with types like orderlies. Of course I told them where to go and put themselves, but I'm beginning to wonder – '

'You are as big an ass as they are,' Robin said wrathfully, and tried to sit up. 'Oh, hell, I'm going to be sick – ' And she was, suddenly and copiously and very shamingly, and Chick shook her head at her and set about cleaning her up and replacing her gown with great dispatch and skill.

'You've had more of a shaking than you know,' she said. 'And I ought to be ashamed of myself for bothering you with nonsense. Sorry, ducks. You need to get to bed if you ask me. Listen, I'll see if I can find his Lordship – '

'No need,' said Dr Landow from the curtain and came in and Chick went pink and laughed and so did he. Robin looked up at him owlishly and thought how agreeable it was to see so friendly a face and then closed her eyes. She really did feel dreadful.

He checked her over with quiet care and warm hands, which made Robin so grateful that tears sprang into her eyes and then said to Chick who was standing by in the time-honoured nurse's pose, with both hands folded demurely against the front of her apron, 'She'll do. Tell Sister she's very shaken up and a bit weepy in consequence. No need to look so annoyed with me, Nurse Bradman. It's perfectly permissible to feel like crying when you've been the target of a bomb. I would if it were me.'

Chick winked at her and went away to deliver her message to Sister Priestland and Dr Landow sat on the end of the couch and looked at Robin and smiled. And she managed to produce in return a smile, though she knew it was a rather watery one.

'I wouldn't tell Sister Priestland for the world, but the worst possible thing to give to people who've been shocked is brandy. But who am I to try to change one of the great British traditions of centuries? Whatever happens, bring out the brandy and then the tea, and best of all both together.'

She managed to laugh at that. 'I know. It seemed like a good idea at the time but actually it doesn't suit me. I hardly ever drink anything. It made me feel awful.'

'Worse than the bomb,' he said and then in the same conversational tone. 'How frightened were you?'

She thought about that. 'Hardly at all. Odd, isn't that?'

'Not really. You had someone with you of course and that helped.'

'Well having someone to take care of takes your mind off yourself,' she said without thinking, and he lifted one brow at her.

'Oh? What sort of looking after did he need? I got the impression he was unhurt too. Just the inconvenience of being buried for a while. Did he have some sort of reaction?'

'Oh, no, not at all,' she said hastily. Too hastily? She couldn't be sure. 'It's just that when there's someone else there you do think about them as well as yourself and it doesn't seem so bad.'

He nodded, seeming satisfied. 'Well, there it is, you're fine now, in a purely physical sense that is. But if you get a few days of depression later on, don't be surprised. No one's got much time for psychiatric problems at present, what with all the surgery that's needed in wartime, and in lots of ways the speciality has a dirty name anyway. The general public tend to see people who can't be soldiers because of some sort of psychological disability as skivers and cheats. Pity really, because they certainly are not. But there it is. We'll teach them eventually, I dare say. But as I say, if you feel at all – shall we say, strange – come and tell me. I'm making a bit of a study of the way people react to raids. And those who've been in incidents, I've

156

found, do get rather low for a while sometime later. If it happens be sure to come and talk to me, hmm? It's a subject I'm interested in. And I'd be glad to help in any way I can.'

'Thank you,' she said and smiled and he turned to go. And then turned back after a moment. 'I've been meaning to ask you. Haven't I seen you at that marvellous little restaurant in Cable Street? I went there a few times when I first came here to the London Hospital, last year it was, and I can remember seeing a girl who looked rather like you – or was I imagining it?'

She smiled then, broadly. 'No, you weren't. That restaurant in Cable Street – I go there quite often – it belongs to my great-aunt. Isn't it super?'

'Super,' he said and then gave a half shake of his head. 'Well, well, well. Who'd have thought it!' And went away, as Sister Priestland came back with Chick.

Not until she had been taken over to the Nurses' Home (in a wheelchair, which she found very demeaning) to sleep off her adventure with strict instructions to be on duty on time the next night, did she think about Dr Landow again and then it was with some puzzlement. What on earth had he meant by that odd little gesture of his head and that 'Who'd have thought it?'

Very strange, she told herself as she fell asleep. But not as strange as the message that wasn't sent but had been received. One way and another she had a good deal to talk to Hamish about next time she saw him.

· 16 ·

Jessie sat at her corner table, staring out across her restaurant and trying to pretend to herself that it was really like the good old days, before the war.

It wasn't of course. How could it be? Then she had sat at this self-same table and watched her customers happily – on these evenings when she wasn't doing the same thing over at her West End restaurant, that was – beaming as they dealt with her superb fish and her delectable chicken and salt beef and her incredible puddings. Those had been the days when she would worry dreadfully if she wasn't left with at least a quarter of what she had ordered for the day, even though the restaurant had been hectically busy from opening time till gone midnight, and the money had rolled into the till as smoothly and as copiously as a waterfall.

But that had been then, and now was now, she thought gloomily, looking at the people who filled her tables. People who in the old days had been chattering and happy but now were quiet, contemplative, downright scowling, some of them. They couldn't help it, of course; they were tired, and the food they were eating wasn't what she wanted to give them. In the past, she'd have been ashamed to set before her beloved customers such offerings as shepherd's pie and chicken casseroles made from very elderly chicken; and as for puddings – who could make decent puddings when eggs were so scarce?

Scarce. That thought made her uneasy, and she moved

in her chair awkwardly, remembering Bernie this afternoon.

'All the eggs you can handle, Ma. And for her bloody canteen an' all. All you want. And butter and a bit of sugar and I've got access to some marvellous salmon, all the way from Scotland. Strictly legal that is. No ration on fish, if you can get it. And I can get it. And when it comes to meat, well, look at that brisket I gave you last week. Isn't that good for business?'

'It's useless for business,' she had told him. 'Useless! You don't think people are stupid, do you? They'll know when I'm offering something I shouldn't have. They'll know I'm getting it on the black market – '

'So what if they do?' Bernie had said and laughed. 'Honestly, Ma, that Poppy's been the ruin of you. You're a real Mrs Milk Toast. Don't you know which way is up? There isn't a house in the West End doesn't buy black-market on account they can afford it. Well, so can you. And it's not as though you were buying for yourself! It's for the business, for your blessed customers, and you know how potty you are about them! Do yourself a favour, Ma, don't be so silly.'

That hadn't settled the matter, of course. Well, not really. He'd gone on and on about wanting access to the closed cellars, the ones she never used because they were so hard to get to; the ones she had one day intended to turn into a decent wine cellar to stock the West End restaurant from. After the war maybe, she could use it for that. Right now Bernie wanted them for some use of his own, and she'd really rather not know what, Jessie told herself, staring sightlessly at her blacked-out restaurant and its few customers sitting quietly at their tables, and eating with so little delight. He'd take them, of course; didn't he always get his own way, one way or another? Of course he did. And it was her fault. She knew that and she sat and struggled with her conscience over it, trying not to remember the way he'd been able to melt her by just glancing at her with those big dark eyes of his, or showing

159

his perfect teeth in a wide and affectionate smile; all her fault. But God's too, for making him so very beautiful, so very beguiling –

The curtain over the door billowed and then flattened as someone opened the outer door to the street and came in, and then once the blacked-out outer door had been carefully closed, it opened to admit the newcomer, and Jessie beamed and surged to her feet, all miseries at once forgotten.

'Robin! It's a mitzvah – it's a blessing to see you! How are you, dolly? And your nice friend? How are you?' And she held out one hand graciously to Hamish who was standing behind Robin, bowing a little regally as she did so. She wasn't as forthcoming to him as she was to some of her customers, and Robin knew it, but she put that down to a sort of shyness because of Hamish's size and also his rather exotic strangeness – for Scottish was very exotic to East End Jessie – and was glad of it. Jessie in a really affectionate mood could be more than a little overwhelming.

She settled them in a quiet table and told the kitchen what to send out to them – for none of her special customers ever actually ordered at Jessie's. She knew what was best in the kitchen, and what was to be recommended and only a fool would argue with her, and then went to find them a half bottle of claret to go with it.

'Wine's getting harder and harder to get hold of,' she grieved as she opened it for them, with an expert twist of her old wrist. 'Since France went – well, it's to be expected, hmm? Anyway, this'll be enough for you two. I know you never drink much, Robin, and I've seen your friend here doesn't either, so – ' And she set the bottle down in front of them and went away to supervise the kitchens, leaving Hamish and Robin alone at last.

Not that they were unduly bothered by Jessie's attentions. Hamish had found her a little surprising the first time Robin had brought him here to have supper, when their nights off coincided, but had found her wholly delightful and said so. And no comment could have made anyone seem more acceptable to Robin than one that approved of her favourite aunt. 'Not that I actually have any others,' she told him. 'But she'd be the best even if I had dozens. Do you have lots of relations?'

Indeed he had, and he had gone on to tell her of them, of aunts with names like Elspeth and Moira and uncles called Fred and Douglas and Jacob, and she had sat and listened, asking questions about his home life in a small and very tightly knit seaside town not too far from Aberdeen, and found him entirely fascinating.

It was inevitable she would, as she had told Chick, once she had discovered about the matter of the message that Hamish had told Sister Priestland he'd taken.

'I mean, honestly, Chick, what more could anyone do for a person? He'd worked out what was going on and marched straight in with the most whopping great lie.' She'd laughed then. 'I told him, for someone with such a tender conscience, he certainly found it possible to lie like Ananias without any hestitation at all. And he said lying didn't matter as a sin as long as it was done for good honest reasons. And he'd lied for me for good reasons, knowing what a battleaxe old Priestland can be. Not,' she had added, 'that I've ever actually noticed it.'

'You will one of these nights,' Chick said with considerable feeling. 'At present you're the blue-eyed girl on account of Meek hates you and anyone Meek hates, Sister likes on account of she loathes Meek. Silly, isn't it? Ah well, women, you know. They make lousy guv'nors.'

'They do not,' Robin had said, flaring at once. 'And you should be ashamed of yourself talking that way! You're a woman.'

'I am at that, and I hope I'd make a better fist of being in charge than the clots we've got here,' Chick said. 'I mean, they give women a bad name. Is it any wonder I get so sour? Look at the way Marshall is on Annie Zunz, and what about that absolute stinker, Mary O'Day, on Cloudesley? A worse bitch never wagged its tail. It's no wonder I reckon women make bad bosses.'

'Watch my mother sometimes,' Robin said. 'She'll show you differently. And Jessie too, of course. They both run their business like – well, like the best of men.'

'There aren't many like that,' Chick had said. 'As well you know. Why else say they run their business like men? See what I mean? Anyway, enough about that. More about Hamish. Do tell me, is this the Big Romance?' And she had rolled her eyes comically and even more so when Robin had blushed a little.

'Such stuff! Of course not,' she'd protested and refused to talk any more about him; but she had wondered. There was no doubt she was getting very fond of him, and she tried to analyse why. The fact that he had lied so gallantly for her, when it looked as though she were about to get into trouble, had of course been very endearing; there could be no better way to make a girl feel affectionate. But then there was the fact that she shared a secret with him. No one in the world, it turned out, not even his own mother or brother, knew of his disability. He'd kept it a secret somehow ever since it first happened when he was just twelve and had been locked in a cupboard by a sadistic schoolmaster. The fact that she knew was an accident of course, but nevertheless, she knew. And that made them feel especially close.

And that closeness did add fun to the night's work on Casualty, when in the middle of the rush and hubbub they ran into each other and shared conspiratorial glances. Indeed she could not deny she was getting fond of him; why else should she bring him to her Auntie Jessie's to feed him? It wasn't just pity for a large and constantly hungry young man with small financial resources and few chances to eat well; it was affection.

Or so Robin thought, and tried not to think of too much. The implications were too complicated, what with the progress of her training to think about, and the war and the family; no, she couldn't think about Hamish at all. So she didn't. She just enjoyed being out with him sometimes, at a film or a theatre, when free tickets came the nurses' way, as they sometimes did, or at Jessie's, like tonight.

But even though she didn't want to think about it, that didn't mean others shared her views. Her Aunt Jessie in particular thought about it a good deal. And talked about it.

She had told Poppy the morning after the first time that Robin had taken Hamish to the restaurant that 'the child has a fella in tow,' and Poppy's brows had snapped together in sudden anxiety.

'What do you mean?' she had said and looked sharply at Jessie. 'Please, love, none of your fancy notions. I remember how you used to be with me, always on about getting settled and trying to find me a man, after Bobby died and – '

'Well, so what if I did?' Jessie said comfortably. 'Isn't it just natural that I should want my girl to be well settled? Just as it's natural I should show an interest in our little boobala, the same way. She's a big girl already, Poppy – '

'Twenty-one, that's all,' Poppy said swiftly.

'A big girl,' Jessie went on inexorably. 'And it's natural she'll be looking at the sort that wears pants and not panties! You'd have more to worry about if she didn't. You want a girl in an Eton crop like those odd ones who only ever talks to fluffy girls?'

'Jessie, for heaven's sake – You can jump from one conclusion to another like – like a goat on a crag. Stick to the point, do!'

'I am! There she is, as pretty as paint, and it's time she was settled. War or not, life goes on, and she's full of life. And she's got this lovely-looking fella, very big he is, looks like a mountain to tell you the truth, and from Scotland. I ask you, Scotland! Brought him here last night and very attentive he was – '

'I imagine he's well-mannered then. Polite men always pay attention to their companions – '

'Well-mannered, phooey! He likes her! You could see that for miles.'

163

'Jessie, for pity's sake, stop it, will you? I'm sure they're just friends. And it's awful to gossip about Robin like this. I won't do it. Now, about that order of herrings from Billingsgate. They could only let us have half of what we asked for and – '

And that had been that from Jessie's point of view, but not from Poppy's. She had worried about Robin's new friend, not simply because he was a man, but because, unusually for Robin, she hadn't told her mother about him. And Poppy found that made her doubtful, to say the least.

So, when she came in tonight to see Jessie and saw them with their heads together in a corner, and so engrossed in their conversation that Robin didn't even see her mother come in, she felt a worm of unease creep into her and wondered why.

Was it just motherly dislike of her child growing up and being adult enough to let men into her life? Hardly that; surely her own experience of love and sex had been good enough for her to want the same for her beloved child? If she could find a husband as loving and as reliable as David was, surely Poppy would feel delight for her daughter, rather than anything else. And yet, standing now in the shadow of the curtained doorway and looking across the restaurant, she felt that unease and didn't know why. And then told herself not to be so stupid and to go and talk to them both.

By this time the restaurant had filled a little more and there were only a couple of tables unoccupied; an unusual thing on a night when there were, for once, no raids. It happened occasionally that the inner part of the East End was left in some peace, when factories and docks further east along the river were the targets, and on those occasions people came creeping out of the shelters looking for peace and comfort and often found it in Cable Street. So there was some animation in the place now, and it wasn't until Poppy was almost beside them that Robin saw her.

She got to her feet at once. 'Ma! How nice to see you! Come and sit down.'

'I won't disturb you – ' Poppy said, looking at Hamish, and at once Robin said easily. 'Oh, do! Hamish – May I introduce my mother, Poppy Deveen? Tell her to sit down, do. She's just being shy.'

'Of course, Mrs Deveen,' Hamish said and held a chair for her. 'You must join us. Mrs Braham has given us this half bottle of wine, and to tell the truth we neither of us really want any. Perhaps you'd have some of it to save our faces a little – '

He seemed assured and relaxed, and looking up at his broad and agreeable face, Poppy relaxed a little. Just a friend, surely. No one special. But nice. A doctor perhaps–

'It was Hamish who bailed me out over that confusion with the message from Norwich.' Robin said with a somewhat studied offhandedness. 'He works in Casualty. He's an orderly.'

Poppy's expression didn't change but at once it all slotted into place. He was a conchie of course; why else would so obviously healthy a young man be working at such a lowly job? And her heart swooped even further and she hated herself for the reaction. A man had a right to have a conscience, for God's sake; who was she to despise one who chose not to join the services because he objected to killing? But it was no good. After her years in the trenches in the first war, and her time as Bobby's wife watching him die from the gassing he had suffered, it was hard for her to accept as fully as she might the conscientious objector; but if he was a friend of Robin's she'd have to. Somehow –

So she smiled as easily as she could, and said, 'How nice!' And then looked over her shoulder gratefully as Jessie came lumbering across from the kitchen bearing plates mounded with slices of pink salt beef and fried potatoes.

'I got something special for these two,' Jessie said and grinned at them. 'This'll make you feel you've eaten for once.' And she slapped the plates down in front of them

165

and then bent again to kiss her niece. 'Poppy, it's lovely to see you – but what are you doing here so late? I thought – '

'I came over for company actually,' Poppy said. 'David's away on a story again, and they don't need me at the canteen tonight and there I was with a night off and all on my own. I could have gone to bed after a hot bath but five inches of barely warm water doesn't seem exactly luxurious even if it is patriotic, so I thought I'd come and have some supper with you. Goosey's been in bed for ages, of course – '

'Lovely,' Jessie said at once. 'Come and sit at my table with me. I'll fetch you some salt beef too.' And with very obvious, even elephantine, tact, she tried to shift Poppy from Robin and Hamish's table.

But none of them seemed to want to be parted. Hamish got to his feet at once and reached for the other chair and said, 'Please, do sit here with us – ' just as Poppy said, 'Oh, I don't know if –' and Robin said, 'Oh, Auntie Jessie, do let's make a party of it – '

And so it was. Extra food was fetched and in a very short time indeed the four of them were laughing and chattering as though they'd know each other for years. Only Poppy was left with a nagging uncertainty as she saw her daughter look at Hamish from time to time and seem to light up at the sight of him; and she worried about that, because as far as she could see, Hamish wasn't at all as illuminated when he looked at Robin. And surely, surely, he should have been if, that is, Jessie had been right in her suppositions?

It was at this point that two things happened; a tall man in a rather rumpled suit got up from his table on the far side of the restaurant and came over towards them and Jessie said suddenly, 'The party, Poppy! Has it been decided? When and where is it? And shouldn't we ask our Robin's friend here to it, as well?'

· 17 ·

'Hello, Nurse Bradman, Mr Todd,' the tall man said, just as Robin said to her mother, 'Party? What party?' and there was a little flurry as the occupants of the table looked round and Poppy opened her mouth to answer her daughter's question, after throwing a dark look at Jessie.

It was the tall man who won the struggle for first place, if there was one; Robin looked at him and then smiled widely.

'Why, it's Dr Landow! How are you? How odd to see you here!'

'Not at all odd. I come whenever I can,' he said. 'It's one of the few good things in a naughty world. I saw you over here and I came to make a nuisance of myself because frankly, I'd like to meet your aunt.' And he smiled at Jessie. 'I'm what they'd call a fan, I suppose, if you were a film star. I just want to tell you how much I like your place and how much I admire you for keeping it all going in these hard times. It's a real oasis in my life, and I'm sure it's the same for many others.'

It was not often that Jessie Braham was lost for words, but this was one of them. She looked at the tall man and blinked and swallowed, and then went as pink as the blouse she was wearing.

'Well,' she said. 'That's very kind of you, Mr er – '

'Doctor,' Robin said, highly amused at Jessie's reaction. 'Dr Landow, from the hospital, Auntie Jessie.

Dr Landow, may I present my aunt, Mrs Braham. Now then! You've been introduced!'

Dr Landow held out his hand and shook Jessie's, and she looked as flustered and as pleased as a girl at her first dance.

'I haven't eaten food like yours since my grandmother died in 1937,' he said. 'Rest her soul in peace. She made the best salt beef in all Manchester but I have to admit yours is even better. And that's quite an achievement.'

Jessie looked at him with birdlike brilliance in her eyes.

'A luntsman!' she said and he laughed.

'Who else could appreciate your salt beef?'

'Sit down!' Jessie commanded and waved at the adjoining table which had no diners at it. 'Bring a chair – '

'Oh, I couldn't intrude!' he said and she became positively vehement and got to her feet and dragged the chair over herself.

'It's no intrusion. Right, Robin? Poppy?'

'Of course not,' Poppy said. 'As long as Robin and Hamish – '

Hamish had said nothing but now he looked at Robin and lifted one eyebrow. 'I've no objection at all,' he said. 'A party's a party – '

Dr Landow stood there hovering, looking at Robin. 'I really do feel a considerable nuisance now – I wish I'd not bothered you – '

'Oh, do please sit down!' Robin said. 'You're no trouble at all. As long as you don't mind if we start eating. This is getting cold – '

Jessie was at once scandalized and surged to her feet. 'Give it to me at once. We'll get fresh for you – for everyone! I can't have you eating cold food!'

'And I can't have you wasting it,' Robin said, holding on to her plate by curling her arm round it like a schoolchild trying to prevent his neighbour copying his work. 'Go and sort out everyone else's, darling, and leave us to this. It's divine. Isn't it, Hamish?'

Hamish, who had been steadily and quietly eating anyway, nodded, his mouth full, and Robin laughed even more. 'You see, Auntie Jessie? Go and deal with everyone else. We're absolutely fine – '

'Dr Landow – salt beef for you and for Poppy and – '

'I've eaten,' he protested. 'I had a plateful already – '

'A little more a healthy man can always manage,' Jessie said and went away, and a little silence descended on the table as the four of them sat there, a little awkwardly. It was as though Jessie had been the glue that held the group together.

'So tell me,' Poppy began just as Hamish looked at Dr Landow and said, 'If I might just ask – '

Landow laughed and held up both hands. 'Nice to be popular!'

Hamish looked at Poppy. 'I'm sorry. I didna' mean to interrupt – '

'It wasn't important,' Poppy said. 'Just making conversation. I was going to – how long have you lived in London?'

'Since I got this job as a Casualty houseman. It's my second since I qualified and it seemed like a good idea to come to London.' His face twisted a little, amused. 'That was before the Blitz started, of course. My mother's having fits, as you can imagine – '

'I can imagine,' Poppy said and glanced at Robin. 'I'm not exactly sleeping easy over Robin being there in the middle of it all – '

'Casualty's pretty safe,' he said. 'Mostly underground – '

'It didn't stop her being buried, though, did it? That could have been a dreadful incident.' And she looked bleak as she contemplated the awful might-have-been.

'But it wasn't,' he said gently. 'And that's the thing to hang on to. We're all doing pretty well, under the circumstances.'

'There was a patient in last night who said she never worried – if a bomb's got your name on it then that's it,

169

and if it hasn't you'll come to no harm. And the child sitting on the bench next to her started to scream blue murder and we couldn't work out why until we managed to get him to explain he was frightened because his name was so easy to write – he's Bill Jones – and he thought the Germans would mark a bomb for him soon. Poor little scrap – '

'He should be out of London,' Landow said. 'It's bad enough for us. For children it's hell – but I must say I do know what that woman meant, and I quite agree with her. A pity a child had to take it so literally, but there it is. I think you *do* have to be rather fatalistic. There's nothing any of us can do to control what's going on. We just have to do our best and try not to think of the might-happens.' He was looking very directly at Poppy as he said it, and she smiled at him, grateful for his sympathy.

'I suppose you're right,' she said. 'I try not to get too agitated, but it's not easy. My husband's a journalist, so he has to go out and cover the most difficult things – he's the London correspondent for a Baltimore paper, so he has to do everything from ship launches to air raids to travelling with the services all over the place. And there's my other two children evacuated to Norfolk, and Jessie to worry about, and Goosey – she's awfully old, and been with us for years and I can't persuade her to use the shelter and if they come to our side of London, heaven help us. And then there's Robin – ' She stopped then, suddenly confused. 'Heavens, how I do chatter on! I do so beg your pardon. I can't think what got into me to be so boring.'

'Not at all,' he said and smiled.

Robin, who'd finished her plateful by now, smiled too, looking at her mother. 'I dare say it's because he's interested in psychiatry. You make people blurt it all out, don't you? Isn't that what psychiatry is for?'

'Not precisely,' Landow said.

'Psychiatry?' Hamish had lifted his head. 'I didn't know that. And I tend to pick up most things around the department.'

Landow's lips quirked. 'I bet you do. Someone as quiet and as observant as you has to – I've watched you doing it and been very amused. Does it worry you that you didn't discover this about me?'

'Not in the least,' Hamish said and bent his head to look at his own plate, also empty now. 'It was just – I thought it interesting.'

'I interrupted you before,' Poppy said then. 'I'm sorry, Hamish. What was it you were going to say?'

'Hmm?' Hamish looked bemused.

'When I started talking you said you wanted to ask something.'

'Oh, yes,' Hamish looked at Landow and lifted his brows in interrogation. 'If I might ask you – what's a luntsman?'

Landow looked amused. 'Ah! A mysterious word, is it?'

'Very.'

'It's a rather altered one. It derives from the German word Landsman – in Yiddish, which itself derives largely from German. It's often mispronounced and it means simply a person from the same place as oneself. In the days when a great many Jewish immigrants fled here from the bad time in Europe, they clustered together in groups made up not just of their immediate relatives, but of people from their home village or district. It was like being related to each other – kith if not kin – but over the years the word has come to mean any Jew. One greets another as one of their own people. There! A very full and frank explanation for you!'

Hamish was looking at Robin. 'So you are Jewish then?' he said. 'I wasn't sure from what you told me – '

'A quarter of me is,' Robin said and looked steadily at him. 'Does that worry you?'

'Worry me? Not in the least! I'm verra interested, is all. My family are good Scots Presbyterians, do you see, and they regard the Jews verra highly as the people of the Bible. I've never had the good

171

fortune to meet anyone who is Jewish. A quarter, you say?'

'My father was Jewish,' Poppy said. 'Jessie's brother. My mother was not – '

'So you aren't' Dr Landow said. 'Are you?'

Poppy smiled. 'Because of lineage only being through the mother? Yes, you're right. I'm not one of the chosen – except from my own choice.'

'How do you mean?' Hamish said, clearly fascinated.

'It's rather practical really,' Landow said. 'The ancients of the tribe reckoned you couldn't guarantee a person's father, but you could always know who his mother was. Maternity can be proven, in other words, unlike paternity. So, they made it a rule – Jewish mothers have Jewish babies. Jewish fathers don't necessarily – '

Hamish shook his head admiringly. 'Well, well, is that so? My father will find that verra interesting. I'll write and tell him – '

Jessie arrived then in a great flurry of excitement, followed by the restaurant's only waitress, who was looking more than a little flustered, and started handing out quantities of food. There was more salt beef and piles of fried potatoes and pickled green cucumbers in quantities and Hamish happily accepted a second helping as did Dr Landow, though with a display of unwillingness that fooled no one, and at last they were all eating contentedly. And chattering away as though they'd all known each other for years, though in fact two of the party were total strangers to both Jessie and Poppy. But it didn't seem to matter and Robin, looking round at them all, had a sudden frisson of pleasure at having been the person who had brought this disparate group together. It made her feel very grown up, suddenly, in a way she rather liked.

'What does your Ma call you, Dr Landow?' Jessie said, now very comfortable with him and beaming at him in an almost proprietorial fashion. 'We can't go on being so formal, can we?'

'Sam,' said Dr Landow. 'Call me Sam. All of you – I'd like that.'

'I daren't,' Robin said. 'It might slip out sometime when we were in Casualty and Sister Priestland would skin me alive.'

'Hospital hierarchies!' Sam said. 'So ridiculous – but useful too, I suppose.'

'How can they be useful?' Robin demanded. 'As far as I can see they're just designed to make fools out of junior nurses – '

'– and drudges out of orderlies,' Hamish said. 'If any of them knew I was sitting here with a doctor and a nurse, talking on equal terms, I'd be – well, you can imagine. There'd be all the hounds of hell called out to gore me alive.'

'Not quite,' Sam said. 'But not far off. But the rules and the regulations are useful, you know. When there's a crisis of some sort everyone does what they have to do because they're more scared of upsetting the people above them or looking stupid to those below them than they are of whatever the emergency is. That's how armies operate, of course. Take away the soldier's individuality and you've got a hard fighting weapon. Let 'em think and do for themselves and you've got mayhem.'

'That's one of the reasons I won't serve in the forces,' Hamish said. 'I'll not kill, no matter what. I'm a good Christian – oh!' He looked awkward. 'I hope that's no offence to you.'

'Of course not! Why should it be?'

'Well, like I said. I'm a good Christian, so I don't kill – but I'm also a man, and God gave us free will to do as we think fit. He didna' make us to obey the rules of other men. So, I'll no' join any army where I'm no' allowed to think for myself.'

'Well done,' Sam said and reached over and touched his arm. 'I feel the same. But in my job I don't have the problem much, of course. I'm not entirely free of it, because there are still the consultants to worry about and the hospital administrators and so forth – but I'm allowed to have my own medical judgement. And that helps. It's not easy being you.'

'It is not,' said Hamish fervently and then smiled, an unusual expression for him. 'You're a pleasure to talk to, Sam.'

'And so are you,' Sam said and Robin lifted her brows at her mother.

'I'm beginning to feel a bit out of place at this mutual admiration society meeting,' she said.

'And why shouldn't they?' Jessie swallowed the last mouthful of her massive supper. 'They're both nice people. You should ask them to the party as well, Poppy.'

'Oh, yes,' Robin said, remembering. 'What's all this about a party, Ma?'

Poppy managed not to look the daggers she wanted to at Jessie.

'It's your grandmother's, not mine,' she said, not looking at Robin. 'There are some cousins coming over, one from Australia, one from South Africa, and she thought a party would be agreeable for us all.'

'Grandmamma said that?' Robin said, staring. 'I don't believe it!'

'I'd hardly lie to you,' Poppy said drily, knowing perfectly well that she had in spirit if not in word. The party had been her own idea in fact. She had felt so low and so tired for so long that she had developed a sort of guilt about it. It was as though she did nothing but work and sleep and all the enjoyable aspects of life had been dropped. A party, she had decided, to welcome the cousins Mildred had spoken of, would be the answer; a chance for everyone to let down their hair a little and relax. She had broached the idea to Mildred in such terms that the old lady had finally not only consented but seen it as her own original notion, and offered to have it in the Leinster Terrace house rather than in Norland Square. Not, she was at some pains to add, that there was anything wrong about Norland Square –

but Leinster Terrace was bigger. And Poppy, not wanting to let Goosey push herself into excessive activity (which only got in other people's way) which she would be sure to do if the party were held on her own territory, had agreed.

Now she said to Robin. 'Your grandmother wants to welcome her nephews, and this seemed as good a way as any other to do it – '

'I'm doing the food,' Jessie said. 'I'm already saving up some special stuff – dried fruit and so forth – ' And she buried her own unease, which had to do with the source of her extra supplies; I won't think about Bernie and his affairs, she told herself fiercely, I won't. 'So that'll be good. And the more people the merrier. That Leinster Terrace house is hell to fill up, believe me. So you bring your friends Robin, boobala. That nice girl Chick as well as Hamish and Sam here, hey? I like Chick. She's got an appetite, bless her, it's a pleasure to see.'

'Well, it's very sweet of you, Auntie Jessie. If Ma thinks it'll be all right with Grandma – '

'Of course it will!' Jessie was at her most beaming and expansive. 'How could it not be? Her lovely little Robin and all her friends? It'll be a pleasure for everyone, believe me.'

'Then we'll all be there,' Robin said and grinned at Hamish.

'Well, as long as I'm no' on duty,' he said and Robin made a face and looked at her mother.

'Hell! I forgot that sort of problem! What do we do?'

'The date's not set yet,' Poppy said, a little unwillingly, feeling herself railroaded and not knowing first of all why it mattered, and secondly why she didn't stand up for her own doubts. 'I suppose it could be fixed to fit in with you – '

'Great! I'll check the off-duty for the next while and let you know when Hamish and I are off duty – ' She stopped then and looked at Sam Landow a little shyly. 'I can't speak for the doctors, of course.'

'No need to worry about me,' Sam Landow said. 'I'd love to come to your party and I thank you kindly for the invitation. And as soon as you let me know the date and the time, I'll make an arrangement with Mike Smith. He makes me change duties over and over to fit in with his elaborate love life, so there's no reason why he shouldn't do it for me for just once! It'll be a pleasure to ask him.'

'So there it is,' Jessie said beaming round at them all. 'It's settled. Poppy and me, we make a party at Mildred's house, and everybody comes. It'll be the best ever, believe me!'

·18·

It had been a raw grey day, and the evening had turned it into a bitterly cold night. Robin, huddled in the corner seat on the bus that was trundling through Oxford Street towards Bayswater and Holland Park, pulled her coat more firmly around her and wondered forlornly how she could possibly expect to look anything but a wreck at the party. She knew her nose was red with the cold, and that her lashes, to which she had daringly applied a coat of mascara, were beaded with the tears that the biting air stung out of her eyes, and that altogether she was anything but the image of a happy girl embarked on a glamorous evening out.

Chick beside her was just as miserable, but not quite as cold, for she had dug out of her capacious luggage a pair of large fur ear-muffs, which sat incongruously on each side of her round face and made her look like a startled and dishevelled rabbit, and Robin turned her head to peer at her in the gloom thrown by the small blue light-bulbs that were sparsely arranged inside the bus and wanted to laugh at her; and felt too cold to do so.

Chick caught her eye and reached up to pull off her earmuffs. 'Here you are, kid. Your turn to be warm,' she said and then huddled more deeply into her coat collar.

'Oh, it's all right.' Robin tried to push them back at her, but Chick growled, 'Put 'em on, you great ninny! Your nose is glowing like a good deed in a naughty world. You can't arrive looking like that. Your Hamish'd be badly put out.'

'He's not my Hamish,' Robin said. 'And anyway, you saw his note – ' But it was an almost automatic retort. She'd got used to Chick's teasing about Hamish. She had for weeks insisted on behaving as though he and Robin were Tristan and Isolde or Abelard and Heloise come again, even though Robin had assured her over and over again that she regarded the big Scot as little more than a very good friend, but tonight she was too miserable to care anyway.

It had not been a good night last night. She and Chick had come on duty full of excitement because the next night was to be the first of four nights off duty, and starting with a party, today, expecting to find good old Sister Priestland – of whom both had grown very fond – bustling about as usual; only to discover that she had sprained her ankle in a bomb hole while crossing the yard and was off sick. Which meant that Staff Nurse Meek was in charge, her eyes gleaming with pleasure at the prospect of harrying all her juniors unmercifully, and Chick and Robin, for whom most of her ire was saved, most of all.

And harry them she had. How Chick had kept a civil tongue between her teeth had been little short of a miracle and Robin too had been goaded almost beyond bearing, with the most ill-named Nurse Meek sending her to do all the foulest cleaning-up jobs she could find for her, and then, after she'd done them, making Hamish go and do them again since Robin's efforts, as she told the entire department, patients and all, in a very loud voice, had been so puerile.

Hamish, who had a good line in dumb stoical acceptance had shown no reaction at all when this happened, except for throwing a sharp and minatory glance at Robin which almost in as many words warned her not to rise to the bait that Meek was so carefully trailing, and even when the Staff Nurse changed her tactics and started sending Robin to redo some of Hamish's jobs, kept his mouth firmly closed and his expression calm and unworried. And Robin, with that example, somehow managed to be quiet, too. But doing so had used up a great deal of her energy and she had gone off duty drooping, as Chick put it, like a lily three days after the funeral.

'That Meek woman is the biggest, most grade-A female animal I've ever come across!' Robin had exploded as they'd traipsed up to the night nurses' supper table. 'One of these days I'll put strychnine in her coffee. I swear it – '

'Not worth hanging for,' Chick said. 'And say what you mean. The woman's a bitch and cow and a – '

'Hush, Chick,' Robin warned, for they were within Night Sister's earshot now as she stood magisterially serving the night staff's meal, her way of making sure they were all present. 'They'll have you up for lèse-majesté or something – '

'The hell with it,' Chick said cheerfully. 'It was a female animal you said, wasn't it? All right then! If anyone listens in we were talking zoology. Oh, God, look at that! Dead baby and mashed innards as well. How can our guardians be so lousy to us?'

Robin had taken her portion of suet pudding with bacon bits in it and the pile of hideously mashed beets to her place at the table to stir it around and pretend to eat, and then had gone to bed to sleep uneasily all day, and had got up with the ghost of a headache to mar her anticipation of at least a better evening than she had experienced last night; only to find waiting for her a note from Hamish explaining tersely that he'd had his duty changed and had to be on until ten pm, so he'd be late at the party if he managed to get there at all, which he doubted, though he'd do his best.

She had to admit her disappointment wasn't so much because she wanted Hamish to be with her, fond though she had become of him; it was more that she needed him as an accessory. The thought of walking into her grandmother's party with just Chick beside her and seeing

179

Chloe's jeering stare made her face go hot – which in this ice-cold bus was at least a little comforting – because she always did manage to make Robin feel inadequate in such matters. To be accompanied by a young man of her own, for once, would have been so nice.

But there it was, she couldn't be, and somehow she'd have to carry it off. And she sighed there beside Chick, a little gustily, and was rewarded with a sharp glance and then a little squeeze of her arm.

'Fed up, ducky? Me too. Last night really was the pits.'

'Well, maybe dear old Priestland'll be back by the time we are,' Robin said, trying to sound optimistic. 'And maybe tonight'll be fun – though I'm beginning to doubt it.'

'Why? There'll be lots of your Auntie Jessie's food and that makes up for a hell of a lot.'

'Not for my grandmother looking daggers at Auntie Jessie and Auntie Jessie just laughing at her, which always makes the old lady worse, and Ma trying to keep the peace between them. This party seemed like a good idea when they talked about it two months ago. Now I'm not so sure. Those two cousins could turn out to be complete stuffed shirts, and there'll be Chloe – ' and again she lapsed into gloomy silence as she contemplated her half-sister's probable behaviour.

'Well, we'll just have to make the best of it. Where do we get out?' Chick peered out at the dark street outside and Robin did too and then jumped up.

'Dammit, we've gone too far,' she said. 'Come on.' And they tumbled off the bus at the next stop, only to find that in the blackout they'd managed to undershoot by two fare stages and so had to walk, in their thin dancing shoes, all the rest of the way.

But at least the exercise warmed them up and they arrived at the house at Leinster Terrace looking better than either of them knew, their eyes bright with the gloss of tears created by the cold, and their cheeks rosy.

The house was already full of people – not all of whom Robin knew – and she and Chick went upstairs to the drawing room, leaving their coats and ear-muffs and gloves and scarves downstairs with a sulky Queenie, who was obviously feeling highly put upon and letting everyone know it, both of them unusually quiet.

The house looked to Robin much more grand than it usually did; Mildred had somehow managed to find someone to collect masses of holly to tie to the wide sweep of the balustrade and its rich green and red glowed against the well-polished mahogany, leading them up to the first-floor hall where a large and surprisingly well-trimmed Christmas tree stood glittering with tinsel and coloured glass balls and a large shining star on the topmost branch.

Chick stopped suddenly and stared at it and then said abruptly in a tight voice, 'Oh, Robin, I do wish I was at home!' And Robin, taking no offence at all but understanding completely, took her arm and led her into the drawing room, determined to put her own ill temper aside and make the best of the evening for poor old Chick's sake. She didn't often give way to homesickness, and sometimes it must be misery for her.

Across the roomful of people a tall man in the elegance of Air Force blue saw the two girls coming in and let a slow smile move across his face. One was small and rather thin and had dark curly hair which she wore in a long bob, and the other was much taller, just as dark and curly but altogether more voluptuously built, and he watched her as the two girls moved across the room towards the corner where the old lady sat in her high-backed chair. And as the smaller of the two girls bent to kiss the old lady's cheek, he moved strategically across the room, making his way around the edges of the groups of talking people in an offhand sort of drifting way that made it seem as though he was doing nothing more than ambling gently with no purpose.

But he undoubtedly had one and it served him well; as

he reached the corner where the old lady sat surveying her party, the smaller of the two girls moved away, her attention drawn by the extraordinary old bat in crimson who had now arrived in the room, leaving the tall one talking to the occupant of the high-backed chair; and the man in Air Force blue moved in closer.

'– glad that you could come,' the old lady was saying. 'I much dislike the thought of dear Robin travelling alone in London during these difficult times. One never knows what might happen – and you too of course are better off with a companion. Now go and – '

'Hi, Aunt Mildred,' the man in blue said. 'I thought I'd just come and talk to you again, you know and – but I hope I'm not interrupting?'

'Not at all,' Chick said and looked at him consideringly. Tall. A definite plus, tall, for Chick, who had been complaining ever since her arrival of the shortage of men in London – 'meaning they're all like shrimps!' she would say to anyone who would listen. 'I can eat soup off most of their heads, and I know too many bald patches a great deal too intimately for my taste, believe me.' There were all too few men around she could, as she would say, look up to. This one was a good three inches above her, which made him six foot two. And there was more. He had an agreeable face and a charming smile and he was looking at her with warm approval. Chick stopped looking at him consideringly and instead beamed on him cheerfully and said again, 'Not at all!' but this time with a whole new emphasis on the words.

'This is my nephew Daniel Amberley from Johannesburg,' Mildred said and looked sharply up at him. 'Daniel, allow me to introduce my granddaughter's friend, Miss Chester.'

Chick put out one hand very directly. 'Hi!' she said.

He laughed then. 'Another colonial, like me? This has to be my lucky night.'

'Canadian,' Chick said. 'Glad you spotted it. I get sick to death of being called an American.'

'And I get just as sick being thought to be Australian,' he said. 'Will you excuse us, Aunt Mildred? This girl looks like she needs a drink.'

'That's what parties are for, I imagine,' Mildred said drily and watched them go, a slight crease between her brows. Chick, noticing it, felt a moment of chill and then forgot it. Old ladies – they had a tendency to look disapproving if you just breathed in. No need to fret over her. And she let herself be taken over to a long table at the far side where a punch bowl and glasses stood looking remarkably festive.

Robin was standing by the table, a punch cup in her hand, talking to the tall and slightly stooping figure of Sam Landow, and she turned as Chick came up to her and smiled.

'Feeling better?' she asked and Chick beamed at her.

'Amazingly better. It was just a moment's lapse, believe me. Here, let me be really cute – I've never had to introduce relations to each other before. Robin, were you ever wrong. This is no stuffed shirt. This is your cousin Daniel Amberley from South Africa, and Daniel, this is your cousin Robin Bradman. There! That's really an all time first for me!'

'Oh!' Robin said and stared at the tall man unashamedly and then, reddening slightly, remembered her manners. 'May I introduce Dr Sam Landow? Dr Landow, my cousin Daniel.'

'In the RAF?' Landow said as he shook hands. 'A South African?'

'Oh,' Daniel said easily and reached for a glass of punch being offered by the maid behind the table to give it to Chick and then take one for himself, 'they're very open-minded, you know. They'll even take some of us raw colonials. These are hard times, after all.'

He laughed and looked down at Chick who laughed too and then moved a fraction closer to him. Robin was startled. It was as though they had suddenly become opponents against herself and Sam Landow, a pair of invaders united against the residents, and she had never felt that with Chick before. And she had opened her mouth to make some sort of joke about England being grateful for all the help she could get these days when Chick moved away from him and whirled around, as on the other side of the room someone started to play a gramophone.

'Oh, lovely,' she said. 'Music! I thought there'd be just chat and eating and so forth – I love that song – ' And she began to sing along to it. '– It's a hap-hap-happy day, toodle-oodle-oodle-ay, you can't go wrong if you sing this song, it's a hap-hap-happy day – '

At once Daniel took her punch glass from her hand and set it down on the table. 'More than music!' he said and grinned at her, a great white glimmering grin, Robin thought, altogether overwhelming, as she watched him pull Chick into the middle of the room and begin to dance an energetic quickstep with her.

One or two people, the older ones, looked first a little startled, for no one else had made any effort to dance, and then moved good-naturedly aside to let the young pair have room. And almost at once other people began to dance and before the record was half over, there were five couples gyrating in the middle of the floor, even though it was carpeted, watched benignly by the people round the edges.

'Oh dear,' Sam Landow said in Robin's ear, as she stood there with one foot tapping in the music's rhythm. 'I wish I could dance. I'm sure you'd love to, but I have to tell you that dancing with me would be like walking a very crotchetty and bronchitic bulldog.'

She stood there and smiled at him, a little disappointed, for indeed the sight of the others dancing so vigorously was inviting, and said as kindly as she could, 'Oh, it's all right! I know it's a silly thing you do when you're young – it really doesn't matter – '

He looked at her with an expression of comical dismay. 'Heavens! How old do you think I am, then?'

'Oh dear,' she said, all compunction. 'Have I put my foot in it? I didn't mean to.'

'Of course not! I just wondered whether you saw me as some sort of old bock who – '

'I only ever heard Auntie Jessie use that word!' she said. 'I'm not sure what a bock is but – '

'Someone old and pretty hidebound,' he said. 'And believe me I'm not. I suppose I'm old in your eyes – no, don't tell me what you think I am, I couldn't bear it if you came out with something on the high side. For your information, I'm thirty-two. Is that past dancing, do you think?'

She smiled at him. 'Of course not! I mean *I* don't think it is. It's just that I thought perhaps you'd stopped liking dancing – '

'I never could do it,' he said and looked down at her with his face now showing just pleasant amusement. 'How old are you, Robin?'

'Twenty-one,' she said. 'It's ridiculous, isn't it? I feel about sixteen sometimes.' And she turned to look at the dancers again.

'Yes,' he said quietly, still looking at her. 'Ridiculous.'

'Chick's older than me, but sometimes she behaves much younger,' Robin said then, unaware of his scrutiny. 'She's great fun, isn't she?'

'Great fun,' he agreed. 'Now, listen, Robin. I have no right to monopolize you. You want to dance and I can't, so let me take you across the room to where there are people who I dare say can dance. Who is that young man there? I don't recognize the uniform – it's Army, clearly, but – '

Robin looked and then lifted her chin in a spurt of recognition. 'I do,' she said. 'I've seen newsreels. Australian army. That must be my other cousin from distant parts.'

'Heavens, do you have so many?'

'I don't really know. I gather there were all sorts of brothers my grandmother had who were far-flung, so I

185

dare say there are – but only two have come here at the moment, as I understand it. I suppose I ought to talk to him. Oh, and there's my mother with my aunt – I wondered where she was – '

The record ended and there was a little splatter of applause and Chick called, 'Oh, more please?' And whoever was looking after the gramophone obliged with 'A Nightingale Sang In Berkeley Square', and the dancers began to move again as Robin crossed the room to kiss her mother and Sam Landow followed her and was greeted like a long-lost relation by the ever ebullient Jessie.

'Ma,' Robin said under the cover of Jessie's loud chatter. 'Is that the other cousin?'

Poppy looked and then nodded. 'He looks rather dour, doesn't he?' she said. And indeed the young man in the rather ill-fitting uniform did look gloomy. He was square and solid, with dusty hair that he kept slicked down rather fiercely and a rather nondescript face. He was staring across the room at the dancers and Robin followed his line of vision and saw that it was Chick and Daniel he was watching so fixedly, and was a little amused. Good old Chick seemed to be doing rather well tonight, and she certainly looked as though she was having fun; she was laughing up at her partner as he swept her around in rather exaggerated foxtrot steps as the music wailed its familiar melody, and her eyes and cheeks seemed to be competing for a shine award. It suited her, thought Robin, and smiled as she caught Chick's eye and her friend winked at her, and she felt a sudden wave of melancholy sweep over her. Here she was at a party and no one to dance with; it really was too bad. And then, there was a little flurry at the door and three more people came in. And one of them was Hamish.

She had no idea how much her face lit up at the sight of him, but Poppy saw it and so did Sam Landow, and they both watched her as she moved quickly across the room to greet him, though each was thinking very different thoughts.

19

For the next hour and a half the party was, Robin felt,
the best she had ever been to. Hamish, having told her
briefly that the good-hearted relief Sister McCann had
let him go, firmly countermanding the egregious Meek's
instructions, had thrown himself into the proceedings
with considerable energy. He turned out, a little to
Robin's surprise, to be a superb dancer, if a little given
to making sudden swerves and twirls, and they danced
to every record played by the indefatigable gramophone
user – who, Robin discovered, was her stepfather, being as
he always was, useful and agreeable.

And when the dancing stopped because supper was
announced, she and Chick and Daniel and Hamish and
Dr Landow, who had been talking to the Australian
cousin Harry, all sat together on the floor of the dining
room, leaving the chairs to the much older guests, and ate
quantities of Jessie's good food, and laughed and joked a
great deal. Or at least Chick and Daniel did, putting on a
sparkling show for the rest of them.

Daniel was obviously a man of considerable social gifts,
with a fund of light-hearted chatter and good jokes that
had just enough edge of malice to make them sharply
witty, and Chick, who was clearly entranced by him,
proved an excellent foil. Robin, leaning against the wall
between Hamish and Sam Landow, watched her friend
and was happy for her; she hadn't looked so pleased with
herself for a very long time.

And Robin was also happy for herself, because the whole evening was turning out so well in so many different ways. First of all her grandmother and her Aunt Jessie hadn't had a spat with each other. This was a remarkable thing in Robin's experience. She had only the haziest notion of why the two of them should be so sharp with each other when they met, though she did know that it had something to do with Poppy's childhood when both had looked after her for a while, and that therefore there was a certain rivalry between them, but Robin had frankly never really cared that much about why it happened. She had just disliked it heartily when it did, and to spend an evening with the two of them under the same roof with no flounces from Auntie Jessie and no dry sharp comments from her grandmother was a delight.

But best of all, she had here just the members of her immediate family she wanted, her mother and stepfather, sitting between Jessie and Mildred at the table and gossiping contentedly, and no one else at all. Most especially there was no Chloe. And she sighed happily and returned her attention to Daniel who was telling a long, involved and apparently enthralling story involving a Boer farmer and a Bantu girl and the local pastor, which was holding the attention of the others like a vice.

Or was it? Her gaze slid along the group and came to rest on the square bulk of her cousin Harry. He showed no sign of any emotion at all. He just sat and ate – a large amount, in fact – and listened and watched them all but said little. When people had offered him a dish from which to help himself he had nodded politely and taken it with brief thanks. When anyone talked to him – mostly Sam Landow – he answered in mono-syllables, and Robin found that puzzling. If he was so unwilling to make any effort to get to know the people amongst whom he found himself, why had he written to his aunt in the first place? Her grandmother had invited them, as Robin understood it, in order not just to meet them but to give them the chance to make new social contacts in a strange city. Well, Daniel was obviously using that opportunity to the point of wringing it out like a piece of tired muslin, but his cousin was doing nothing at all. And Robin felt irritated by that, rather than sorry for him. She wondered why, and then realized it was because his face wasn't entirely expressionless after all. Looking at him again she thought – he's jealous. Jealous of Daniel, that's what it is. And she glanced again at Daniel and saw how closely Chick had placed herself next to him and the way she looked in the tall man's face, and understood. Poor Harry, she thought then. He'd like to be with Chick himself. And preened a little on her friend's behalf.

But then sharply the bubble of pleasure in which the party had wrapped her burst and all its iridescent charm vanished. She was a dull ordinary girl sitting on the floor with her back to the wall and surrounded by sticky plates, staring at the doorway in which a vision was standing.

'My darlings!' fluted the vision, which was closely draped in shimmering blue silk which swept to the floor, at which point it was edged with very soft white fur. 'Did you think we were never coming? Well, here we are and the party can start at last! Madly sorry, but we simply had to go to the old War House. The General's pre-Christmas do, you know – he'd have been livid if we'd missed it – '

A silence had fallen on the room as everyone had turned to stare at the doorway's occupant and then David got to his feet, and Robin, in the middle of her own sense of lurching disappointment, was aware of how typical it was of him to walk into any awkwardness and try to smooth it out.

'Well, better late than never, Chloe, my dear,' he said. 'And how are you?' And he bent forward and kissed her cheek, which she proferred in what Robin regarded as the silliest film-starish manner imaginable. 'And your friend too – ah – Captain Stanniforth, wasn't it? I think we met at Ley On's one night – '

'Yes, indeed, yes, we did, sir.' The vision's companion stepped forward, very dapper in a perfectly pressed dress uniform on which a good deal of red braid was scattered. 'How de do – '

The room became noisier then as people at the table and around it, sitting on the floor like Robin's group, relaxed and began to chatter again, as David took the newcomers towards the food and drink.

'Well!' Daniel said and grinned down at Chick. 'As my old Daddy used to say, there's nothing quite like putting all your goods in the store window, is there? Question is, are there any wares inside to match up to what's on offer?'

Chick, whose face had fallen at the sight of Chloe, for she really was breathtaking to look at, at once lightened. 'You have a point there, my colonial friend! We're a bit leery about that sort of lady where I come from too! Who is she, Robin? Do you know?'

Robin, watching Chloe sparkling and performing for the delectation of everyone around her, and especially for her straight-backed Captain in his over-garnished uniform, looked miserable. 'She's my half-sister,' she said shortly.

There was an appalled silence and then Chick, mortified, scrambled across the space between them to put her hand on Robin's knee.

'Oh, pull my tongue out with red-hot pincers and feed it to the wolves! I'm sorry, ducky – '

'It's all right,' Robin said a little wearily. 'She has that effect on everyone. She's a bit – well, my mother says she was rather spoiled. And you have to admit she's marvellously good-looking.'

'Not at all.' It was Harry who spoke and everyone now stared at him in some surprise, except Sam Landow who was still looking at Chloe with his brows slightly creased. 'She thinks she is, and so she sends out a message telling everyone that she is. So that's what everyone else believes. It's a common enough trick.'

Again there was a silence and then Sam laughed.

'I couldn't agree with you more, Harry. I have nothing against the lady at all – agreeable to look at and so forth. But I am intrigued by someone who finds it so necessary to make an impact. She comes late, dresses in a way that you can't deny is outrée, if interesting, and manages to make a room full of people talk about her and only her. Just look at those over there. All fascinated by her. But when you really look at her, it's a pleasant enough face but fairly ordinary. She's a self-created thing – make-up, and clothes and manner. Quite fascinating – '

'Yes,' Harry said. 'That's what I thought,' and lapsed again into silence.

'Well, I'm not talking about her,' Hamish said and there was something a little wooden in his tone. 'I don't think it's verra kind of us to be criticizing a relation of our hostess – '

'Oh, don't worry about that, Hamish,' Robin said, a little bitterly. 'We all have our problems with my sister Chloe! All except Grandmamma, that is, but then she's special. Anyway, let's all go upstairs, shall we? Maybe someone else can play the gramophone as David's busy, and we can dance again – '

It was suddenly important to Robin that they all escape from what she regarded as Chloe's baleful influence, and she was very relieved when they all got to their feet obediently.

'I'll deal with the gramophone,' Sam Landow offered and Robin smiled at him gratefully.

'That would be lovely,' she said and gave Hamish a small push so that he led the way to the door. If they could just get out of the dining room and upstairs before Chloe saw her and her friends, perhaps it could all be all right – still –

And at first it seemed it would be. Sam played a tango and then a rumba record and that made them all laugh immoderately as they struggled to deal with the steps, and when the record finished it was generally agreed that Hamish, with Robin battling gamely to keep up with him, had been far and away the best; and then as Robin protested her shame at her own inability to dance as well as her partner, the hated voice broke in from the doorway.

'You're absolutely right, Robin, darling. A man who dances a rumba like that deserves a chance to really show it off. Darling – there at the gramophone – do I know you? Well, never mind. *Do* put that divine thing on again and we'll have another try at it. It will be bliss after dancing with you, Colin, my sweet. There are a number of things you do superbly well but the rumba isn't one of them.'

And she moved towards Hamish as the record started again, though with a little jerk, as though the person putting it on had been clumsy for some reason, and then, as the sickly sweet sobbing of the violin began, she put her arms up to Hamish, and he, apparently unable to do otherwise, accepted her as a partner.

There was no doubt she could dance. Robin watched her, trying as hard as she could not to let her anger show in her face, as Hamish threw himself into his dancing with even more fervour. Now he had a partner who understood the dance and could do it well, he was even better than he had been. They swooped gloriously about the room, Chloe with her head thrown back in true Latin American haughtiness and Hamish looking quite magnificent with his bulk and his swiftness. So much so that when the record came to and end everyone in the room applauded them, and there was a good deal of badinage from some of the other people who had come up from the dining room, which made Hamish go red with pleasure and made Chloe, thought Robin spitefully, preen like a demented bird.

From then on, Chloe and her partner seemed to become part of the group that had been formed by Chick and Robin as naturally as though it had been ordained by some higher power. The sharp remarks they had shared earlier about her seemed to have had no effect on either Chick or Daniel, and Harry remained his own silent self, and Sam too, who, when he wasn't playing records for them all, watched with quiet interest but contributed little. Now it was a threesome who sparkled, rather than just a duet, and Robin felt her throat tighten and the muscles across her back become ever more tense as she watched her happy evening break up around her.

Because there was no doubt that Chloe was flirting quite shamefully with Hamish. She would make some wicked little remark and then look at him sideways with a twinkle that made his stern face relax, and then would say something wheedling that made him actually laugh, and Robin got angrier and angrier. How dare she steal her escort like this when she had a perfectly serviceable one of her own? And she looked at Colin Stanniforth and felt a little better, for he too was watching Chloe's efforts with anger in his expression. And Robin, with a rare touch of malice said quietly to him, 'Well, I never knew my sister to be so attracted to a man who's one of the quiet sort! She does seem to like him, doesn't she?'

Colin made some sort of noise indicating acquiescence as he watched the dancers come to the end of a waltz, during which Chloe had brought her face as close to Hamish's as it could be without their cheeks actually touching, and then as they came up to where he was standing, said in what seemed a pleasant enough voice but which to Robin had an edge of dislike in it, 'Well, well! That's quite a grasp you have of the art of ballroom dancing, Mr ah – ah – '

'Todd,' Hamish said quietly and looked down at Chloe, who still had her hand resting on his shoulder as though she had inadvertently forgotten to let go when the music ended. 'I learned from my older sisters. They were very keen, and needed a tall partner to help them along with their own efforts.'

'Oh,' Stanniforth said and smiled a little thinly. 'I thought perhaps you'd learned it in the officers' mess somewhere. We have regular dances in ours. Don't you?'

Hamish looked at him. His face, though still a little flushed from the effort of dancing in a room which was getting steadily hotter, was composed enough. 'I'm not in the Army, Captain,' he said.

'Ah! My mistake! Navy then? Air Force?'

'Neither of them.'

'Oh! I imagined you must be on the sick list or something of the sort. One usually does get that notion, don't you know, when one sees an able bodied chap in mufti – unless you're in one of these what-do-they-call-'em reserved occupations? Doctor, perhaps, or such like? Though most of the chaps with that sort of training I know couldn't wait to get into uniform to do their bit.'

Around them the rest of the group had gathered, all except Sam Landow who had gone back to deal with the gramophone, and Daniel, one eyebrow cocked, looked at Chick and then at Stanniforth and said easily, 'Hey old man, lay off! Chap'll think you're accusing him of a being a conchie next! I dare say there's a good reason for him not being in uniform. Not fit maybe. You can't always go by looks, can you? Could be he's just not able to do the sort of concentrated hard work that's necessary in the mob – ' And then he looked at Hamish and nodded cheerfully at him. 'Eh, fella? You tell him!'

'I am perfectly fit,' Hamish said steadily. 'And I work hard. As a hospital orderly. And you were perfectly right. I *am* a conscientious objector.'

The silence that struck them was made even sharper by the wail of the record that Sam had put on before being relieved at his post by David, who had just come up from the dining room. 'It's a lovely day tomorrow,' the saxophones wailed and as Sam joined them he looked at Robin's face, which was stiff with embarrassment and anger, and then looked around at the rest of them, and said with cheerful good humour, 'No more listen-to-the-music for me! It's time I learned to dance, I think, useless as I am. Robin, could you bear to teach me? I'd be most grateful – ' And not waiting for a reply he took her elbow and drew her into the middle of the room.

He knew how to go through the motions of dancing, at least, and put his arm around her in the approved manner and took her right hand, and began to walk a little awkwardly to the rhythm of the music. 'What was all that about, then?' he said quietly. 'You looked as though you'd caught a direct hit.'

Robin was almost in tears of mortification and had to swallow hard before she could answer.

'It's my sister – oh, I do hate her sometimes! I know I shouldn't, but she makes it impossible not to.'

'Why shouldn't you hate her?'

'I told you. She's my sister.'

'A very good reason to hate someone, I'd say,' he said judiciously. 'I've a brother I simply loathe. Have ever since he was born. We do fine as long as we're not within a hundred miles of each other.'

She managed a watery little grimace of a smile. 'Well, I wish Chloe kept herself a hundred miles away. That horrible friend of hers is having a go at Hamish for being a conchie, just because he's jealous of the way Chloe was flirting with Hamish. I could see it in his face – '

'Are you jealous too?' he said, even more quietly, and managed to make a sort of reverse turn as they reached the end of the dancing area and were at real risk of going into the wall.

'Me, jealous?' She managed to laugh then. 'As if I'd be jealous of – oh, damn it, of course I am! She's so pretty and looks so marvellous all the time and she's – it's the way she doesn't *care* about anything. I couldn't be like that, even if I tried.'

'Would you like to be?'

'Oh, sometimes, of course I would. Wouldn't you? Wouldn't it be lovely to just do what you like when you like and never have to worry about anyone else's feelings? Me, if I go to bed in the morning before calling Ma I get swallowed up in a guilty conscience. Not Chloe – she doesn't bother to call anyone for weeks and weeks and then if anyone says anything she gets simply hateful. Of course I get jealous of her – '

'You needn't be. Being the way you are makes you a much nicer person.'

'To other people maybe,' Robin said gloomily. 'But she has more fun.' And she watched over his shoulder as the conversation between Chloe and Stanniforth and Hamish and Daniel went on. At least he hadn't walked out in a rage as she would have thought he might –

'I wondered actually if you were jealous because she was flirting with your Hamish,' Landow said then.

'Jealous of – such stuff! And he's not my Hamish! It's just that he's a friend and – oh, I don't know! Let's not talk about it, for heaven's sake.'

'By all means,' he said courteously. 'Just tell me where I'm going wrong with these steps. I know what we're doing isn't dancing. So what should I do with – Oh! The record's over. Shall we try again when your father – '

But she's slipped away from him, back to the group; but she was too late. Hamish was no longer there, and Chick was speaking heatedly to Stanniforth as she came up.

'– it's no one else's business anyway!' she was saying and she turned as Robin came up to her and said impulsively, 'Look, ducks, I'm sorry, I've been a bit overheated with one of your guests – I'm truly sorry. But I just get so mad sometimes – ' And she broke away and headed for the door, with, after a moment of surprise, Daniel at her heels.

'Well!' Robin said and glared at Chloe. 'I hope you're satisfied!'

'Darling!' Chloe opened her eyes wide. 'What did I do? Not a thing, believe me! It's dear old Colin here who got hot under the collar and put the old foot in it. But you can't really blame him. Here he is, giving his little all for king and country and so forth and it's maddening to see these other characters skiving off – '

'Absolutely got it in one, old thing, naturally gets a chap's back up. Don't mean to offend your guests though, I must say – ' Colin Stanniforth looked as pleased with himself as a well-fed baby, in spite of his words, and Robin threw him a withering look and then ignored him.

'Hamish is not a skiver,' she said hotly. 'He's a damned hard worker. If you or any of your friends had to do some of the ghastly work he has to do you'd know. Not that you lot do much at the War Office but polish seats with your bottoms, as far as I can tell! I'd like to see you deal with the buckets of blood and – and – mess he deals with night after night. So let's have a little bit of – '

Chloe lifted her brows at her, looking angry for the first time. 'No need to be coarse, sweetie,' she said sharply. 'We all do our bit in our own way. And less detail, if you please.' She smiled then, suddenly emollient. 'Leave it be, there's a lamb. No harm meant and none done, I'm sure. Just a few ruffled feelings. You go and tell your little friend we're all madly sorry to have hurt his sensitive feelings, though seeing he's got so many of them, it's hard not to, of course – '

Robin opened her mouth again to argue and then shook her head and turned away furiously. 'Good night,' she said, almost spitting it. 'I have to get back. Chick'll be waiting for me – ' And she went stomping off across the floor to say goodnight to her grandmother and stepfather and then marched out of the room, totally ignoring Chloe and Stanniforth, and necessarily, Sam Landow who was still standing beside them, watching thoughtfully.

There was a silence after she'd gone and then Chloe, seeming unaware that Sam was still standing there said softly, 'Well, well! Who'd have thought the little one'd ever be so spirited? Pity she got herself mixed up with a conchie, though!'

'Disgusting, if you ask me!' Stanniforth said. 'I'd stand the buggers against a wall and shoot 'em, begging your presence, of course. But really, it's a bit much when we're fighting a bloody war to have these fellas sneaking off under cover of their so-called consciences and getting away with it.'

'Oh, he's not that bad,' Chloe said and still she stared at the door, a little dreamily, as though she could still see Hamish and Robin on the other side of it. 'It's my bet he could be made to see the error of his ways. He needs someone to make a real man of him, wouldn't you say?'

'Can't be done,' Stanniforth said. 'He's just a coward, a damn useless coward – '

'What would you put on it?' Chloe looked at him sharply.

'Eh?'

'You heard me. Put your money where your mouth is, darling. Make me a bet I can't get that man into uniform. I know I can do it. You say I can't. Well, how much says I can't? I'll bet you ten to one, in fivers, that I *can* do it.'

He looked at her dubiously. 'In fivers –?'

'In fivers. Ten to one. Well?'

Stanniforth managed a smile, but it was a strained one. 'Really, Chloe, you do go a bit far, sometimes.'

'Not as far as I'd like to. Listen, are you on? I'll have that great lump of porridge dolled up in a uniform of some sort or another before the summer. I need a little time, of course – '

'Three months,' Stanniforth said promptly, grabbing at the slim opportunity he saw; and then his face fell, because she nodded emphatically.

'You're on! I'll keep you informed of what's going on, I promise. But you'd better start saving.' And with one last smile at him, she turned and went to get herself another drink from the diminishing store of punch, as Stanniforth stared gloomily after her.

20

'So, there you are, Poppy.' Jessie leaned back and took a deep breath which turned into a huge yawn. 'We've done it. But ain't it enough we got all the rest of the business to worry about without having to deal with an audit? You'd think, wouldn't you, in these hard times they'd leave us in peace?'

Poppy managed to laugh, but it was a tired one. She had in fact done most of the necessary extra work demanded by the approaching audit, and that had needed perforce to be left till after the restaurant had closed, eating away at her canteen hours. But she'd still tried to put in some time there, so as not to exploit Maria and Flo and Edna and all the rest of them too much; so she was as near to total exhaustion as she had ever been. Even breathing seemed to be an effort, let alone laughing.

'It's necessary, darling, and you know it. It's not as bad as the next one, though – the end of the financial year – '

Jessie groaned. 'Enough already! Let next April worry about itself. I got enough with the Christmas one. Listen, you'll have something to eat before you go home?'

Poppy hesitated. She'd had a long day, acting as waiter as well as bookkeeper and cashier over at her own restaurant, because both Horace and Minnie were off sick with heavy colds, and what she needed most of all was sleep. But she hadn't eaten all day that she could remember, apart from snatched cups of tea – blessed tea! – and there was no need to hurry home. David had warned her he might not get home tonight, because something big was blowing up, he'd been warned, and he'd probably stay at the office. To return to a silent and shuttered house occupied only by the sleeping Goosey wouldn't be any real pleasure, after all. She had a moment of pricking conscience over Goosey and then dismissed it. The old lady would sleep late as she always did these days, and wouldn't even know Poppy hadn't got home till all hours.

'A little something easy,' she said. 'I couldn't manage anything too heavy, so late – '

'Soup,' Jessie said, looking at her with sharp anxiety. 'I had some marvellous bean and barley today, best you ever tried. Decent beef bones for once – it'll take only a minute.'

When they were both sitting over the big bowls of fragrant soup and pile of rolls that Jessie had inevitably added to the meal, Jessie said with studied nonchalance, 'So – the little one, how is she?'

'I wish you wouldn't call her that,' Poppy said with sudden sharpness. 'She's not a child any more.'

'She'll always be the little one to me,' Jessie said comfortably. 'Just as you'll always be my Poppela.'

'Fiddle-de-dee,' said Poppy and drank more soup.

There was a short silence and then Jessie said, 'All, the same, how is she?'

'Oh, damned irritating!' Poppy burst out and put down her spoon with a little clatter. 'She does nothing but work and work. Swotting for exams and so forth, I know, but all the same – '

'Won't talk, huh?' Jessie said sympathetically.

'The proverbial oyster,' Poppy said with some bitterness. 'But I'm not as silly as she thinks. It's that wretched Hamish who's upsetting her.'

'You think it's serious then?' Jessie looked almost comically dismayed. 'He's not right for our little – our Robin.'

'Who can say who's right for anyone? All I know is that something happened at the party to upset her over him and ever since there've been all sorts of problems. I talked to Chick and she was unwilling to gossip – '

'Nice girl, that Chick,' Jessie said and reached for a roll and pushed the plate towards Poppy. 'I always say you can tell what people are like from their friends and that Chick proves what a lovely girl our Robin is.'

Poppy had to laugh. 'Darling Jessie, does everything have to revolve around you and yours this way?'

Jessie looked surprised. 'Of course!'

'Well, I suppose – anyway, Chick said that it was because Chloe was making a pest of herself.'

Jessie looked dark then. 'Chloe makes a lot of trouble for all sorts of people. Not just now, either. Always did – '

'We won't talk about that, Jessie,' Poppy said firmly, and for a moment there was a chill between them inhabited by Bernie. 'All I know is she seems to be seeing something of Hamish and – '

'And Robin's annoyed. What girl wouldn't be?' Jessie got to her feet and went to fetch the inevitable pot of tea and with it a plate of her apple strudel. 'It doesn't mean a lot. It doesn't mean she wants to make it a serious thing.'

'I wish I could be so sure,' Poppy said, almost absently, and Jessie looked at her and smiled in satisfaction.

'So you don't think he's right for Robin, either.'

'It's none of my business,' Poppy said. 'She's an adult now, for good or ill, and she has to make her own choices.' But she was uneasy and it showed.

'Maybe I shouldn't have made so free with my invitations to your party,' Jessie said after a while and Poppy made a face.

'Mildred's party as much as mine, and yes, you're right. Maybe you shouldn't have. But since when did you ever stop to think when you wanted to invite people anywhere? Especially when the food's in your department? No, don't blame yourself, love. This would have happened anyway.'

She got to her feet and stretched. 'Time I was going home. I'll be at Poppy's tomorrow at the usual time. With a bit of luck Minnie'll be back, and that should help. But

201

if you can spare a pair of waiters' hands I'd be grateful. Is Jessie's staff doing all right?'

'Touch wood. No one off at all. I'll send old Ivor, if you're pushed. Give me a ring.'

'I'll do that – ' Poppy began to shrug herself into her coat and searched her pockets for gloves and scarf and Jessie watched her and then said awkwardly, 'You need some more stuff for the canteen?'

Poppy had her head down as she fixed her scarf, and her hands stopped moving for a moment but she didn't look up and then went on with what she was doing.

'No thanks,' she said lightly. 'I've managed to make an arrangement with the M of F. They've agreed to send me the same supplies they're giving the British restaurants. So we're managing fine – '

'I can get you fish,' Jessie said. 'There's no black market in fish. Some kippers, maybe, or salmon? They'd like that, your firefighters and wardens – '

'No doubt,' Poppy said and now she did look at Jessie. 'But I wouldn't. I'm sorry, Jessie, but it was bad enough I accepted things that once. It helped at the time and I won't deny it, but I felt dreadful about it and still do. Thank heavens I've got enough now not to need to take anything from – from you.'

'From Bernie you mean,' Jessie said flatly. 'Oh, Poppy, I wish you didn't hate him so!'

Poppy shook her head. 'It's not as simple as that, though, is it, Jessie? I'm not just being awkward. It's not like Robin finding Chloe so tiresome. It's that Bernie is bad news. He treats you abominably and always has – '

'He does not!' Jessie flared. 'He's a good son to me – '

'When it suits him, darling,' Poppy said gently. 'When it suits him because he wants to use you in some way, he's all over you. But when all is well with him, do you hear a word? You know you don't. That's why I won't get involved with him. He's a – '

Jessie was on her feet, her face red. 'It's enough,' she said and her voice was husky. 'It's enough already. I should know better than to even ask. Listen, take care of yourself on the way home. Get a taxi if you can. At least it's quiet tonight. No sirens – '

'Maybe they're sick of it. Maybe the raids are going to stop – ' Poppy said, glad to change the subject, and headed for the door. 'Who knows?'

'Who knows indeed,' Jessie said grimly and then reached for the light switch. 'Here. I'll turn off so I can come and see you off the premises on your way – '

'Thanks,' Poppy said, knowing the old lady needed to make the gesture. She hated arguing with her aunt as much as Jessie hated crossing swords with her; and the only time they ever did was when Bernie came into the picture. Poppy had seen nothing of him since his reappearance last autumn, but she was very aware of the fact that he was still around and still using the cellars here at Cable Street for his own dubious purposes.

Poppy had actually wondered what would happen if she turned informer and directed the police to the cellars. That would deal with Bernie in a very satisfying manner, but what would it do to Jessie? And what would it do to the business? Possibly the police wouldn't believe that the whole thing was Bernie's doing. They'd be sure to think that Jessie and Poppy themselves had benefited; and hadn't she been stupid enough once actually to accept goods from Bernie via Jessie? The fact that it had been only once and that she had been in dire need for her firemen and wardens was beside the point. The police would be sure to see the worst side of it all. No, she couldn't dispose of the hateful Bernie that way, no matter what. But she could pray and often did that he would disappear again out of their lives as suddenly as he had returned to them.

Outside the street was bitterly cold, and she hugged her gloved hands under her arms to protect them from it, and waited a moment till her eyes had become accustomed to the darkness and could see the faint clouds of her own breath steaming in the bitter air.

'I'll be sure to get a taxi at Aldgate,' she said. 'Or a train. One or the other. Goodnight, darling. Speak to you in the morning – ' And she kissed Jessie and then went, leaving the old woman to lock herself back inside and to brood over her son. Poppy knew that she did that, knew she spent more time thinking about him and worrying over him than he could ever have deserved, and it made her bitterly angry. Jessie was worth more than that, and once again she marvelled that so warm and good a woman could have reared so unpleasant a son.

A thought that made her think of her own mothering. She walked quickly through the dark streets, knowing almost by instinct where the kerbs were, and where the dangers might be, the faint light of her pocket torch bobbing ahead of her (and heaven knew where she'd next get any number eight batteries for it; they were like gold dust these days) and thought of her children.

Lee seemed to be the only happy one, or at least contented one. She wrote long solemn letters about her schoolwork and her life on the farm with Goosey's nephew and his wife and in the village where she had made enough friends to fill page after page with her round writing of accounts of their exploits and activities. She ended each letter by telling her mother to take care of herself and make sure she kept out of the way of the bombs and added rows of kisses that straggled off the page. Lovely warm comforting letters, Lee's were.

Joshy's weren't. He poured out his misery and his home-sickness in spidery writing well illustrated with blots and exaggerated accounts of his anguish. He would tell her he didn't get enough to eat, which Poppy knew to be untrue, for one of the things that Lee's letters tended to include was detailed accounts of their meals; all of which, as far as Poppy could tell, were embellished with quantities of the sorts of treats that only farmers could possibly enjoy these days. Eggs seemed to be plentiful and so far they ate only butter at the farm's kitchen table, and scorned margarine. So Poppy had written back to assure Joshy that she wasn't worried about how much he ate, at which he'd changed tack and wrote piteously about his bad dreams and sleepless nights. Poppy had phoned the farm then, taking ages to get through and had been greeted with clucking and some laughter by Goosey's nephew.

'That lad?' he burred at her. 'That little lad sleeps right fit to bust hisself and there's the truth of it. I'm late to bed and early up and he's always spark out when I look in on him. Believe me, Mrs Poppy, the lad's a-teasing of you. He's as happy as a sandboy most of the time. It's only when he has to go to school on Fridays when they do music he gets upset – '

'Music?' Poppy said then, remembering Mildred's words. 'Music upsets him?'

'He reckons Miss Summers don't know so much as he does about it,' the voice said and laughed fatly. 'And he's right. She doesn't. Other than that, he ain't got no cause to complain. He's as brown as a nut and getting that chubby – he'll need new trousers he will, any minute now. An' shoes and underwear, the missus says – '

So Poppy had sent new clothes in her next parcel and at the last moment had collected the trumpet her mother had told her of from the attics at Leinster Terrace, and sent it as well, together with a request to Mr Gosling to seek out a teacher in Norwich who might be able to help Joshy with it. Maybe, she told herself now, as she reached the main road and could at last glimpse the dim glow across it that showed where the entrance to the underground station was, maybe that would help him settle better. It would be dreadful if he ran away again –

And then she thought about Robin and felt the black curtain come down over her. She loved all her children with an equal passion, but it could not be denied that there had always been and always would be a special emotion saved for Robin. She was the child of her first and deepest love, as well as her first-born, so how could it be otherwise? And to see Robin as miserable as she now undoubtedly was, was sometimes more than she could bear. It made her so angry that there were times that she could have shouted aloud her fury, but she dared not, knowing she would direct it wrongly, at Robin herself. The girl was unhappy enough without being blamed as the author of her own troubles, though in truth that was how Poppy saw it. To fall in love with someone who allowed himself to be beguiled by someone like Chloe – how could she be so silly? And even as she thought about that, she knew how unjust she was being, for how could she help falling in love, poor child? How could anyone? And she thought confusedly of Bobby who had died before his daughter had been born, and of David who had been for Robin the best father any girl could have wanted and felt her eyes fill with tears, and then sniffed them away angrily, knowing them to be born as much of her fatigue as her concern over her children. It really was a miserable business being Poppy Deveen at the moment, she told herself drearily as at last she reached the station and saw on the board that there was another train still expected to run to the West End, and plunged gratefully down to pick her way past the sleeping shelterers to wait for it. Once she got home she'd be fine, she promised herself. There'd be peace and comfort there and a chance to sleep away her miseries.

But it wasn't to be so. She came in to find not the half-lit silence she expected but the hall light on and the wireless playing, muffled, from the kitchen, and alarmed, she hurried downstairs to the kitchen to see what was wrong. For Goosey to be up at this hour there had to be something badly amiss. Or was it David? Had he perhaps come home after all? And she was furious with herself for not being here if he had.

But it was just Goosey sitting there asleep in her chair, while the wireless on the dresser played organ music by Sandy McPherson, and Poppy stood at the top of the steps looking down at the familiar old kitchen with its polished black range and its rag rug and tried to find the sense of security and comfort in it that she usually did, and couldn't, for she was filled with anxiety. Why on earth was Goosey sitting up so late? It was now past midnight –

She woke her more sharply than she meant to and the old woman dragged herself out of her sleep in response to Poppy's hand shaking her arm and stared at her with confused milky eyes, bewildered and frightened; and then her expression cleared and she was Goosey again, dear familiar old Goosey.

'Well, there you are, Mrs Poppy – I thought you'd be back long before this, but there, with these dratted raids and that there canteen o' yours who can know what's what? So I thought I'd better just sit here and wait for you and not just leave the letter for you – '

'What letter?' Poppy could have shaken her again, she was so frustrated, but she controlled her impulse and said again more gently, 'What letter, Goosey?'

'Mr David's.' The old woman hauled herself out of her chair and went padding across the room to the dresser, and then Poppy saw it and darted in front of her to pick up the big white envelope that was leaning against the blue and white willow pattern teapot, and had it open and the pages smoothed out even before Goosey had reached the dresser herself.

'Darling,' she read. 'I hoped you'd be home in time for me to say a proper goodbye, but I couldn't wait any longer. The thing is, they want me to cover a convoy of merchantmen from the US. Don't panic – they're not all sinking by any means. And I'll be very carefully looked after. Foreign correspondents tend to be coddled – dinner with the captain and all that – so there's no need to fret yourself. The trip starts in Boston and takes the route that runs north of Ireland to Liverpool. It's well accompanied – corvettes, cruisers, the lot. (Is that info. me indulging in 'Careless talk'? Of course not – *you* won't tell Adolf, will you?) Anyway, it may take a while. I go to Liverpool tonight and they're taking me out to meet the convoy on one of their smaller corvettes or whatever they call them.

By the time I get back I'll be deeply knowledgeable about nautical terms, take it from me. Don't worry, darling, but it will take time – I may have to go further than at present is planned, and that means I could be away as much as four weeks. I've made sure that the Admiralty will have all the information about where we are at all times (to the best of my ability, that is!) so don't worry, you'll get news of me as often as possible. But remember that "often as possible" could turn out to be hardly at all. They're fighting this war as best they can and putting things in order of priority, and let's face it sweetheart, our billets doux aren't exactly top priority. But you are with me and always will be and I'll be thinking of you. This could be the best piece of reporting I've done yet, you know that? Take care, sweetheart, I love you absolutely ever so much all the time. D.'

She put the letter back in its envelope carefully and lifted her head and looked at old Goosey who was making the inevitable pot of tea from the kettle which had been sitting hissing quietly to itself on the range.

'It's all right, Goosey,' she said and was enormously pleased with herself, for her voice was as steady as it normally was. 'Mr David's had to go on a special job and he'll be away a while – '

'How long a while?' Goosey said bluntly, still bent over the kettle, her plait of thin grey hair flopping over her shoulder to make her look like a very elderly baby. 'And where?'

'Maybe a month or so,' Poppy said, and was still steady. 'As to where –' And she looked down at the envelope in her hand and then folded it carefully and put it in her pocket. 'To sea, Goosey,' she said and this time her voice shook a little. 'He's going with an American food convoy, on the North Atlantic run – '

And then she turned and went upstairs, leaving Goosey alone with her tea, unable to stay another moment. Because she knew there were tears of desperate fear in her own eyes, and greatly suspected they'd be in Goosey's too. And she couldn't have borne to see them.

· 21 ·

Christmas came and went in a flurry of activity, but not much fun. At the hospital great efforts were made to provide the patients with a little Christmas cheer, with boxes of last year's decorations being dug out of ward cupboards and arranged hastily on battered walls, and a measure of beer provided for every adult male patient and a glass of sherry for every woman. The children were lavished with sweets from staff and from parents, so they had a lovely time making themselves thoroughly sick, and by the end of Boxing Day Robin and Chick, like most of the nursing staff, were exhausted and thoroughly out of temper with the whole notion of Yuletide.

'As if there wasn't enough to do without all this!' Chick said disgustedly on the Sunday after Christmas, looking at the rows of drunks, sporting assorted examples of battered anatomy, who filled the waiting hall benches in Casualty. 'It's odds on they'll start raiding us again tonight – it hasn't been that much of a respite, Christmas or not – and the last thing we want is boozers getting in the way.'

'You wouldn't mind so much if you weren't tired out,' Robin said and lifted her head from the pile of mackintoshes she was scrubbing. Staff Nurse Meek was still being as hateful as she knew how to be to Robin and Hamish, and Robin consequently spent more of her time up to her elbows in dirty water than any other nurse. 'What time did you get to bed today?'

Chick was evasive. 'Early enough,' and went on spreading kaolin and lint to make the antiphlogistine poultices that the department used in such vast amounts for the treatment of infected wounds and boils. 'God, I hate this job. It's like putty, this stuff, and the smell of it – '

'I rather like it. It beats crappy macks, anyway,' Robin said, and wiped her forehead with the back of her hand. Her fingers were red and swollen with cold because the hospital's hot water was at low ebb following a raid earlier in the week which had caught the big boiler-house at the rear of the courtyard. 'And don't change the subject – '

'The only reason I have to do 'em,' Chick said, studiously not looking at Robin, 'is because that grade-A bitch Meek, may she rot, has taken it into her head to punish anyone who dares to be a friend of yours. I've heard of vindictive, but she honestly is the end – '

'She's going next week. All you have to do is be patient,' Robin said. 'And the Main Theatres can have her and welcome. It'll get easier then. So, tell me – were you out with both of them again today?'

'Oh, damn you, Robin Bradman,' Chick said. 'You're as bad as my mother used to be, always quizzing – all right, so I did. So what? Work's so miserable at the moment that I have to do the best I can with my days to make it tolerable.'

'Just make sure Night Sister doesn't find out you're not in your room by noon, that's all,' Robin said. 'She can't be fooled by a bolster in the bed for ever. What I can't understand is why you go out with both of 'em at the same time.'

'It's a bit tricky – ' Chick agreed, and began to spread gauze over the layer of grey kaolin she had at last finished applying. 'But what can I do? They're both staying at your grandmother's house, and it's difficult for them not to know what the other's doing, if you see what I mean. So whenever Daniel makes a plan with me, somehow Harry turns up too.' She chuckled then, a self-satisfied little sound that irritated Robin greatly. 'It makes Daniel absolutely furious, but I don't really mind. It's rather fun to have two chaps fussing over you.'

'I dare say it is,' Robin said shortly and slung the huge mackintosh she had at last finished over the drying horse, and then bent to mop up the inevitable puddles she had made. Staff Nurse Meek would bawl at her at the top of her voice if she didn't, as she knew from bitter experience. 'I wouldn't know.'

'Oh dear,' Chick said sympathetically. 'Did Chloe horn in again today?'

'I really have no idea,' Robin said, even more shortly. 'And what's more, I don't care. For heaven's sake, Chick, do move over. I can't get this one done properly if you keep your trolley so close. And anyway your poultices might get contaminated.'

'Don't take your fury out on me,' Chick said comfortably, though she did move her own working trolley out of the way. 'Save it for the person it belongs to.'

'Chloe? I wouldn't waste my breath on her – ' Robin began.

'Actually, I was thinking of Hamish,' Chick said mildly and shot a glance at her from beneath her lashes. 'He's not exactly a baby doll, is he, lying around for someone to pick up as and when she fancies? I mean, he is a person with a mind of his own. If he accepts the wretched woman's invitations, he's the one to blame, rather than Chloe – '

'I really don't know what you're talking about,' Robin snapped. 'And that's the last mack, thank God. I'd better get those drums packed now, or Meek'll explode.' And she flung the last mackintosh into place to dry, mopped out the sink, and fled to the other side of the department. Talking to anyone, even Chick, just made matters worse.

Maybe especially Chick, she thought then, as she began to pull pieces of cotton wool off the big roll to make them into swabs ready to be packed in the big metal drums in which they would be sterilized. She had too shrewd an idea of what was going on in Robin's life and was far too pushy about meddling. It was all very well, Robin told herself with some anger, to be a free and easy Canadian and all that, but there had to be times, surely, when you showed a bit of tact, and tact was the one quality Chick conspicuously lacked.

But she didn't lack common sense and Robin had to admit that what she said about Hamish not being a helpless doll was absolutely true. He was a person with a mind of his own – more mind than most, in fact, for hadn't he set himself against all conventional thinking in refusing to put on a uniform? – and if he let Chloe with all her obviousness take him in, surely the fault was as much his as hers?

Robin's hands slowed down as she thought of it all, and her eyes felt hot and tight. It had all seemed so silly at first; she had just been amused. But not for long. They'd come off duty one morning, she and Chick, to find Chloe's small car in one of the spaces in the courtyard reserved for the consultants. Robin had recognized it at once, for it was a rakish little red roadster with huge headlights that made it look as though it had a face on which a positively wicked leer could be seen. It suited Chloe exactly, Robin had always thought, and to see it in the hospital's yard was amazing and she stopped short to stare. Chick, who had been chattering at her, had gone on several yards before she realized that Robin was not beside her and turned back to see what had delayed her.

'What on earth is she doing here at this time of the morning?' Robin had said, and then reddened as Chloe, seeing her, had got out of the car and came over to her.

'Morning, ducks!' she had said. 'My word, but you look rough. Too awful working at night. I'd loathe it.' And she'd given a pretty little shudder and then nodded coolly at Chick. She herself was looking chic and elegant as only she could in beautifully cut black slacks and a little red jigger coat. Robin looked at her almost despairingly, well aware of her own straggling hair and shiny nose on a face which was quite innocent of any make-up.

'Looks as though you loathe working during the day too,' Chick had said, looking at her watch with some ostentation. 'Shouldn't you be at your madly important job in the War Office by this time?'

Chloe had looked at her with naked dislike. 'Actually, my dear,' she had said, 'It's Saturday, and we don't go in on Saturday unless there's a madly big push. Some people do, of course, but I'm not one of them, glory be. One needs some time to call one's own, war effort or no war effort.'

'We wouldn't know,' Chick said and smiled at her, a glittering, rather wolfish grimace that had no pleasantness in it at all. 'Time to ourselves is something we don't expect. And we're right not to on account of we don't get it.'

'Poor you,' Chloe said and flicked her eyes away from her and back to Robin. 'Darling, your poor hands! They look like a pile of pork sausages! You ought to use some cream on them. I'll try and get some for you. It's madly short in the shops but I have one or two useful contacts.'

'I'll bet you do,' Chick said, looking at the car. 'How else would you get petrol?'

Chloe didn't look at her but couldn't resist answering, 'I get a special allowance because of my job,' she said. 'Essential services, you know. Now, Robin darling, do remember to remind me about that cream. I do so want to help you. And you could do with some new lipstick too. Can't you get any? I've a few ends I'm sure that you can have.'

'We aren't allowed to wear it in uniform,' Robin said. 'I've enough for off duty, though, thanks all the same. No need to give me leftovers of yours – '

'Oh dear, oh dear! You sound just like you did when you were small, complaining because you couldn't stay up late like me! No need for that, sweetie! We're all grown up now.'

'Some more than others,' Chick said nastily and then tucked her hand into Robin's elbow. 'Come on, Robin.

We've been working all night, unlike some people, and we need our sleep.'

This time Chloe ignored her completely and kept her eyes on Robin. 'Any news from home?' she said. 'I never seem to get a moment to phone Poppy, what with work and one thing and another.'

'I'll bet,' Chick murmured.

'No,' Robin said. And her voice sounded husky suddenly and Chick, knowing how anxious she was about her stepfather, tightened her grasp on her arm. 'Ma's working all the hours God gives of course, and we haven't heard anything about David. So I suppose everything's all right – ' Her voice had sharpened then. 'Is that why you're here? Have you heard something that – oh, my God, Chloe, do tell me! What is it?' And her eyes had widened in sudden terror. Standing now at the dressings table and rolling her cotton wool swabs with savage little movements of her wrists, Robin remembered the way fear had leapt in her, how certain she had been that Chloe's unexpected appearance at the hospital had been because she was the bearer of some awful news.

But Chloe had just lifted her brows and laughed. 'My dear infant, why on earth should I have any news for you? I told you I never get round to calling poor old Poppy as it is – '

'The War Office,' Robin said. 'I thought perhaps – '

'No, my dear,' Chloe said. 'I deal with quite different matters.' And she put up her hands to pull her red woollen cap to a more becoming angle as her glance shifted over Robin's shoulder. 'Ah! Here comes the reason I'm here. Good morning, Hamish! Have you had a ghastly night too?'

Robin had turned her head and seen him coming from the direction of the porter's rooms, where he was accommodated. He had clearly hurried off duty at a great rate to wash and change, for his hair was clinging damply to his skull and his face had a newly shaved look about it. He was wearing a thick woollen jumper with a

214

round neck, rather like the ones the women patients in the wards spent hours knitting for the Sailors' Comforts Fund, and looked a totally different person from the bedraggled man in the shabby brown overall which was the insignia of a hospital orderly and in which Robin usually saw him.

'Good morning, Miss Bradman,' he said and then nodded at Chick and Robin. 'I can hardly bid you good morning since we were all on duty together the night.'

'Oh, I don't know,' Chick said tartly. 'You certainly look as though you're a different person to the one we worked with, so have a go. Where are you two off to?'

Robin was mortified. She wouldn't have asked the question had her life depended on it, though God knew she wanted to. The sight of Hamish looking so very well spruced up had rendered her almost speechless. And then angry. It wasn't that she felt she had any right to be consulted about his comings and goings; they were, after all, only friends and no more than that. She had no special claims on him and would have been very alarmed had he attempted to consult her on all he did or planned to do, but still the sight of him so obviously prepared as he was to meet her half-sister had filled her with a great rush of feeling, and she had to admit to herself, shaming thought though it was, that it was sheer jealousy.

And that had confused her. Staring at her hands, which were now quite still instead of rolling swabs, she tried again to deal with that. Hamish was a friend, that was all; or was it all? That was the thought that had been forced to the surface of her mind by his appearance that morning, and she still hadn't answered it satisfactorily. It wasn't that she didn't care about such matters as boyfriends and falling in love, or that she wasn't aware of how important they could be. Didn't she hear the other nurses talking interminably about their own adventures – or lack of them – until her head buzzed with it? It was just that she didn't know what her own feelings were. Yet she suspected they were a good deal stronger than she had realized, for why otherwise would that morning encounter have upset her so?

It had been Chloe who had answered Chick's question. 'Oh, nowhere you'd be interested in,' she had said airily and moved forward to link her arm with Hamish's in a proprietorial fashion. 'I just happened to know of a marvellous exhibition all about Scottish involvement with the English, you know, James the First and the Fourth and all that stuff, not to speak of Bonny Prince Thingummy. It's at the London Museum, so that's where we're off too. Toodle-oo, my dears!' And she had swept Hamish away into her small car and with a last flip of her hand out of the window had taken it noisily out of the gates and into the Whitechapel Road.

They had stood there in silence for a moment and then Chick had said disgustedly, 'Well, what a stupid lie that was!'

'What?' Robin said vaguely, still trying to deal with the confusion of feeling she had experienced.

'I said that was a stupid lie. Of course they're not going to any museum! She must think we're really barmy to swallow that!'

Robin had looked at her, trying to pay sensible attention; it was difficult but she had to try.

'Why?'

'Because everyone knows they've closed the museums, or most of 'em, for the duration. Sent all the exhibits off to Devon or somewhere to keep them safe, and shut up shop. So why try and tell us that's where they're going?'

Robin had felt her face go stiff with dull anger. 'Hamish wouldn't lie though – ' she had to say it, knowing him as she did. He might be quiet, but that he was honest and cared a great deal about what he regarded as right and wrong was undoubted.

'Wouldn't he!' Chick had said and taken her arm and forced her to start the walk to the dining room, and ultimately bed. 'He lied over that message that wasn't sent, didn't he?'

'But that was different – ' Robin had said, and then no more. They had both dropped the matter as though they'd agreed to, but it had rankled with Robin and it still did.

Since that morning she had seen Chloe's car twice more in the yard, and had hurried on, her head down, affecting not to have noticed. But all the same, she had been stung, and had kept well out of Hamish's way ever since. If that was what he wanted, she had told herself furiously, that's what he can damn well have. I don't care tuppence.

She jumped then as Staff Nurse Meek's voice came from behind her, as strident as ever, if not more so. 'If you've nothing better to do than stand there cuddling that cotton wool, Nurse Bradman, I'll find something for you. One of these drunks has been sick in the far cubicle. Go and clean it at once – '

'I've done it, Staff Nurse.' This time it was Hamish's voice that made Robin's head snap round and she stared at him as he went stomping past them with his covered bucket and mop and he looked at Robin with a faint smile and then at Nurse Meek with an expression of stolid stupidity which, had Robin not been so angry with him, would have made her laugh aloud.

'Oh, trust you two to hang together!' Meek shrilled. 'It's no more than I'd expect from the likes of you, Bradman – hanging around with domestics. It's all you're fit for, isn't it? Well, then – '

It started suddenly, almost overhead, and they all stood silently as the noise swooped on them and then Hamish said loudly, 'I didn't hear them start over the docks the way they usually do – ' just as another siren took up the clamour.

Sister Priestland, hitherto locked in her office, appeared from nowhere out on the tiled floor, surging into the middle of the waiting hall like a very small but very wind-filled galleon, her full bust seeming to pull her forwards.

'Right!' she called. 'Get yourselves together and start moving, everyone. There's sure to be big touble here soon. Get those drunks on their way as fast as you can and make sure every cubicle is set up and ready. I want all the available blood there is and then plasma, and the wards checked for available beds. Nurse Bradman, leave those drums and get the anaesthetic equipment checked. Nurse Chester, I want dressing packs and drips set in every cubicle, and Todd, bring in all the spare oxygen and nitrous oxide cylinders as well as the CO_2 – '

The instructions came out in a steady stream and the whole department seemed to scatter in a maelstrom of movement as the sirens went on and on shrieking overhead and others took up the noise. And then there was the even more ominous sound of planes, flying low and in large numbers. The London Hospital's Casualty Department braced itself for a heavy night.

· 22 ·

The readiness was the easy part. Within fifteen minutes of the sirens sounding the alarm, the Casualty department was poised and able to deal with a positive flood of casualties. The drunks were gone, banished for treatment elsewhere in the hospital – Robin never did find out where – and the benches in the waiting hall all stretched silent and glossy with the polish imparted by thousands of serge-clad East End bottoms over the years. But the casualties didn't come. The sirens stopped their noise and the doctors and nurses braced themselves for the usual din of whistling bombs and explosions and gunfire to come but none of it did – not even the ack-ack response from Victoria Park they were so used to – and still there were no ambulances shrieking up to the doors outside, still no stretchers dragged in by sweating First Aiders and ARP post wardens.

It was Dr Landow who found out what was going on. He went out into the street to see what was happening, which scandalized the gate porter, Thomas, who believed that everyone but himself must be kept within doors while an alert was in progress, and came back to head for the phone in Sister's office. When he emerged his face was grim.

'It's different this time,' he said, and Sister, who had set her nurses to rolling those interminable cotton wool swabs on the principle that they'd get tired out from doing nothing at all, turned her head and said drily, 'We'd guessed as much. What is it? Gas? I've just the three emergency respirators, you know. It's the one I've always told everyone we'd not be able to handle so well – '

He shook his head. 'Not gas, thank God. Not really all that many people either, which is what matters most. It's the City – '

'The City?'

'I've talked to them at Bart's and Guy's. They're pounding the city with fire bombs. None of your big stuff, but it's doing terrible damage. It's burning like crazy, according to old Geoff Lovell at Guy's. He says the Thames is at low tide and the fire service have no pressure in their hoses and there are whole streets burning and nothing to stop 'em. It's 1666 all over again.'

'The City,' Sister Priestland said and then rubbed her eyes with the heels of both hands. 'Bloody vandals,' she said loudly. 'Bloody vandals!'

The nurses stared at her, amazed and shocked. Sister Priestland to swear? And even as they looked at her she blushed and muttered something that sounded as though it might have been an apology.

'It's the only description,' Sam Landow said. 'Wren's London up in flames – it's worse than vandalism. But at least it's not too many people. Most of the buildings are empty and locked at weekends, you see, especially now, between Christmas and New Year. Most of the people they're getting in at the other hospitals are firefighters and wardens and so forth – hang on – here we go!'

They had all heard it, and pushed the dressing preparation trolley into its cubbyhole and made for the big doors as a group, ready to take their first patients. It was Sam Landow who opened the big doors and the stretchers came bustling in, and with them the reek of burned rubber and cloth and leather.

They filled the cubicles at once, but unlike the bedlam caused by other raids, especially of high explosives, there were few bewildered people sitting or lying in the waiting hall until they could be treated. The place was well in control of the amount of work there was, and Robin and Landow, who were working together in her usual far cubicle, had actually finished their patient and seen him, his dreadfully blackened face well covered with vaseline gauze, off to his bed in the ward, and had stopped to tidy their dressing trolley when Sister Priestland put her head round the curtain.

'Dr Landow,' she said. 'You've got your obs. training, haven't you?'

He lifted his chin sharply. 'Yes – Got one coming in?'

She shook her head. 'Guy's called. They've got a domiciliary case calling from Fenchurch Street, would you believe. Caretaker's wife at a bank – in the first stage, they said. The woman sent for a midwife but all theirs at Guy's are out or involved in the pressures they've got on their Casualty department and they can't help at Bart's either. Our midwives have a full ward and can't go and anyway they want a doctor. The girl's had a pre-partum haemorrhage already – '

'Jesus, why didn't they admit her?' He was half-way out of the cubicle. 'I'll deal with it. Give me the address. And Sister – ' He stopped and looked back over his shoulder. 'I'll need another pair of hands. Can I take Nurse Bradman here? She's deft enough to make up for not having a midder training and she takes orders well – can you spare her?'

'Off you go, Nurse.' Sister Priestland nodded at Robin and she, staring with shock at them both, opened her mouth to speak, closed it and then opened it again like a half-witted fish.

'No time for that,' Sam Landow said briskly. 'Come on.' And she was off, almost running behind him.

He stopped at the instrument cupboard. 'Get me dressing towels, big swabs, some small ones and a roll of gamgee,' he instructed over his shoulder as he pulled items out of the cupboards. 'And a bottle of Lysol and some mercurochrome and ask Sister for a sterile drum of gowns and gloves. They'll have nothing there, I'm sure.'

Staff Nurse Meek came surging across the waiting hall and tried to put herself in between Robin and Sam.

'I'll deal with this, sir,' she said smoothly. 'Nurse, get back to your work. Now, Doctor – '

'No, thank you, Nurse Meek,' he said firmly and handed the instruments he'd collected to Robin. 'Sister's sent Nurse Bradman to help me. Put those in the bag you'll find in the corner of the office, nurse, and make sure all its bottles are full, will you? There should be spirit, some carbolic acid and silver nitrate as well as the other things I asked you for. I'll check the ergotamine and the needles and suture materials. Excuse me, Nurse Meek.' And he pushed his way past her.

And Staff Nurse Meek, who didn't know whether to be more mortally offended because Dr Landow had addressed her simply as 'Nurse' instead of her justly entitled 'Staff Nurse' or because she had been passed over in favour of a much-hated junior, stood there blankly without a word to say. That was, Robin decided, the sweetest moment of her entire life so far.

But there was a great deal more to come. She had pulled on her cape, well aware that it was a cold night and prepared to be chilled to the marrow, but when she got into the yard and followed Sam Landow's headlong rush towards the parked cars on one side, she was startled to find that the wind that was blowing strongly from the west was a warm one. But it was not the normal warmth of a spring breeze. It came in hot gusts and brought thick flakes of soot and the stench of burning wood, and beneath that an even more ominous smell that she preferred not to think about. There couldn't be that sort of smell, could there? Not *people* –

The car bore a large white cross painted on its roof and on both the front doors, as well as white paint on its mudguards and running boards, and she bundled herself into it as fast as she could as Sam Landow stowed the bag and the dispensary basket, now containing the dressings drum and the extra lotions he'd asked for, on the back seat, and then came and clambered in himself.

'I've been expecting calls like this from the beginning,' he said, as he pulled the steering wheel round and hauled the car into the main road. 'Painted the crosses on, the lot, to be ready, but this is the first time I've needed it. But it'll show the rest of 'em I was on the right tracks. They'll stop laughing at me now – '

'Who laughed?' Robin almost gasped it as she hung on grimly, for the car was not as well equipped with springs as it was with white crosses, and the bumping was horrendous.

'Oh, the other fellows in the mess – listen, I'd better give you a quick lecture on the normal delivery. Listen hard. It should help. Don't think you can remember it all at once because you can't, but once we're there and in the thick of it you'll have an idea what's going on. So, here goes.'

She would never forget the next ten minutes, not if she lived to be a hundred, Robin decided. As the crazily painted little car careered along the Whitechapel Road towards the crimson glow that now filled the sky ahead, she listened to his shouted account of a baby's birth. She knew the basic female anatomy and physiology well enough, but had only the sketchiest notion of what happened to the anatomy when it was in full working order, and listening now as he spoke of the cervix dilating and the infant pushing its head against the perineum she began to feel decidedly alarmed. It wasn't just the fact that they were heading for the centre of what looked like the most incredible inferno, but that she was to help someone with what was obviously a great deal more complicated procedure than she would ever have imagined. He spoke of the baby's neck flexing, of the crowning of the occiput and the risk of the umbilical cord being round the neck and how to deal with it after the presenting shoulder delivered –

Her head spun and she knew that she wanted more desperately than she had ever wanted anything to get out of this hateful little car and away from this implacable man talking still at the top of his voice of the most unspeakable things while he drove them both into hell and seeming a totally different being to the friendly one she had worked with hitherto. But the car was going too fast for her to escape. To have left it would have been even riskier than staying. She was appallingly trapped and there wasn't a thing she could do about it.

They shrieked to a stop just outside Aldgate East Station, as a policeman, looking very odd because most of his face was black with soot, flagged them down. Sam leaned out of the window to explain to him, at the top of his voice again, because the din that exploded over them when the window was open was immense, an amalgam of fire bells and shouting and shrieking burglar alarms. Whatever Sam said clearly worked, because the policeman jumped up on the running board and waving his other arm over his head as he held on grimly, got them through the hubbub and the twisting snakes of fire hoses, onwards towards the City.

Inferno was too weak a word for it. Everywhere they looked buildings were burning, and the crackling roar of the flames got louder and louder as they moved ever westwards, past Whitechapel High Street and on over Middlesex and Mansell Streets, inching their way towards Aldgate proper and thence to Fenchurch Street.

Outside the remains of the façade of Aldgate Station, the policeman thumped on the car roof and Sam stamped on his brakes and the car stopped, almost throwing Robin forwards into the windscreen, and the policeman jumped down and shouted, 'You'll get no further than this, sir. The Malay Bank's about half-way down on the other side. It's not been burned yet, but it will be. I'll get the ambulance up as close as I can and we'll load the lot of you into it. You be ready for us!' And he jumped down and disappeared into the mêlée behind them.

'Here we go,' Sam said and got out of the car, reaching back to fetch the gear as Robin sat there, unable to move. She had been overcome by a wave of fear so powerful that it had seized her muscles in a harsh grip and she could not have moved out of the small safe place that was the car she had so recently yearned to leave, to save her life. She knew it and she knew too that she couldn't explain to him why she was still sitting there, because she couldn't speak either. It was an extraordinary way to feel and she sat and stared at the fitful light ahead of her, thrown by the flames, and thought – I'm breathing. I can breathe, please don't let that stop too –

It was as though he knew. He had come round the car to her side, and had opened the door to let her out, but still she sat there, her head held rigid, and after a moment he crouched down beside her and said in a conversational tone, 'It's all right. This happens to a lot of people. It's a sort of paralysis – nothing to get agitated about. I'm going to touch you, on your face, and that will be the thing that makes your muscles work again. You understand me? When I touch you on your cheek, your muscles will work again and you'll get out of the car and come and help me.'

Still she sat and stared ahead, her eyes so hot with her staring that tears were running down the sides of her nose, not tears of misery, but of stillness. And he put out one hand and touched her cheek and at last it was all right. The touch of his fingers on her cheek, just at the side of her nose, felt like the touch of something very cold, and the cold slithered inwards and downwards and then she was moving without knowing quite how she'd done it, lifting her legs to put her feet outside the car as he straightened up and stepped back.

When she was standing beside him he peered into her face and then put a hand in his pocket and hauled out a handkerchief. 'You'll need this or your eyes will hurt,' he said. 'Dry them carefully,' and she obeyed. The handkerchief smelled of ether and tobacco smoke and an indefinable something else which she found she rather

225

liked and then didn't, and she scrubbed at her eyes and handed it back to him and said huskily, 'So sorry. Don't know what happened there – '

'A moment of hysterical paralysis, that's all,' he said conversationally. 'Common in crises like these. You behaved extremely well. You'd be a joy to hypnotize, I suspect. A fast responder.'

'What?' She was alarmed, and he laughed.

'Not now, idiot! We've got a baby waiting for us right now. Some other time. Come on!'

She followed him blindly, knowing she was safe now. It was a silly way to feel. There they were in the middle of a positive holocaust, as flames licked the City of London into rubble with the dome of St Paul's, outlined by the glow of the innumerable fires, cut out against the night sky – at least that hadn't burned yet – and she felt safe. 'That's mad,' she whispered to herself and he half turned his head and said, 'What did you say?' But she shook her head and smiled at him and he turned back and went on with his half-crouching, half-running walk that made her think absurdly of Groucho Marx for a moment, and she followed him.

'Found it,' he said after a moment. 'Malay – here it is. They said the basement but I can't see – oh, yes, there. A small area. Great. Underground has to be safer than this – ' as overhead a flame leapt from a high roof and then over their heads to the other side of the street and seemed to lick at the brickwork there greedily.

There was a gate half hanging off the railings and below it a short flight of steps and he went down, lugging the heavy basket he was carrying, and she brought the bag and for the first time they stood fully upright and he took a deep breath and said, 'Thank God for that! I was beginning to feel like the Hunchback of Notre Dame.'

'You looked like Groucho Marx,' she said and he gave a snort of laughter and then banged on the door.

It moved under his attack and he pushed it open and peered in. There was blackness so thick it was like fabric, and he reached into his coat pocket seeking a torch, and at last found it, to send its tiny beam to cut the inkiness ahead like a needle, albeit a very small needle.

'Probably didn't want to leave her,' Sam said. 'Come on,' and she did, wondering if he ever said anything else, and they shuffled their way along what seemed to be a narrow corridor until they reached a dead end.

'Another door. Open, I wonder?' he said and pushed, and this time a faint rim of light appeared and she took a deep breath of gratitude. The heavy blackness had started to make her feel very jittery indeed.

The rim of light became a square and then filled itself in with a fitful glow. They were on the wrong side of a heavy curtain, she realized, and he reached up and pulled it to one side and the rings above it clattered and rang and then there was a good deal more light, and she blinked over his shoulder to see where they were.

It was a cellar, a common enough place to use for an air raid shelter, but this one was not equipped like the usual sort. In the middle there was a table, which looked like a common or garden kitchen table, and all around this were chests and boxes, piled higgledy-piggledy on each other. Not that Robin paid much attention to them; it was the table's burden which interested her most.

A woman was lying there, with hair so long that it hung down at the back of the table, and almost reached the floor. At her side sat a man, holding her hand tightly as she rolled her head from side to side on the bare boards of the table. He jumped up as they came in and stood with his back to the woman on the table, clearly terrified, and then at the sight of Robin his face cleared and he ran forwards, and totally ignoring Sam Landow seized her hands in both of his and dragged her over to the table, chattering loudly all the time in a rather shrill voice, and Robin, like it or not, had to go with him. Not that she minded; but she was undoubtedly bemused.

Because the chattering meant not a thing to her. The man, and the woman on the table, were both Oriental, with the narrow eyes and the high cheekbones that looked so familiar to her from performances of *Chu Chin Chow*. But these two were not pretending to be Oriental people; they really were, and she didn't understand a word they were saying. And she realized, as she looked over her shoulder at Sam, neither did he. And the woman on the table was crying bitterly and the man now pushing Robin at her was too, and both were looking at her appealingly, begging for help. And she hadn't the remotest idea what to do.

· 23 ·

'It's your uniform,' Sam said then. 'That's what makes
him trust you.' And he took the bag from her and set it
down on the floor beside the table. 'Get your cape off,
and see if you can bring over enough of those boxes to
make into some sort of working surface. Then lay out the
gear on it while I look at her.' He sounded crisp and a
little remote, with none of his usual relaxed friendliness,
and that helped her feel more able to cope, oddly enough.
He was so coolly professional that it was as though he had
brought a small part of the hospital with him to wrap them
all around in its safety.

She obeyed without hesitation, using her cape after a
moment's thought to cover the feet of the girl on the
table, for she had no other covering and was wearing just
a thin nightdress, and the man, who had returned to the
woman's side and was murmuring rapidly at her, looked at
Robin and then smiled suddenly, a wide sweet smile that
she found herself returning almost automatically.

When she went over to the side of the room to start
dragging boxes to the table, he understood quickly and
came to help her, and soon they had a broad, if rather
low, surface prepared, and Robin began to empty the
dispensary basket as well as the bag, first setting a
dressing towel to cover the rough cardboard.

Sam, who had moved to the girl's side and had been
checking her pulse as she stared up at him in clear alarm,
nodded approvingly.

'I'll need to wash,' he said then. 'See if you can see any water sources, will you? We won't need all those buckets of water they always boil up in the films, but I'll need some – '

She looked around and could see no taps or sinks and turned back to the man, and mimed what she wanted; turning a tap, washing her hands; and he stared for a moment and then nodded and went off at a trot, leaving her to follow as he plunged into the shadows deeper into the cellars.

There was a tap over a dirty sink there in the dimness and beside it a crusted old gas ring with a battered iron kettle on it and she looked around for matches and found some in a dirty box on a nearby shelf. All was covered in old cobwebs and she bit her lip hopefully as she wrestled with the stiff gas tap and then breathed again at the blessed sound of hissing and the smell of town gas which emerged. She struck a match and lit the ring, praying inside her head with a garbled fervour that the so far unbroken gas main which serviced it should remain that way; and was amazed that in all the conflagration outside it was still possible to find a gas ring that worked.

The little Malaysian had wasted no time, but had filled the kettle and now he hauled it on to the ring and then went trotting back into the middle of the cellar to where Sam was with the girl. She had twisted herself up again into a posture of agony and her face was twisted too into a tight rictus, but she made no sound and Robin realized that so far she hadn't uttered a word, and she went over to her, as Sam looked up and summoned her with a little jerk of his head to come to join him.

Robin reached out and took the girl's hand, and she grasped it convulsively and Robin looked at her more closely, for the hand was wet with sweat, and now she could see that her face was too, and she lifted a corner of her apron, for want of anything else to use, to mop the girl's face dry. Nothing felt worse, she knew, than having a sweat-streaked face that itched –

Sam had arranged Robin's cape as a sort of blanket to protect the girl's modesty as much as he could, and had gently pulled up her nightdress to reveal the pregnant belly beneath. It looked dome-like to Robin, who stared with fascination at the almost translucent skin, marked with even more translucent stretch-marks, which covered it, and the everted umbilicus on top looking absurdly like a cherry on top of a great cake. And then her eyes widened, for there had been a shiver of movement that passed right across the taut belly and Sam grunted in approval.

'Well, the infant's lively enough,' he said. 'Even though the head's well engaged. Let's see, now, this matter of bleeding – '

Gently he lifted the cape to cover her belly and then, carefully pulling on the girl's knees persuaded her to relax and let him see further.

'I'll risk a vaginal examination,' he said, speaking almost to himself. 'I can see a small trickle of blood, but it could be just what's left after the show – ' And then he looked at Robin. 'You remember what I told you in the car about the show? When the operculum comes free?'

'Yes,' lied Robin and then nodded as some of his words came back into her memory. 'Yes, I really do!'

'Don't sound so surprised.' He had turned back to his makeshift trolley. 'Now, that water – will it be hot yet?'

'Not very,' Robin said. 'But just about warm enough to wash, I think – '

'Let's see if we can make our friend work for me as well as he does for you,' Sam said and turned to the hovering man and mimed hand-washing and then held out one of the enamel bowls to him. The man nodded at once and took the bowl and trotted away as fast as ever, to re-emerge with the bowl filled with lukewarm water.

Sam took it and grinned at the man who essayed a grin back, and bent to wash his hands, using some ether soap from one of the bottles that had been in the dispensary basket, as the woman's hand tightened in Robin's grasp and again she twisted herself into a tight posture of pain.

'Is she having another contraction?' Sam asked, looking over his shoulder. 'Looks like it. Put a hand on her belly – tell me what it feels like – '

Shrinking a little, Robin did as she was told and set her hand flat on the great mound and felt the rigidity beneath her fingers and her eyes widened. 'It feels like wood,' she said. Sam, now drying his hands on a sterilized dressing towel he'd taken from the drum of dressings, nodded approvingly.

'Keep on holding your hand there and you should feel it relax and fade away.' And even as he said it the softening came, and Robin stared down, a little overawed. It was as though the girl's body was acting of its own volition and with no reference to the mind and spirit that inhabited it; and then she thought – it isn't the girl who matters to this body now; it's the other body, the baby's.

It was a confused thought and it vanished as Sam turned back to the table, pulling gloves on as he came. She watched him, still holding on to the woman's hand, as he began to examine her, and winced a little at the inevitable invasion of her body that was required and then her original thought came back: it's not her body now. It's the baby's, at least until it gets out, and wondered how it would feel to be the girl on the table and to her amazement found herself wishing it was her. She would have expected to be appalled, revolted even, but she wasn't. What was happening right now to this girl seemed more important than anything in the world, even the huge fires overhead which were swallowing up the City of London and for all they knew might swallow them up too eventually. And it would have been a wonderful thing if it was happening to her.

Under her fingers she felt the belly tighten and harden again and she let out an involuntary exclamation, and Sam, withdrawing his hand said, 'Another one starting?

Good girl – well spotted. She'll start to show – yes, there she goes – ' And again the girl on the table tightened herself into a grimace of pain, an even tighter twisting this time.

'We've got to try to stop her doing that,' Sam said. 'It'll make delivery devilishly difficult. We've a bit to go. The cervix is almost dilated and I can't feel any placenta in the way. As far as I can tell. Just pray it isn't a praevia.'

'Praevia?' Robin asked.

'If the afterbirth is across the birth canal, she could bleed to death before the baby's delivered and it could be dead too,' he said. 'She bled earlier in the pregnancy, apparently, but maybe it isn't a true praevia. Sometimes these smallish haemorrhages can be due to a stretched and torn vein – nothing too dangerous. We just have to wait and watch – ' And he nodded encouragingly at the little man who was still hovering outside the group of patient, doctor and nurse.

'She all right?' he said then and Sam stared at him.

'You speak English then?'

'Small. Small,' the man said and nodded anxiously at the girl on the table. 'All right? Wife baby all right?'

'I hope so,' Sam said. 'Why isn't she in hospital?'

'No go.' He shook his head. 'Wife not go. Me here, you see? Me here. Boss say, me in charge. No go. So wife no go – ' His face creased in anxiety. 'Wife strong lady – '

Sam laughed then. 'She's a very strong lady,' he said cheerfully. 'So far she seems well – '

There was a rattling sound from the depths of the cellar and the little man brightened. 'Hot water. Tea,' he said and disappeared into the darkness. And Sam laughed.

'So it's not just the English. Everyone makes tea at the drop of a hat, all over the world – '

'I'm not surprised,' Robin said. 'It helps. What happens now?'

'We wait for the ambulance that policeman promised and pray it gets here before the baby does. But at the rate she's going' – for another wave of pain had moved

233

over the woman's body – 'the baby'll beat it. She's almost ready to push – '

'How do you know when she's ready?' Robin was fascinated. 'I mean, how do you know to tell her?'

Sam laughed. 'I need tell her nothing. Her own body does it without any prompting. As soon as the cervix is really dilated and the head gets down far enough to sit on the perineum, she'll start to push. She won't be able to help it. All we'll have to do is guide the little beggar on his way – '

'Why do you need to? I mean, women haven't always had doctors to do babies for them, have they?'

He looked at her sharply. 'Good for you, Robin! The London hasn't managed to stamp out your questioning yet! I'm one of those who think that women themselves know best how to have their babies, and how to look after them. Too many damned experts get involved these days. It confuses women – I suspect sometimes it makes birth harder – but there it is. That's the way it's been done, so that's it. If I, as a doctor, don't handle pregnant women according to the rules, then it's my fault if it all goes wrong. If it all goes well, it's luck. If I do obey the rules and it all goes wrong, then it's an act of God. No one ever blames the doctor or gives credit to the mother. That's the way medicine is – Ah! There we go again. It'll only take a few more contractions – '

The girl on the table had closed her eyes and was pushing downwards, clearly trying to expel the baby from her body, and Robin stared fascinated as the face reddened and began to sweat. And then after a long moment relaxed, breathlessly, and the girl opened her eyes wide and stared fearfully at Robin and then at Sam.

'I think we can give her some help,' Sam murmured. 'No need for her to go through hell if she can have something to take the edge off. Give me that small nitrous oxide kit – that's it. With the oxygen. It was damned bulky to carry but well worth it – '

Quickly his hands moved in the equipment, setting it up, as the little man returned with mugs of tea on an old lid from a biscuit tin for a tray and he stood and hovered as once more his wife gasped and began her pushing efforts.

Sam had the equipment ready now and held the mask over her face and at first she fought it, trying to push him away, and then as the deeper breaths she was taking because of her efforts filled her with the nitrous oxide, relaxed and stared a little glassily at them both.

'That's the way to do it,' Sam said with great satisfaction. 'As Mr Punch would say – Here we go again – '

It seemed to Robin that the next half hour took a week to pass, and yet at the same time was over in a flash. It was as though time had been poured into a crazy kaleidoscope and shaken up so that it presented first once face and then another. She was bewildered and exhilarated and more fascinated by what she was seeing than she had ever been in all her life.

The pushing and the breathing of the nitrous oxide went on and on, and the tea cooled, ignored on its biscuit-tin lid, and the little man hovered on the fringe and Robin listened with one ear for the sound that might mean the ambulance had arrived. But they could have been alone in the world, just the four people and fifth as yet unseen, in their half-lit cellar.

When it happened it was sudden and shocking.

'Come on,' Sam said with abrupt urgency, holding the girl's knee hard against his chest, as Robin, working by imitation, did the same on the other side. 'Like that – push. Keep on pushing – keep on and on and on – ' And the girl tried to pull away from their controlling hands on her legs, and Robin, feeling wrong somehow, fought to keep the knee she was holding well back against her apron.

'That's it – hang on – ' Sam said breathlessly. 'I have to see what's happening here – good girl! No bleeding yet – push! That's it – push – harder – harder!'

And there at the edge of her body it appeared – a crumpled furious face that emerged as far as the chin and then remained there as the woman gasped and seemed to lose all awareness of what was happening, as again she breathed in great gasps of nitrous oxide which smelled sweetish in the warm dull air of the cellar. And then there was another push and this time the rest of the head and neck appeared and one hunched shoulder as Sam reached down and hooked one finger beneath the emerging armpit. The head turned, the baby turned, and with a sudden swirl of pinkly stained water it was there, the whole streaked wet body, bright pink in the poor light, and with a great twisting snake of pulsing blood vessels emerging from its own domed belly.

Robin stared and blinked, startled to find that she was weeping and Sam picked up the child by his heels and held him high and with a long tube taken from the piled-up boxes behind him began to suck the baby's mouth clear, and there was a moment and then a gasp and at last a mewing sound as the baby opened its mouth and began to wail, and this time Robin's tears clouded her vision and she had to sniff hard and rub her face.

'No need to slap the baby to make it breathe?' she managed to say and Sam shook his head.

'None at all. Why hurt the child as soon as he leaves his safe warm home? To prove this is another world? He'll find out soon enough! I reckon that first wallop can have effects that last a lifetime – '

'More psychiatry,' Robin murmured and he laughed and agreed.

'Lots more,' he said. 'I promise that. Stick around till say – what – 1950? You'll see where I'll be by then!'

The girl on the bed lifted her head now and was calling something loudly and Robin looked at her and laughed aloud. It was the first time the girl had uttered a sound, but it was a sound that had been worth waiting for. Her face that had been twisted in pain was as smooth as a schoolgirl's and she looked as though someone had lit a lamp inside her, she was so excited, and she reached her hands out for the baby, and Sam said a little abstractedly, 'Hold on, my love, just hold on there – you shall have him – ' And he set the baby down on his mother's belly and with one of his Spencer Wells' forceps grasped the bulging cord and then used another to clip it again a couple of inches away. He sliced between the forceps with a pair of scissors, making Robin wince, though it seemed not to bother the baby or the mother at all, and then wrapped the child in a dressing towel and gave it to the girl, who at once pulled down her nightdress and set it to her breast, and the baby, feeling it on his cheek, twisted his mouth and then his head and found her nipple and clamped himself on like a leech.

'Clever girl,' Sam said, though he was involved still at the other end of her body. 'Knows just what to do better than I could tell her, you see – she pushed the child out a treat, and now she's making sure the placenta'll come as easily – here we go – ' And he delivered the afterbirth, a great reddish brown thing, into one of the basins and for the first time Robin was repelled by what she was seeing and looked away to the mother's face again.

She was staring down at the baby still with that expression of vast excitement, and above her the little man stood and stared down too, his face quite smooth and apparently blank. But then he looked up at Robin and she saw the blaze of excitement in his eyes and said, 'Well done,' to him and he too lit up and laughed and stood up a little straighter and said, 'My son, yes? Son?'

'Very much so,' Sam said then, as he swabbed the girl with some of the lotions that they had brought from the London, and set a pad of gamgee there, and pulled down her nightdress and rearranged Robin's cape as a blanket. 'As fine a set of male equipment as I've seen in a long time, eh, Nurse Bradman?' And Robin, who had indeed noticed the child's sizeable genitalia, blushed a little, and was furious with herself for doing so.

'Your name, sir?' the man said as he stood there very straight behind his wife and baby. 'Your name, missee?'

'I'm Sam,' he said. 'You don't have to, you know – '

'I choose,' the man said with great dignity. 'And you, missee?'

She shook her head. 'But I'm a girl,' she said gently. 'Not a name for a boy baby like yours.'

The Malaysian looked at her a little sadly. 'Yes – next time – you come again?'

Sam roared with laughter at that. 'Give the poor girl a chance!' he said. 'She's barely had this one. Next time, for a girl, the name is Robin, though, when you get to it. Try and put that into good Malay.'

The little man looked thoughtful. 'Is not easy. Sam is easy.' And he bowed slightly. 'My son,' and he indicated the child, who had stopped sucking and was now sleeping with every appearance of content. 'My son Wong Tu Sam.' Sam bent his own head in reply and said gravely, 'How do you do, Mr Wong,' and then smiled at the baby's father. 'And you too. How do you do.' And the two men shook hands, after Sam had taken off his gloves, and seemed highly pleased with each other.

Tidying up took a little while and still the ambulance hadn't arrived, and when the dispensary basket had been repacked and the instruments washed in the remains of the hot water and returned to the bag, and the placenta wrapped in a great many sheets of newspaper ready to be disposed of, Sam and Robin stood there waiting. And then Sam said, 'We can't stay here like this! They'll get here, and in the meanwhile these two are all right. We'll get back and I'll call Guy's – '

It was as though his decision had speeded things up, because they heard it then, the sound they'd been waiting for. Voices and footsteps along the corridor outside and then they were there, two men with a stretcher, both built on the large side and filling the cellar so full that it seemed to have shrunk.

'Great timing,' Sam said a little sardonically. 'We're done here. Baby's in a good state, but should be checked when you get to your unit. Mother's fine, no placenta praevia as feared, loss of blood minimal. Placenta delivered complete, and it's here to be taken back for checking and disposal. Where're you taking them?'

'The London,' one of the men said as the two of them began to get the woman and the baby wrapped in blankets and on to the stretcher. 'Bart's and Guy's are full to the brim and goin' potty. They've lost some buildings of their own, and staff and patients. It's a right bugger out there and no error.'

Sam looked grim. 'A lot of damage?'

'There won't be no city left tomorrer mornin',' the man grunted as they picked up the stretcher. 'They'll come in for business as usual and there won't be none. Gawd, but I'd like to get up there and kill those bleedin' German bombers. This is just stupid – docks is one thing – war effort stuff and so forth – but historical old buildings, there's another.'

'And people,' Sam said quietly.

'People?' The ambulance man had the girl on the stretcher now and they were taking her towards the door, her anxious husband close behind. 'Much they care about people, that lot! Listen, the copper outside said if that there car with the white crosses on it was yours, it ain't no more. It's bin burned like everything else. You'd better come back to the hospital with us, eh? It'll be a hot ride, but not much worse'n it would have been in your own car, I'll tell you that. We got blankets you can use to shield yourself. Come on then. Into the jaws of hell we go. Welcome to the world, nipper. It's all yours and ain't it a beauty!'

· 24 ·

That she was being extremely edgy Poppy knew. What she couldn't know was just how far along the road to behaving foolishly her edginess had driven her.

She should have talked about it, she knew. She should have found a sympathetic ear into which she could pour all her misery, her fear and above all, her conviction that David wouldn't get back safe from this mission. It was natural enough she should be so frightened. Day after day the papers were full of it, the dreadful risks run by the merchantmen and their accompanying convoys who were bringing supplies to the beleaguered station. There were constant exhortations to save food, to use it well and not to hoard it, to be unselfish and caring of other people's needs and regular attacks on the 'vermin' who were the black-marketeers. Poppy felt battered by it, and also felt that much of the progaganda was directed at her personally. Here she was, frantic with anxiety about David at sea with those same merchantmen, while Jessie's son, her own partner's son, had filled their cellar with – oh, it didn't bear thinking about.

But she couldn't help thinking of it, and in particular dreaming of it. Night after night she had dreams in which she saw David in a ship's cabin with the water rising inexorably until it submerged him, as she watched paralysed with helplessness, only to wake sweating and trembling to face another day of terror for him. Days in which she had to go to Cable Street and do her usual work, then to the restaurant in the West End and finally back to the canteen at night. She became obsessed with David and his safety, and the more obsessed she became the less she talked about how she felt.

Even to Robin. She had told her that David had gone to sea and been as casual as she could about it, trying not to show the deep river of fear that ran through her and, she told herself, had succeeded in beguiling her. Robin, Poppy assured herself, had no idea how much danger her stepfather faced and therefore wouldn't worry. It never occurred to her that Robin too might be anxious and hiding her own feelings for fear of upsetting her mother.

She was the same at Cable Street too, refusing to allow Jessie to see anything of what seethed under the surface of her mind all the time, even when she was talking about the business or doing the books, or working out what had to be charged for the day's food as it was served in the restaurant. That added to the pressures, because the prices had to fluctuate constantly because of the fluctuation in the cost of raw materials and that made some customers complain and behave as though Jessie's Ltd was making a vast, indeed a profiteer's, margin for themselves. Added to all of that was Goosey's constant lamentations about 'Poor Mr David' and her constantly repeated hopes that the 'dear man was all right and keeping himself safe', which so far she had managed to bear without complaining. But she was dangerously near the end of her rope. How close even she didn't know.

The morning after the massive raid that left the City a heap of smouldering rubble she left the house in Norland Square a little later than usual because Goosey had been querulous on the subject of laundry.

'I can't get them to come to collect it, and getting it back – well, you can imagine. It'll only be a matter of weeks before there won't be a laundry service at all and we'll have to get it all done at home, and how am I to manage that, I ask you? I don't want to be thought lazy or anything, Mrs Poppy, but there's only me and no one to help at all and how am I to cope with such things as sheets and shirts as and when and if dear Mr David gets back – '

That had been the point at which Poppy had cracked and suffered the first spurt of temper. How dare the old woman say 'If Mr David gets back'! The mere sound of the words had sent such a shaft of cold sick terror through Poppy that it left her shaking and she had exploded into rare wrath and shouted something confused about throwing the damned laundry out if it couldn't be washed, and not bothering her with such things at this hour of the morning, a reaction which made old Goosey's chin tremble and slow rheumy tears run down her grooved old cheeks. And that made Poppy feel so dreadful that she had done the only thing she could, and snatched up her bag and her gas mask and gone slamming out of the house. Without her gloves or scarf, so that by the time she got to Cable Street she was almost solid with the cold, for it was a dark and miserable New Year with dirty slush in the streets and icy patches underfoot, to add to the hazards of broken pavements and heaped rubble when you got to the East End.

When she arrived at the office and put away her coat and gas mask and fetched herself a cup of hot coffee to thaw her frozen fingers she thought she'd feel better; but the memory of Goosey's stricken face staring at her as she slammed the front door behind her still haunted her and she had to bend her head to her ledgers early to try to banish it. And then Robin had put her head round the door and interrupted her just as she got to a particularly complex area, and she lost the thread of what she was doing so completely she knew she'd have to start all over again.

But she closed the book patiently, or so she thought and tried to look at her daughter. And was horrified at what she saw.

Robin's eyes were red, so red that for a moment Poppy thought they were bleeding, but she looked again and realized it was inflammation and she shook her head with disbelief as she gazed at them and at the swollen puffy skin around the eyes which clearly had suffered the same attack as the eyes themselves.

'Robin, whatever has happened to you?' she gasped and Robin managed to blink at her and grin.

'Not as bad as it looks, Ma, though it's got me an extra night off so I can't complain! It was the raid on Sunday night – wasn't it ghastly? It was the heat and smoke – it made my eyes dreadfully irritated – though it looks worse than it feels. Listen, I must tell you what happened – ' And she launched herself into an excited account of the birth of Wong Tu Sam and her part in it, as Poppy sat and listened in increasing horror.

'Are you telling me that they let you – dammit, that they *sent* you to go out in those conditions? Are you mad, Robin? I thought you'd be reasonably safe there at the London. They've got these raid-proofed wards and you told me Casualty was largely underground – though that didn't stop that damned incident when you got buried – but to send you *out* in that – that hell of a raid? How could they? And why on earth didn't you refuse? You must be – '

Robin's eyes opened as wide as they could, which wasn't much. 'Refuse, Ma? Don't be daft! As if I would or could. I was thrilled to be chosen – it was marvellous of Sam Landow to ask for me and – '

'He should have known better,' flared Poppy. 'I thought he was a sensible sort of man – if it had been that wretched Hamish who seems to have no more sense of a man's duty than – than a flea – it would have been different. But Landow? To take you out in all that – and now look at your eyes. You could have damaged your vision for good, for heaven's sake – '

'My vision will be unimpaired,' Robin said quietly. 'This is just a severe reactive conjunctivitis because of the smoke. It'll be clear by tomorrow. What do you mean about Hamish having no sense of duty?'

'Oh, for God's sake, Robin! These objectors – selfish most of them, that's all they are – they make a great song and dance about their damned consciences while the rest of us get on with it and take appalling chances. People like the soldiers and the airmen who turn out night after night to fight those damned planes – and at sea – ' Here she had almost choked as her throat had closed on her and had stopped, and Robin had jumped in hard.

'You've no right to say that about Hamish! How many objectors do you know, anyway? Jumping to conclusions like that – I thought better of you. He works like – like a lunatic at that hospital, do you know that? As for taking chances – aren't we all taking them these days? Why pick on him? He's a – an honest and caring person, and it's beastly of you to say such a thing about him – '

'I'm not going to argue about him,' Poppy said, knowing she had been unjust. 'I'm only concerned about you. For God's sake, Robin, you've got to leave that hospital. You can if you choose to, and I'm telling you it's high time you made that choice. It's not fair to me, to the people who love you, to go on like this. It may seem a huge lark to you, but to go out in a raid like that – it was the most lunatic thing I've ever heard of – '

'It may be,' Robin said quietly. She had got to her feet now and was staring down at her mother. 'But it's the sort of lunatic I am and am going to remain. I am not going to leave the hospital just to give you peace of mind. I know what it's like to worry – and I know you're worried about David as well as me, but that's the way of it these days. Don't you think I worry over David and over you and Auntie Jessie being here so much? This place – it's right in the danger area. But you don't run off and nor does she, and you've no right to ask me to, either. So forget it. I'm going back to the hospital right now and I'm going to tell them I don't want the night off to go home, which I told them I did. I'm going to go on duty tonight, sore eyes or no sore eyes. They'll find some way to make use of me, no doubt. I'm certainly not coming home to you if all I'm going to get is this sort of attack just because you're feeling miserable about things. I'll call you in the morning as usual if I can. And I hope you'll have the grace to apologize about Hamish when you've thought about it. He's a friend of mine and I don't intend to tolerate any attacks on my friends, wherever they come from. Goodbye, mother, I'll talk to you tomorrow if I can.'

And she was gone, leaving Poppy staring at the door she had closed behind her with a firm snap that only just stopped short of being a decided slam, and feeling fury and distress in equal measures filling her up; she was almost sick with it. Too much feeling altogether.

After that it was almost inevitable she'd have a row with Jessie too. She was reverberating like an overstrung guitar when she took the books to Jessie, as she usually did at eleven in the morning to go through the day's accounts, and she bit her lip hard as she went slowly down the familiar stairs. I won't rise to her, she told herself. I won't. I'm in a filthy mood and I must control it, I must. Robin was right, damn it. I have no right to attack people just because I'm feeling miserable –

But as soon as she walked into the big preparation room and saw them together, her good resolve melted and vanished. The women who did the work of preparation were there rushing around, doing twice their usual stint, because so many hadn't come in today. That always happened after a bad raid in the area – the news travelled fast, and the women got nervous, only a few stalwarts being prepared to take a chance and come so near the danger area; the rest came back in a few days when things quietened down a little and all would then be as usual. But today was not a usual day. Jessie was up to her elbows in flour, beating out her strudels unaided, while leaning against the warm oven behind her Bernie stood and watched her. And the sheer rage that lifted in Poppy actually made her vision dazzle for a moment so that when she looked at him she could hardly see him for glitter.

'That does it,' she announced loudly. 'I've had as much of this as I can take, Jessie. He's got to go. He's got to take his stuff with him and leave the premises. I've had all I can cope with and he's got to go – '

They both stared at her in the way they sometimes did, showing clearly their likeness to each other. Even now in her old age, when her face had collapsed and her large body had settled into anything but agreeable lines, Jessie still showed signs of the handsome woman she had been, and standing there beside her son with her head up she looked formidable and not at all the adoring aunt and good friend she usually was.

'Just a minute, Poppy,' Jessie said very deliberately. 'This ain't the time or the place,' and she began to pound her strudel dough again after casting a warning look over her shoulder at the working women and then back at Poppy. 'Some other time maybe – '

'Right now,' Poppy said, all control and good sense quite gone, and there was a dangerous note in her voice. 'I'm not interested in excuses or anything else. I've had about as much as I can take of this – this man and his – ' This time caution did catch hold of her by the coat-tails and she bit off what she had meant to say and ended instead, 'And his affairs. I want him out of here now.'

'And just who do you think you are?' Bernie was standing upright now, no longer leaning, his hands in his pockets in what was meant to be a relaxed posture but instead looked very tense indeed. 'You can't give my mother orders, and you sure as hell can't give me any – '

'I'm not giving orders,' Poppy snapped. 'I'm just telling you. I've had enough. If I have to – ' Again she glanced over Jessie's shoulder at the other women who were agog, while pretending carefully not to be listening. 'If I have to pass on the problems I have with you to – to other agencies, then that is what I will do. I'm an equal

246

partner in this enterprise and I won't be tainted by you and what you do. Is that understood?'

'It's understood.' It was Jessie, who was standing tense and very erect now. Her hands were still floury and that made a comic touch, but there was nothing at all comical about her face. She looked tired and drawn and very old. 'You hear her, Bernie? If you don't start to do it her way then she'll find other ways to make you. Fair enough? There are ways, as well you know. It's decided, dolly. If I had my way I'd help you no matter what, on account of you're my boy and always will be. But my partner says different – ' And she looked at Poppy so bleakly that some of the anger in her dribbled away, and left her feeling flat and miserable.

'Oh, Jessie, I don't want to pull any sort of rank here! It's just that I've told you I'm not happy about – about Bernie's involvement in the business. Yes, you're his mother, and I've no right to step between you and him. But I have a right to step between him and the *business*. Our business. My business, damn it. Don't I give as much to it as you do? I know it started out yours, that I've given no capital input, but it's had my heart and soul these many years and – and I can't live with myself if he's involved. You must understand me, Jessie.'

'I understand,' Jessie said again. 'You hear what she says, Bernie? It's all got to be settled. New arrangements will have to be made – '

'Oh, yes. Just like that. It's so easy, isn't it?' Bernie said savagely. 'Little Miss Goody Two Shoes here says it's all got to be done different, so different it's got to be done even if no one knows how to. Between now and tonight I've got to find new premises, just like that? I should cocoa!'

'It's got to be done,' Poppy said implacably. 'I say again, Jessie, I'm sorry. But I've got enough to cope with without worrying about this as well. It's all wrong – '

Again Jessie looked over her shoulder at her workers and this time she snapped at them, 'So stop staring already! Ain't it natural enough partners have business differences? Go and get yourselves your coffee or something. Work can wait ten minutes. Go on – '

The women went, wiping their hands on their aprons as they passed the three of them, their eyes well averted and with an air of tension across their shoulders, and Poppy knew what it was. As soon as they were in their crowded little rest room they'd fall into such an orgy of gossip it would take over twenty minutes before they got back to work. God, I'm stupid, she thought. If I'd made Jessie and Bernie come up to my office we could have sorted this out without wasting so much working time, and we're shorthanded too – I'm a damned fool –

When they'd gone, her sense of anger at herself made her more pugnacious than ever. 'Well, they've gone,' she said. 'So now I can spell it out. I will not have any truck with the black market, Jessie. I know you gave me some stock for the canteen a while back, but I'm still kicking myself over that. If we hadn't been at the very bottom of our resources I'd never have allowed it. As it was – well, I took it as a gift. I certainly didn't pay for any of it, so I feel less evil than I might. But I'm having no more of it. He's got to get his stuff out of our cellars. He can come here as often as you and he likes, of course – I've no way of stopping that and I wouldn't dream of attempting to do so, much as I can't stand you, Bernie. But your stuff has to go, and no later than tonight.'

There was a silence, and then Bernie shrugged. 'Well, it was time I was getting out anyway. I can move a bit north of here where the bombers won't come, and maybe do better business at that. I could end up thanking you for doing me a favour, Poppy, you know that? I really could. So get yourself down out of the high trees and take it easy. You'll blow a gasket, you go on like that. And then where'd your David be when he gets back from sea? *If* he gets back, of course – ' And he grinned at her winningly and went back to lean against the oven once more.

248

Jessie went white. 'Bernie! How can you be so – '

'Oh it's easy, Ma,' he said, not taking his eyes from Poppy's stricken face. 'Just as it's easy for her to be so high and mighty over a bit of business. She chooses to do it her way, and because I choose to do it mine, she's full of judgements. I wouldn't like to be in your shoes, Madam Self-Righteous, if anything ever goes wrong because of your high-minded meddling!'

'I'm not acting this way because I want to be self-righteous,' Poppy said, and her lips were stiff and that made speech difficult. Under the surface her pulses were thumping with sick terror. *If* David gets back, of course, *if* David gets back, of course – 'It's just that I can't stand black-market profiteers. I won't be associated with them. If you want to make your living that way, that's up to you. I won't turn you in. But I will if you go on involving me and Jessie in your rotten business. And there's an end of it.'

'I told you, Poppy,' Jessie said wearily. 'You win. All right, you win! It'll all be taken out tonight, right Bernie? You can get the van and shift it out?'

'If I must,' he said.

'You must.' Jessie stopped pulling on her strudel dough and stared at Poppy. 'Poppy says you must, so you must. All right now, Poppy? You feel better?'

Poppy had turned to go and was standing now by the door that led to the restaurant. Jessie was very clear to see, standing as she was right in the pool of light over her pastry table and a corner of Poppy's mind thought – why do I care? Why not let it all ride and let Jessie be happy? Times are so lousy, isn't it more important that people be happy than be good?

But she said nothing. She turned her head and went back to the restaurant and then on to the West End and finally that day to the canteen, and all the time she refused to think of Jessie's stricken face as she had stood there with her big red arms covered in flour and her face so bleak and miserable, as Bernie, the beautiful and unscrupulous Bernie, stared at her over Jessie's shoulder with malevolence in every line of his face.

Even when she went home to find Goosey sulking and the house undusted and unswept – Goosey's usual form of reprisal when she felt she had been at all put upon – and took a sleeping pill and went to bed, desperate for the peace of sleep, she still saw Jessie's face staring at her. And Robin's. And she felt deeply at odds with herself and everything and everyone else that was in her world.

· 25 ·

Robin was still seething when she got back to the hospital. How dare her mother speak so? How dare she try to interfere in her life that way? I'm twenty-one, Robin thought furiously, twenty-one and she still carries on as though I were an eleven year old. It's too much –

Somewhere deep inside her mind a little voice whispered at her – but she's frightened. David's at sea in the most dangerous area, and she's frantic, and Joshy and Lee are away and she's got a lot to cope with – but the angry Robin refused to listen. Her mother had no right to speak to her so. Mothers were supposed to be caring and supportive and never like that. Robin was close to tears of anger and a sort of fear as she reached the last hundred yards or so that lay between her and the hospital courtyard. Things were difficult enough without her mother showing her clay feet this way –

There was a good deal of traffic along the Whitechapel Road, buses and lorries of course, but some private cars too, and she had to wait on the corner of New Road for two of them which were waiting to find a hole in the traffic and turn left, when she saw her, and all her anger, which had begun to subside, came back in a rush.

Was her entire family against her? What had she done to deserve it? And her sore eyes filled up with stinging tears, and she bent her head, hoping the little red car would speed past her without its driver noticing her.

It didn't. As she crossed the road and began to hurry on to the hospital, the small red car which had been about to turn out into the traffic stopped, and the window was wound down.

'Ye gods,' Chloe said. 'What's happened to you then? You look as though you've been in a prizefight.'

'I was out in last night's raid,' Robin said, and couldn't resist the spiteful dig that rose to her lips. 'While you were no doubt snoring safely at home in Bryanston Square, I was looking after people in that awful raid.'

'Oh, do tell!' cooed Chloe. 'The little heroine, are we? When do you get your George Cross, then?'

'Oh, shut up, Chloe. If you can't say something decent – '

' – then don't say anything at all. For God's sake, you don't have to quote Goosey at me. Where are you going now, then?'

'To bed,' Robin said nastily. 'As soon as you stop gassing on in this stupid fashion and let me go.' And the question she hadn't meant to ask, the question she'd promised herself she wouldn't ask, was there, spoken, and she hated herself for letting the words out. 'What are you doing here, anyway?'

Chloe smirked. As far as Robin was concerned that was the only word for the expression that flitted across her face.

'Oh, just bringing Hamish back,' she said with studied nonchalance. 'He had nights off, you know, and he's due back tonight.'

'Really?' Robin said, knowing perfectly well what Hamish's off-duty was.

'Mm. So last night he – um – stayed over at my place. He's madly sweet, you know. Terribly naive and inexperienced, but awfully sweet – ' And she let her lips curve into a reminiscent smile, never taking her eyes off Robin's face.

Her meaning was unmistakable and Robin felt the pain in the middle as surely as if she had been hit by a piece of

252

shrapnel. It's none of your business. You don't own him and anyway there's nothing special between you. He's just a friend, only a friend, and not a very close one at that. But she didn't believe the small voice. She believed Chloe, who was still looking at her with that smirk on her face and Robin had to tighten her hands into fists inside her cape to stop herself hitting out at her. She'd never done that even when she'd been a child and Chloe had been hateful to her. She wasn't going to start now, please don't let me lose my temper now.

'If you say so,' she managed to say, though her lips felt stiff and unmanageable. 'But I haven't time to stand and chatter, I really must get to bed. See you again, no doubt.'

'No doubt,' Chloe said sunnily and let in her clutch. 'Bye, darling! By the way, how's Poppy and Co.?'

'Fine, fine,' Robin said, desperately needing to get away before she lost all control and the tears of fury that were rising in her throat like sharp points of shattering glass overwhelmed her, and she moved a little sideways to get round the car and escape, and Chloe watched her and then laughed.

'Try not to be too hard on your friend Hamish,' she said lightly. 'Poor darling – didn't know what hit him! Putty in the old hands, wasn't it – ' And this time she did put the car into motion and went, leaving Robin standing there as it disappeared into the traffic heading west along the Whitechapel Road.

Somehow she managed to get herself into the hospital grounds and on her way to the Nurses' Home without anyone she passed noticing how distressed she was. Chloe and Hamish – it didn't bear thinking of; and therefore she wouldn't think of it, she wouldn't, no matter what. It wasn't important, anyway; why should she worry about it? Let him do as he chose. If Hamish wanted to play at tomcats with her sister that was his affair. Nothing to do with me, Robin told herself, struggling to believe it. Nothing at all to do with me –

She turned the corner by the emergency dispensary unit that had been set up in a Nissen hut after the original one had been damaged in a raid, her head down and the tears running down her cheeks. Her eyes stung dreadfully and her face seemed to be flaming as though someone had set a match to her cheeks. She didn't see him until she almost ran into him.

'Robin!' Hamish said and put out a hand to hold her shoulder. 'What happened to ye? They told me where you were last night when I called in at the porter's lodge – let me see – '

She lifted her face and glared at him. 'What do you care?' she snapped and tried to get past him, needing to be alone in her own room where she could let out all the confused feelings that were pounding in her own aching head.

He dropped his hand and said in a clearly startled voice, 'What did you say?'

'I said what do you care? You were having a great time with my sister – my half-sister – while I was out in that raid. What do you care about me or what happens to me?'

He took a sharp little breath. 'I thought we were friends,' he said. 'That's why I – '

'So did I,' she snapped. 'Now I know better.'

Why am I talking this way? the little voice in her mind whispered. Why let him know how hurt you are, how angry, why make a fool of yourself? Where's your pride, for God's sake?

'Now you – ' He shook his head. 'You'll need to explain.'

'I saw Chloe,' she said and had to work hard not to shout it. 'Outside. Just brought you back, I imagine. Glad to hear it was all so – oh, leave me be. I'm going.' And she pushed past him and went running across to the Nurses' Home, her cape flying behind her, leaving him standing staring after her with his face as still as a piece of his native hillside.

Chick was in her room when she got to the Nurses' Home and Robin stood at the door and said tightly, 'What do you want?'

'Mm?' Chick looked up from the book she had on her lap as she sat curled up on Robin's bed. 'Oh, it's your Anatomy and Physiology book. Lost mine. I'm just mugging up on the arteries that supply the kidneys, ready for the test next week. I've done no work at all, what with all the gadding about I've been doing. I thought I'd try to get something into my thick head before I went to bed. There's sure as hell no time to do any swotting on duty – ' She stretched and yawned and then, half-way through, stared at Robin and said, 'Hey – what are you doing here anyway? I thought you said you were going home till your eyes were better?'

'Changed my mind,' Robin said shortly. 'Listen, do you mind? I want to go to bed. I'm tired – '

'You're more than that,' Chick said and sat up more erectly, staring at her. 'My child, you are in a state of – well, tell me what happened to get under your skin this way. I've never seen you so screwed up. And it's not just the eyes I'm talking about either – '

'Oh, it's nothing!' Robin snapped. 'I'm just tired, that's all – '

'Oh, sure, that's all,' Chick mocked. 'Come off it, ducky. This is me, the old Chick, still selling at the old stand, remember? Don't try and tell me I'm a fool who can't see beyond the end of her own nose, on account I won't stand for it. Something's got under your skin very badly and I insist you tell me – '

'Chick, go away!' Robin said and stamped her foot and burst into loud and uncontrollable tears.

It took Chick almost half an hour to sort her out. She got her undressed and into the bath and then into bed, scolding her all the while, but without any real opprobrium, for all the world like a younger version of Goosey, Robin thought at one point, and then brought her a cup of cocoa from the little gas ring at the end of the corridor, together with one for herself. And then flopped down on Robin's bed, making her push her legs to one side, and glared at her with affectionate reproval.

'Okay, little one, spill it,' she said and when Robin started to shake her head in refusal, lifted one imperious hand. 'You'll have to tell me everything as well you know, so you might as well get on with it, and then we can both get some sleep.'

And Robin, knowing when she was beaten, and filled with the languor that comes after a great emotional flood of the sort she'd just been through, told her. Of Poppy's behaviour first of all, for that still hurt, and then haltingly of what had happened with Chloe and Hamish.

'So there you have it,' she said at length. 'I feel – oh, it's hard to explain. I just thought he was a friend, that's all – '

'Rather more than a friend,' Chick said. 'Love and all that, I reckon. It does get in the way, doesn't it? Spoils some good friendships – '

'No – ' Robin protested, but Chick shook her head.

'Listen, ducks, will you? You're in a great state on account of Hamish curled up with your sister. Sorry, half-sister. It's really got under your skin – and that wouldn't have happened if you didn't want to curl up with him yourself – '

Robin's already red face got hotter. 'I never thought of him that way,' she protested feebly.

'Maybe you didn't, not with your head. But your body did, didn't it? Bodies can be a goddamned nuisance, take it from me.' Now it was Chick who looked a little pink. 'That cousin of yours – '

'Mm?' Robin looked at her, glad to be distracted from her own tale of woe. 'What do you mean? Daniel?'

'Daniel,' Chick said. 'As smooth as butter and then some. And rather on the gorgeous side, wouldn't you say?'

'I suppose so,' Robin said and Chick laughed.

'I guess when it's a relation you don't notice it. Take it from me, he's pretty as guys go. And very pushy – '

Robin looked alarmed. 'I hope he's not – not – ' and again Chick laughed.

'Oh, don't fret! I can take care of myself. It's just that – ' She shrugged. 'I'm just glad I can talk to Harry now and again.'

'He's still seeing you then?' Robin was deeply grateful for the turn the conversation had taken. The more they talked of Chick's affairs, the less they'd talk of her own.

'In a vague sort of way. He's really rather nice in his own dour fashion. Getting him to talk is like walking over a ploughed field in high-heeled shoes, mind you, but it's worth the effort, you know what I mean?'

'Yes,' Robin said and managed a smile. 'Yes, I think so. Listen, tell me more tonight. I must get some sleep and then I want to get up early and go over to the Nursing Office and arrange to go on duty tonight. My eyes don't bother me too much, and I know they're short in Cas. Especially now that Meek's gone to her new post – '

'Alleluia, praise the Lord,' said Chick. 'Without her we all do much better, believe me. They'll never let you go on duty tonight. You look as though you ought to be in the sick bay.'

'Oh, nonsense, I'm fine. Just a bit sore is all. Are you going then?'

'If you promise me you won't fret any more over this business with your – with Hamish and Chloe.'

'I won't,' Robin said knowing she lied. 'Go on now.'

'I'll go.' Chick got to her feet. 'But I'm not leaving it at that. I've got a feeling about your half-sister.'

'So have I,' said Robin with sudden malice in her voice.

'Not like yours,' Chick said. She had reached the door now. 'I think she's a born troublemaker. I think she'd say anything to upset people, just for the hell of it. Really spiteful – '

'Is Churchill Prime Minister?' Robin said wearily and put her cup on her bedside table, so that she could slide down in bed. It felt very welcoming and sleep was beginning to creep into her.

'So I'm going to do a bit of research,' Chick said. 'Sleep well, ducky. See you tonight,' and she was gone, closing the door softly behind her, and Robin slid into sleep almost at once, worn out with the pain of her eyes and last night's exploits and the emotional maelstrom that had followed. She tried to think about what Chick had said and what she might mean but couldn't catch her own thoughts; they kept sliding away into dreams of flames and the sight of St Paul's Cathedral outlined in crimson against a black sky.

Poppy sat at the kitchen table, hunched over a cup of cocoa, staring at the blackout that covered the big window. Its thick stuffy folds seemed to echo her mood, and she wanted to bury herself in it. To be able to sink into blackness, to have no painful dreams, no fears that twisted themselves into hideous images of death and disaster as she slept – that was the only sort of bliss she could imagine.

Upstairs Goosey was sleeping. She'd been in her room all day, and Poppy, when she had climbed the steps to the front door and gone into the house to stand and listen to the silence had thought for a while of just leaving her there to sulk, and then had sighed.

She couldn't do that to the old thing. She'd meant no harm, after all. Just moaning on about the laundry; and it was difficult for her, because wasn't she too fretting over David? Oh, David, prayed Poppy, standing in the hall in the cold winter light, come home safe, please come home safe. I need you so much, don't let them drown you. And so terrified was she by the word that had come into her mind that she ran upstairs to speak to Goosey as though she could run away from her own thinking.

The old woman was sitting in the chair beside her window staring out at the garden when Poppy had followed her knock on the door by immediately putting her head round it, and at first, she wouldn't speak. But eventually Poppy had coaxed her round and she had wept a little and sniffed a lot and then opted to go to bed, though Poppy insisted that she eat some supper first.

'I'll bring you something on a tray,' she said. 'I'm not sure what but – '

'There's a bit of cheese in the box,' Goosey said, looking animated suddenly. 'It would toast up lovely on a bit of bread – ' and she had sniffed again and mopped her old eyes and crept into bed, and Poppy had gone down to make her supper.

Now she sat in her silent house, almost straining her ears to hear some sort of comforting sound from outside, but there was just the hiss of the coals on the fire and the faint murmur of the kettle lid on the hob as steam lifted it in a steady rhythm, and she sighed and tried to pretend there wasn't a war on at all, that this was the ordinary old days when she'd been busy of course, but it had all been so comfortable and easy; and she couldn't. The layer of fear that was always there at the bottom of her belly these days wouldn't go away, and while it was there no amount of effort to exercise her imagination could possibly help her.

She dozed a little, sitting there at the table, her head propped on her hand and her empty cocoa mug in front of her, and dreamed again; this time it was Robin she saw, running through leaping flames with her cape streaming behind her like a crimson wing, and then she saw it wasn't just crimson on the inside but on the outside too, and the colour came from burning – and she woke suddenly to stare sightlessly at her quiet kitchen, trying to banish the image that was still there in front of her eyes.

Quite what made her do it she was never to know, and in years to come she was to think about it often; all she knew now was that while she sat there willing the image of Robin in flames to leave her memory, she had a sudden urgent need to go to Jessie.

259

She could see her staring at her, standing there in the middle of her kitchen with her red arms dusted with flour and her face glowing with the reflection of her pink blouse, and Bernie standing behind her looking sullenly at Poppy, and she had to go and see her. Perhaps after all she'd been unduly unkind to her this morning; she wanted Bernie and his hateful black-market dealings out of the business's premises, of course, and that was reasonable enough, but she needn't have been so short with Jessie, so very hard.

And she got to her feet almost without realizing she was doing so and headed for the hall to pick up her coat and hat and scarf and go back to Cable Street. It was dreadful to leave the people you loved in a bad temper at any time, and perhaps worst of all now, when all around them all was so fluid, so ever-changing, so desperately, constantly dangerous.

She closed the front door gently, praying Goosey hadn't heard it, knowing she'd worry if she had, and then set off at a jog for the Bayswater Road and the first bus that came along. A train from Marble Arch, that was what she wanted, and then Aldgate East and the chance to tell Jessie she was sorry to have upset her this morning.

And then, perhaps, she told herself as the bus came trundling along, looking like a faintly blue ghost in the darkness as its shaded bulbs glimmered coldly in its depths, perhaps even to make some sort of peace with the hated Bernie. He might be despicable but he was, after all, Jessie's son. And for that reason alone it would be worth making the gesture of friendliness to him. It would make Jessie happy, certainly. And she sat in her corner seat as the bus started up again with a low growl, feeling suddenly a little better.

·26·

The bells were ringing at Aldgate East station when the train got there, and she swore softly under her breath. An alert in progress; and she stood on the platform as other arriving passengers moved into the crowds, looking at the rows of occupied bunks and people on mattresses and rugs who filled the whole area as far as she could see, very aware of the fetid air laced with the smell of hot winter clothes and rubber shoes and tobacco and above all of human sweat, and tried to think.

To go out into a raid would be foolish and anyway the chances were a warden would appear to bundle her into a shelter again; but to stay here would be worse, and she hesitated, not able to decide what to do.

Somewhere up the platform someone was playing a mouth organ and a couple of children, a little boy with crisp curling black hair, a wide grin and enormous energy, and a small round girl who was just as eager as he was, were tap-dancing to it, and she stood and watched them for a while, diverted.

They were both obviously blissfully happy, their feet twinkling in practised unison, and grinning at their audience with practised skill as a small neat woman, obviously their mother, sat and watched them with bursting pride all over her face.

'That's it, Lionel – keep it going – good girl, Joycie!' she cried and clapped her hands in encouragement, and the children danced even more energetically as their mother laughed delightedly, and Poppy thought – they've forgotten why they're here, forgotten they're here for the bombs and the sirens. They're just happy dancing, and she looked at the other people around them who were watching them. They looked tired and white about the mouth, but they were amused by the children and enjoyed them, following their mother in clapping their hands in time to the music that the mouth organ churned out perkily.

'On the good ship Lollipop,' Poppy whispered under her breath in time to the music. 'It's a short trip to the candy shop, where the bon-bons are, happy landings on a chocolate bar – ' and suddenly her eyes smarted with unshed tears.

Lee had loved that silly song, had learned to sing it in her tuneless little voice almost as soon as she could speak; and Poppy tried to imagine her here beside her, dancing like these children, and couldn't. She was safe and happy enough where she was, however much she might be missed here, and Joshy too, and the tears came closer to the surface. I must see Jessie, she thought then with complete inconsequentiality. I must see her, raid or not. It had become the most important of matters, more than just a desire to calm the morning's spat, more than a wish to make peace. It was an imperative that pushed her to the exit and the stairway to the surface.

She arrived at the top a little breathless, for the escalators had stopped, to find the warden standing near the half-drawn iron gates across the entrance. It all looked very odd; the ticket office and the cigarette kiosk and newspaper stand shuttered, but otherwise the usual messy Underground station, and she stared round, trying to remember it all as it had been. A silly thing to do – another attempt to escape from what was really going on. And she shook herself mentally. There was no escape from the here and now. There never would be.

The warden turned his head as she came up. 'You want to stay down there below, missus, where it's safe.' He returned his gaze to the street. 'The buggers are really after us tonight and no error – '

She looked out over his shoulder and saw it; the glow in the sky ahead, just at the far end of Leman Street across the wide road that was Whitechapel High Street, empty now of moving buses and lorries, for they were all abandoned at the kerbs, their occupants gone to seek shelter. It looked unreal and yet menacing out there as the glow in the sky ahead was reflected off such shop windows as had survived, and the patches of worn road where the gleam of tar showed through. And suddenly she caught her breath. Leman Street – close to the shop and restaurant and Jessie –

'Where's that coming from? That glow there – any idea?' she said as she came closer to the man, and peered through the gap between the gates.

'Last I heard from the fellers over at the Post, it's a direct hit on Cable Street,' he said, peering out into the dimness. 'And 'ere they come again, the devils. Get down!' And he turned to run towards the head of the escalator as above them the low roar of aeroplanes shook the sky.

She pushed the gates open wider and wriggled out. A direct hit on Cable Street. Oh, God, she thought. Oh, Jessie. Oh, God, and began to run as the man in the station behind her, suddenly realizing what she was doing, shouted after her and the noise of the planes overhead got louder.

She ignored his shouts and ran on along the familiar route, staring ahead with her eyes wide for fear of missing her footing in the blackout and then realized that with the light overhead as well as the other fires burning around her and lighting up the sky, there was ample illumination. Fire engines were everywhere, with police and more wardens, and she dodged arms put out to stop her as she ran on, getting first dreadfully breathless and then at last finding her second wind, which made it possible to run even faster.

The planes overhead grew quieter, and she thought – thank God, they're going over to somewhere else and then felt a great stab of shame. Wishing bombs on other people. Is this what we've been reduced to? Wishing others hurt, anyone as long as it's not ourselves –

She came bursting out of Leman Street to make a great curve to her left, and at last was in Cable Street. And then stopped and stared and knew that this had been entirely what she had expected. It had to be. There couldn't have been any other outcome. From the moment she had left Norland Square, she told herself with a sick certainty, this was what I expected. I knew, somehow I knew –

She began to run again, until she was up to the edge of a depression in the ground which was almost deep enough to be called a crater, and which had on its far side a heap of battered remains of the building, great slabs of concrete and piled dusty bricks, and, incongruously, a broken table lying helplessly on its back with the legs in the air like a stranded tortoise, and she thought – it's mine. From my office. Oh, God, it's my table. And she stood and stared over the rubble, trying to see, and a warden shouted ahead somewhere and she looked up, almost frightened to see what was beyond.

And for one moment felt a stab of hope. It was the restaurant that had gone with the office over it, but the building alongside where the kitchens and the shop were was still standing. Fire licked along the crest of the roof, but there were firemen up there and hoses played elegant dancing arcs of water across the darkly orange sky above. If she'd been in the kitchens she'd be all right, Poppy told herself, almost whispering the words aloud. If she'd been in the restaurant – and then caught her breath in a half-sob, half-shout as a warden appeared out of the hubbub and looked out towards her.

'Hey, you,' he bawled angrily. 'Take cover – '

'Tom?' she called, recognizing him even under the layer of soot that covered his face. 'It's me – Mrs Deveen

– do you know who was here? Can I come and see what's up and who was here? I just got here – '

The man peered at her in the fitful light, as a couple of firemen went by her hauling another hosepipe, and she stepped sideways to keep out of their way and almost slithered into the crater, and the man Tom cursed loudly and came slipping and stumbling over the pile of rubble to reach her.

'I told you to take cover – oh, Gawd, Mrs D – I didn't hear what you shouted – didn't know it was you. Listen ducks, nothing you can do. The place got a direct hit – I'm that sorry.'

'Who was here?' she said and her voice amazed her by its steadiness. 'I must know – who was here?'

'Place had almost shut for the night, according to the man we got out. Old fella – head waiter?'

'Horace,' she said and caught her breath. 'He came over tonight to help out.'

'He's all right,' the warden said quickly and then, amazingly, laughed. 'Dead annoyed, mind you. They took him off to the hospital to get his broken leg sorted out and he was cursing a treat. He was just counting up the tips or something – the tronk, is it? – anyway, sharing out the moolah, he said, and the bloody Huns come and scattered the lot. Steamin' mad he was – '

Poppy managed to laugh. It was so very much a Horace sort of thing that, and the relief of hearing the irascible old man had been up to form, in spite of his injury, was huge. But there had been others there and she caught her breath again and said, 'Tom – my aunt was here tonight, wasn't she?'

'Mrs Braham?' Tom said and swore again. His language was rich and rounded and seemed to help him. 'Here, Dave!' he bawled over his shoulder. 'Dave! Mrs Deveen says as how the old girl's in there – any luck looking?'

'No one on the ground floor or the upper ones,' a hidden voice roared back, barely audible over the sound

265

of the spluttering hoses and the crackling of flames greedily eating wood and throwing an incongruously cheerful kitchen-in-the-early-morning sort of scent into the air. ' – take another look – '

'The cellars?' Poppy said then and tried to follow Tom as he turned to clamber over the rubble towards the distant shouting voice. 'She may have been down there. It's pretty deep – she could be all right, but we've got to get her out – '

'Leave it to us, for Gawd's sake, Mrs D – ' The warden turned and looked down at her and she saw him brilliantly outlined against the smoky light of the fire that was now taking hold of the kitchen and shop building and which seemed to be defeating the sweating, shouting firemen. The sound of crackling wood had become an ominous roaring now. 'We got enough to sort out without having another civilian down there to worry over – we'll look for her, trust me – Cellars, you say – ' And he turned and slithered away to the other side of the heap of rubble, leaving her staring impotently after him.

It seemed to be an eternity that she stood there waiting. There was nothing else she could do. To have insisted on following Tom would have been stupid. He was right to tell her she'd be in the way. But she couldn't go away, either, and she stood there, her head thrown back, staring up at the roof where the years of Jessie's and her own hard work seemed to be about to be slowly eaten away into a cloud of white ash and broken bricks, and waited.

And then suddenly there was action, loud action, and she strained forwards to try to see what was happening and frustrated by the heaping of the rubble which obstructed her view, made up her mind and began, slowly and awkwardly, to climb it.

Her feet slipped and twisted on the broken bricks and timbers which lay drunkenly across it and she almost fell on her knees at one point, but managed to regain her balance just in time. And got to the top of the pile of rubbish that had once been the best restaurant in the East End to stand staring down on the other side.

It was like a scene on a stage. At the rear the glow of the fire and at ground level, the bulk of the building with its roof ablaze, and in front of that a little group of slowly moving people lit by flashes of light from above as the fire on the roof leapt up in response to the sudden bursts of breeze that came swooping over the roof tops from the river. She stood frozen into stillness, watching as they inched their way across the remains of the pavement and blinked as the heat made her eyes smart and run tears and rubbed them and stared again.

Two people carrying a stretcher and on it a figure that didn't move. Behind them another stretcher with three men carrying it this time, and a figure that seemed to be moving a little. Or was it an optical illusion due to the leaping firelight? And then she knew it wasn't. She could see arms waving about and hear the sound of voices, but it was hard to hear properly for the roaring of the fire was now very loud. She strained her eyes and ears even more, but it was useless. There was only one thing to do and she did it.

She slid precariously down the other side of the rubble heap, bringing a good deal of it down with her, and tearing her legs painfully on bits of twisted metal that stuck out of it, until she was on reasonably safe ground and then, holding her hand in front of her face, because the heat from the fire was now almost searing, pushed towards the stretchers.

By this time they'd reached the edge of the cleared area, where an ambulance stood waiting, its doors gaping wide, and as she came up to it, the bearers began to push the first stretcher with its still burden into it. And then she was there at last, standing beside the second stretcher with its three bearers and she looked down at it, almost too frightened to focus her eyes and saw the glimpse of red under the rough blanket and swallowed hard.

'Jessie,' she said very softly and the head on the stretcher moved and then turned and the husky voice said, 'Poppela – I knew you'd come, dolly. I knew you would – ' And then stopped in a little sigh.

Poppy was crouching beside her, trying to see in the unreliable light and the man behind the stretcher said kindly, 'She's all right as far as we can see, lady. Friend of yours?'

'My aunt,' Poppy said, and set her cheek against Jessie's. 'She's my aunt and the best woman in the world. She's not too hurt – ?'

'Legs seems funny,' the other stretcher man said. 'Couldn't feel nothing when we moved her. There was this thing across her back. They'll sort her out at the hospital though. She's on her way – '

Poppy got to her feet then and peered into the ambulance where they were settling their first passenger, arranging the blankets neatly across the stretcher and she called out, 'Who's that?'

'No idea,' the stretcher man said, and looked down at her. 'Might you know if you was to look?'

'Yes – ' she said breathlessly, trying to think who it might be. Lily? Had she stayed late tonight? One of the waiters or the chef? And, fearful and unwilling, she climbed into the ambulance, not wanting to look.

The stretcher man stood aside courteously and she wanted to giggle. It was just as though he were one of her own waiters showing a customer to a table, and she almost expected him to use a napkin to flick an imaginary speck of dust away. But she controlled herself and looked down at the face on the stretcher.

The eyes were half open and the hair was rumpled over them. It made him look, down one side of his face, like a child who had fallen asleep so suddenly he hadn't even had time to close his eyes properly. But the other side of his face showed no expression at all. It couldn't. It was a mass of bloody tissue which had been torn from the bone so deeply that she could see a white gleam in

268

the depths, and experienced though she was in seeing battlefield wounds, the sight made her head swim and her belly heave with nausea.

'Do you know him, lady? It'd help for the labelling,' the man at her side said and she looked at him and again at the stretcher and shook her head to clear it.

'Yes,' she said dully. 'I know him. His name is Bernard Braham.'

·27·

Robin stood at the far side of the casualty waiting hall, pretending to look through the bundles of patients' record notes she had in her hands, but in fact watching Hamish. She had to talk to him; that ten minutes she had spent listening to Chick as they came out of Night Nurse's breakfast to go on duty had shown that. He deserved an apology. But the trouble was, if she apologized would he read more into it than she intended? Could he perhaps think she was being the same as her half-sister? The mere idea of that was enough to make her feel hot with shame. She couldn't bear to let him think so. Yet, equally, she couldn't bear to let him go on thinking she had been rude and hateful and didn't want him to be her friend any longer. She sighed. Whatever she did she was in trouble. Devils and deep blue seas just weren't in it.

Chick came out of her cubicle with a swish of the curtain behind her and made her way to the sterilizer in the corner, making a detour in order to pass Robin, and as she went she hissed, 'Ass! talk to him now. Tell him I told you what he told me – that your Chloe lied like a Persian rug and then some – he's entitled to know. And the longer you put it off the harder it'll be – go *on*!' and then caught Sister's eye as she went bustling across the waiting room and smiled beatifically at her. Robin, also seeing Sister, was forced into action. She couldn't just stand here watching Hamish any longer.

He had just finished scrubbing the walls of the soiled cubicle when she went in, and was about to start on the floor. It smelled foul – beer and worse – and she wrinkled her nose a little, wishing they could talk somewhere else, somewhere quiet and decent and –

'I'll be away from here in about five minutes, Nurse,' he said in his soft burr, not looking at her. 'If you need the cubicle urgently – '

'I don't need it, Hamish,' she said. 'I need you.'

He went on mopping the floor in long practised strokes and then hauled the mop into its bucket and screwed it into the squeezer. He didn't look at her.

'I thought you didn't want to speak to me,' he said at length.

'I was wrong.' She managed somehow to keep her voice steady. It really was difficult. 'I have to apologize.'

There was a long silence and then he looked at her, and just for a moment leaned on his mop. 'Well, who'd ha' thought it? And you so convinced I was some sort of – of – '

'Don't say it,' she said swiftly. 'Please don't. I – it wasn't entirely my own fault. My half-sister – Chloe – she always manages to – '

'Ah, Chloe,' he said thoughtfully and started mopping again and Robin sidestepped to get out of the way. 'Poor soul.'

Robin stared at him. 'Poor soul?' she echoed. 'She's about as pathetic as a shark!'

'Oh, you're wrong there! She's had a bad time of it one way and another, you know – '

'I know a lot about Chloe!' Robin said and began to feel angry again. How could he defend her when she'd told such a thumping lie, and made her, Robin, so miserable? 'More than you possibly can – '

'I wouldn't be so sure. Outsiders sometimes see a good deal more of what happens in families than the members of it do.'

271

'Oh, I see!' Robin was sardonic now. 'She's been telling you tall tales about how unkind everyone is to her and how Ma and David didn't let her do this and that when she was younger and how they stopped her from spending her money and – '

'Were they? Unkind? I'd doubt that. From what I've seen of your mother.' He was leaning on his mop again. 'Certainly Chloe said nothing derogatory about them.' He looked reflective then. 'Unless it's derogatory to say that her family are all stick-in-the-muds and boring and have no fun in them and so forth. But there. I'm the same sort, so I don't think it's a bad way to be. I dare say you know she thinks that – '

She stared at him. 'Well, yes. She says it all the time. She said nothing else about us?'

'Not a word. That's why I'm so sorry for her.'

'Indeed.' Again she let the sardonic note sound.

'Aye,' he said with equanimity, ignoring her edginess. 'A lonely creature when all's said and done. Wants so much to be part of you all, and simply doesna' know how to be. So all she can do is dig away at you and try to deal with her jealousy that way. As I said, poor soul.'

Robin was silent. This was a version of her half-sister she had never seen before, but she had to admit that there was some sense in what he said. At family events of any kind Chloe was always rather on the outside looking in. They had tried to make her comfortable with them, of course they had. David alone was too generous a character to do otherwise, and Robin knew her mother had been trying for years to be closer to Chloe. But whatever they did there was always that air of remoteness about Chloe and over the years perhaps they had all rather stopped trying, had turned their backs on her –

He was watching her closely and now he smiled. 'You're seeing what I mean,' he said quietly.

'I – perhaps.' She straightened then. 'Anyway, let's leave Chloe out of it for the moment. Just let me say I'm sorry I got so upset. It was – it was just I believed her when she said – anyway you know what she said. Chick told me she'd talked to you. I have no right to get so bothered anyway. I mean, I should have realized she was lying to me and you didn't – you hadn't – ' She couldn't stop it then, the hot blush that climbed her cheeks and made her forehead sweat and he smiled again.

'It mattered to you that I hadna' accepted her invitation to get into her bed?'

'I've no right to care either way,' she mumbled. 'I mean, I shouldn't have said anything – it was none of my – '

'I'm glad it mattered to you,' he said and looking over her shoulder to see if they could be seen from the waiting hall, leaned across and drew the curtain, and then bent his head and kissed her mouth gently and without any urgency, but for all that, it made her hotter and pinker than ever. 'Very glad,' he repeated.

'That's all right then,' she managed and put up both hands to wipe her face and found the notes she was still clutching in the way and giggled. 'Then we'll say no more about it? Just go on as we were and – well, get to know each other better?' There were images in Robin's head of herself and Hamish walking hand in hand along the streets, herself and Hamish at parties, herself learning to dance his special way – and her eyes glittered and her smile widened. She didn't know it but she looked suddenly prettier than she ever had.

'I'd like that. It won't be so easy of course, but I'd like that.'

'Won't be so easy?' There was a note in his voice that sent the pretty imaginings away in shreds. 'Why not?'

'There'll be letters, of course. I hope you'll write to me?'

The glitter vanished suddenly and she looked at him with her face puckered. 'Where are you going that you'll want letters?'

He began to mop again, his head down over the bucket. 'Wales.'

'Wales – what's in – I mean, you're needed here!'

'I'm needed more there.'

'Doing what?'

'Mining.'

There was a long silence and then she said, stupefied, '*Mining*? Underground? In the *pits*?'

'Yes,' he said steadily and looked at her. 'Underground, in the pits and the shafts. In the dark.'

'But Hamish, you – I mean – how will you cope with – ' She could feel it all again with a great vividness; his shaking body beside her in that small place, the dampness and heat of him, his rushing pulse. If that had happened after just a few minutes in an enclosed space, how would he cope in a mine for a whole shift?

'I'll have to,' he said. 'It's time I did a better job. I – call it a bit selfish if you like, but I canna take the jibes any longer. Every other man who walks in here or in the street sneers at me – calls me coward. I've worked all the hours God sends here, doing tough and foul work, but it seems to make no difference. So I'll be away down the mines and there'll be no question then.'

She stood silent for a moment and then held out her hand. 'I do congratulate you,' she said. 'You're just about the bravest person I know. If anyone ever again calls you a coward, just let me know – '

He took her hand and held it tightly. 'You couldn't have said anything to please me more,' he said gravely. 'Thank you, Robin.'

She went pink again. 'I'll miss you,' she managed.

'And I'll surely miss you. But that's wars for you. They kill all sorts of things and not just people, bad as that is.'

'Yes,' she said. 'Oh, yes.' And somehow she managed not to get tearful. It wasn't easy.

The curtain rings clattered and they sprang apart almost guiltily, though they'd been doing no more than talking, and Robin said in a rather loud and

274

oh-so-professional voice. 'Well, if you've not seen it, then I'll have to look somewhere else,' and then lifted her still rather flushed face as Sister Priestland appeared.

She looked from one to the other and for a moment it seemed she would offer some sort of rebuke, but then she stopped herself, and turned to Robin.

'I've been looking for you, my dear. We've just had a couple of casualties in from an incident not far from here – '

'Oh!' Robin said and tidied the notes in her hand. 'I'll get rid of these, then, Sister, and finish them later. Which cubicle do you want me to – '

Sister Priestland put out her hand to set it on her wrist and Robin stared down at it and then at Sister Priestland to find some clue to this remarkable behaviour, and the older woman said gently, 'Now, at present there's no need to worry too much about her, but I have to tell you your aunt is involved – '

'Aunt?' Robin said stupidly and Hamish set down his mop and came to stand protectively behind her. 'Aunt?'

Sister looked down at the notes she had in her hand. 'Mrs Braham,' she said. 'Your mother's with her – she's fine, not involved – just happened to visit, I gather, after the raid had – '

Robin waited for no more. She pushed past Sister and, breaking all the rules, ran out into the waiting hall to look around wildly and then run full tilt across it, almost pushing other people out of the way, to where her mother was standing beside the corner cubicle into which a trolley was just being taken. And even from the far side Robin could see on it the flash of crimson that was Jessie's dress.

This was, Poppy decided, the worst time of her life hitherto – or almost. Sometimes she tried to put it all into perspective by deliberately looking back over the years to her days in the horrors of Verdun, or the agonizing time when Bobby had been gassed and she'd had somehow to get him back to England and especially to the time of the flu epidemic when he and his sister Mabel had died, indeed to anything she could that would take her mind away from the here and now. But none of it worked. She just had to cope, somehow, a day at a time.

That first night in Casualty at the London Hospital with Robin, white-faced, hovering to find out what was happening – because Sister Priestland was adamant that she mustn't help Dr Landow since the patient was so close and beloved a relation – and waiting to hear the diagnosis, had been a painful exercise in patience. It was fortunate, Sam Landow had told her, that the number of raid-injured people had been low that night. They had time to deal with Jessie properly, and in consequence she spent long painful hours being prodded and checked, having a blood transfusion set up, for she had lost a lot from a wound in her left leg, and being X-rayed.

And when at last she had been taken up to a ward and settled to an exhausted drugged sleep, Sam sat down with Poppy and Robin and talked to them.

'I'm not sure what to tell you first,' he said. 'I think I must be sensible and start with the worst news. About Mr Braham – '

Poppy had stiffened. 'I saw his face,' she said huskily. 'It was – I can't tell you how – he's so very good-looking, you see. It'll be a blow and – '

'No,' Sam had said gently and put out both hands to take one of Poppy's cold ones in his. 'It won't be a blow to him, I'm afraid. It's more a blow to you. He died, my dear. I'm so sorry. He was dead by the time we received him.'

There was a long silence and then Poppy's face crumpled and she began to weep, a great storm of tears that flooded her face and twisted her mouth in an ugly grimace and Robin reached out and held her until the storm had passed and she was just sobbing, a little spasmodically, and hiccupping.

'I'm sorry,' she managed at last. 'I'm truly sorry – '

'You needn't apologize,' Sam said and at last let go of her hand, for he had held her all through her paroxysms. 'Grief is natural enough and – '

'Grief?' she said hoarsely. 'How can it be grief? I hated him. He was the most – I loathed him. Have for years. But Jessie – my Jessie – she'll be devastated. I can't tell her and I have to because no one else can and she'll – oh, God – ' And she closed her eyes tightly, willing herself not to weep again.

'That does make it more painful, then,' Sam said. 'I know. In the weeks to come, maybe we can talk about it? It might help – '

She had managed a watery little grimace at that. 'Robin told me that you were interested in psychiatry – '

'In helping people with emotional pain,' he said. 'Yes.'

'I'll think about it – ' Poppy had straightened then and put up her hands to wipe her face. 'Tell me about Jessie. She's – oh, God, I have to say it, she's the only one I really care about.'

'She'll live,' Sam said very positively. 'You hear that? Her life is in no danger.'

Poppy swallowed hard and closed her eyes. 'That's something to be – ' And then shook her head. 'Thank you.'

'But there is a problem.'

'What sort of problem? One you can't deal with? Does she need an operation or – '

He shook his head. 'I'm afraid it's not as easy as that. As far as I can tell – and I'm not a neurologist, you understand – she has an injury at the level of lumbar – let's say just that she's broken her back. The bones will heal well enough, but the nerve supply – '

There was a silence and then Poppy said carefully, 'She's going to be paralysed.'

'I think so,' Sam looked at her and shook his head. 'But don't just believe me. We can get her transferred to a country hospital – there's one of the London specialist nerve hospitals with a branch in Hertfordshire, well away

277

from the bombing, and they do excellent work there. I'll try tomorrow to arrange her transfer. There they can do a full appraisal and start whatever treatment might help. I think at this stage, though, the wisest thing to do is expect her to be wheelchair-bound for the rest of her life. But her life need not be shortened by that. She's a strong lady for all her years – '

'Seventy-five,' Poppy had said clearly. 'I never thought of her as old, but I suppose she is.'

'Yes. Getting old anyway. But she could have five more years of happiness, as long as she has good care – '

'Five years,' Poppy had whispered. 'It sounds so little.'

'I could be wrong! I'm only guessing. If she's got a good family history of long-living people and if she's happy she could live to be ninety! The important thing though is to help her accept her condition if it is in fact irremediable. If she fights it, then – ' He had shrugged. 'Well, it might make her ill.'

Robin had spoken then for the first time and she was never to know how the words came to her. But they made Poppy laugh and look, just for a moment, hopeful.

'Oh, she'll love it! She'll run circles round everyone and boss them about and make everyone jump when she speaks to them – oh, Ma, can't you just see it?'

And Sam had looked approvingly at her and sent them both to get something to eat and drink, determined, he said, not to have any more members of the family in need of loving care.

But that had just been the start of it. Over the next two weeks Poppy needed all the strength she had, and then half as much again.

There was, first, the matter of telling Jessie of Bernie's death. She had tried to convince herself it would be better to wait until Jessie was transferred to the specialist neurological hospital and was a little stronger, better able to take it in, but she knew she was really protecting herself, not Jessie. Soon she'd ask anyway – and she

278

went up to the ward where Jessie was at the London on the next day to tell her.

Walking down the long expanse of polished wood, between the serried rows of beds, each bearing a face that watched her mutely as she went by, was agony. They'd put Jessie at the far end, and every step that brought Poppy nearer made her pulse rate rise by a couple of beats. By the time she got to her, it was racing.

Jessie was lying flat on her back with a pair of metal hoops linked with a dish of weights holding her head still and stretching her neck. 'It's a device to stop any further damage being done to her spinal cord,' Sister had explained before allowing Poppy to go in. 'She has traction on her legs too, especially the left one because there was a break there and a major soft tissue injury which is now in plaster. She's had that repaired and it shouldn't be too bad afterwards. Not that she'll ever walk again, you understand – ' Sister had been as clinical as the smell of carbolic which surrounded her and Poppy had looked at the bleak blue eyes that looked at her with calm common sense but little warmth, and longed to have Sam Landow with her. A good man, Sam, and she liked him a lot. And thought, just for one mad moment, of the way he had looked at Robin, and then forgot it. It was Jessie who mattered most, now, not Robin.

Jessie had swivelled her eyes sideways as Poppy came up and as soon as she saw her, managed a smile.

'Poppela,' she croaked. 'Is it good to see you! Tell me all about it. Everything. I can't remember properly. It's just like it never happened. I keep trying to remember and they say forget it, but how can I? I was sitting there having a bit of supper with Bernie and the next thing I know is I'm here lying like some beetle turned on its back. Can't move – where's Bernie, Poppy? I know he makes you mad, but dolly, if I'm hurt you can't mind him coming – '

'Jessie,' Poppy said and took her hand tightly, and Jessie moved her eyes and looked up into hers, and

279

Poppy stared down at her. And in that moment Jessie knew. Poppy saw the truth come into her eyes and then a look of horror.

'What is it, Poppy? Tell me,' the thick voice said and Poppy did.

'It was instant, Jessie. He didn't know, they swear that to me. Just as you didn't know you'd been hit, didn't hear the bomb, neither did he – '

Jessie was staring at the ceiling, her face as rigid as though it had been carved out of mahogany.

'I – his face had been injured, darling. If he'd lived he would have been scarred. Dreadfully. He wouldn't have wanted to live like that – '

'A judgement,' Jessie said. 'A judgement.'

'Darling? What did you say?' For Jessie's voice was very low and Poppy had to bend to hear her.

'A judgement. He wouldn't move it, you see. Said you were – said he wouldn't move it. Came to put in new invisible locks so you wouldn't know he had anything, and so couldn't get it out – a judgement. If he hadn't been doing it, he wouldn't have been there. A judgement – ' And she closed her eyes and in a suddenly loud voice began to chant, 'Yiskadal, Yiskadach, Shamai Raboh balmah nov' and then went on and on, in Hebrew, and Poppy thought – that's the prayer for the dead. She's praying for her dead child – and closed her eyes, needing to make some response.

The curtains parted and Sister came in, and Poppy opened her eyes to glare at her, for the woman had her mouth open to protest at the noise Jessie was making, but Poppy hissed, 'I've had to tell her her son was killed. She's praying for him – ' And Sister looked at her and then at Jessie's closed eyes and moving lips and then crisply nodded and went away. A good woman after all, Poppy thought. A good woman.

They talked a long time after that, Poppy and Jessie, of the old days of Bernie's childhood sins. 'A lobbas,' Jessie said fondly and wept again and Poppy bit her lip and tried, very hard she tried, to think good of the dead. But it wasn't easy.

After that, there was so much to organize, to deal with and to plan that she had hardly any time to think about anything, and certainly not of her own feelings. There was the matter of Bernie's funeral, first, and that was difficult with so few rabbis around and the cemeteries sadly depleted of gravediggers, but that was managed, somehow; and then there was the even more painful matter of what to do about the business.

She went again in daylight to look at the damage and had to face the truth; there was no possibility of restoring the premises in the makeshift way other business people tried to do when it happened to them. There could be no 'Business as Usual' signs on these doors. Lily, who had come to work as usual the morning after the raid, had taken one look and then, frozen-faced, had told Poppy she'd had enough. She was going to live with her sister in High Wycombe till it was over.

'I'll come and see Jessie wherever she is, and I'll go to the funeral for that Bernie, the – well, I'll be there. Right's right. But after this, there's nothing left for me here. I'm old now. I have to go.' And she had looked at Poppy bleakly and then wept on her shoulder, and Poppy had stood there, dry-eyed, patting her shoulder and wondering when there would be someone for her to lean on. Oh, David, she prayed. Be safe, my darling. Be safe.

There was worse to come. When she investigated the situation she realized that the other restaurants, in the West End and in Knightsbridge, had to go too. They might have intact premises, but without the kitchens in Cable Street to back them, she couldn't maintain any sort of service. Better to let go, especially as she discovered that her insurance policies covered such an eventuality. And she remembered the long hours she had spent, back in the early 1930s, hammering out these policies to make sure they were well protected and was grateful for her own past perspicacity. There were no clauses to exclude enemy action damage in her policies, no chance for the insurance company to renege on its deal. And the cheques were paid into the bank and there she was. After all the years of running three restaurants and a busy factory kitchen supplying half of London with Jewish delicatessen, and also their own shop, it was all over. There was only money to show for it – a sizeable sum, but still only money – and a crater in Cable Street.

That, Poppy told herself, was her nadir. And then castigated herself for her own wickedness. Jessie was alive, wasn't she? That was what mattered. And though David was far away and she had heard no word from him or about him, to the best of her knowledge he was all right. He would get home, he would, he would. How could she be at her lowest, she asked herself passionately, when the people she most loved were all right? Or comparatively so –

She accompanied Jessie on her journey to the hospital just outside Bishops Stortford, in Hertfordshire, and was comforted to see how well cared for she would be. The place was set in the middle of a country park, having been adapted from an old manor house, and was beautifully equipped and, as far as Poppy could tell, staffed by gentle sensible people. She had no qualms about leaving Jessie there, though the old woman had clung to her hand, weeping bitterly, not wanting to let her go.

'I can't be alone, so far from home,' she wailed. 'So much nothing out there – ' And she looked towards the wide window and the vista of fields and hedges and trees it showed her, with disgust. 'I'll go meshuggah here. Don't leave me, darling – '

But she'd been able to persuade her of the need for being there, and by the time she actually left, Jessie had accepted the necessity, albeit grudgingly.

'As long as you come to see me often, dolly,' she said. 'And bring me something to eat from the kitchens. It won't be like I make myself, but it'll be all right, the girls'll make for me – '

And Poppy, who hadn't yet been able to tell her that the business had gone too, promised she would, and tried to think feverishly of where she could get the sort of things she knew Jessie wanted.

Well, she told herself as the train limped its slow way back to London through anonymous country stations and bleak wintry fields, that's that. Now what? What will I do tomorrow with nothing to get up for but the canteen? At least I've still got that – and she had fallen into an uneasy sleep and dreamt of being at the canteen and having no food for the customers and Bernie appearing in the doorway with a case full of stale bread to sell, and she woke with a start and shook herself for being so stupid. It would be all right. *All right*. It had to be. Somehow it would be all right.

And then at last, the only thing that could make her feel really better happened.

· 28 ·

She was woken by the phone shrilling downstairs, and somehow she dragged herself from the depths of sleep – because the night before she had in the desperation of an exhaustion that had robbed her of sleep for the past two nights, taken a pill – and managed to find her way downstairs to answer it.

'Mrs Deveen?' the voice clacked in a maddening singsong tone. 'Ai have a call for you. Kaindly hold the line – '

An official voice, Poppy thought, staring blearily at the front door, outside which the dark night pressed in on her. An official voice – at this time? What time is it? And she managed to lean across, while still clutching the phone to her ear, to kick open the dining room door and peer across at the clock on the mantelshelf. Half past five in the morning; and she thought – who's the fool calling at this time? And then went cold.

It had happened. The worst thing she could have imagined, and it had happened. David had been badly hurt. Worse, David was dead. He'd never come back to her. She'd lost the only bulwark she had in a dreadful world and –

'Mrs Deveen? Are you the-ere, Mrs Deveen?'

'Yes,' she said and her voice was thick. 'For God's sake who is –? What is it? What – '

'Hold the laine per-lease,' And she could have screamed at the delay and held the phone so tightly that her knuckles were white and her fingers began to tingle, not that she paid any attention.

'Mrs Deveen?' Another voice this time and now she lost her temper. 'For God's sake, what's happening? People keep coming on the line and saying my name – who are you? Where are you calling from? What's going – '

'Poppy?' the voice said in her ear and the words dried in her throat and she stared even harder at the front door, trying to concentrate.

'Poppy? Darling, it's all right. I'm all right. Stop fretting. Are you okay, sweetheart? I heard the raids got bad again – I've been frantic – Poppy?'

'Oh, my God,' she whispered and again began to cry. She wouldn't have thought she had any tears left, she'd shed so many.

'Poppy, are you there?' Anxiety sharpened his voice and now she found her own.

'Oh, David, David, thank God! I didn't think I could go on another moment and now you're here, and oh, David – ' And she could say no more for a moment.

'It's all right, sweetie. It's just a small thing really. They can take the plaster off in a few weeks and – '

'What did you say? Plaster?' Her voice came back with a rush. 'Oh, darling, what's happened?'

'Nothing dreadful. Slipped on a wet deck in a heaving sea. But, oh Poppy, have I got some material! I've got the story of the century, believe me. If I don't get a Pulitzer Prize there's no goddamned justice in this wicked old world. I'll be writing for weeks, believe me. Just as well because I won't be able to get around much – maybe you can spend some time at home with me, darling? Let Jessie get on alone, just for one – I'm aching to see you – '

'Oh, David, I've so much to tell you. The business is gone – '

'Gone?' He was horrified. 'How do you mean, gone – '

'Bombed. I can't tell it all now. And Jessie – she's in hospital and – oh, darling when will you get here?

I need to see you so much and tell you so much and – '

'Goddamn!' he said and the line crackled and went dim for a moment and then cleared. 'That's the bloody thing about it – they won't let me travel alone. I have to be collected. The Navy brought me this far, to Liverpool, but the sods won't take me any further. I'm not Naval personnel, you see and – '

'It's all right,' she cried joyously. 'It's all right! Where are you? Tell me all I need to know and I'll be on my way. The first train I can get. Oh, David, I'll see you soon! It's wonderful!'

Nine hours after Poppy's train snorted its majestic way out of Euston, on its way to Crewe and an interminable delay there for the connection to Liverpool, the small fussy train from Norwich settled itself against the buffers in Liverpool Street and the doors all along it opened like so many gunshots, slamming against the sides with a very satisfying bang, and the small boy who left the third carriage from the engine waited just for a moment to give the door another bang, just for the joy of hearing it.

The man getting out behind him snapped, told him not to do such stupid things, and immediately, Joshy attached himself to him.

'Why not?' he asked, his eyes wide and his head tipped back to stare up at the man's face. He was wearing what Joshy always thought of as butler's clothes, ever since he'd seen one of those august beings in the house of a friend of his when he'd gone there for a tea party; a fusty black jacket with tails behind and a high collar that looked as though it were cutting into his neck, under a very round and clearly painfully hard hat.

'Because making a noise is selfish and bad manners,' the august being thundered, fiddling in his waistcoat pocket for his ticket. The crush of people leaving the station slowed down as it reached the bottleneck of the ticket collector's gate and Joshy, looking ahead, skipped nimbly to the man's other side.

'Why is it bad manners?' he demanded and the man beside him snorted.

'Because it is,' he said. 'And it's bad manners to make a pest of yourself asking silly questions as though busy people hadn't better things to do than waste their breath on children who ought to know better – ' He handed over his ticket, still talking and Joshy, close by his far side, kept step with him. They were through the collector's gate and no one had spotted him; another couple of seconds and he'd be able to get away. And he walked alongside the still lecturing august person till they were in the middle of the station and then nodded brightly at him and said cheerfully, 'Thank you, sir. Very kind of you, sir!' and skipped off, disappearing into the surging mob of khaki and naval and air force blue and WVS green like a ferret going down a hole. The large man blinked and just for once revised his opinion of small boys. That one had been really quite well brought up, considering –

Joshy was extremely pleased with himself. It had been a long time since he'd run away and he was bigger now. It should have been harder to get away without a ticket than it had been last time, but thanks to that chattering old idiot he'd done very well and he grinned to himself and whispered aloud, 'Old idiot,' knowing he would never be cheeky enough to say such a thing to a grown-up's face.

He made his way through the station, still pleased with himself for remembering the way to the Underground, but when he reached the ticket office and handed over the sixpence he had so carefully hoarded for this purpose his courage began to ebb a little. All he'd thought of for the past two days had been this journey, and the planning and the execution of it had been dramatic enough to keep him at high pitch. But now, standing on the platform amid all the people on their bunks and blankets, waiting for the right train, anticlimax swallowed him up and his bravery seeped away like rain on a dry flowerbed.

What would they say at home? Would Mummy be as angry as she had been last time, and would she make him go back? That possibility hadn't been one he'd been willing to think of so far, but now he had to. The next stage of his journey was home, that much longed-for place where all should have been peaceful and loving and welcoming. And which, now he came to think of it, was likely to be anything but.

He made up his mind suddenly as the train limped into the station and the scrimmage of leaving passengers caught him in its current; he wouldn't go home at all. He had a much better idea, and he climbed on the train and stood staring up over the sliding doors at the map of the Underground with its brightly coloured lines, trying to work out which station was the one he needed. From now on it really would be lovely, he promised himself, and he held on to the rail beside the sliding doors, because he was still too short to reach the leather straps that swung so invitingly overhead, and began to whistle softly between his teeth.

Mildred woke suddenly as a coal fell in the grate with a little rattle and then stretched stiffly. It was really dreadful the way she fell asleep in her chair these evenings, since it so often made her go past her bedtime, and that really was foolish. It also made her ashamed of herself; such behaviour had always been despicable in her eyes, so loutish was it, and suddenly she remembered her father stretched out in this self-same drawing room and snoring in a singularly unlovely fashion, and gave a little shudder. She hadn't thought of him for many years; why should she when he had been so altogether hateful? Thinking of him now was stupid; she must be getting old. And the thought slid into her mind that she was now older, a good deal older, than her father had been when he had died. But that was an insupportable thought and she set it aside at once.

Below her the door bell rang, and she lifted her head eagerly. Poppy? Who else could it be at this time of night? And she glanced at the clock, which read eleven, and got painfully to her feet. It would be wonderful to see her; she had been worried about her these past two weeks, for she had heard nothing from her. That she was busy was undoubted. Jessie kept the poor girl constantly on the go, she told herself censoriously, but then Jessie always had. And she looked back down the years at her feud with Jessie and sighed. A pity really. It had been so good between them once, long ago. But not now, with Poppy being kept away from her own mother, even when the phone at her wretched office was constantly out of order, and she was never in when her mother called Norland Square.

But she was here now; and Mildred straightened her back as she heard the steps on her stairs and the burr of Queenie's voice. And then frowned. Why should Queenie drag herself up here to bring Poppy, who never needed announcing? And she pulled her shawl a little closer round her throat, filled with a sudden doubt.

The door opened and there was Queenie. 'Well, Madam,' she said sourly, glaring at Mildred over her thick glasses. 'This'll not please you, I'll be bound,' and she stepped aside and Mildred stared and then couldn't help herself. Her face cracked into a wide smile and she held out her arms.

'My dear Joshy!' she cried. 'My very dear child! How delightful to see you!'

He was across the room like a scalded cat, and threw his arms around her and held on, his head half buried in her skirts.

'Oh, Grandma, I'm so pleased to see you! I was so afraid you'd be angry with me!'

She put her hands on his shoulders and made him stand back a little so that she could look down into his face, which was streaked with railway soot.

289

'I'm very cross indeed with you, you naughty boy,' she said but her voice was filled with affection. 'You know you must stop this running away! Your Mama will be very put out, and rightly so!'

'But Grandma, I had to! I wouldn't have if he hadn't done it, but I had to!'

'If who hadn't done what? Have you had supper?'

He lit up. 'Oh, no. Nor tea either. I'm empty. I could be a drum, I'm so empty.' And he beat his hands on his belly. 'Hear it? I can.'

'Don't be vulgar,' Mildred said. 'Queenie, bread and milk, I think, with honey in it. And a cup of cocoa and he can have a ginger biscuit from the special tin. Hurry along now.' And as Queenie turned to go, moving with all the speed and elegance, Mildred thought impatiently, of a farm cart drawn by an ox, and with a sulky look on her face that Mildred considered it best to ignore.

'Well now,' Mildred said as soon as they were alone. 'Come and sit by the fire and tell me all about it. Why did you have to run away? And what did he do, whoever he is, to make it necessary?'

Joshy took a deep breath. 'It was the trumpet,' he said and suddenly his grimy face looked bleak. 'I was getting on ever so well with it, truly I was, Grandma, and I think he was jealous – '

'He?' Mildred said patiently.

'A horrible person. His name's Ted Thaxted and I hate him. He was in the choir with me and everything and came to have lessons on his stupid cornet from Mr Rawlings who was my teacher before rotten old Ted Thaxted started going to him and I was much better than him even though he's twelve and I'm ten and he got jealous and he got hold of my trumpet and he stamped on it and bashed it with a stone until it got nearly flat and then he ran off with it and threw it into the dyke and I wish I could kill him and – '

'Now just a moment!' Mildred held up one minatory hand. 'Didn't you tell any of the grown-ups about what he did? Surely someone would have dealt with the matter – '

'Oh, yes of course I did,' Joshy said disgustedly. 'I didn't care if it was sneaking, a chap can't have his trumpet stolen and spoiled and still not be a sneak can he? But Mr Rawlings said he couldn't do anything about it because when they got it out of the dyke it was too spoiled to mend and you can't get new ones in wartime and he said I could have Ted Thaxted's cornet but I hate the cornet and I didn't want to play it. I wanted my trumpet.' And for the first time he looked tearful. 'The trumpet you gave me.'

'My dear, I am so sorry,' Mildred said. 'That was a dreadful thing to have happened – what a very wicked boy that must be!'

'He got a whipping anyway,' Joshy said with some satisfaction. 'And I thought serve him right but then some of his friends sort of started getting mad at me and it got rather awful at school – and well, I had to come home, Grandma. You can see that, can't you?'

There was a silence as they heard Queenie's creaking steps on the stairs. 'Yes,' Mildred said then. 'Yes, I can see that. But all the same – well, eat your supper first – then we'll talk.'

Joshy found that bread and milk which he had long ago dismissed as horrible baby food didn't taste half bad when you were as hungry as he was and when it had been as plentifully laced with honey as Queenie had prepared it, and he swallowed every drop as well as the cocoa and three biscuits she had brought him. Sour as she was, even Queenie had a soft spot for Joshy.

He was leaning back in his chair with a visibly rounded belly, for it had been a very large bowl of bread and milk, and looking decidedly sleepy and Mildred stared at him for a long moment, smiling a little, and then sighed.

'You'll have to go home, Joshy,' she said. 'No, don't look like that. I dare say your mother will be cross at first, but once you tell her what happened over the trumpet she'll understand. You must go now.'

'Oh, Grandma, I'm so sleepy!' he said and looked at her winningly. 'Can't I go to bed now and p'raps go in the morning?'

She shook her head, smiling. 'I never thought the day would come when you didn't plead passionately to stay out of bed at all costs. No, my dear, home you must go. This happened once before you see, and I took time sending her home and – '

'What do you mean?'

She shook her head. 'It's an old, long story. Ask your Mama some time, or ask Robin. Anyway, I really must send you straight home now. I wish I could take you there, but – well, I can't manage that. Not at my age and at this time of night. I'm not happy about sending you, but it must be done. We'll get our usual cab driver. He understands me, since he's getting on in years himself, and he takes me everywhere I have to go when I do go out. Which isn't often these bad days – but there, I know I can trust him to take good care of you. Just touch the bell there, Joshy, and we'll make all the arrangements.'

'Will you talk to Mama on the telephone and explain first?' Joshy said and Mildred smiled.

'I think that's an excellent idea. I will. Let me get the matter sorted out first though. I don't want to call her too soon or she'll get over-anxious. As soon as the cab comes and we can see you on your way, then I shall indeed call her. So you have no need to fret yourself – ah, Queenie. We must telephone Albert and get him to come round at once.'

'Albert? But it's nearly half past eleven, madam!' Queenie looked horrified.

'That cannot be helped,' Mildred said with all the imperiousness of one who takes good service for granted. 'Tell him my grandson is here and has to be taken home at once and I can trust no one else but him with the task. He'll understand. See to it that he gets twice the usual fare for the journey. He'll have earned it – '

The cab pulled away from the kerb with Joshy, looking rather subdued as well as sleepy now, sitting in one corner of it and Albert, who was far from pleased to be called from his bed at this hour of night, even for twice the fare, in a decidedly bad temper, not that Mildred knew, or would have cared unduly if she had. After the years of tolerating Queenie's sulks she took such moods for granted in those who looked after her needs.

She stood by the window peering round the blackout curtain, watching the cab disappear into the darkness, and then reached for the phone. Poppy might be in bed herself, but what did that matter? She would have to get up; and a frisson of mild malice entered Mildred. She loved her daughter dearly and understood the pressures on her, but there were times when she felt herself overlooked. After all, she hadn't called her for almost two weeks now. And waking her with this news would in a sense serve her right. And she picked up the telephone.

But however long she hung on, however often she replaced the receiver and then called again, there was no answer, and she stood there and stared out at her blacked-out window with her face puckered. Perhaps she shouldn't have sent Joshy back until she had been certain they were there at home waiting for him, and she prayed that Albert would have the sense to bring him back if no one answered the door when they arrived.

The cab went remarkably quickly along the Bayswater Road, heading west, and Joshy leaned forwards to stare out of the window, trying to see. But it was very dark, not so much as a hint of starshine, let alone moonshine, and everywhere muffled in blackout shutters and curtains, and he caught his breath as the cab swerved to the left. Clearly it had been too near the middle of the road and the oncoming car which passed them going in the other direction had nearly hit them.

'That was close,' he said through the little glass shutter that separated him from Albert, but he just grunted, 'Stupid devil that was – ' and went on, and again Joshy stared out of the window ahead, trying to see over Albert's shoulder what might be coming towards them.

There wasn't much traffic and Albert put his foot down and again the cab shot forwards, and this time Joshy held on like grim death to the leather strap beside him, because the cab was decidedly old and rattling rather ominously. It would never do to be landed on the floor and arrive home with bruises. That would really make Mummy get in a state –

When it happened it was so sudden that Joshy didn't hear it, let alone see it. There was a shuddering bang and then the cab turned right round and hit a lamppost on the kerb, flinging Joshy to the floor in spite of his holding the leather strap, and then out on to the road, where he actually bounced, grazing the side of his leg as he did so. He shouted in protest, but there were other noises now, more shouting and running feet and he sat there dazed, for what seemed a long time, trying to get his head to stop spinning.

Someone appeared beside him, bent down, prodded him. 'You all right, kid?' he said in a throaty voice.

'Think so,' Joshy said. 'Got a grazed leg – ' And then he was suddenly copiously sick, sending half-digested bread and milk in all directions.

'Strewth,' the man jumped back. 'Better get you to the hospital – Fred!' he bawled then. 'Got a kid 'ere. Throwing up something rotten. Get him to the next ambulance will you? How's the other one?'

'Looks dead to me,' a voice came back from the darkness. 'Can't be sure but he's pretty battered. The other one's got a busted leg and 'e's unconscious – '

Joshy was looking a bit better now, and he reached out and pulled on the trouser leg of the man standing beside him.

'Is Albert all right?'

'Who?'

'The driver of the cab I was in – that's Albert – '

'Hmm. Well, sonny, he's the one with the broken leg, I think, and the knockout. Gone to the hospital – St Mary's down Praed Street. We'll get you there soon – '

'No, I've got to get home – ' Joshy said and struggled to his feet. He really was feeling rather awful again.

'What's the address, sonny?'

Joshy, bewildered as he was, didn't stop to think. 'Endlane Farm, near Forncett St Paul, Norwich – ' he said. It had been his address for so long now that he'd almost forgotten the Norland Square one.

The man bent and peered into his face. 'Ah!' he said with great satisfaction. 'Runaway vaccie, are you? Well, well, who'd ha' thought it? We'll soon get you back there, sonny, and no error! Come on now. Get you cleaned up and settled. Here's the ambulance, thank Gawd. Come on then. On your way – '

· 29 ·

The train pulled into Euston so slowly that it seemed to Poppy it was hardly moving at all, but at last it touched the buffers and there was a shudder and finally it stopped, and she stretched a little in her seat and peered across at David.

He was sitting bolt upright in the corner, his head resting against the criss-crossed sticky tape that adorned the window, and his mouth half open, snoring. Lucky man, she thought for a moment, to sleep like that through such a pig of a journey, and she moved awkwardly as the man beside her got up and collected his bag from the rack and picked his way out over David's outstretched leg. He gave Poppy a glare as he passed her, and Poppy almost stuck her tongue out at him, knowing it would be childish but wanting to all the same. It hadn't been her fault that David needed to take up so much space with his massive plaster.

Really he should have travelled by ambulance, but there were simply none to spare for such a long journey from Liverpool, which had had more than its fair share of raids, too, and they had been lucky to get on to the train at all. But then a woman who had been squeezed into the far corner came picking her way out of the carriage too, and she leaned over Poppy and patted her shoulder and said in a breathy little voice, 'My dear, I do hope your poor husband is well again soon – such a worry when one's loved ones are hurt, isn't it? Do let me give you this – ' And she pushed a piece of paper into Poppy's hand and beamed at her and climbed out of the train.

Poppy looked down at the paper and shook her head in mild exasperation. It was a tract from a religious society of some sort, exhorting its readers to take up their consciences and follow their God, rather than their country's flag, because that was the best way to deal with an enemy – and she looked over at David's exhausted face and remembered the tales he had told her of the way German U-boats has pursued the convoy for a large part of their journey and how they had attacked unarmed merchant ships, and her gorge rose. She had never been particularly patriotic, had never found herself waving the Union Jack with fervour at Empire Day parades, but she knew with every fibre in her that this was a war that had to be fought; and she remembered Hamish and how Robin had looked at him, and frowned and then shook her head. No time for that sort of worry now.

'David.' She leaned over him and gently shook his shoulder. The carriage was empty now, and she could get him out. 'We're in London, darling. Almost home – wake up.'

Even before his eyes were open his arms came up and wrapped themselves around her and he pulled her down until her face was buried in his coat and she laughed, making a muffled protest, and he hugged her even more tightly.

'Of all great words of tongue or pen the greatest are these, "We're home again!"' he said and let her go. 'I swear I'll never complain of anything ever again. To be home – and have a bath – '

'Not in that cast you won't,' Poppy said, and he made a face.

'Damn it all to hell and back, would you believe I'd forgotten it? I shall just have to stink then, I suppose.'

'Not if I have anything to do with it.' Poppy was collecting his luggage from the rack. 'I'll blanket-bath you. I haven't forgotten how.'

'That sounds exciting.' He gave her a lascivious leer and reached up and pinched her bottom and again she laughed, absurdly happy.

'You've spent too much time with lustful sailors,' she said. And he laughed too and began to haul himself to his feet.

It took them a long time to manoeuvre themselves along the crowded platform, because even with his crutches David found it difficult to walk, for his plaster was hip high and very heavy, and as they went she thought – I didn't know how much I loved him. I thought I'd only ever felt real passion for Bobby, but it's all right – I feel the same for David now, and he's mine and I'm the luckiest woman in the world – and then felt a great pang of guilt. How could she feel so light-hearted when Jessie was in hospital with her legs paralysed and her business a ruined, useless mess? But she couldn't help it. She was happy, war or no war, injuries or no injuries. The people she loved were all alive. She couldn't ask for more than that.

Goosey greeted them at the doorstep as they got out of the taxi, and with a great deal of exclaiming about how thin poor Mr David looked and her with nothing in the larder to build him up with and mind his poor leg, oh dear, oh dear, it must hurt something cruel, fussed round them so much that it took twice as long as it should have done to get David in and upstairs to the bedroom. Poppy was determined that that was where he was to go to start with, so that she could get him cleaned up and the doctor in to see him and, over his protests, that was where she took him, while Goosey kept getting in the way and trying to hiss something in her ear.

But at last he was there and Goosey was able to grab Poppy's arm and tell her whatever it was that was clearly bursting out of her.

Poppy, only half listening, because she was thinking about what she'd need to get David comfortable and clean again, suddenly heard what she was saying and she stopped and stared at Goosey, her eyes wide and dark with shock.

'What did you say?'

'Oh, Mrs Poppy, hush do, you'll upset poor Mr David –' Goosey said, fluttering her hands, but Poppy ignored that.

'Tell me what you said. I didn't – disappeared? What are you talking about?'

Goosey shook her head and threw a look at David who was now regaining his breath – because despite his denials, getting up the stairs had been an enormous effort for him – and he said curiously, 'What's up, Goosey?'

She waved her hands around distractedly, not seeming to know what to do with them.

'I wouldn't have fretted you for the world.'

'Out with it, ducks,' David said firmly and Goosey, who had always behaved as though men were slightly alarming if beneficent gods, obeyed.

'It's Joshy, Mr David. Run away again –'

David lit up. 'That boy is too much – where is he?'

'That's the trouble, Mr David, that's what I was trying to tell Mrs Poppy without worrying you and –'

'How can he have *disappeared*, Goosey?' Poppy demanded and made the old woman sit down in the small armchair beside the dressing table. 'Short and sharp, for God's sake. Tell me.'

Goosey looked up at her with swimming eyes. 'He run to his grandma, you see, Mrs Poppy, on account you was annoyed with him last time, she said, and she sent him home sharpish and the taxi cab had a crash in the blackout and there was one of the drivers killed and the other one in the taxi with Joshy, he was unconscious and never came round to be asked and they found out Joshy was a runaway vaccie and sent him off again –'

'They sent him back to Norfolk?'

'If only they had! I've phoned up there, talked to my nephew –' She swallowed and David reached a hand out to her and said, 'That was brave of you, Goosey,' for everyone knew how terrified Goosey was of the phone.

'Well, that's as may be. And he was that upset! They've been looking everywhere. It seems there was some trouble over some of the local boys picking on our Joshy and it all turned nasty, and well – '

Now she was frankly weeping. 'No one knows where he is. Your Ma, Mrs Poppy, she's been that upset. On the phone ever since it happened, she's been, talked to them at the rest centre and the office that looks after these evacuees and no one knows nothing. There was three trains going out of Liverpool Street that day and no one knows which one he was put on. They say they're trying but it's all right on account he'll be safe being out of London and he'll write home soon enough – but oh, I'm that upset – '

Poppy was standing very still and then she turned and looked at David. 'Darling – can you manage? I'll go and phone Mama and see what she can say and then I'll have to go and look for him, won't I? I can't just have him adrift somewhere and not know – ' She swallowed. 'Please, can you cope if I – '

'Go on,' he said at once. 'Right now. Phone me when you can. You've got enough money on you?'

'I've got enough.' She ran over to kiss him and then shrugged back into her coat, which she'd only just got out of and headed for the door.

'Look after him, Goosey,' she called and was gone.

I never want to see another train as long as I live, she thought, staring out at the blank greenness outside the window. The train had been standing silent like this for over half an hour, and the crowded carriage was cold and foully stuffy at the same time. She was lucky to have a seat, and she knew it, but that didn't make her feel any better. There ought to be a better way of finding him, there had to be, and temper rose in her until she almost shouted her fury aloud. But she controlled it and started to take deep, slow, even breaths to give herself something else to do until the train moved. Counting her own breaths was better than nothing.

But it didn't help. All she could do was go over and over it all in her mind. The uselessness of the people at the air raid post who had salvaged Joshy from the Bayswater Road that night, and taken him to hospital; the officiousness of the Sister at the hospital who had told her the child had been handed over to the evacuation authorities as soon as he was fit enough to go, and she had no more news than that – all accompanied with the sort of accusing glare that made it clear how much she despised any woman whose child created so much trouble in wartime – and finally the sheer ineptitude of the woman in the office that had supposedly dealt with Joshy's re-evacuation.

'I can't say, my dear, I'm sure,' she had bleated. 'I've told the boy's grandmother that, and really what more can we do? The children who came back were so silly, yes silly, and now we have to get them all away again – ' And she had looked helplessly at Poppy as though the unhappiness of evacuees which drove them to abandon their safe country billets in order to get home again was all her fault, and again shook her head.

'I'm sure he'll get in touch with you and tell you where he is,' she said. 'Won't he? I'm sure he's a good boy and can write his own name, and knows his home address.'

'Oh, of course he does, but I can't wait until he's able to get in touch – I have to find him *now*. He's my son, for God's sake. Can't you understand?'

'They're all somebody's child, Mrs Deveen,' the woman said reproachfully. 'I wish I could help, indeed I do, but I've no assistance here and all the paperwork that has to be done, it's really too much for one person. I keep telling them that. Don't worry, dear. I'm sure he'll turn up somewhere and as long as he's out of London he'll be safe enough – '

'But can't you see, you stupid creature!' Poppy had blazed. 'He ran away before when he was with his sister and with people he knew and who loved him. Don't you see he'll obviously run away again now he's with strangers? And he'll be frightened to come home because he thinks we'll be angry, and anything could happen to him. He's only ten – '

The woman had gone glassy-eyed with affront at being called stupid and simply shrugged her shoulders. 'Nothing else I can do,' she'd said frostily and bent her head to her work with some ostentation, leaving Poppy to turn away, sick with frustration and fear.

At least she'd been able to find out the trains that had left at the same time from Liverpool Street that evening. They'd taken him to the office directly from the centre, barely half an hour after they'd received him from St Mary's Hospital, she had been told, but no one could remember which of the trains he'd been put on. Yesterday she'd gone to Colchester and scoured the area with the help of a reasonably sensible billeting officer, but there had been no joy there. This morning it had been Sudbury where the billeting officer had been less helpful, but the local vicar was very concerned. She was sure he wasn't there. Now, it had to be Bury St Edmunds, and after that – but after that there was only a blank. He had to be here, somewhere.

The train shuddered, jerked forwards a few yards and stopped again, but at least it had moved, and she closed her eyes and began to beg it to move, staring into the pinkly tinged darkness behind her lids and knowing she was behaving like a frightened child. As if her desires could have any effect on inanimate objects –

But they did, for the train started to move, sluggishly, but at least it was going forwards and she opened her eyes and stared out at the telegraph poles with their wires swooping oh so slowly down to be caught again by the next telegraph pole, and felt a sudden surge of hope. He had to be here. It was logical he should be. She'd find him, somehow –

The town was cold and wet, with a little snow lurking in the gutters of the narrow streets and across the broad expanse of Angel Square, and she walked over to the hotel, knowing that there at least would be a place where people would have information. They'd know the identity of the local billeting officer for evacuees if anyone did. And full of hope and tension, she took herself into the slightly dusty wood-smoke-scented interior and across to the reception desk.

The very young girl sitting there looked up blankly when she asked to be directed to the billeting officer responsible for the town's evacuees, and then scuttled off to bring someone else, and the tall man who came towards her with polite enquiry on his face looked as old as the girl had been young. No ordinary middling people left anywhere, she thought then. All the vigorous ones gone to fight and the country run by the children and the decrepit.

But he was far from decrepit when he spoke and her spirits began to lift.

'You want our billeting officer? A problem with your foster children, madam? Or perhaps you feel able to take some more? We have a great many in Bury who – '

She shook her head. 'I'm not – I don't live here,' she said hastily. 'I've come up from London. It's – my little boy – ' And suddenly she couldn't go on. The fatigue of the past few weeks, from the night that Jessie's had been bombed until now, overwhelmed her. She had hardly slept for days, had travelled hundreds of miles, first to settle Jessie in her country hospital and then to Liverpool to fetch David – and those two journeys had been quite horrendous – and for the past two days she had been criss-crossing Essex and Suffolk like a thing demented, sleeping in hotels where she could find one and all the time praying and worrying about Joshy. She

303

had managed to phone home only once, and knew that at least David was all right, but now she could do no more. She just stood there with her face white and her eyes blank, and the thin old man behind the reception desk said, 'Tsk, tsk – poor lady, I think you need a nice cup of tea.'

At which point Poppy couldn't help it. She started to laugh. A cup of tea. That cure for all ills, a cup of tea – and the laughter built and increased and then ran over into tears and she was sobbing miserably on the old man's shoulder as he half dragged her, half led her to a sofa in the adjoining lounge, the little girl from reception staring round-eyed all the time.

'Tea, Ellie,' he called over his shoulder. 'Hot and strong, and bring two cups. I wouldn't mind one myself.'

He settled Poppy on a sofa in front of the fire and then bent to throw a log on it, and the flames leapt cheerfully and she thought – they looked like that on Jessie's roof – and took another deep breath to try to control her tears.

She managed it eventually, and when the tea came, took it gratefully and sipped its over-sweetened strongness without complaint. It wasn't the delicate China tea she much preferred but it was warming and sustaining and she needed it.

'Well now,' he said comfortably. 'I think perhaps you'd better tell me all about it.'

'Oh, I can't bother you!' she said, filled with embarrassment. 'I've used up enough of your time already, and been a fearful nuisance – '

'But you said you wanted to see the billeting officer,' he said mildly.

'Well, so I do. If you could just direct me.'

His smile widened and she thought – he's not so very old after all. Or if he is, he doesn't let it stop him at all. And again she thought of Jessie and had to take a deep breath to push her distress down where it belonged, under control.

'I don't need to. I'm Jeremy Markham. I'm the senior billeting officer. I have two or three assistants, you know, but I am the one who does all the paperwork. So if – '

She almost dropped her cup in her excitement, and set it down on the table beside the sofa with a little clatter and leaned towards him with her eyes wide and hopeful.

'It's never occurred to me I'd find you here – I – '

He smiled. 'We aren't full-time billeting officers, you know! It's our bit of war work and we do it in our own time. Otherwise we're busy earning a living, you see. I'm the book-keeper here at the hotel and so it's convenient for me to be in charge. They all come in and out of town and I'm nice and central. And of course I have a phone here. Not everyone does, in the country – '

'Yes – yes,' she said. 'Well now, let me tell you what happened – ' And she told him as succinctly and as quickly as she could, watching his face all the time.

He listened courteously and then very slowly smiled.

'He sounds a resourceful child,' he said. 'Full of devilment – '

'Oh, yes. He *is*. He's – well, I think he's a delight, but he isn't easy, I know that – '

'So we've found,' he said drily and then held up both hands as Poppy shrieked and almost threw herself at him.

'He *is* here, then? Oh, thank God, I knew he'd have to be – Where is he? Where can I find him? Shall I – '

'He's in the hospital,' Jeremy Markham said. 'But don't jump to conclusions! He's very fit. It was simply that he kept trying to run off and it was impossible to ask any ordinary home to deal with him. So, I had him admitted to the children's ward at the cottage hospital because there're lots of other children to play with, and plenty of control over him. There's no way he'll be able to run away from Matron there.' And he chuckled. 'I thought he'd give in and tell us who he was eventually, once he knew he couldn't get away on his own. But he's been holding out for three days so far, and refusing to speak to anyone, which is quite remarkable. Never mind.

I shall take you along there at once and see if he's yours. But from all you say I rather suspect he is.'

It had to be Joshy, it had to be, and she almost ran out of the hotel dragging a rather puffing Jeremy Markham behind her, to go to the hospital to get him. They had to walk all the way. 'No car available, I'm afraid, or rather no petrol at present!' the old man said cheerfully, but at least she was on her way to him. She repeated that over and over in her head. I am going to Joshy, I am, I am. It has to be him. Doesn't it? It has to be him –

There was no doubt in anyone's mind that it was, once she got there. The small and crowded children's ward, where some children were sitting round a long table having tea, was rent with the loudest of joyous shouts that had ever been allowed to shake its hallowed walls, as Joshy, seeing her, hurled his dressing-gowned self down the ward and into her arms.

· 30 ·

It was tea-time in Laburnum Ward, and beyond the windows the thin sunshine gilded the dregs of the laurel bushes that straggled across the flowerbeds that flanked the gravel paths, or rather what had once been the flowerbeds; now they showed long rows of sprouting young carrots and onions and beets. The hospital took the injunction to 'Dig for Victory' very seriously.

'So, listen, what have we got?' Jessie demanded. 'This you can't call cake. It's a nasty thin bit of cardboard, that's what that is. This place is great on bedpans and sore bottoms and such like, but when it comes to food – pfui' And she made the familiar old dismissive noise that had always made Poppy laugh.

'I managed to save up our egg rations for two weeks – didn't dare hold them longer in case they went bad – and we've made some pretty nice egg sandwiches, with some watercress I managed to get from the market. And then there's a pile of Goosey's best malt bread – she got her nephew to send some things down for it, and I didn't ask any questions – and I managed to find some strawberries. See?' And she showed her the precious punnet. .

'Hmm,' Jessie said. 'One each if we're lucky.'

'And we are,' Poppy said serenely. 'So stop nagging. And remember the hospital are doing their best, you know. They've laid on toast and jam – '

'Plum and apple,' said Jessie with terrible scorn.

' – and some rock cakes – '

'Rocks is about right.'

' – and a bowl of ice cream.'

'Ice cream!' This time Jessie was impressed. 'How did they manage that?'

'I gather from Sister that they've put themselves out because they're seeing you off.' She grinned wickedly. 'Can't wait to get rid of you.'

'Me? I've been no trouble to no one,' Jessie said complacently. 'Ain't I worked harder than anyone to get up on my feet?'

'Haven't you just,' Poppy said and hugged her. 'You're amazing. They all say so.'

'Well, they helped a bit,' Jessie said. 'I mean, it was good, the operations they did. Didn't like them at the time, but they worked and that's what matters, ain't it?'

'That's what matters,' Poppy said. 'And so does your own hard work. Show me again. I can't get over it!'

Jessie grinned and reached for her crutches. She was sitting very upright in a high-backed chair, beside her bed, and the crutches were propped beside her, well within reach. Now, moving extremely slowly, she took hold of them and as Poppy, sitting on her hands, literally, to prevent herself getting up to help her, watched together with the other five women in the ward, she just as slowly straightened up. Her legs were encased in very widely cut crimson slacks, which looked a little incongruous because beneath them appeared large boots, out of the sides of which thick metal callipers disappeared into the legs, but that didn't matter; the frilly purple blouse she had on over them distracted attention from anything but itself.

She looked a lot thinner when she was standing. The old bulky Jessie, so blooming in her roundness, had given way to a wiry figure with a stretched neck and sagging little jowls beneath her chin, but they disappeared when she laughed, and she was laughing now, so pleased with herself was she. They'd cut her hair too, into a neat crown of curls, and somehow she'd managed to persuade one of the nurses to colour it for her, having found her natural greyness much too depressing, and the curls bounced in their henna'd excitement as she set one crutch in front and swung her hips to make her left leg go forwards. She stopped to catch her breath, still grinning from ear to ear, and then swung her crutch forward again, and her hips the other way and her right leg swung out heavily and awkwardly to land a foot or so in front of the other. And still she grinned.

It took enormous effort to do it, and almost ten minutes, but using the same swinging motion she crossed the fifteen feet of floor space that lay between her and the facing bed and then, as slowly as an ocean liner being pulled into a dock by tugs, turned around and came back, a little more quickly this time. And when she finally collapsed into her straight-backed chair the whole ward applauded.

And so did the people in the doorway and Jessie turned her head eagerly and then squealed with excitement.

'Joshy, Lee – come here, you two lobbusses – oh, come here, will you?' And the two children came a little shyly into the ward, watched benevolently by the other patients, and came to be hugged.

'The train was on time, believe it or not,' David said in Poppy's ear. He had hobbled in behind the children and was now looking at them with enormous satisfaction. 'Did you see how nicely they behaved? I gave them socks on the bus, telling 'em we'd both scrag them alive if they didn't show the world what marvellous parents we are. I think it worked.'

'It worked,' Robin said from behind him and bent to kiss her mother. 'I've brought Chick too – is that all right?'

'Wonderful,' Poppy said and kissed them both.

'And – er – we hoped you wouldn't mind if I joined in.'

Poppy turned her head and laughed.

'How on earth is the hospital managing with all of you here? Hello, Sam! How good of you to make the effort.'

Sam shook her hand warmly as Robin and Chick went to fuss over Jessie. 'Never forget that Jessie's restaurant was my second home! I miss it – and her – dreadfully. So when Robin told me she was coming I sort of tagged on.' He made a little grimace. 'I usually do when I can. Tag on to Robin, I mean.'

She looked at him thoughtfully. 'She's all right, then? Not missing Hamish too much?'

'How can I know? She doesn't say. But I'm on the premises as it were – to keep an eye on her and – er – be with her – and not in Wales. So – ' He left the rest unsaid, but they understood each other well enough, and Poppy smiled at him, and said quietly, 'Thank you.'

'While we're on the subject,' he said then. 'As we are, in a way. I'm – er – keeping an eye out for Chick too. Seeing she's Robin's friend.'

'Oh? In what way?'

'I'm a bit concerned about that chap Daniel. I know he's a cousin of yours, but there's something about him I'm not sure about.'

Poppy looked relieved. 'Is that all? Bless you, no need to worry over Chick. She's told Robin he's a pest as far as she's concerned. It's Harry she's involved with. Well, as much as anyone can be involved with someone as taciturn as Harry! She'll be fine.'

He looked amused. 'Is there anything you don't know about Robin and her friends?'

'Well, we do talk quite a lot. Especially since we – well, we had rather a fight, but we made it up when Joshy had his adventure, and since then we've been even closer.' She looked fondly across the ward at her daughter, who was talking animatedly to Jessie. 'Not that I ever quiz her about her love life, of course. I've got more sense than that, I hope.'

'I hope so too,' he said gravely. 'It's usually better to say as little as possible.'

'I take your warning. Not a word, ever – ' And she turned away and caught David's arm.

'David, did they like the cottage well enough?'

'Well enough?' he said, turning back from Jessie's side. 'They're crazy about it. And when they worked out how much nearer to London it is than Norwich there was no holding them. *And* they like Mrs Freeman and what's more to the point, Goosey likes her. I think it's going to work.'

'I wish we could have persuaded Mama to come here – and to the cottage,' she said, watching the children who were now enthralled with showing the various pieces of drawings and toys they had brought with them, ostensibly for her pleasure, though what she would do with a child's sewing kit and a balsawood model aeroplane was anyone's guess. 'She has to be the most stubborn woman I know.'

'After you,' David murmured and tightened his hand on her shoulder. 'And I wouldn't have you any other way.' He shifted his weight on his heels then and she said anxiously, 'Are you all right?' and he grimaced.

'We made a deal, right? You'd stop asking me if I hurt and I'd stop telling you if I did. So shut up.'

'Yes. But take some of the painkiller. He said you could – ' And he made another face and reached into his pocket.

Well, even if David's still having pain from his injury, Jessie seems all right, Poppy thought, looking at her aunt, and then realized that she was deluding herself. There was a tightness about her mouth and shadowing under her eyes that showed she was less than comfortable, but it was overcome by the grin she was spreading across her sagging cheeks as Joshy, demonstrating some complicated manoeuvre with his aeroplane and chattering like a cage full of monkeys, stood beside her, and that had to be admired. Dear old Jessie, she thought.

They said she'd always be flat on her back and now look at her. Tough old darling. And impulsively she got to her feet and went over and hugged her.

'Tea-time,' she said. 'And don't interfere, I've got it all organized.' And Jessie looked at her and nodded contentedly and returned her attention to the children.

It all went very well, just as Poppy had planned it. The Sister and her nurses came in, and the physiotherapists and the young houseman Jessie had driven nearly mad with her demands for all sorts of things and some of the patients from other wards, and they all had tea together, getting through every scrap of food that was there, even the much despised cake and sandwiches provided by the hospital, which weren't all that bad, after all. And when they'd finished, David, behaving a little like a conjurer, pulled out of the overcoat inside which he'd smuggled it in, the largest box of chocolates any of them had seen since before the war.

'Never mind how I got it,' he said airily as the nurses opened their eyes wide, gasping and excited at the sight of it. 'Just say I had a favour to call in. Listen, I'm going to make a speech.'

Joshy groaned loudly and they all laughed, and David cuffed him cheerfully and went on. 'I just want to say, on behalf of the family, how grateful we are to Sister Trent and all the nurses and the doctors and Miss Henson from the physio department and all the girls on X-ray, and, well, all of you. She's done incredibly well, our Auntie Jessie, and we're very grateful. She's going home now to a really pretty cottage we've found for her and the children and another special person in our lives, Goosey, who's been in our family for the – well, for ever – and we'll be there too as often as we can get out of London. Even though the raids are over now – '

'I wish I could be so certain,' Jessie growled.

'Oh, they are, Jessie. I swear to you they are. There hasn't been a raid now for almost seven weeks. May the seventh ended the Blitz, truly it did. They're too busy elsewhere now, those Germans. No more raids – the Blitz is truly over, I promise you. And as I say, we'll be down here as often as we can and life might be a lot easier, war or no war – '

'Can we call on you to help with the summer fête in August, Mr Deveen?' Sister called. 'A man who can get his hands on a five-pound box of chocolates in wartime has to be well worth cultivating – '

'We will,' Poppy promised. 'Just tell us what you want – '

'I'll do some sewing for you if you like,' Jessie said. 'I used to work in a factory making coats and dresses, long ago. When I was young, younger than my Poppy here.' She smiled at Poppy. 'Ask your Mama some time, Poppy. Why ain't she here today?'

'What, get her out of her house?' David demanded. 'That'll be the day – '

'She'll have to get out sometime,' Joshy said. 'After she's dead, she will. You can't keep dead bodies in houses. It's not legal. I asked my teacher and she told me – '

'Joshy, that's enough,' David said firmly. 'There are things we all know and don't have to be told, believe me.'

'Well, I was just saying that – '

'Enough! Listen, everyone, the car's outside, and I think it's time we took our Jessie home. Come and wave us goodbye, hmm? If you can – ' And he smiled at the woman in the bed next to Jessie's, who had been lying flat on her back for weeks and showed no sign of ever trying to get out again.

The next half hour was exhausting. The children ran to and fro with Jessie's collection of personal belongings, and her books ('How can a person be in a hospital for five months and not pick up a few bits and bobs?' Jessie demanded when Lee commented on the quantity. 'I'll bet you've got more than me, anyway. I was bombed out, remember?' And she said it almost with pride) as David dealt with the details of payment outstanding with the

Sister and her clerk, and Poppy tried a little hopelessly to control the hubbub and stop people from being too upset by Jessie's magisterial progress out to the car on her own two crutches because she was not, she assured everyone loudly, going out any way but under her own steam.

The only difficult moment for Poppy was when they were standing in the hospital's main doorway watching the children bustle round the car to get her place ready for her.

'It's when children turn out good that life makes sense,' Jessie said suddenly, standing there four-square between her crutches and following them with her eyes as they darted busily about. 'It's what we're for, hmm, Poppela?'

'Not the only thing,' Poppy said and tucked her hand inside the taut elbow beside her. 'Life's about being happy and loved and busy – and – and good yourself. Like you. You've done well, sweetheart, and never think otherwise. No matter how our children turn out, we matter too. Otherwise it means the children were only as important as the sort of children they have themselves eventually, and that can't be right, can it?'

'You're a good girl, Poppy,' Jessie said. 'You always have been. As far as I'm concerned you're my child too. Let your mother go and jump in the lake if she don't like it. My Poppela, hmm?' and she turned her head and grinned at her. And Poppy smiled back.

'Got it in one,' she said. And Jessie nodded and set out to take herself and her crutches across the gravel to the car.